I0738642

10¢ AND A SILVER STAR...

A SARDONIC SAGA OF PTSD

A NOVEL

Bruce D. Johnson

Copyright © 2018 by Bruce D. Johnson

All rights reserved. No part of this book may be reproduced or transmitted in any form or by any means without written permission from the author.

ISBN 978-0-578-42041-7

Printed in USA by Ingram Spark & Lightning Source® for Edit Ink Publishers.

This is a work of fiction. Names, characters, businesses, places, events, locales, and incidents are either the products of the author's imagination or used in a fictitious manner. Any resemblance to actual persons, living or dead, or actual events is purely coincidental.

Some of Many Book Reviews

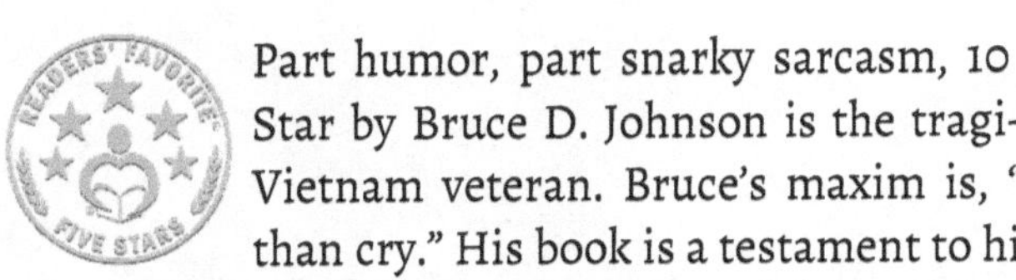

When I was growing up, and still to this day, I loved to watch M*A*S*H and Bruce D. Johnson has captured a similar vibe with a humor similar to the famed TV series. If you were to bring Hawkeye into a more modern context, this would be a very close result. The humor was great and really lightened the horror being experienced by the characters. There are many memorable lines, chuckles, and even darker moments, as you would expect from a work of this style. Bruce D. Johnson's 10 Cents and a Silver Star only briefly touches on the gore side, keeping it manageable and less horrific than actually being there would be. I thought the dialogue was well scripted and enjoyable and the issues were handled in a very sensitive manner. This book gives you a good, but light-hearted perspective on life in war and the camps and the array of characters are diverse, and each has their own important role in giving a glimpse into this war-ridden chaos.

Reviewed by K.J. Simmill for Readers' Favorite. *K.J. Simmill is an award-winning British author with books released in both the fantasy and non-fiction genres.*

Part humor, part snarky sarcasm, 10 Cents and a Silver Star by Bruce D. Johnson is the tragi-comic memoir of a Vietnam veteran. Bruce's maxim is, "It's better to laugh than cry." His book is a testament to his sense of humor as he grows into manhood during one of the world's most confusing and senseless wars and beyond. Spiked with (at times, sardonic) humor, and many heartwarming incidents, this book will take you on a unique journey through the depths of the hazardous Vietcong jungle, to the mad jungle of Chicago as the author learns how to curb his bitterness and heal the scars of the war. What better way to mend than with humor and penning a great novel? Written in a delightfully snarky first-person narrative, this book will have its readers laughing out loud, crying, and smiling warmly as they experience the wonder of unconditional love, understanding, and hilarious moments. I appreciated how the author shakes the perception of the crazed Vietnam veteran while touching on the more painful and sensitive issues such as PTSD and the resulting trauma of war. I recommend this book to readers that have family in the military or would like an inside peek into the life of a soldier at war.

Reviewed by Alyssa Elmore for Readers' Favorite, one of the most prolific reviewers at 287 reviews and counting.

Bruce D Johnson's 10 Cents and a Silver Star is a gripping blend of humor and a military story, a narrative with strong emotional and psychological underpinnings, featuring likeable and well-developed characters. Johnson has a unique sense of plot structure and develops very interesting relationships between the characters. Character development is impeccable, and it combines with the humor to make for a delightful read. The quirkiness, the focused scenes, and the emotional strength of the narrative are elements I enjoyed the most in this engaging tale. It will get your emotions rattled, have you laughing at unexpected moments in the story, and you will learn to see painful situations differently. I enjoyed every bit of this story. An eye-opening read.

Reviewed by Ruffina Oserio for Readers' Favorite

This book is dedicated to:

Ron Johnson, who struggles with PTSD, one day at a time

and

Erik Enstrom, who tragically lost his battle with PTSD

and

the 500,000+ lives impacted by this disorder.

ACKNOWLEGEMENTS

This novel is not finished. Admittedly, it boasts a plot, conflict, a point of view, a setting, characters, and even a theme . . . lots of neat literary stuff, but, it's not finished. However, like an airplane, barreling down the runway on its takeoff run, it has reached V1, the "commitment to fly" speed. The book is with the publisher. Not a day goes by that I don't conceive of another amusing or salient tidbit that I wish I could pop in here or there, but, for better or for worse, this is what the reader gets. For the sake of my dear wife Gail, I hope you enjoy it. She has been amazingly tolerant of my choice of a leisure recreation. Now, I'll have more time for watching YouTube videos depicting people attempting wacky stunts that, more often than not, end up causing agonizing trauma to their groins.

CHAPTER ONE

The Silver Star

"Hey Ken," I greeted Ken Quidero, our commonly capable company clerk, as I stepped through the flimsy screen door into the less than orderly, orderly room. "You wanted to see me?"

"Not *me*. Captain Riley sent for you," Ken replied without looking up, a filtered cigarette dangling precariously from the corner of his mouth as he continued typing.

With his sleeves rolled up past the elbows, Ken sat behind an Underwood Standard #6 typewriter, factory-painted, matching the hue of his olive drab jungle fatigues. The massive manually manipulated machine sported a white-stenciled, 16-digit U.S. Army inventory control number and a polymerized ethylene-vinyl acetate, adhesive-backed decal that read: "Join the Army; See the World; Meet Interesting People; and Kill Them."

"Is that Specialist Johnson?" came the captain's thick baritone voice as he emerged from his rear office, reading glasses low on his nose, a holstered Model 1911 sidearm on his belt, and a fat Corona Gorda cigar between his pudgy fingers. He wore olive drab jungle fatigues with the sleeves rolled up past the elbows and a class of 1965 West Point ring on his left hand.

"Bruce, thanks for reporting. It seems that Military Assistance Command, Vietnam has approved your recommendation for a Silver Star."

He raised the volume of his voice a few decibels to compete with the din of an Eagle Flight of departing Huey helicopters.

"Sorry we can't do this presentation with a kitschy ceremony, but I wanted to get this decoration into your hands just as soon as possible; while you're still alive, that is. I can't tell you how much I detest awarding these things posthumously. It's so, so disconsolate, and double the paperwork."

I had no inkling I was under consideration for a commendation, nor did I have any reason to suspect such. In fact, I aspired to be accused by the U.S. Army of a cowardly reaction to enemy fire (which could be easily corroborated), and discharged for unbecoming behavior, or disrespect, or insubordination, or disobedience, or dereliction of duty, or fraternization, or malingering — anything to get me out of this shithole country and back to the United States of America with her spacious skies, fruited plains, amber waves of grain, purple mountain majesties, and one lawyer for every 265 citizens. Nonetheless, Captain Riley handed me the medal in its cardboard-sleeved presentation case along with an official-looking certificate in a white envelope.

"Here you go, kid. Back in the world, this and 10 cents ought to get you a cup of coffee just about anywhere." (Nobody had ever heard of Starbucks back in those days.) "Go ahead. Read it. I think you'll appreciate the sentiment, if not the graphics, which I'm of the opinion is on the amateurish end of the aesthetic scale. Uncle Sam needs to recruit some more adroit graphic artists, in my opinion, but I'm just an airborne infantry captain, so what the hell do I know?"

Ken and the Captain looked on while I opened the envelope bashfully, as if it were a birthday card from Aunt Clara, with a crisp $10 bill enclosed.

"You're not going to sing, are you?" I asked sardonically. (For you're a jolly good killer. For you're a jolly good killer. For you're a jolly good kil-l-l-l-er. That nobody can deny.)

I read:

On March 2, 1969, while engaged in military operations involving conflict with an opposing foreign force, in the Republic of Vietnam, Specialist Fourth Class Bruce D. Johnson distinguished himself by extraordinary heroic achievement and conspicuous gallantry in action, beyond the call of duty; blah; blah; blah; at the voluntary risk of his own life; blah; blah; blah.

Richard M. Nixon, Commander in Chief

I glanced over to my friend Ken (a "grunt" by association), squinting my right eye and raising the palm of my left hand slightly upward as if to ask, "What's going on here?" He shrugged his shoulders, then continued typing the standard-form condolences letter he worked on: *I wanted to let you know how much we regret the loss of your son (Fill in the blank). Please accept my deepest sympathy . . .*

By this time, the cigarette in Ken's mouth had grown a disconcerting ash three quarters of an inch in length (or about 19 millimeters for those of you who subscribe to the metric system).

"Well, take care now, soldier."

The captain patted me on my scapula through the blouse of my olive drab jungle fatigues, that I wore with the sleeves rolled up past the elbows.

"I've got to get back to work now. I'm knee deep in KIA paperwork and body count reports."

"How's that going?"

"Well, as a matter of fact, so far, this month, our unit's winning by a landslide; twenty-eight to seven to be exact, if you count women and children. And that's with a first lieutenant grappling with a ulnar collateral ligament tear, and one of our key automatic riflemen on injured reserve for a groin strain."

"It's too bad about those seven, however."

"That's like saying the glass is half full. You need to be mindful, son, that back in the world, more people perish in automobile accidents each year than die in combat here in Southeast Asia. You might just be safer walking point on a long-range patrol in the A Shau Valley than you would be backing out of your own driveway."

"I'll try to remember that. It's an intriguing statistical hypothesis. But, is it substantive and replicable?"

"Yes! And that's not even factoring in passengers of Senator Ted Kennedy's Oldsmobile."

"Thanks for the insight. I'm feeling a little more invulnerable now."

"Great! But, I sort of hoped for invincible. It helps greatly when the 18-year-olds I send into combat feel themselves to be invincible."

"I'm not sure about invincible. Would you settle for indomitable? I think I could muster indomitable; especially with your inspiration and demonstrated superior leadership ability."

"Sure. Anything I can do to help. However, I want you to also think of me as your mentor, not only your commander."

He seemed to have no idea that I was being flippant.

"You're my commander?"

"Of course I am. Who did you think I was? Cool Hand Luke?"

"I couldn't tell you. I don't relate well to the concept of superiors and minions. I come from a staunch union family, you see."

"I understand. It's a confounding notion for some white folks who never lived in the South. You need to be able to just put your faith in the system, however. The Army's got it all figured out for us. Trust them just like you might trust Jesus Christ himself."

"I'll work on it."

"Don't just work on it. Pray on it. Pray for the gift of understanding."

"Understanding, you say?"

"No, you're right. Washington certainly doesn't want that! The Pentagon prefers to keep us baffled by the war. On second thought, pray instead for, for deference."

"Okay. Great. I'll be sure to do that," I lied. "And, thanks for the cool medal. Bye."

"It's my pleasure. Take care now, son. There's no need to salute me. This *is* a combat zone after all."

"I wasn't going to."

"Well, just in case you were."

"It never crossed my mind. Bye, Ken."

The ash from Ken's cigarette (just like I knew it would) had fallen into the mechanics of his typewriter, and he was blowing on the keyboard. He looked up and gave me a big wave.

"See you later, Bruce."

Surprised that I had exited the orderly room with no reduction in rank, as would typically be the case, I stepped outside into the scorching subtropical sun. Tom Kline sauntered down the lane, singing:

> *Wait until the war is over*
> *And we're both a little older . . .*

Returning from the showers, he wore only a towel and flip-flops, carrying a double zip-top leather shaving kit. I was more accustomed to seeing him in olive drab jungle fatigues with the sleeves rolled up past the elbows, carrying a badass M60 machinegun, and belts of ammunition draped over his shoulders, Pancho Villa style.

"Get busted down to private again?" he asked with a smirk.

"No. I got a Silver Star."

"A Silver Star! Are you shittin' me?"

"No. Look."

I showed him the box and envelope.

"I can't figure it out."

Tom took the box from me, examined it top and bottom, and shook it close to his ear.

"Are you sure that this thing's not some sort of a sick gag?"

"What do you mean?"

"I mean, when you open it, does a spring-loaded snake come shooting out?"

"No! It's real."

"Are you sure?"

"Positive."

"You know, probably what happened is, they ordered this Silver Star from headquarters for someone else, like Bill Hastings, and when he got killed over there in Phu Yen Province, they decided to give it to you instead; just so it wouldn't go to waste. I mean, these things can't be cheap for the government to procure. They're probably much like those $600 toilet seats. I bet, if you look closely at the accompanying certificate, you're going to find that the original name is obscured with whiteout ($50 a bottle whiteout) and yours has been typed over it. You *know* how much Captain Riley hates awarding these things posthumously."

"Not as much as I'd hate *getting* one posthumously," I added as I turned away and continued walking.

Tom could be a such a putz sometimes.

Back at my hooch, which I shared with my solid brah, Loren Anderson, I sat down on the edge of my squeaky, saggy-sprung bunk and carefully opened a flap on the end of the plain cardboard box that securely housed my prestigious medal. Shaking the box gently, the presentation case slid out and into my left hand. The hard, flat, clam-like container, encased in a supple leatherette material, reminded me of a wristwatch case. I started to open the lid, but hesitated when I considered Tom's suggestion about a spring-loaded snake. Holding the box at arm's length, aimed away from my face, I popped it open.

"Whatchagot?" asked Loren as he walked in with an armful of mail.

He sported olive drab jungle fatigues with the sleeves rolled up past the elbows.

"A Silver Star," I casually answered.

"Why are you opening it like that? Did you think it was possibly a Viet Cong booby-trap masquerading as a respectable military decoration?"

"Just being careful. Awhile back, I heard, a fellow over in the second battalion picked up a Seiko watch case he found, while engaging in a little recreational looting, and when he lifted the lid, it blew his right hand off."

"Bummer. I hope he was left-handed, or ambidextrous."

"He is *now*, and perplexingly problematic to shop for at Christmastime."

"Well, for sure, you wouldn't want to give him a watch."

"I agree. That would be sadistically inappropriate, to say the least."

"You *could* give him a glove, however."

"I suppose so. To me, it just sounds like one ugly product liability lawsuit for the Seiko Company. So, where did you get that Silver Star, anyhow? From a Cracker Jack box? I *know* that's not yours. I don't want to hurt your feelings, but you're no John Wayne, Bruce."

"It *is* mine. I received it from Captain Riley just now."

"From Captain Riley? Oh. Of course! I bet that medal was originally meant for Bill Hastings, but when he came back in one of those blasted black body bags, they gave it to you instead."

"No way! This medal is mine."

"Yours? What for? People like you don't get Silver Stars; they get dishonorable discharges; or prison time; or firing squads."

"I don't know. I was awarded it for something I did on the second of March, according to the accompanying documentation."

Look out kid, don't matter what you did

"It's subscribed by President Nixon, after all, and he's about as incorruptible and upstanding a man as you're likely to find. Wouldn't you agree?"

"Now you're name-dropping, but no, I don't agree. If I were old enough to vote, which I won't be for a couple more years yet, I would have cast mine for Humphrey."

"Coming from a staunch union family, I suppose I would too . . . if I were old enough to vote, that is . . . for sure, not for that racist rat, George Wallace."

"Look. All I'm saying is that if you did something to warrant a Silver Star, you'd know it. Not just the date. You've got to do something really insane to be worthy of a Silver Star."

"You mean like actually *vote* for George Wallace . . . if I were old enough to vote?"

"I mean you've got to carry a half dozen wounded comrades to safety on your shoulders while under heavy enemy machinegun fire, or something like that, to earn a Silver Star. And even then, you've got to do it while wounded yourself and with total disregard for your own personal safety."

"Total disregard for my personal safety? How would one *do* that? It's not natural. . . at least for a non-Marine."

"I don't know. That's a profoundly probing question. Let's split a fatty and contemplate it. I picked up your mail. Feels like there may be some more of those lewd Polaroid snapshots from that hot little girl-friend of yours. *How* old did you say she is?"

"Oh, Toni? She's sixteen."

Loren lit up a *Bong Son Bomber* (pre-rolled joint), took a long toke, and then handed it to me.

"Whoa, man. *Sixteen*. Damn! How do you stand it?"

"Stand what?"

"Being over here while she's like 10,000 miles away."

"I don't know. How do you enjoy being over here?"

I passed the joint back to him.

"It sucks."

"Well, it sucks for me, too."

"Oh, really? That surprises me. You see, I thought it would be different for someone who sports a Silver Star."

"How do you mean?"

"I mean, if you received a Silver Star, you must be *one* gung-ho son-of-a-bitch. Do you mind?" Loren asked, nodding towards the packet of photos.

I nodded in the affirmative. Loren opened the hand-cancelled envelope with extra postage affixed, then casually thumbed through the naked snapshots of Toni. In one, she sat seductively on a park swing, and another in the crotch of a sprawling white oak.

"I really like this one of her with the American flag," he commented.

The next photo in the deck portrayed Toni, fully clothed, cuddling her pet schnauzer.

"What's this?" Loren asked, holding the picture in the air.

I snatched it from his grip and exclaimed, "Whoa! How'd that one get in there?"

"These pictures probably violate one or more United States postal regulations for indecent content."

"With a ZIP code in Indian Country, I doubt that any postal inspectors will be tracking me down anytime soon."

Jim Mullen appeared at the door of our hooch, wearing olive drab jungle fatigues with the sleeves rolled up past the elbows.

"I smell a party in here. Y'all going to bogart that stuff or are you willing to share some with a good old boy?" he asked in a slow and lazy Kentucky drawl.

"Hillbillies don't smoke pot," Loren replied. "They drink white lightning moonshine."

"That's redundant."

"Pardon me?"

"White lightning and moonshine. It's redundant, and not grammatical."

"Well, let me give *you* a lesson in the productive rules of grammar, Corporal Smarty Pants. It just so happens that you can't use the words *y'all* and *bogart* in the same sentence. It's linguistic ineptitude. Maybe not morphologically, although I think it very well may be; something having to do with dangling your participle by mixing your misplaced modifier metaphors and ending them in a preposition that doesn't agree with your antecedent, or something along that line. I can't site the exact infraction off the top of my head. You'll have to trust me on this one. It's just not syntactic."

Noticing the envelopes and a package sitting on my footlocker, Jim quickly changed the subject. He had to know he was losing the syntax argument.

"Did we get mail today?"

"Yeah. Came in by that supply chopper this morning," Loren replied, releasing a plume of smoke as he spoke. "How's your hand?"

"Oh, it's better, but it still hurts when I scratch it."

"Then don't scratch it."

"Thanks. I'll try to remember that. Let me tell you. A valuable lesson I learned from that last Zippo raid is to never pet a dog that's on fire. Any mail for me?"

"Nope. Do any of your kin know how to write?"

"Up yours! Who's the package for?"

Brown paper packages tied up with strings.

"Bill Hastings. Probably some more of those cookies his fiancée bakes. I guess she mailed them before she received the news of his death."

"I *love* her cookies. Are you going to open them?"

"Of course we are! Loren and I are working up a major case of the munchies as we speak. We're going to *need* those cookies."

"Too bad Bill's fiancée has to get such terrible news. She'll probably stop sending treats now."

"War is hell, my friend. Haven't you heard?"

"That's what I've been told; and combat's a motherfucker."

"You could always talk to Ken Quidero," Loren suggested. "Perhaps he hasn't typed up Bill's K.I.A. paperwork yet."

"What exactly are you suggesting?"

"I mean, if he sits on it for a couple more weeks, we could still get another cookie shipment or two."

"Would that be ethical?"

"Ethical! What are you talking about? You torch villages, burn peoples' rice, and shoot their livestock, you shithead!"

"I suppose you're right, but those are Vietnamese people, after all. Doesn't that make a mitigating difference?"

"The Army would like you to think so, my friend, and if you buy into that, you might just as well reenlist and become a sorry-ass lifer."

From outside came the dull thuds of mortar shells exploding. I could tell that they had started at some distance and were walking their way closer and closer.

"Incoming! Incoming!" Some newbie, fresh out of charm school, wearing stiff new olive drab jungle fatigues, his sleeves rolled up past the elbows, shouted as he ran from hooch to hooch, spreading the word as if he were frigging Paul Revere. Having been in-country for over six months, with fewer than 180 days left until my DEROS (Date Eligible to Return from Overseas), I got up reluctantly to look out the door just as a mortar round caught the new kid with a virtual direct hit, essentially transforming him into a pink mist of blood and a scattering of body parts. His left boot, with his bloody severed foot disturbingly still in it, landed at my feet.

"What's with *this* crap?" I rhetorically asked my dumbfounded buddies. "This is absolutely nauseating."

"And the kind of thing," Loren added, "that can spoil a fellow's whole day."

"Well, it sure as heck spoiled mine."

"Ah. Don't mean nothin'."

Holding the roach between the nails of my thumb and index finger, forming an "O," I sucked the last glowing embers out of it.

"Now, what do you say we open those cookies?"

These are a few of my favorite things.

"And how about those snapshots of your little X-rated girlfriend?" asked Jim. "May I see those, too?"

"Knock yourself out. My only stipulation is that you've got to look at them here. No taking them with you into the latrine when you go. That would be disrespectful."

Excitedly, Jim thumbed through the photos.

"Holy crap! These things just keep getting better and better. Don't you ever wonder just who the photographer might be? I mean, he sure does have a knack. The camera *loves* her!"

"He?"

I never thought of that before. It made me a little jealous.

"Well, you don't think her *mother* is taking these pictures, do you?"

"You perverts stay away from those photos."

"But you said we could look at them."

"I changed my mind."

"Well, good friends are golden, while numb-nuts like you are fickle."

"War is a fickle business, my friend."

Darnell, one of our company medics, ambled in the door, pursuing the rumor that I had received another packet of pornographic photos. With the sleeves rolled up jauntily past the elbows, he wore faded, olive drab jungle fatigues. An ineffective African elephant good luck charm dangled around his neck.[1]

"Whose boot is this?" he queried.

"It belongs to the newbie from Recon."

"Did you know that his foot's still in it?"

"Yeah. I saw that. If I weren't so stoned, I'd be horrified!"

---

1. Darnell died less than a week later, during a firefight, while attempting CPR on a wounded comrade, who also died.

"I get you. Vietnam is the insane asylum of this planet. Where's the rest of him?"

"Over there, by that M-41. Why do you ask?"

"I'm betting he's going to need a tourniquet."

"Or, more pragmatically, a Graves Registration representative."

"Those guys have got a tough job. I don't envy them."

"I agree. Those bodies can get mighty ripe after a day or so in this tropical heat. Do you smoke?"

"Yeah, man. Whatchagot?"

"Come this way, my friend. I've got the perfect remedial herb to take the edge off a taxing and stressful southeast Asian day."

"*Cambodian Red*?"

"You bet!"

"Exquisite. I fancy myself to be a bit of an aficionado, you know."

"I didn't know that."

Darnell sparked the pre-rolled joint I offered him, and took a deep deliberate drag, then another, and another still.

"Mmm. Great construction and nice draw. Very full-bodied . . ."

"You are so full of shit, Darnell. Now pass that thing around. This isn't some sort of 'spliff gremlin' soirée. We subscribe to the puff and pass rule in these parts."

Darnell reluctantly passed the joint clockwise, then accused us all of being racists (as he did on pretty much a daily basis), but that certainly didn't stop him from hanging out with us white guys for the balance of the afternoon, smoking pot, munching Bill Hastings' homemade peanut butter cookies, and listening to Grand Funk Railroad on Jim Mullen's Channel Master 6313 cassette player.

And then I don't feel so bad.

CHAPTER TWO

Dust-Off

Old men start wars; young men fight them. At 18, I fought as a ground-pounder with the 173rd Airborne Brigade based at Bong Son, Vietnam. Although Sergeant Washington informed us, during a brief orientation on our arrival, that the area boasted a rich history, culture, and tradition, I found the people of the province a decidedly disagreeable lot, regularly employing extempore weapons of opportunity to discourage our enjoyment of the amenities and picturesque countryside. These people intend to create "maximum consternation," General William Westmoreland once explained it to the national press. I can't speak for the rest of the guys in my company, but I know I felt consternated. When I told this to my buddy Loren, he suggested I take a laxative.

Since our country's leaders in Washington embraced the staunch opinion that these people's ill-temperedness arose from an ignorance of capitalism and elective government, it became our crucial mission in Bong Son to win their hearts and minds, and to get a toehold on democracy. The way we did this, for the most part, involved going on long range patrols. Our commanders, for enigmatic reasons, possessed a passionate penchant for patrols. At their fancy, we engaged in combat patrols, Zippo raid patrols, ambush patrols, security patrols, night patrols, and reconnaissance patrols, the latter being subdivided into route reconnaissance, area reconnaissance, and zone reconnaissance. It grew dizzying. Who would have ever thought that patrolling could be so perplexing and convoluted an endeavor. It also raised havoc with my circadian rhythm.

Essentially, in any genre, a patrol consisted, basically, of walking in knee-deep water under the hot tropical sun for a few days at a time without changing our socks or underwear. We all suffered from perennial jungle rot, Malabar ulcers, and tropical phagedena. When encountering a village, we then proceeded to make all the people come out of their houses and stand off to one side while we shot their pigs and burned their rice. You might think of us as the Peace Corps in reverse.

As a natural consequence of these antagonistic asocial activities, the villagers started to become agitated by having their hearts and minds won, and their livestock perforated. The mainstream press of the time, commonly referred to it as the "domino theory." Henceforth, these otherwise apolitical peasant people grew to become communist sympathizers *(Oh dear!)* who, just like the major in NVR training back at Fort Campbell, Kentucky, warned us they would, started leaving booby traps and thin wires connected to hand grenade pins all around, which could put a damper on the mission, and, quite frankly, proved extraordinarily aggravating. Think about it.

Regrettably, when the situation had degenerated to this lamentable low point, the only plausible option left shrunk to shooting the sons of a guns. It's a pathetically sad fact, but once a villager had experienced the intoxicating opiate of retribution, by successfully maiming or killing constituents of the occupying army (us), he or she couldn't be effectively or methodically rehabilitated to a satisfactory extent. This did not, however, discourage the bozos at Psychological Operations from employing assorted featherbrained strategies to influence target citizens' values, beliefs, emotions, motives, reasoning, and behavior. For the prisoners we handed over to them, self-evaluation, introspection, intimidation, torture, and execution were just a few of the many, diverse, and imaginative techniques employed to induce confessions or reinforce attitudes and behaviors favorable to the singularly virtuous objectives of the United States of America. Unsurprisingly, and unfortunately, Psy Ops tended only to reinforce the resolve of the locals to kill more Americans, more ruthlessly. In short, it proved counterproductive.

This sparked a serious situation, that we in our platoon all agreed, demanded to be addressed at a fundamental level. It would be necessary to get to the root of the inconvenient problem, and not simply address the repercussions with a reactionary response. In a nutshell, we needed to be more proactive. The guys in our platoon, accordingly, talked it over in depth and concluded that the best thing to do, under the circumstances, would be to drink a beer over at the Enlisted Men's Club and play some pool. The way we had it figured out, the guy who lost would have to shoot our lieutenant, whom we all agreed instigated much of this aberrant behavior and, in general, tended to be a poor moral role model for some of the younger, more impressionable fellows in the platoon. Me for one.

Damian, a swell guy from Puerto Rico, whom I liked a lot, lost by sinking the eight ball, but — I should add — took it like a man. He demonstrated exemplary sportsmanship. (Especially when you consider that he didn't even have a voting representative in Congress.) The only thing is, as a devout Roman Catholic, of a more traditional (i.e., Pre-Vatican II) and conservatively orthodox persuasion, he didn't possess the conviction necessary to shoot the lieutenant in the chest, where it would do some serious damage to the critical organs of the thoracic cavity, and thus count for something consequential. So instead, incredibly, while out on our next patrol, Damian shot the lieutenant in the left elbow. (Actually, a trickier target.) In Damian's credulous mind, the Sixth Commandment germanely applied to officers as well as enlisted men.

"I think this is a big mistake," I frankly told Damian, as we incredulously watched the lieutenant thrashing insanely around there in the mud, grasping his shattered elbow.

Damian had a terrified look in his eyes.

"You better finish him off," I implored. "It's got to be done."

"Look, man, I'm not the one with a Silver Star for valor. I can't do this. Please. Please. You do it! I just don't have the stomach for this business."

"Frankly, I don't believe this to be my responsibility," I argued. "And besides, I'm not as gallant as one would infer from the commendation I received. You need to understand, my being awarded a Silver Star was more of a fluke . . . a big bureaucratic blunder."

Loren Anderson walked over to where we were standing.

"You dudes have really done it now," he said, looking down on the lieutenant. "He seems pretty pissed off. You better go fetch Sergeant Washington," he suggested to Damian. "He'll know what to do."

The sergeant joined the growing circle of people forming around the wounded lieutenant. This included a rabble of highly amused Vietnamese street urchins who appeared out of thin air. He looked Damian square in the eye.

"Good initiative; bad judgment." `

"I'm sorry," Damien whimpered, close to tears. "I called the two ball in the corner on a bank shot, intent on cheating the pocket. I don't know what I was thinking. I never gave any consideration to the position of the eight ball . . ."

"That's all in the past. But, what'll you do now, in the present, my brown-eyed son?"

Damian looked horrified. It shown on his face like a scene from "Night of the Living Dead."

Sergeant Washington strode up to the wounded lieutenant. The platoon cringed in anxious, uneasy anticipation. Tentatively poking the officer with the barrel of his M-16, he asked broadly, "Well. Did anyone see what direction the sniper fire came from?"

"Huh?" asked Damian.

"Well, he was shot by a sniper, wasn't he?"

In extraordinary situations, when it became necessary to shoot an overly rambunctious junior officer, blaming it on a sniper proved to be, customarily, reliably convenient. Ninety-five percent of the time, you might be interested to know, when the official cause of a combat death is reported as "sniper fire," that guy was shot by one of his own men.

"Yeah. Yeah. Sniper fire," we all agreed, nodding our heads like bobble dolls.

A sense of relief enveloped the patrol. I lit a cigarette. Leaning up against a post, I smoked it slowly and sensually. It seemed to me that Sergeant Washington deliberately took his sweet time before calling in a Medevac chopper. The lieutenant's incessant yowling began to get on my nerves.

"Are you going to call this one in?" Loren questioned.

"But many who are first shall be last, and the last first," the sergeant quoted the Bible, as he often did.

I suppose he figured that if the lieutenant lost enough blood, at least the son-of-a-bitch would have the courtesy to pass out or choke to death on his own vomit, but I'll be damned if you couldn't still hear his primal screams of pain over the whine of the Huey as it lifted off the LZ (landing zone) in a vortex of purple smoke, and what a foul mouth this man had for an officer and all. It shocked and surprised me and certainly not what I would expect of an officer's code of behavior.

"Fuck Captain Riley. Fuck Major Wilhelm. Fuck Colonel Barrows."

He went right up the chain of command.

"Fuck General Abrams. Fuck Melvin Laird, Fuck Richard M. Nixon."

"Melvin Laird! Who the heck is Melvin Laird?" I asked Sergeant Washington.

"He's President Nixon's new Secretary of Defense," the sergeant tolerantly explained to me. "He's been charged with the 'vietnamization' of the war, and achieving peace with honor."

"Well, good for him. I wish Mr. Laird the best of luck, but he certainly has his work cut out for him."

"And, if there's anything I can do to help bring about his goal of peace," Loren added, "just let me know."

"The Lord gives strength to his people; the Lord blesses his people with peace," Sergeant Washington pulled another Bible verse out of his butt. "What did you have in mind?"

"I don't know. I suppose I would go along with a comprehensive stratagem to cease terrorizing the local citizens in a manifestation of imperial provincialism, if that would help, and spend more time making love to the attractive young females amongst them."

"I'll pass it on. I'm sure headquarters will be gratified to hear that, and appreciate your sacrifice. Now, grab your gear and saddle up. We need to *Di di mau*. That dust off likely attracted the attention of every Ho Chi Minh loyalist within 10 miles. In the future, you gentlemen are going to have to start clearing it with me before you pop an officer. We have a chain of command in the Army, and for a good reason. If enlisted men just went around gunning down ham-fisted officers willy-nilly, this war would be chaos. We'd be facing anarchy. Sometimes there can be ramifications to your actions that you dunderheads can't foresee."

As an aside, this approximated about the same time that the following jokes began to circulate:

Question: What do you do if a second lieutenant staggers out of the officers' club, stumbles, falls, then gets back up?
Answer: Shoot him again.

And:

Question: Where can you find a fearless lieutenant?
Answer: Right where you shot him.

Indeed, the whole affair, unfortunately, turned out to be a nightmare for poor Damian, who was charged with, and later convicted of shooting a congressionally represented white guy. He received a sentence of three years in Leavenworth (I told him that he should be able to do that standing on his head), plus a dishonorable discharge for unbecoming behavior and gross battlefield indiscretions. For the rest of us, though, the shooting accomplished the intended purpose.

Word got out around the Officer's Club, and the next lieutenant we were assigned knew damn well what happened to the last one. Since he liked his elbows just the way they were (as a matching pair), he seemed content to let us hang out all day, doing what we liked to do best: shuckin' and a jiving, jaw jackin', lolly-gaggin', bull-shittin', eating C-Rations, popping pills, drinking beer, scratchin' our nuts, playing gin rummy, smoking pot, and reading *Playboy* magazines, while he filed reams of phony-baloney After Action Reports to III Corps about how we were burning *barge*-loads of rice, shooting *whole* herds of pigs, and having the time of our lives doing it.

As you can well imagine, this impressed Command. So, for his extraordinary effort, Lieutenant Holstein received a Commendation Medal for " . . . meritorious service in the face of great hardship and hostile enemy action," a big promotion, (that got him transferred to Bien Hoa) and later, I understand, a well-paying job as the assistant acting, second assistant secretary to the senior secretary for the undersecretary of the Secretary of the Department of Health, Education, and Welfare, in the Nixon administration.

The crux of the matter is that I was assigned to the 173rd Airborne Brigade at Bong Son, Vietnam, didn't care for it terribly, and acquired an unbecoming cockiness and bad attitude that I would, regrettably, carry home, and find exasperatingly difficult to conquer. As an explanation for my incessant inexcusable conduct, people who knew me would persist in whispering, to those I offended or otherwise appalled, that I had "Vietnam issues." Meaning well, my very closest friends would add, as a mitigating codicil: "And a Silver Star."

CHAPTER THREE

Letters from Home

War is endless boredom punctuated by unspeakable letters from home. I made it an ironclad policy not to reply to any of the garrulous mail I received. Doing so only encouraged them to write longer, more fatuous letters, more often. From my mother's dispatches, I received such interesting news as: using peanut butter for bait, my dad trapped a mouse in the basement; a robin built her nest on the ledge outside the dining room window and now had four eggs; the Putnams put their house on the market for $19,900; and Grandpa Schultz died.

I thought a lot about Grandpa Schultz the day I received the heart rending news. I remembered how he regularly took an afternoon nap. I remembered his treasured stamp collection. I remembered shaking his hand at the bus stop when I shipped out.

All my bags were packed; I was ready to go.

There were tears in his disconsolate eyes.

"Don't be a hero," I recalled his admonition.

Grandpa Schultz emanated wisdom. He had fought in World War I at Saint Mehiel as a teenager and hated war. I took his advice to heart, and no more so than on Oct. 3, 1969. We were on a long-range reconnaissance patrol. Although nicknamed "Sky Soldiers," for an Airmobile unit, we did a lot of walking in those days. Sergeant Washington explained to us that it was the only way to truly experience the natural richness and cultural profundity of the country.

"Regrettably, we take too many of God's gifts for granted," he expounded. "What with all of our daily diversions and distractions."

I held Sergeant Washington in high esteem. He became a father figure to me. Despite his persuasion as a born-again Christian, he fortunately exhibited none of the offensively condescending, intolerant, and narrow-minded hallmarks of Christian fundamentalism. His faith manifested itself in an unassuming, genuinely virtuous man.

"Yeah," I said, attempting not to laugh. "Like trying to stay alive."

"The fact that you are so eager to live testifies that you are fiercely alive, son. That's a positive attribute in combat. Dead boonie rats don't earn their keep, and put an unwelcome additional burden on their comrades."

That October day, 15 klicks west of Dak To, our advance progressed swimmingly, a sure indication that we were indeed walking straight into a Viet Cong ambush. In a combat zone, you may be interested to know, there is nothing more lethal (to his own men, that is) than a second lieutenant with a map and a compass. We suffered from one of those.

The first sign of an ambush came with the sickening thunk of PFC Crosby taking a bullet in the jaw, then the succeeding report of a sniper's rifle.

Holy shit! I thought. *We're being ambushed.*

Although I truly felt terrible about Crosby "getting it" the way he did, I was, nonetheless, appreciative that it was him and not me. If that makes me a hopeless narcissist, so be it.

"Somebody help that man!" Sergeant Washington yelled.

Pinned down by heavy enemy gunfire on the bank of a shallow stream, I figured he *couldn't* be talking to me.

"You, Johnson! Get over there and help that man!"

There were two Johnsons in our platoon.

He must be talking to the other Johnson, I thought.

"You! The one with the Silver Star and scat in your shorts. Get over there and help that man."

I crawled on my belly over to Crosby. I easily found him. I just wormed through the elephant grass towards the gurgling sounds he made while struggling to breathe. When he spied me, PFC Crosby reached out to me like an infant for his mother. I could see the terror in his blue eyes. Horrifyingly, his remaining lower jaw hung grotesquely by tatters of tenuous tissue.

I'll never get used to this blood and guts business, I thought to myself.

If his jaw were to fall completely off, which it appeared about to do at any moment, I feared that it would be just too much, on top of everything else.

"Don't talk," I stupidly instructed Crosby.

Blood gushed from his wound. I removed my belt to fashion a tourniquet, in conjunction with my bayonet, as we were trained. Hastily assessing the situation, the only place I figured it could effectively go would be around his neck. As I attempted to position my improvised medical appliance thusly, Crosby frantically fought me, desperately shaking his head from side to side, pleading with his eyes, *No! No!*

So, ruling out that proposition as imprudent and not practicable, I instead grabbed his personal medical kit and removed the sterile pads. Pressing them into his wound, I took his right hand and told him to hold the package to his face.

"We've got to get the hell out of here!" I yelled over my shoulder in the direction I last saw Sergeant Washington. By this time, however, he had made his way, with our radioman, to where we were.

"Keep calm, Johnson, and try not to draw fire. It irritates those around you."

"If I could be calm, it would only mean that I wasn't fully comprehending the gravity of the situation."

"Try not to be so negative, son. You can't control everything that happens to you, but you can control how you react to it. Now, look on the bright side. The lieutenant's dead . . . shot in the head, so from here on I'm in charge of this monkey show. Your chances of getting out of here with your pretty blonde scalp just got a little more promising. Now, lay chilly while I call in some air support. You can do *that*, can't you?"

"Sure, but you say the lieutenant's dead? Damn! He was the most courageous officer I've ever served under."

"Yeah. I guess that's what I always hated about him. That plus the fact he was, of course, a racist blue-eyed devil and Citadel graduate. I would have shot him myself, long ago, except it would diminish my chances for a promotion — and consume crucial ammunition."

Grabbing the radio's handset, the sergeant called for an extraction, a dust off, and some gunships. Mulling over his muddy map (or funny papers as we called them), he transmitted our calculated coordinates. Meanwhile, the rest of the patrol were assiduously squirming, crawling, and wriggling to where we lay in the mucilaginous muck. Incredibly, within minutes, the radio crackled back to life. The pilot of a Huey Slick called us to confirm that he was in the air and heading to our location.

"We're in some deep doo doo down here," Sergeant Washington radioed in reply; some strong language for the perennially decorous gentleman.

"No sweat, G.I." the pilot calmly answered. "I can put this Slick down anywhere, anytime. Plus, I'm bringing some Snakes (Cobra gunships) with me, because that's just the kind of guy I am."

The incoming fire was intense, from all directions, but mostly the east. "Reefer" John Humnicky joined us, diving to the ground at my left, squeezing me between him and the radio. As usual, he had been smoking quite a bit of weed on this patrol.

"Wow, man. Every day here is like the Fourth of July," he observed. "Apparently, these 'little people' take profound exception to being invaded and occupied by the likes of us."

"Yeah. And, regrettably, they know the territory better than we do," Sergeant Washington added.

I was, at once, reminded of "Rock Island," the opening number of "The Music Man" by Meredith Wilson . . . *you've got to know the territory, territory, territory.* Shaking my head, I tried to evict the nagging tune from my sub-consciousness.

"That same thing happens to me every time I hear Yellow Submarine by the Beatles," Reefer John reassured me. "Don't worry about it. Just do what I do and go with it."

"Johnson! Humnicky!" ordered Sergeant Washington. "Lay down some suppressing fire there to the east of you — at the base of those Mia Chau trees."

I expressed, I'm confident, a confused look on my face.

"They're the trees with androgynous panicles consisting of a central pistillate surrounded by staminate branches or catkins."

Sergeant Washington, you may be interested to know, stood out, amongst other pursuits, as a preeminent amateur botanist and a respected authority on the morphology of the local flora.

"I think I see the ones you're referring to," I replied, "but from this distance, there seems to be a confusing range of ploidy, with some plants appearing diploid, and others tending to be either triploid or tetraploid."

"Now you're being a wise guy, Johnson. Just lay down some suppressing fire — yonder."

He pointed east.

"I'm down to only three magazines of ammo," I argued. "Are you sure you want me to expend them? How long do you expect three magazines will last in a ferocious firefight like this?"

"Based on the way the situation is *currently* deteriorating, I'd say the rest of your pathetic life. Now stop questioning my authority, son. It's presumptuous to assume that such profound matters as tactical battlefield management can be explained in terms that you could grasp."

In the distance, I could hear the distinctive *thup, thup, thup* of the choppers as they approached. I needed to focus on the immediate state of affairs. A war enveloped me, and I needed to realize a way out, other than death or dismemberment. The radio crackled again.

Mad Dog Three Zero. This is Control. Are you going to want smoke when you get there?

That's affirmative. I'm going in for a look right now. Checking out the pucker factor. I'll be coming west to east.

"I copy that," Sergeant Washington jumped in on our radio. "This is Mustang Six. We're all in one spot now. I'm popping smoke at this time."

He pulled the pin on a smoke grenade.

"Do you see my smoke sir? Do you have a visual?"

I don't see you yet. Can you see me?

"Negative on that."

OK. OK. I see you now at three o'clock. Is that your yellow smoke?

"Roger that. Come on in to the yellow smoke."

"Actually," Reefer John argued, "I'm thinking that smoke is more of a saffron or a mustard color, rather than a true lemon yellow. I sure hope the pilot is clear on that."

Mad Dog Three Zero overhead at this time . . . just checking things out.

The first Snake arrived on the scene, banking hard, followed by the Slick. Hanging precariously out of the Huey, the door gunner opened fire. I could see his tracers penetrating the underbrush and the hot brass spewing from his gun. Fragments from the M13 disintegrating ammo belt links rained down on us like metal confetti. On one of the passes, the co-pilot extended his gloved hand out the window and gave us a friendly wave. In his bulbous helmet and goggles, he looked like a six-foot-tall grasshopper. Reefer John, I could tell, was visibly shaken by the disconcerting sight of a giant (and likely radioactive) insect piloting a helicopter. The radio crackled to life again.

Get your heads up! To the east . . . two fast movers closing.

As a pair of Phantom jets roared low overhead, shaking the ground, John observed, "Whoa, man. This is some far-out air show these dudes are putting on. I hope we get those Blue Angels for the finale. They give me goose bumps every time I see those F-4s performing that Delta Formation maneuver."

Uh, Control. This is Mad Dog Three Zero. We just had a couple of "lead sleds" pass right through us in a brazen triumph of thrust over aerodynamics. Do you want to do something about that, sir?

This is Control. They were probably just having a look.

Yeah. Well, can you keep those jet jocks, and their flying footlockers out of our sector while we're working? We almost had a midair . . . and also, can you tell me if there is any other fixed-wing traffic in the area . . . any AC-47s?

Control here. Looks like there may be a Clutch Cargo at above 10 thousand, I have no explanation for the flight suit inserts, and there are no Spookys airborne at this time.

I copy. No Spookys.

That's affirmative.

Well, if you F-4 pilots are on this frequency and listening, I just want you to know that wings are for fairies.

And helicopters don't actually fly, they just beat the air into submission, came a sneering reply. *They're so ugly that the earth actually repels them.*

Fixed wing pilots were once kids who dreamed of becoming an aviator, but were too lazy to learn.

The reason you guys don't have ejection seats is because, in a helicopter, the difference between flying and crashing is not black and white. It's more of a gray area.

How do you know if there's a fighter pilot at your party?

I know, I know. He'll tell you. Remember, my little friend, gravity never loses. The best you can hope for is a draw.

I'm guessing that Will Rogers never met a fighter pilot.

"What station you got on there, bro," Reefer John asked the radioman. "Is that WBBM? Have you heard a business report yet? I was sort of hoping to learn how the Dow did today."

PFC Crosby moaned in pain. Sergeant Washington grabbed the microphone.

"OK. We're going to need that dust off just as soon as possible. Also, could I get some suppressing fire along that tree line to the east . . . and . . . uh, I've got a man down here who could use a market report, if anyone can help us out with that."

Last I heard, all of the major indices were down fractionally in moderate trading.

"Thanks. I copy you as down fractionally."

Roger, Roger. I'm rolling in at this time, charming the cobra and spellbinding the snake. You say that tree line is to the east of you?

"That's affirmative. About 50 meters to our echo. Could you make that a mini gun run through there?"

Roger. I have 21 thousand rounds left in this old mountain magnet heap of spinning metal fatigue, surrounded by an oil leak, on the way to a crash site. I'm beginning my pass now. Comin' to ya' . . . down on the deck, rockin' and rollin'.

The Cobra lowered its nose. The eerie resonance of its minigun reverberated through the valley, like the sound of a powerline transformer shorting out. A second Cobra fell in behind the first. The radio continued to spew incomprehensible chatter.

Hold your fire, Mad Dog. This is Gunfighter Four. I need about ten seconds to get behind you and bless the altar boy . . . OK. I'm lined up now.

Roger. We're going to start our approach at this time.

Multiple firings of the gunships' twin 70 mm rockets from their launch tubes hissed just over our heads and hit their target about 15 meters from our position. Tiny pieces of hot shrapnel from the explosion rained down on us.

How was that, Mustang Six?

"Good shooting," Sergeant Washington replied. "That's how I like it. Nice and close."

"What about me?" I piped up as I swatted at the dozens of glowing embers burning little doughnut holes in my jungle fatigues. "Did anyone ask *me* how I like it?"

"I thought about it," Sergeant Washington answered, "but since your previous opinions have proven to be both uninformed and irrelevant, what would be the point?"

I'm clear now. Dust Off Two. Are you still in the area?

This is Dust Off Two. We're orbiting about one mile to your whiskey . . . Winding the Jack In The Box, and waiting for you to do your thing.

We'll be coming back the other way just as soon as we get turned around. Keep an eye out. OK, I'm inbound from the southwest now. Over.

"Oh crap," I exclaimed as I flattened out and covered my head with my arms.

Roger. Holding high and dry on this frequency.

I copy. We need that extractor chopper and, uh, we'll also need his call sign if you've got it.

This is Control. I'm working on that now.

Be advised that we're receiving all sorts of fire from the tree line on the low passes. We need more ordinance on this area before attempting a dust-off. The LZ is still too hot. I repeat. The LZ is still hot. Do you copy?

OK. Mark it on your next run and we'll suppress that tree line when we pass over it. This ain't no pigs and rice mission. I'm beginning to think that the only possible way we're going to win this pointless war is to exterminate the entire domestic population.

Roger that. OK, we're on the go at this time . . . Takin' Herman to the circus. It's a laugh a minute.

Yep. Just a walk in the park . . . Duck soup.

A mortar shell exploded about 10 meters away, followed by a hail of AK-47 fire. The gunship's rockets ripped over our heads again, this time finding their mark even closer to our position. This proved to be far too much variety for me. Reefer John buried his face in the soft mud. His helmet, I noticed, had a peace sign on one side and the image of a cannabis leaf on the other. After I determined it was longer than any person could possibly hold his breath, I shook him vigorously.

"Hey John. Are you alive?"

"Yeah man. I'm OK," he replied, coming up for air. "This is some crazy shit, but I'm dealing with it. I'm fine. . . just fine."

"Well, you'd never know it to look at you."

"I'm good. I'm good. Just thinking about geography."

"Geography?"

"Yeah, and I've concluded that of all the places in the world I'd *least* like to be, this one has got to be on the top of my list. What about you?"

"For sure! But East Chicago, Indiana, along with Calumet City, Illinois, still round out my top three."

"Then, I take it, you've never been to Flint, Michigan."

"Can't say that I have."

Another burst of AK-47 fire. More merciless mortar bombardment. I couldn't believe I signed up for this shit.

"Someday, they're going to throw a war," John prophesized, "and nobody will show up."

"Well, the next time the pleasure of my company is adjured, on the occasion of a military police action, war, armed conflict, or crusade, I'll be sending my regrets, if it's all just the same, thank you. That's for sure."

Dear Mr/Ms President:

Thank you for your public-spirited behest to report for induction into the Armed Forces of the United States. It sounds exciting!

Unfortunately, due to a previous obligation, I will be unable to attend. . .

A mortar round exploded just to our left. We both flattened out again.

"Damn! That was close," John understated the obvious.

"Yeah. I sure wish my grandpa Schultz were still alive," I responded.

"What? What's this about your grandfather?"

"I said I wish my grandpa were still alive. I think I'm really going to need to talk to someone about this shit when I get home. Someone who *gets* it."

"I sure as hell wish I would have listened to *my* dear old gramps before I enlisted for this insanity. He was the wisest, most rational, level-headed man I ever knew. But, like your grandad, he too has gone into the fertilizer business."

"Did he advise you against military service? Or implore you go to college and procure a deferment? Or to move to Canada? Or feign bone spurs in your feet?"

"Honestly, I don't really know. As I just said, I didn't listen to him."

"Well, I'll always remember the last thing my grandfather said to me before he bought the farm."

"What was that?"

"He said 'Bruce! Guess what? Your grandmother and I sold our condo, and we're buying a hobby farm outside Matteson.' That's what he said."

CHAPTER FOUR

The Extraction

I understand you want an extract, Mustang Six, the radio crackled.

"Roger that," Sergeant Washington responded. "First chopper in, we're going to need a medic on board."

I copy. We have a dust off orbiting a mile to your west, but that's some hot Lima Charley you've got down there.

"We're taking some wicked fire from that tree line to our echo."

I can see that. You guys must have walked into a Viet Cong convention. We're going to need to soften that area up to the east of you before we attempt. I understand you have one wounded.

"That's affirmative. One whiskey and a dead officer — and we also have two captives we'll need to load."

I copy. Continue to monitor this frequency while we work. I'll drop a body bag for your lieutenant when we pass over. Sometimes it helps prevent the temptation of the men to mutilate his corpse. You might want to put those entrenching tools of yours to some productive utility, and dig in. This may take a while.

"Roger. Roger."

OK. We're going to start another approach now. Get your heads down.

A Cobra gunship skimmed over our position.

Rockets away!

The incoming from the tree line to our east grew so intense, that I dared not raise my head for a peak at the carnage, let alone attempt to return fire. It seemed best, in my humble judgment, to just let the gunships ameliorate the situation. My whole world shrunk to this one square meter of soggy humus. It smelled like gun powder and dog shit. My mouth felt dry. When I licked my lips, I tasted bitter insect repellant. Inches from my nose, a dung beetle, oblivious to the battle, busily burrowed into some rotting plant material. Crackling from the transceiver next to me, radio traffic dominated my consciousness.

Gunfighter Four. Follow me in and commence suppressing fire at that tree line. Cease it when you get to that open area to the south, and climb out to the west. If you receive fire, throw some smoke and get out of there in a hurry.

OK. What's the terrain like around there?

There are some small hills to the south, but otherwise, it's pretty level.

Roger. I'm going to start our approach now. Turning in behind you.

The haunting, harmonic hum of the Cobra's miniguns climaxed with a flaming explosion from the tree line. They probably hit a cache of mortar shells, I guessed.

Control here. Outlaws are inbound with three more aircraft.

Three Zero copies.

Six copies.

Gunfighter Four . . . I copy.

Outlaw Seven here. I think I have you in sight. I see yellow smoke.

That's affirmative. Yellow smoke.

We're about three minutes out. Can you give us some idea of the "political climate" in the area?

"Well, I'm black," Sergeant replied, "and I feel slightly less accepted here than when I was back in Alabama."

The pair of Cobras made a wide turn around our position.

How was that last pass, Gunfighter One?

It was a little too hairy for me.

If Lynch got shook, it must have been bad.

The shark's teeth painted on the Cobra's noses gave the aircraft an evil grin.

We need more ordnance on this area. It's still too hot.

How was that minigun run? How did that last one look, Rich?

Was that your burst, Pat?

Affirmative.

Well it was about twenty low.

Gunfighter One is on location, overhead, and ready to go to work for you. I'm low on fuel so I may only have a couple of good runs. Where do you want my first pass?

The tree line to the east of the smoke. Don't expend everything you've got, and divert to the river when you're down to about 250 pounds. Control tells us we have three more snakes inbound.

"Mustang Six here," Sergeant Washington radioed. "This soldier is going to need that evac right now! We can't stop the bleeding down here. He needs to get upstairs."

Uh, Dust Off Two. This is Batman Three Zero. Do you copy that? Mustang Six is trying to contact you.

Roger Batman. Dust off Two copies and we're inbound at this time.

In the distance, I spied a Huey, sporting a big red cross painted on its nose, and heading in our direction.

Holy firefight, Batman! Those Airborne Rangers have gotten themselves into a pickle.

That would be a colloquialism for a predicament, I presume, came the terse reply. *Always remember Dust Off, when communicating on the Bat Radio, precise phraseology is critical. You might want to commit to memory this astute haiku: The magnitude of a word misconstrued . . . ineptitude!*

Holy diction, Batman! I never looked at it that way before.

Happy to help. We're working the people on the ground here. Do you understand where the friendlies are?

Yes, but have them give us some more smoke if they've got it.

We'd like to hose this area down better before you attempt to go in, if that's okay. I want to light up that hot spot just to the east of the smoke.

Negative on that. We're just to the southwest of the LZ at this time. I'd like to do a one-eighty for a short final. The way things look now, it's going to be a low hover. After we load, I'd like to go through transitional and make two hard lefts out.

Uh, Dust Off Two. This is Dragon Three Zero. Gunfighter One is just finishing his pass at this time; then we'll all be out of your way. I'm afraid they're still taking a lot of fire down there. We put quite a bit of ordnance on that tree line, but it's still alive. Be advised that winds are light and from the southwest. Good luck, sir!

The Medevac chopper approached — fast and low. He headed directly for our smoke. At first, due to his speed, I thought the pilot was going to over-fly our position but, at the last instant, the Huey's nose flared up and its tail nearly struck the ground as he transitioned into a hover just above us. From the wash of his rotors, the tall grass we were hidden in parted like the Red Sea. I could hear rounds piercing aluminum as the Huey took several hits while settling to the ground.

"Get that man loaded fast," the medic screamed. "This LZ is too hot to be lollygaggin'."

We put Crosby on his feet, and shoved him in the door. He was still desperately holding the blood-soaked dressing to his face. With the flight medic holding him under the armpits, Crosby's legs dangled out of the helicopter as it banked left and upwards, disappearing from sight within seconds. The oily smell of kerosene lingered.

Dust off completed at this time. We're balls to the walls and out of here!

Congratulations. Great job. Your heading will be one four zero degrees. Looks like you took some serious hits back there. What's your damage assessment . . . and can you make it home OK?

I think they got a fuel tank. We certainly lost pressure. I have a cracked canopy, and I took some hits in the tail somewhere. We've got good instruments, however, and three hundred pounds of fuel. We appreciate your help, sir.

See you later aviator!

"I hope Crosby makes it," someone who had dug in near me said. "He owes me forty bucks."

Batman Two. I'm on station at this time . . . just to your west. I see their yellow smoke by a small stream to my echo. This is not a bad place to orbit until you need our help. You can call me back toll-free when you're good and ready for us, Scotty. As card-carrying members of the 180-degree club, we won't be conducting any absurd heroics like that Medivac crew.

The sky was now swarming with aircraft.

What's your position, One Zero?

Say again.

What's your position . . . and are you hot?

I'm having some problems with my radio. Say again please.

Are you loaded . . . and what is your position?

You're coming in broken. I don't copy.

For another 20 minutes, the gunships continued their punishment of the tree line, tipping their noses down, as if genuflecting to Satan, while their miniguns spewed their wicked bile. The stench of war pervaded deep into my sinuses. A burnt metallic sulfur taste clung to the roof of my mouth.

Did you see where that came from?

One one zero degrees . . . about five meters.

Are you going to be working the area where the dust off was just completed?

Roger that.

How many people are left?

I understand we have seven extractions to make. You can turn left to four zero degrees. Mustang Six, are you receiving fire at this time?

Sergeant Washington grabbed the handset again.

"Most of the fire coming from the tree line seems to be directed at you guys now. We took a straw poll, and my boys down here tell me that any time you want to extract us, it would be fine with them."

Roger, but be advised that your ballot is adjudged to be nonbinding. As per the Deputy Staff Judge Advocate for this sector, your vote tally does not directly determine the outcome of the evac. Instead, Tactical Air Control has the discretion to decide whether or not to implement your request, even if the majority of those on the ground support it.

During my thirteen months in Vietnam, I never heard Sergeant Washington curse, and this time was no exception. He looked, however, to be acutely exasperated.

"Just ask yourself: *What would Jesus do?*" I put forward, familiarly aware of his fervent faith in Christ.

"Not this," he grumbled. "Not this."

"Hey, Sarge. We're going to make it aren't we?"

"I'm not sure anymore, Son. I'm afraid that if they don't get that hot-spot neutralized soon, we'll all be brown bread."

"Huh?"

"Dead."

"Can't you be just a little more positive than that? I look up to you."

"Alright. I'm *positive* that if they don't get that hot-spot neutralized soon, we'll all be brown bread."

The circling Slick, which had been making wide, lazy circles while the Cobras worked out, now headed in our direction.

Mad Dog Three Zero here. We're inbound to your location now, Mustang Six. What am I going to need to know about this Lima Zulu?

"We're taking mortars and small arms . . . mostly from the east. I have seven U.S., a body bagger, and two straw hats now . . . and . . . uh . . . make that one straw hat. This guy just got shot by one of his own people."

Dragon Six. This is mad dog three zero. Are we still going in direct or are you going to route us through?

Mad Dog. This is Dragon Six. I suggest you come into the LZ from the west with a departure back to the west. Stay away from that tree line. We've had a little difficulty mitigating the situation over there.

Control here. I just received a fresh NOTAM (Notice to Airmen) across my desk. It's marked 'urgent.' According to this, you're requested to make that departure to the southwest for noise abatement protocols.

For noise abatement? We're in a firefight down here for God's sake!

Well, uh yeah, but some of the residents of a nearby hamlet, evidently, have been complaining about the racket you're making.

Roger. We are beginning our descent now. We are on final to the LZ at this time.

The Slick arrived, looking like an angel of mercy. Eagerly our platoon climbed onboard as the chopper hovered just a few feet above the ground.

"Go! Go! Go! Go!" Sergeant Washington screamed.

I stepped on the chopper's skid tube, extended my hand to the door gunner, and he yanked me into the craft with such force that I sprawled face down on the sand-textured metal floor, abrading the skin on the palms of my hands. My attempt to get back on my feet was impaired by the swaying motion of the hovering aircraft. Just as I gained a half-standing position, the Huey lurched and banked simultaneously as it lifted off the LZ, nearly ejecting me out the door opposite the one I had entered. Only grabbing, with my bloody hands, the nylon webbing that lined the helicopter's interior, saved me from a freefall back into the battle.

This is control, Mad Dog Three Zero. I need to know how many souls you have on board.

We have one ship loaded. I had a real problem with all of these guys jumping on the aircraft at one time. I've got seven or eight right now. I think I already lost one man falling off the skids. I don't think he was U.S. though.

Grab some altitude getting out of there.

Roger.

Once at safe altitude and level flight, the door gunner addressed us.

"Shit, man," he drawled with a Kentucky coal miner's accent. "I've got 10 days, a wake up, and I'm out of this hellhole. I'm way too short for this sort of nonsense. You guys have got to stop pissin' the Viet Cong off like that or you're going to get me killed before I'm able to go home to see my sick mama and my mule . . . I'm getting married when I get back, you should know."

He proudly pulled a photo from his breast pocket of a homely girl who appeared to be about fourteen.

"Is that your fiancée," I joked, "or your mule?"

"I don't know. I don't speak French so I can't answer that . . . but she's my cousin if that's what you're asking."

"That was going to be my next gag, but you stole my punch line!"

"Perhaps, you need to be more creative, then . . . more original. Not only are you recycling stale old comedic formulas employing infelicitous stereotypes, you're also overworking the material. You need deeper, more interesting jokes, and better timing. The use of rhythm and tempo can have a profound effect on how well your jokes are received . . ."

"Where do you come up with this shit, you pretentious little prick?"

"Before I was drafted, I was the entertainment critic for the *Marrowbone Mountain Messenger*."

CHAPTER FIVE

Eagle Flight

Six pairs of legs dangled from the two open doors of the Huey as we thrashed our way through the sky towards home. Mine were not amongst them. If I should die in Vietnam, it wasn't going to be from falling out of a helicopter. I seated myself safely in the interior of the craft near the door gunner.

"Where are *you* from?" he yelled over the sounds of rushing air and relentless rotors.

"I'm sorry. I can hardly hear you."

"Here put this on."

He handed me a helmet with built-in headphones and a foam-covered microphone.

"How's that?" I heard his voice clearly now, accompanied by a soft hiss.

"That's much better."

My own voice in the headset, boomed a little louder than comfortable and sounded dorky.

"I'm from Chicago. . . that toddlin' town."

In the background, static-filled radio traffic from the battle we just escaped continued.

Be advised that you currently have Stinger Six working in sector three.

Roger. Roger. I'm breaking right. We will not be expending any more rockets after this.

Hey! That bastard just about shot me down! I'm doing a one-eighty. I'm going back to get that son-of-a-bitch.

Roger that. I saw exactly where the fire came from. Stand by and I'll vector you in if you want.

Mayday! Mayday! Mayday!

Can anyone see where that distress call came from?

Roger. I think Witch Doctor Five is down . . . just to the west of the smoke. He's crashed into the trees.

Dragon Two. Take over the flight. I'm going in to see what I can do.

OK. Be advised that we are taking heavy fire at this time.

Divert south of the river if you can.

Taking fire! Taking fire!

Six here. We're also taking fire . . . we've been hit! . . . I'm losing power. We're going in!

Uh, Control. We now have two downed ships and are receiving heavy fire. This mission is deteriorating into a real cluster-fuck.

Radio etiquette please!

Sorry. Disregard my previous transmission. Correction. This mission is deteriorating into a real Charlie-Foxtrot.

Sir?

Uh, er, soup sandwich.

We copy that. Proceed with your SOP if you can. Is someone able to give me a fix on where that last aircraft went down, please?

One and one-half clicks west of the LZ. We have two ships down now. One just crashed and burned. I'm going back to see if those guys are OK. I saw right where they went in.

Who was it?

I don't know. I think he ID'd himself before he went in but there was too much static. I saw one aircraft explode. The other looked like he set down. I see three crew members outside. The copilot looks like he's still inside. The ship is burning pretty bad. Uh . . . there's another ship right next to it. The other one is not on fire. I see four crew members outside this one.

Was that a midair collision?

It could have been. I can't say.

Do you know what happened to his copilot?

Negative.

Did anyone just see that? There was a Cobra on his run and he just exploded midair.

What? Are you saying we have three aircraft down now?

That's affirmative.

OK. I understand we have two recovery ships on the way.

Roger. Roger. We have a recovery in progress.

Did anyone see if the copilot got out of that aircraft?

Negative. But I saw the gunner get the pilot out and he's walking around the crash site. This is a pretty helpless feeling.

"Sounds like those guys back there are catching all sorts of trouble and strife," the door gunner broke in over the intercom. "That's always been one of my worst fears . . . becoming a crispy critter like that."

"Yeah. If I live to get out of here, I'm guessing that years from now I'll look back at these times as my misspent youth."

Uh, control. Are you copying this? We have two Slicks down. One's burning, one's turning. We also had a Cobra explode midair.

I copy. Can you get a tail number off the Slick that's on fire?

Looks like the tail number is two one five . . . let me see . . . seven one six. Oh crap! I have another Snake down over here on this ridge.

That one's been there a while. It's one we lost last week.

No. This one's turning. I don't know what he's doing. But there is a lot of black smoke coming from his engine.

OK. Let's get a Slick in there and get that crew out.

Control here. Do I understand that you now have four downed aircraft?

Roger. Two Slicks and two Snakes, plus we have at least four more of us with moderate to severe battle damage.

If you have any ordnance left, One Zero, try to put it down on that tree line where all of the fire is coming from.

Uh. Roger. I'm a Slick. I'm expended at this time. I'm trying to pick up that crew that's down.

Oh. OK. Sorry for the confusion.

No problem. It's nothing but confusion up here. I think you need to withdraw some of these aircraft. There's a good possibility that two of those down were the result of a midair.

Meanwhile, we enjoyed a scenic flight over the lush Vietnamese countryside. Below us, rice paddies, punctuated by artillery impact craters, glistened. Whenever we passed over a small hamlet, I could see the occupants running for cover.

I just lost one guy. He's turning back now with heavy damage . . . and apparently, no radio. Does someone want to accompany him . . . in case he can't make it home?

Six here. I'll go.

Thanks. He's a good friend of mine.

We approached Bong Son. After executing a big wide circle around the airbase, our Huey settled on its hardstand. I pulled off my helmet. The pilot shut down the motor while we disembarked with the rotors still turning. My buddies all headed for their hooches while Sergeant Washington chatted with our pilot.

"I'm going over to the mess hall," I called to them. "I need to get something to drink."

As I walked across the airfield, a major stopped me.

"Hey, Specialist. Where's your hat?"

I answered with a shrug of my shoulders.

"You're out of uniform," he warned me. "I could put you on report."

"I'm pissing in my pants," I replied, turned my back on the clown, and walked away.

I hadn't had someone hassle me, or care about, whether I was wearing headgear since training. I took basic training at Fort Leonard Wood, Missouri and it was an interesting nine weeks. At first meeting, our drill sergeant delineated some of the expectations he had of us, and looking around at our group, I tell you, this guy was *California Dreamin'*. In fact, I told the fellow standing next to me as much.

"What did you say, recruit?" screamed the drill sergeant.

"Oh," I extemporized, "I was just saying that those are some pretty ambitious benchmarks you've outlined, but that I'm confident, with your leadership and our determination, we can all pull together to not only meet those noble goals, but exceed them, and become better soldiers in the end."

"Is that so?" responded the drill sergeant calmly. "Because it sounded to me exactly like you asked the recruit standing next to you what planet I was from."

"Well, that too," I replied, "but it was a rhetorical question."

"A *rhetorical* question, you say? Well, that's a pretty sophisticated word to be using on a poor white boy from Mississippi, educated in a one-room schoolhouse. Let me see if I can figure it out from its context. Would that be, by chance, the same thing as sayin' that it was a *smartass* question?"

"I suppose so," I meekly responded.

"Well, what do you think happens to smartasses in the Army?"

"Ugh, they do pushups?"

"That was a rhetorical question," snapped the Drill Sergeant, "characterized by mere rhetoric . . . asked for effect only, to emphasize a point . . . no answer being expected."

"Do you still want me to do push-ups?" I asked, afraid of the answer.

"No," he replied after contemplating the question. "As a matter of fact, I don't. I want you to stand there and ponder this conversation while the *rest* of the platoon does push-ups."

He paused dramatically, as if deep in thought, then continued,

"On second consideration, it's a real scorcher out here today. I wouldn't want you *standing* in the hot Missouri sun in weather like this."

He ordered a recruit to run over to the senior drill sergeant's office to procure a chair. Placing it in the shade of a live oak, he offered me the seat with an exaggerated gesture.

"Young man," he addressed one of my platoon mates, "Run over to the mess hall and tell the cook to serve up a nice tall iced tea with plenty of ice for my good friend here. We wouldn't want him writing home to his mommy that the United States Army isn't taking excellent care of her baby now, would we?"

"No, Drill Sergeant."

"Because if he becomes dehydrated or suffers sunstroke, I'm going to hold you personally responsible. Do you understand me boy?"

"Yes, Drill Sergeant."

The overweight and out of shape recruit ran to the mess hall and returned with the tea, panting. Our drill sergeant took it from him and handed to me with contrived obeisance.

"Recruit!"

"Yes, Drill Sergeant," Fat Boy responded.

"How come there's no straw in my friend's tea?"

"Oh, I'm fine," I insisted. "I'll just drink it like this."

"Are you sure? Because it wouldn't be any trouble for me to send this thoughtless recruit back to get one for you."

"No. No. Really, I'm fine."

The drill sergeant then conducted the rest of our platoon in 45 minutes of rigorous calisthenics, followed by a mile run, which he personally led without breaking a sweat. Comfortably watching all this strenuous activity, from my pleasant spot in the shade, I sipped my cool drink, enjoying the slight breeze, and thinking that I should have mentioned to the drill sergeant that I take lemon and sugar in my tea.

That evening, back at the barracks, some of the guys had a "conversation" with me about keeping my comments to myself. It seemed a challenge enough to stoically finish basic training with two broken ribs. I really didn't feel further motivated to keep these recruits' spirits up with any more levity — with but one small exception. Just to mess with the drill sergeants' heads a little, I started acting as if I were a Marine recruit. It was an idea that just popped into my mind.

"Everybody line up for formation!" our senior drill sergeant announced, blowing his referee's whistle.

"Oohrah-oohrah!" I screamed.

The drill sergeant gave me a curious look.

"Kill! Kill!" I persisted, standing at stiff attention, the veins in my neck protruding.

"Are you feeling alright? Do you need to go on sick call or something, Johnson?"

"No Sir! I'm gung ho, Sir! I want to improvise, adapt, and overcome, Sir!"

"Please don't call me *Sir*, Johnson. I work for a living. Now, just calm down a little. Relax. It's way too early in the morning for this."

"Yes Senior Drill Sergeant!" I screamed at the top of my lungs.

"Look kid. If you're bucking for some sort of an entry-level separation discharge for mental defect, I'm not buying into it. In fact, if you keep behaving like this, I'm going to promote you to a prestigious, permanent fire guard position."

Actually, my little charade completely backfired. Upon graduation from basic, I received my MOS (Military Occupation Specialty) of Eleven-Bravo, and proceeded on to infantry (bullet catcher) school at Fort Benning, Georgia. They decided it would be a splendid fit for someone with my enthusiasm. Our sergeant there told us we were the most sorry-ass, funky-smellin', momma's boys that he ever had the misfortune to train. My guess, though, is he said that to all his recruits. He also predicted that most of us would be killed if we ever saw combat. I looked at the guy on my left, and then the guy on my right, and wondered if the sergeant might tell us that *one* of us wouldn't be coming back. He didn't. A missed opportunity for some good melodrama, and I have to say, I felt deeply disappointed.

The conventional wisdom in infantry training maintained that troops perform best with a motto. For good measure, we had two. The first was: "I am the infantry, the queen of battle. Follow me!" Just in case some of the fellows found that to be a bit swishy, or couldn't remember a three-part motto, we had another, more succinct one: "Forever Forward." I could see now where our high school football coach, who had been a ranger in World War II, had likely gotten most of his material.

Overall, infantry training seemed very much like football practice — only with assault rifles. I had done pretty much all of this before, so, naturally, I wanted to try something different. Something intrepid. I don't know what came over me, but for some inexplicable reason, I decided I wanted to jump out of airplanes. All I can think of now, it must have had something to do with being 18 years old.

Before reporting to Ranger School, it was necessary to receive a "ranger haircut" and a special, extra *heavy-duty* physical exam.

"Hey Doc," I protested while bending over the exam table with my shorts down around my ankles. "What the hell are you doing back there?"

"I'm checking your warrior ethos," he replied. "What did you think?"

"To be perfectly candid with you, I was thinking that this is *exactly* why I'm not gay."

"Hold your horses. I'll be getting to that part of the exam just as soon as I finish up here."

Only a couple of days into training, it became obvious that Ranger School was, for me, a poor fit. This is not just an arbitrary statement. I'm able to submit several facts to support that assertion. First of all, I came to realize, I did not possess the *esprit de corps* and intestinal fortitude required to fight on to the Ranger objective and complete the mission. There seemed to be a strong emphasis on this. Another thing that didn't resonate with me (and I have to say, they really weren't up front about) was their *obsession* with moving further, faster (in full *battle-rattle*), and fighting harder than any other soldier. These guys really needed to mellow out.

On top of that, I have to tell you, jumping from airplanes was a grand disappointment. After ground instruction, tower training, and aircraft orientation, we learned more than anyone ever wanted to know about parachute malfunctions. When I asked one of the parachute packers just how long he had been doing this sort of thing, he told me, "Six months, and I've never had a complaint."

"What if my main chute fails to open? How much time do I have to open my reserve?"

He shot me a pathetic look.

"The rest of your life, of course."

As a matter of fact, on our second jump, the main chute of one of our fellow trainees *did* fail to open, and when he went to his reserve, it opened only partially and with twisted lines. He hit the ground at like 40 miles per hour. I landed nearby, and as soon as I freed myself from my suspension lines, sprinted over to see if he was dead. Both of his femurs suffered compound linear fractures, his shoulder was dislocated, and he appeared to have a broken nose.

"Hey dude," I asked. "Are you alive?"

"Yeah man," he answered groggily. "But if this ranger training gets any tougher, I'm quitin'."

The main thing I came away with from jump (dope on a rope) school was that, assuming it's not on fire, there is absolutely no good reason to jump out of a well-maintained, expertly piloted aircraft with an adequate supply of fuel.

Having completed five anguished qualifying jumps there at Fort Benning, Georgia, I, fortunately, never had to put on a parachute again for the balance of my airborne career. After that, we just flew places in helicopters, which after all, made a whole lot more sense. Helicopters had the distinct advantage of being capable of hovering just a couple of feet off the ground. When we got to our destination, all we needed to do was just step out.

CHAPTER SIX

Fire Support Base Charlie

Our platoon received a week off to recover from the unfortunate October 3rd ambush west of Dak To. Captain Riley told us that he felt very sorry about everything.

"According to intelligence, there weren't supposed to be any V.C. in that sector," he explained. "Those devious little tunnel diggers can be so sneaky at times. It makes it exceedingly difficult for me to command effectively when the enemy roves with impunity as they do. They have absolutely no concept of sportsmanship or fair play."

So, while we were giving peace its proverbial chance, by soaking up some rays in sunny Bien Hoa Province, bothering no one, and getting some much appreciated R&R, high-ranking U.S. military officers were back at it, provoking the locals. This is something these "ring-knockers" were, evidently, taught to do at West Point. I'm thinking it to be most likely a Political Science class with a turgid title like: *Ensuring the Universal Hatred of America in the International Community*. It must have been a graduation requirement, the way I see it.

"Johnson!" Sergeant Washington barked, startling me. "When you finish masturbating, pack your gear, and see the armorer for as many bandoliers of ammo as you can comfortably carry, along with a half dozen M61 fragmentation grenades. Here's your paperwork."

He handed me a single sheet of paper printed with a long series of numbers punctuated by snippets of text . . . something like this:

15:00HRS 28 OCT. 1969, HQ 3087COMD. BON SON 173rd

000016354/1897357 RE: JOHNSON, SPC/4 322-18-0153

DIRECTIVE 00009764725357-17635 ACT #33265AR 15011

IS TO TRANSFER TO FSB C 15211-2456727/18753 . . .

I scratched my head. As best as I could decipher them, the orders decreed that I report to a fire support base "over the fence," i.e., in Cambodia. I was to relieve some guy who had, imprudently, stood up during a firefight to urinate. As a result, he received a radical, non-religious indicated circumcision.

"I'm going to relieve a guy who took a bullet while relieving himself?"

"According to 'rumor-control,' that just about sums it up. Now get moving."

Begrudgingly, I slid my *Playboy* magazine, and Playmate of the month, Shay Knuth, under my mattress. At age 24, Shay studied sociology at the University of Wisconsin, Madison, and moonlighted as a bunny at the *Playboy Club* in Lake Geneva. We had a singular relationship. Her turn-ons: Italian food and groovy clothes. Her turnoffs: Insincerity and conceit. Although easy-going, she could be strong-willed.

"I think I've found my one true love, Sarge."

"I thought that too . . . when I was fourteen."

"What ever became of it?"

"I discovered that I was ambidextrous."

"You mean you're *black* and *ambidextrous*?"

"Yep."

"You're not transgender too, are you?"

"No. That's plenty enough."

"I should think so."

As instructed, I visited the company armorer.

"Hey Shawn," I inquired. "Do you think these jungle fatigues, under certain circumstances, could be considered groovy?"

"Nope."

"And what about the spaghetti with meat sauce C-Rations? Would that be like Italian food?"

"Nope."

"And also, do I, by chance, ever come across to you as insincere or conceited?"

"Nope."

"And what about women? Do you like strong-willed women?"

"Nope. I like guns. I like guns a lot."

"Well then, you'll be pleased to learn that the Second Amendment is very much alive and well here in Vietnam. Did you hear that I'm being shipped out to Fire Support Base Charley to replace that fellow who got his pee-pee shot off?"

"Some people have no consideration for how their actions might inconvenience others. Here's your stuff." Shawn slid the cumbersome pile to me, "and thanks for shopping with us today. Would you like to contribute to our campaign to find a cure for *Abdominal chemodectomas with cutaneous angiolipomas?*" He indicated a clear plastic receptacle with a bright red cap and slot on top. It contained a couple of Military Payment Certificates and a few ten and twenty dong coins.

"No," I alibied. "I gave at the office. Besides, I'm pretty involved with a different good cause."

"Oh? What's that?"

"The prevention of ballistic trauma."

I flew into Fire Support Base Charlie on a supply helicopter during a monsoon. From the air, it looked to be uninhabitable; a one hundred meter in diameter circle of mud, ringed by sandbags and concertina wire, punctuated with discarded empty ammo cases and shell casings. It sat on a small rise surrounded by a grove of burnt, branchless, barren trees lying helter-skelter on the scorched earth. The *Apollo 11* lunar module landed on a less desolate place than this. I threw out my gear and climbed circumspectly off the Huey into the muck.

> *One small step for a man,*
> *one giant leap for mankind.*

The guy in charge at the FSB was a captain. The reason I knew this was because he walked around the base all day singing, "*I'm your captain, yeah yeah yeah yeah.*" He smoked a lot of that Cambodian pot.

The captain told me that this was just a temporary assignment for him while he was waiting for a slot to open up in helicopter flight school.

"I really wanted to get into Sommelier School, but it turns out, the Army doesn't *have* one of those. So, now I'm stuck at this stinking FSB where the closest thing a man can find to a glass of potable wine to enjoy with his meat chunks and beans in tomato sauce MCI (Meal, Combat, Individual Ration) is some warm *Red Ripple*. Let me tell you, kid, this place is a oenophilic desert."

He assured me, however, that a couple of his men knew how to shoot the 105 mm Howitzer, plus one guy had a copy of the gun's manual, and was reading up on how to aim it. When I got there, he was on the chapter titled *Friendly Fire*. From what he had read so far, he learned that you didn't want to shoot one of those puppies straight up in the air. *Always aim gun in the direction of the enemy*, the instructions cautioned.

"That sounds like excellent advice," the captain conceded. "I haven't complied with a single regulation since I landed in this crappy country, and nothing bad has happened to me yet, but I think I'll go along with this one."

I felt a sharp cramp in my bowel, probably from the malaria pill I took earlier in the day. From experience, I knew I had but about sixty seconds to find a toilet.

"Hey buddy," I asked some guy standing nearby, with a shell-shocked look on his face. "Where's the latrine?"

"Over there."

He indicated a slightly elevated, rickety plywood hovel perched over two rows of 55-gallon drums cut down to about 18 inches.

I stepped inside, quickly dropped my trousers, and positioned my butt uncomfortably on the hole over one of the drums. A fellow sat across from me, intently reading his *Stars and Stripes,* a roll of toilet paper within arms-reach. When he caught me eying it, he discreetly moved his hand to the M-16 at his side and flicked the selector switch from "Safe" to "Semi."

"There's something not right with this setup," I commented.

"Welcome to the boonies. Try jiggling the handle," he suggested.

On the map, Fire Support Base Charlie resided in Cambodia. Cambodia was a beautiful country with lush tropical forests, so that's why they invented *Agent Orange. Agent Orange* was a chemical defoliant containing dioxin. The theory was that if you made all of the leaves fall off the enemy's trees, he would be kept too busy raking them up to fight effectively.

I'm confident that some university received a substantial government grant to come up with the plan, and a lot of effort and brain-power went into it. The problem was that it turned out to be an ill-conceived battlefield tactic that, as we all know now, caused chronic illness in our soldiers who were exposed to *Agent Orange.* This did not discourage the relentless university researchers though, who rushed back to their proverbial drawing boards to come up with their new big idea: depleted uranium artillery shells.

That first night at the fire support base, I was able to find a piece of culvert, some sandbags, and half a sheet of plywood, so I built myself a shelter. As a devotee of Frank Lloyd Wright's Usonian philosophy of architecture, I incorporated native materials into the construction to achieve an organic design that clung to the earth, using horizontal lines and broad overhanging eves. From the veranda of my new prairie-style master bedroom, I had a great view of the Howitzer's brilliant flash upon each firing of the gun. Coupled with the streams of small-arms tracer fire, flares drifting to earth on tiny parachutes, and the rockets and mini-guns of the dizzily circling helicopter gun-ships, came an impressive fireworks display nearly every evening.

And the rockets' red glare, the bombs bursting in air.

Before long, some of the Viet Cong were starting to show up regularly outside the perimeter with their lawn chairs, picnic baskets, and little kids waving sparklers. On a good night, commerce on the Ho Chi Minh Trail would dip 10 percent due to our considerable draw. All in all, we were making a significant impact on the enemy's supply channels, and their ability to sustain the offensive.

Catering to the audience's demographics, (they were predominantly Communist Asians) the company armorer even fashioned a crude Viet Cong flag out of some gunpowder and plastic explosives. He lit it off as part of the grand finale one evening. It was a real crowd-pleaser. (Forgive me, but that's just too much.) Even though I knew these were the "bad guys" outside our perimeter, I experienced a troubling embrace of melancholy when the Phantom jets dropped napalm on them. Though more than a 200 meters away, I could feel the singe from the boiling black and orange ball of fire that rolled along the landscape. I had to remind myself, however, that this was war.

So, when the F4-Gs thundered in from the east to make their second pass, I didn't allow myself the luxury of lamenting. I knew all too well from my school lessons in the '50s that democracy comes at a price. If these people wanted their children to be able to go to the polls some day and pull that lever for the library board member of their choice, then some of them were just going to have to get toasted that night.

As I watched the conflagration in awe, a cannon cocker (artilleryman) walked over to join me.

"And to think," he commented. "I could have bought *Dow Chemical* when it was at 31. By the way, what the hell do you do here?"

As it turned out, nobody at the fire support base had a clue as to why I had been assigned to them, and the captain was just as unsuccessful at deciphering my orders as was I. One fellow suggested that, perhaps, I was being punished for something.

"You didn't happen to have anything to do with that lieutenant getting shot in the elbow, did you?" he asked.

I acted like I had no idea what he was talking about.

Another guy, who had dropped quite a bit of LSD that afternoon, thought maybe I was with the Bob Hope Show. He wanted to know if I had brought Ann Margret with me.

"No," I had to explain to him, "She doesn't play small venues."

The captain, on the other hand, told me he didn't care why I was there or how I spent my time so long as I didn't eat the flaming saganaki C-rations or hoard toilet paper.

"Let me know if you need any orders or what-not," he generously offered, "I've been to leadership school you know."

After a couple of weeks, Lima Company left and Bravo Company rotated in on an ungainly *CH-47 Chinook* helicopter that, aerodynamically, defied most of the laws of physics governing flight. I can better understand how reindeer fly than a *CH-47*. Sergeant Washington once cautioned me to never board a Chinook that wasn't leaking hydraulic fluid. It was a clear indication that something was seriously wrong with the craft.

These new artillerymen all had identical Mohawk-style haircuts and treated me as if I were a stray dog. They were an odd lot. They didn't know the meaning of fear. In fact, there were a lot of words they didn't know the meaning of . . . like: "ebullient," and "ubiquitous," just to name a couple. There was also this unsettling war cry that they howled each time they fired the Howitzer. Even more disturbing was when I would hear a plop, then the identical "yeehah" bellowing from the latrine when they used it. After only a couple of days it proved to be unnerving, so I was, understandably, looking forward to the next rotation. I sort of hoped it would be the singing captain from leadership school again. The last time I saw him, he had taken up playing the harmonica and began learning to juggle. I found him to be quite amusing.

The weather in Cambodia sucked. Not only was it hot and humid, but also it rained just about every day I was there. I developed some strange fungal skin disorders and my jungle fatigues and boots began to disintegrate. By the time the next company rotated in, my clothes were in tatters and I had acquired several nasty-looking open sores. When it appeared there resided maggots in one of my wounds, I decided it might be prudent to show them to a medic.

"Geez, man! They never taught us about anything like *this* in training," was his horrified response. "Now if your intestines spilled out of a nasty stomach wound, and you walked up to me holding the slimy jumble in your arms, struggling to keep them off the ground, I could deal with it. . . that's what I trained for. But this! This is way outside my realm. I'm afraid that all I have to offer you in my magic bag of medical tricks is a soporifically lethal dose of morphine. . . that and a prayer for mercy on your soul. You're suffering a grave malady there, Bro."

"I'm thinking I'd like a second opinion."

"Okay. Well let's see. You also appear to have some pretty acute dandruff."

I stayed well clear of that battle-fatigued medic until he was relieved with the next rotation. The new captain I received there at the fire support base, who had smuggled in his Vietnamese girlfriend, stopped me one day while I was mucking through the mud.

"Hey, kid. You're freakin' me out," he complained. "Why don't you catch the next chopper out of this place, burn those clothes when you get back, and go down to the post exchange and buy yourself some *Selsun Blue*?"

He had been curiously studying the Howitzer ever since his arrival. "By the way," he added, "You don't happen to know if this thing has a trigger or something to fire it, do you? Some Navy Seals have been on the radio grousing about getting some artillery support now for the past half hour."

In total, I ended up spending one and a half months at the fire support base. When I returned to Bien Hoa Province, Captain Riley spied me and asked where the hell I'd been. I explained to him I had been at Fire Support Base Charlie for the last six weeks. I showed him a copy of my orders.

"Well, I'll be screwed nude." He scratched his head. "I wonder if it's too late for the company clerk to stop that Missing in Action notification we sent to your family. We were looking everywhere for you," he explained. "Perhaps these orders weren't as clear as they might have been. You see, it was only intended that you go to the FSB for the *day*."

He tilted his head to one side and squinted squeamishly as he studied me.

"And, by the way, you might want to have that sore looked at. I think I see something nematode-like crawling around in there."

"I was just on my way to sick-call."

"Good. Good. And also, Johnson."

"Yes?"

"When was the last time you had a haircut?"

"Two or three months ago. Why? Do you think I need one?"

"Well, at least a half inch or so . . . you know . . . to get rid of your split ends. It's not very becoming let alone, regulation. If this were the Marines, you'd be written up for wearing your hair that long."

"But this isn't the Marines."

"You're right. But, on the other hand, this isn't some sort of a hippie commune either."

"No. I agree. In a hippie commune, there'd be a lot less recreational drug consumption."

As it turned out, it was just as well I returned from Cambodia when I did. Not only was it necessary for the doctors to treat me with a powerful larvicide, but also, two days after I left Fire Support Base Charlie, it was overrun by the Viet Cong. After an intense firefight, followed by some vicious hand-to-hand combat, everyone on the base, including Thuy, the captain's girlfriend, was massacred.

I was in the orderly room playing gin rummy with Ken, our company clerk, when the radio distress call came in. Ken was ahead 196 points to 173.

"What do you say we make this interesting," I challenged Ken, pulling a wad of Military Payment Certificates from my breast pocket.

"Okay. Here you go. That will be 10 bucks."

Ken slid a hit of *Orange Sunshine* across the table.

"This stuff will make shopping for underwear at *Walmart* more interesting."

Major Wilhelm was at his desk casually smoking a cigar, as usual, and drinking brandy as the radio blared:

. . . Broken arrow. Broken arrow. We have Victor Charlie inside the wire! Do you copy? We cannot hold this position. I repeat. We cannot hold this position! Do you read me? We need an immediate evacuation. Do you copy? Does anyone copy?

"That's the fire support base in Cambodia calling for help," I spoke up. "Isn't anyone going to respond?"

Mayday! Mayday! Mayday! Do you read me? Our position has been overrun. We have VC inside the perimeter! Do you read me?

"Didn't you hear the president's address to the nation on the radio last night kid?" the major calmly replied. "We don't have any troops in Cambodia."

CHAPTER SEVEN

The Safe Conduct Pass

In December, our platoon was assigned a Vietnamese interpreter. Previously, while on patrols, we had been having difficulty communicating perspicaciously with the local residents, all the while being sensitive (as prescribed in the Army Manual) to their cultural differences. For example, in one village we came to, Corporal Stockley, holding a 50-caliber machine-gun at his hip, Rambo style, yelled to the terrified occupants of a thatched-roof hooch, "Everybody outside with your hands behind your heads, you little slant-eyed, zipper headed, gook bastard, piece of monkey shit, dinks." (*This was insensitive.*)

Due to the language barrier, however, the family inside mistakenly thought he was instructing them to go hide in the livestock pen behind the feed bunk.

When nobody emerged from the tenuously teetering stilt house, Tom Kline suggested, "I bet they're hiding in the livestock pen behind the feed bunk."

We trudged in that direction.

"You know, what we really could use on these patrols would be someone who spoke Vietnamese."

"Well if you're looking for someone who speaks Vietnamese, you came to the right place," I said.

"I heard that."

As it turned out, and to our astonishment, Colonel Barrows, evidently, completely agreed with us. The interpreter we were subsequently assigned, introduced himself to me as Luong Phuc. Noting the curious expression on my face, he added, "It means 'lucky one' in my language."

"Same in my language!" I told him.

II Corps employed Phuc as an English/Vietnamese translator. He also spoke French. He augmented his meager salary as an interpreter by a brisk business he conducted on the black market. Phuc's credentials as a translator gained him important access to U.S. military installations where he could procure the goods he needed to sell in the underground economy.

"You get me Claymores," (a directional anti-personnel mine) he beseeched, "I make you rich G.I."

Although strictly against regulations, Phuc and I made an unofficial excursion to a small hamlet in Binh Dinh Province where, he told me, he had family. He promised me a date with his attractive seventeen-year-old cousin. On the way to Phuc's ancestral home, a teenage Vietnamese boy, dressed in traditional black pajamas and a straw peasant hat, appeared on the trail, quite excited to see us. He waved a slip of paper, and grinned ear to ear. Phuc had a brief conversation with the intrepid traveler, and then turned to me.

"He tell me helicopter drop paper."

I looked at the slip, one of those ubiquitous *Chieu Hoi* safe conduct passes, printed in both Vietnamese and English. It promised humane treatment for the bearer if he were to surrender to American troops. To my knowledge, this may have been the first time in the history of the U.S. occupation of Vietnam that someone had ever tried to use one of these things for something other than tinder or toilet paper.

"What do I do?" I asked Phuc.

"Shoot him in the head," he insouciantly replied.

"I can't do that," I argued. "Not with him smiling at me like that. We need to take him back to the base."

"You no want to meet my cousin? She be *beaucoup* sad. I tell her you very handsome American. . . want to meet nice Vietnamese girl."

"No," I insisted. "We should take this guy back to Bong Son."

Heading back with our cheery prisoner by the way we had come, our party encountered a long-range patrol from the 4th Battalion.

"What the hell are you fools doing out here?" their lieutenant asked us. "We just about took you out."

I explained to him about how this *rallier* in the black pajamas had presented himself to us with a safe conduct pass. I told the officer I wasn't sure what to do with him.

"He sure is a happy son of a bitch," the lieutenant observed. "How about we shoot him in the head. I bet that will wipe that annoying grin off his face. One bullet. One dead gook. That would be friggin' cost-effective, wouldn't you say? Efficiency, you should know, is nothing but a highly evolved form of laziness."

"Maybe instead, you could call this in on your radio," I suggested. "He might have valuable information for our intelligence people."

"Who told you we had intelligence people?" the lieutenant snapped.

"I just assumed."

"This is the Army kid. Never assume intelligence when stupidity will suffice. 'Military intelligence' is an oxymoron."

"Pardon me?"

"Forget it. Just ignore my grumbling. I was only venting. This has been a crummy assignment for me . . . a number ten thousand! I'm going dinky dau, diddy-bopping through rice paddies. I think I'm contracting 'jungle madness.' I wouldn't even be here in *Funny Country* if I could have afforded to pay for my own college education . . ."

I stared at the officer, bemused. He picked up on the befuddled look on my face.

"Look, I'm sorry. You seem like a nice kid. I'll tell you what. I'll call this thing in for you and see what they have to say about it at headquarters, but remember . . . we never had this conversation . . . you understand?"

I nodded in the affirmative. The lieutenant signaled for his radioman, picked up the handset of the PRC- (Prick) Twenty-Five, and after some preliminary nonsensical radio jargon protocol, he tried to explain to someone on the other end of the line about our situation. He then waited for a minute or two for an answer. There seemed to be some confusion, however.

"No. No," the lieutenant argued with headquarters. "I don't need air support. I don't need artillery. I don't need a medical evacuation! I just want to know what to do with this prisoner. The guy who captured him seems to think he might have valuable information on enemy positions . . . Okay. Okay. I see. I'll tell him."

He handed the handset back to his radioman, then turned to me.

"They say take him up to at least 3,000 feet in a helicopter, get what information you can, then push him out."

"A helicopter?"

"Yeah. It's like an airplane, but with one of those spinney things on top."

"I don't have a helicopter!" I raised my voice in frustration. "Where am I going to get a helicopter?"

"No sweat *there,* my friend. I'll just call one in for you. That's why we have these nifty radios, you know, and my man Joe here to lug the ponderous gizmo around."

His radioman smiled at me meekly. The words *You must have me confused with someone who gives a shit* were neatly painted on his helmet.

"Please. Call them back and tell them we don't have a helicopter," I pleaded, "and ask them what to do with this prisoner."

The lieutenant magnanimously granted my request, spoke to someone on the radio for a few seconds, and then thanked him.

"The guy at headquarters says to shoot him in the head," he reported.

Frustrated by our encounter with the L.R.P., Phuc, the prisoner, and I continued along the trail in disbelief.

"Good luck to you," the lieutenant called after us. "Remember, the *journey* is the reward."

"That man *beaucoup* crazy," Phuc editorialized.

"He's an officer," I explained.

As we traveled along the trail, Phuc and the prisoner were having an animated conversation.

"He say his name is Trung Tuan," Phuc told me. "He want to be like American and smoke cigarette."

I gave Tuan one of my *Kools* and lit it for him with my 'Damn you Charlie Brown' inscribed *Zippo*. When we came to the spot where our trail met the half-mile wide Mekong River, we hired a sampan to take us across. There were heated negotiations between Phuc and the boatman. The price settled on was 12 dong and a sincere promise that we would not dangle our feet over the side. The operator fired up the two-cycle motor (which resembled a *Sears & Roebuck* string trimmer) and we were tenuously underway. The motor smoked, sputtered, and spat. The waterline splashed a disconcerting two inches below the gunnels. I looked around to see if I could find something to bail with if it became necessary.

At about the midpoint of our marine adventure, a Brown Water Navy swift boat sounded its siren and pulled up alongside us. On the bow of the ship, a talented artist had painted a beautiful Vietnamese woman in black, weeping over a coffin, and the words *The Wake Maker* arching through the illustration.

"What the hell are you imbeciles doing out here?" the officer in charge asked us as our sampan banged up against the aluminum hull of the swift boat in the choppy water.

Two of his men used long grappling poles to keep us close. Once again, I explained our situation. I told him all about our prisoner and his safe conduct pass.

"Have you given any consideration to shooting him in the head?" the officer asked me.

"I won't do that," I insisted.

"That's understandable. It *is* a messy business, but I'm afraid you're going to have to dispatch him, one way or another. Only the method, I'm sorry to say, is negotiable. I'll tell you what. We've got plenty of rope on board. How about we just tie his hands behind his back and push him in the river. That should take care of your prisoner dilemma and reduce the boat's draft as a big bonus."

I refused the rope but took him up on his generous offer to tow us three kilometers up the river in order to save the hike. I'm guessing that we were doing close to fifteen knots behind that swift boat. The sampan operator looked scared shitless, holding onto his straw peasant hat with one hand and the gunnels with the other.

"He Buddhist," Phuc hollered over the wind. "He believe he on eightfold path to Nirvana."

Papa-ooma-mow-mow, papa-ooma-mow-mow

Once back at Bong Son, I proudly delivered my grinning idiot of a prisoner to the company headquarters. I felt confident that I would surely receive some sort of a medal, and perhaps a three-day pass to China Beach, for capturing a dangerous V.C.

"Specialist Johnson here to see Captain Riley," I announced myself to Ken, our company clerk.

"Look out! He's got a grenade!" shouted Ken as he hit the deck.

A loud explosion hurtled fragments from the grenade, ripping through the office, blowing out the windows. Captain Riley charged in from the backroom with his *Model 1911A1* semi-automatic pistol, cocked and in hand. Quickly assessing the situation, he shot Trung Tuan square in the head making quite a mess all over Ken's typewriter.

Later that evening, Phuc and I were discussing the day's events over a beer.

"You crazy G.I., Johnson," Phuc told me. "How come you no shoot V.C. in head when I say."

"Oh. Don't you worry about that, my little chink friend," I assured him. "The next person who presents me with a safe conduct pass will be . . . Well, let me put it this way: It's just not going to be his day."

CHAPTER EIGHT

Guard Duty

You might be interested to know, I didn't enlist in the Army per se. Instead, I idiotically *volunteered for the draft* . . . just to get it over and done with, then get on with my life. The outcome: Selective Service fixed me up with a free, swell-as-can-be physical exam, down there in the induction center at 400 S. Jefferson. This turned out to be a metaphorical foreshadowing of the next two years of my life: *Bend over and spread your cheeks.*

Just inside the entrance, we were required to produce our *Order to Report for Armed Forces Physical Examination.* Our Selective Service System forms number 223 were carefully scrutinized to ensure none of us had gotten up at 4:00 a.m., to be at the induction center by 6:30, without proper paperwork. Apparently, this had been a problem in the past.

Once our orders were authenticated, we were required to fill out a brief medical questionnaire. It was explained to us that our responses would greatly assist the physicians in their examinations. For example, Part Five, *Have you ever had any of the following cardiovascular or heart problems?* Item "d." listed *Heart Failure; Yes/No.* Evidently, having your heart fail is a serious medical condition that impedes one's ability to perform at the minimum threshold of military physical standards. I circled *No*, and moved on, skipping over Section Seven, which, even if it hadn't been clearly marked *For Women Only,* based on the personal nature of some of the questions, I would have inferred it to be such. Nonetheless, more than one of the male respondents went ahead obliviously and duly answered that no, they did not *suffer abnormal vaginal discharges, yellow or green in color, chunky in consistency, and accompanied by a foul odor.*

After completing the medical questionnaire, I offered a silent prayer, thanking God I didn't suffer from oozing lesions, swollen or tender testicles, a burning sensation when urinating, genital ulcers, abscesses in the groin, or milky discharges. In consideration of these possible consequences, I decided right then and there that I would never again go on a date with Dee Baker, whom up to that point in my life, was my "go to" person for coitus, as she was for the majority of sexually active young men in the Garfield Ridge neighborhood.

Next, we were required to strip to our undershorts, placing our street clothes and personal belongings into a basket for safekeeping. In single file, clutching our manila files tightly to our chests, we proceeded from station to station, getting poked and probed, X-rayed and palpated, measured and weighed, degraded and humiliated. In fact, there are aspects of the experience that my mind has so deeply repressed, it would take innumerable sessions in psychoanalysis to reconstitute them for the controvertible purpose of sharing them here. I do remember, however, after the exam we all did this funny little walk outside and a few of the guys there at the bus stop, I could tell by their hollow eyes, empty gazes, and blank expressions, were visibly traumatized by some of the horrors they had seen inside. They were subsequently classified 4-F, *not acceptable for military service . . . under established physical or mental standards.*

Despite my shameless attempt to feign *Autism Spectrum Disorder*, I was unable to demonstrate, beyond a reasonable doubt, that I failed to possess the rectitude or moral character required to serve in the Armed Forces of the United States of America, and arbitrarily kill and maim denizens of French Indo-China. So, woefully, on the prescribed day, I gathered up my conscription papers, took the "elevated" into the loop, and rode a number seven bus over to the induction center. Once there, I handed all of the documentation provided me to a grumpy old fellow wearing a tweed sport jacket, reading glasses, and a rubber tip on his index finger. Sitting at an old oak desk, armed with an arsenal of rubber stamps and a master list, he had no record of me whatsoever. He thought it a curious thing that I was there at all, but as long as I was, and since all of my papers seemed to be in excellent order, he put me in the Army.

"If you're feeling particularly gung-ho this morning, I can arrange to put you in the Marines," he commented to me, "but after that Tet Offensive business, the Army's going to need all the fresh meat they can get."

That's how I wound up on perimeter guard duty in Bong Son, Vietnam with Loren Anderson, in December of 1969. Don't laugh. This was serious stuff . . . guarding the perimeter with our trusty 50 cal. Those shifty Viet Cong had been known to abscond with unsurveilled sections of perimeter. One time, in fact, the Army Corps of Engineers installed gravel on the entrance road to our base, and by sunup the next morning, every last nugget of stone was gone; purloined by an army of Vietnamese women with woven bamboo baskets.

That night, Loren and I were both pretty stoned while engaged in an animated conversation about a couple of guys who shared the hooch next to us . . . Diego and Ernst. Now which one of those two would you guess was Puerto Rican? If you're thinking it's Diego, you'd be wrong because he was from Cuba originally, and it wasn't Ernst either. He was a *Charismatic Pentecostal.* Now, I know that *Charismatic Pentecostalism* has nothing to do with a person's origins, but I'm confident they're quite rare in Puerto Rico, and when you add that to the fact that his name was Ernst . . . well, I just don't think so, but he *was* very annoying, with all of that speaking in tongues business, so some of the English only speaking guys in the company (believing that he was speaking Spanish) would yell at him, "Why don't you go back to Puerto Rico, you bum."

I think it may have been because many of those same guys had seen that *West Side Story* movie when they showed it over at the enlisted men's club, but failed to absorb the central message which has something to do with how people of different ethnicities can love, just as well as kill each other. That made me think Diego and Ernst's hooch was like a microcosm for the war.

When I explicated all of this to Loren, he just laughed and said, "Maybe you've smoked enough pot for one night, Bruce."

"Hey, Loren."

"What is it now, Bruce?"

"What's your worst fear being over here?"

"I'd have to say, waking up on fire."

"That's a real thing, you know. I read about it in the *National Inquirer.*"

"What is?"

"Spontaneous human combustion."

"I didn't know that. I always assumed it was just an urban legend."

"Did you know that I'm an only child?"

"No. I didn't know that either. Did you read that in the *National Inquirer* too?"

"No. I just figured it out for myself when each morning I'd sit down for breakfast, and there were no other kids at the kitchen table. There's lots of interesting stuff besides that you may not know about me."

"Is that so?"

"Yeah. For example: I bet you didn't know that Janis Joplin and I went to different high schools."

"Really?"

"I'm not shitin' you."

"So, then I presume you didn't take her to the prom."

"Oh. I didn't say that. I've taken her to the prom plenty of times."

"You did?"

"Yeah. My mom used to yell down the hall, 'What's all that racket you're making in that bedroom of yours, Bruce?' and I'd call back to her that I was shadow boxing."

"Well, you don't want to tell her you're dating Janis Joplin."

"Not if you're Catholic. It's a venial sin, you know."

"Not a mortal sin then?"

"No. To be a mortal sin it would need to be like your sister, or a nun or something like that. You know, if you're shadow boxing, and your shadow kicks your butt, then you should probably do something to get in better shape . . . like push-ups, don't you think?"

"Or get a punching bag."

"You want to know something else?"

"I'll tell you what, Bruce. Why don't you write a book, if you get out of here alive, and I'll read all about it. You're a good storyteller, and a master of hyperbole. I'm confident you can come up with plenty of amusing anecdotes to embellish."

"I think I *will* write a book. And also, I think I'll do something really avant-garde, like I might have a little book within a book."

"That would be called a *chapter*."

"Oh, yeah? Then I'm going to have chapters in my book, and lots of them."

"Now *that* would be avant-garde!"

"Do you think? I also know how to write like Hemmingway."

"Good for you."

At about this time, the V.C. started lobbing mortar rounds at the base.

"Looks like enemy fire," I observed, sucking the smoke from my joint deep into my lungs.

"We get that a lot around here . . . and some friendly fire, too."

"Friendly fire would be far more accurate than this stuff."

"I thought that this sector was supposed to be secure," Loren commented as he lit another doobie.

"Well, I guess no one communicated that to the V.C."

"We can't. Their phone system is not compatible with ours. For some reason, it operates on a different format. Ours is PBX, I think, and with theirs, you have to dial *nine* to get a dial tone then *one* before the area code or something. It's all very confusing."

"That's goofy."

"It sure is."

A mortar round exploded near the mess tent, sending a dozen or so guys, who were eating midnight chow, scrambling for cover.

"Don't you ever wonder if one of those rounds might have your name on it?" I asked, trying not to exhale too much smoke as I spoke.

"Or *To whom it may concern*? No. I'm not superstitious. I'm a practicing atheist as a matter of fact, thank Almighty God."

"No wonder I've never seen you in a foxhole. Whom do you think is going to win this crazy war?"

"Oh, that's an easy one. The side with the simplest uniforms always wins. Didn't anyone ever explain that to you?"

More incoming ordnance fell inside the wire.

"We should probably call this in."

"You're right. This may very well come under the purview of the third general rule of guard duty: *I will report violations of my special orders, emergencies, and anything not covered in my instructions to the Commander of the Relief.*"

Loren cranked the little handle on the side of our lima-lima (field telephone), but the line was completely dead.

"I wonder if Ken neglected to pay the phone bill," Loren speculated. "He's been discernably overwrought since he came out of the closet last month."

"No. That's not it. Look at this." I offered, "Here's the problem. This wire isn't connected to the phone."

Loren studied the double-strand wire end I was holding.

"You're right!"

Stubbing out his joint Loren took the muddy wire from me. He cut about six inches off the end with his bayonet, splayed the two halves, then removed about an inch of insulation from each.

"Where do you think it goes?"

Pointing, I indicated, "On those two terminals, there."

We scrunched down with our faces close to the phone. I struck my *Zippo* for light as Loren looped the thin wires around the posts, then tightened the corresponding wing-nuts. Before snapping my lighter shut, I lit another blunt.

"Now try it," I suggested.

Loren cranked the handle again. This time, the result was a brilliant flash of white light and a huge concussion as shrapnel ripped through and shredded the vegetation in front of our position. We both hit the deck.

"*Choi oi!*" I exclaimed. "What the hell was that!? You got one insanely wrong number dude."

"You stupid shit!" Loren screamed at me. "That was the det-cord for firing the Claymores you handed me."

"What?"

"Those wires should have been connected to the clacker, and these commo wires here go to the field phone."

"How was I to know? Do I look like the *Wichita Lineman* to you?"

"That's it! That's who you look like. . . Glen Campbell."

While I watch the cannons flashing
I clean my gun and dream of Galveston

Meanwhile, sirens began to wail.

"Listen! Now the alarm is going off because of us."

"What are you talking about? It's going *on* because of us."

"The reason it's going on is because some mortar rounds have hit the mess hall! Now the mess hall is burning up."

"No, it's burning down."

"God almighty! I wish this war would be over."

"It pretty much is . . . except for the shooting."

"Well, you can include me out."

"Do you mean *exclude* you out?"

At once a jeep driven by a half-dressed Sergeant Washington raced to our position, and out jumped three junior NCOs.

"Search that area there," he ordered. "And as for you two . . . what the heck's going on here?"

"They started it!" Loren expounded, referring to the Viet Cong.

The buck sergeants scrambled over the sand bag wall, carefully cut their way through the concertina wire, and disappeared into the bush.

"I don't care who started it. What I want to know is who has the wisdom to end it?"

"Henry Kissinger?"

"That was a rhetorical question."

After a couple minutes of rustling noises coming from the vegetation, one of the Buck Sergeants called out, "I think we've got something here, Sarge."

As it turned out, they found six dead V.C. sappers all carrying satchel charges of high explosives. Their grossly perforated bloody bodies were dragged out of the brush and lined up in a neat row just inside the wire.

"Looks like these guys were up to no good," Sergeant Washington observed. "Obviously that mortar barrage was just a diversion for something far more sinister. If you boys hadn't set off those Claymores just when you did, it's my guess that you two would have had your throats slit, and there would have been a lot of fireworks coming from the ammo dump behind us."

Wide-eyed, Loren and I just looked at each other in dismay.

CHAPTER NINE

The Bob Hope Show

Loren Anderson and I were solemnly celebrating the Christmas season at the Enlisted Men's Club. Our eyes all aglow, we were brimming with holiday spirit and Jack Daniel's No. 7. Merle Haggard's *Okie from Muskogee* was playing insufferably in the background.

> *We don't smoke marijuana in Muskogee*
> *We don't take our trips on LSD*
> *We don't burn our draft cards down on Main Street*
> *We like livin' right, and bein' free*

I could tell some of the black guys in the club were having a difficult time dealing with the choice of music. They squirmed in their chairs, wearing the facial expressions of someone who had just witnessed a beheading.

"What *is* this shit?" Private Jimar Jackson asked the bartender, as he gathered the beers he had just ordered for his table.

"It's the beer that made Milwaukee famous."

"How come all the white guys are drinking 'the champagne of bottled beers' and we're served *Schlitz*? This stuff will gag a maggot."

"It's what they ordered."

"It's what they ordered?"

"Yeah. That's what I said. It's what they ordered."

"In that case then, I'll take five *Millers*."

"We're all out."

"You're all out?"

"Yep. You heard me."

Jimar rolled his eyes, collected his beers, and started to return to his table, but hesitated and turned confrontationally back to the bartender.

"And what about this music?"

"What about it?"

"Is this country and western bullshit all you've got for that *Sony* eight-track of yours? What's next? Are you going to be playing some *Buck Owens and His Buckaroos* and have a fuckin' barn dance?"

Without looking up, the bartender calmly answered, "Anything that helps to keep you niggers out of the place, I'm willing to try."

With that, Private Jackson spun on his heels and charged out the door, leaving behind his bottles of beer on the bar.

"He's gone to get his M-16," Loren guessed aloud.

"I'm out of here," I announced, and the two of us pushed back our chairs and exited the club leaving our drinks behind too.

"Wait up boys!" shouted Sergeant Washington. "I need to talk to you, Bruce."

Catching up to us, he walked with Loren and me towards our hooch.

"The captain wanted me to speak with you. Inasmuch as you received a Silver Star, he thought that you might enjoy going to the Bob Hope Christmas show as sort of a perk. He said that you could take a buddy along for company, if you wish."

"Even if my buddy and I are helicopter-borne air mobile infantry rangers with no will of our own, sometimes walking around blindly with dead eyes, following orders, not knowing what we are doing, not caring?"

"You mean like Democrats? Sure. You can be a Democrat and still go. After all, you can't really be much of a threat to the party in office if you're not even old enough to vote, and burning your draft card would be inefficaciously belated, now that you're in the thick of the fight."

"What do you say, Loren? Do you want to go see Bob Hope?" I asked.

"Sure. I'll go . . . so long as I don't have to walk point. You know, it pays having friends in high places."

"There will be a special 'Santa Claus' flight to Da Nang leaving shortly before midnight tomorrow," Sargent Washington briefed us. "I'll have Ken type up some travel orders for the two of you."

In the darkness, Private Jackson brushed past us, headed back towards the Enlisted Men's Club. He was carrying his weapon, loaded with a thirty-round banana clip.

"Yeah. Sounds fun," I answered. "We'll be on it."

"You boys have a good time now, and don't be getting into any squabbles with those guys from the 101st Airborne there at Camp Eagle. They'll kick your sorry butts, you know."

By this time, there was a lot of automatic weapons fire coming from the Enlisted Men's Club.

"It's like the wild, wild west around here every night," Loren commented. "Just imagine if that bartender had been playing the *Harper Valley PTA*."

"I don't even want to think about it," I agreed. "With as much cultural diversity as exists here in the U. S. Army, it demands a musical score with a broad societal appeal to accompany the war. I think it would be judicious to generate a sound track that is, at once, inspirational yet unobjectionable to all participants . . . a theme that would do for Vietnam what *The Blue Danube* did for Stanley Kubrick's *2001: A Space Odyssey*."

"That's true! As pathetic as it sounds, for some of these young enlistees, this war is going to be like the biggest deal in their tedious little real lives. It demands a soundtrack deserving the magnitude of such."

"I'm thinking *Wagner's Ring Cycle*."

"So am I."

We high fived.

"Right on! Tell me, Loren. Do you ever fantasize about being in an uninhibited venereal orgy with those Rhine maidens?"

"Every now and then. However, as seductive as they may be, mostly I find them to be elusive and ambiguous."

"Yeah. I know what you mean. That can be a problem with water nymphs at times."

Shortly before midnight, Christmas Eve, Loren and I boarded our flight to Da Nang. The plane we were to fly out on was a *de Havilland CV-2B Caribou*.

"I once toured the factory in Canada where they build these planes," Loren commented.

"Oh yeah. Was it interesting?"

"Riveting."

Although our aircraft commander/pilot appeared to be no older than 16, he assured us that he was indeed 20 years old and had a license to fly one of these things. I asked to see it.

"Well I do *have* one," the pilot replied defensively, patting the pockets of his *Nomex* flight suit. "I just don't make it a habit to carry it with me."

"I'd still like to see it," I insisted. "I'm pretty sure it's my right as a consumer. I know that's the way it is back in Chicago with cab drivers."

"I've been flying airplanes now for six months, and you're the first person who ever asked to see my license."

"Just being careful, my friend. Just being careful. Now, I count two engines on this aircraft so I'm assuming that you're multi-engine certified with, I presume, an instrument rating and perhaps a high altitude endorsement. Am I correct?"

"Yes. Yes."

"Good. Then, I trust, you should be able to get us to Da Nang without too much drama. I usually like to nap when I travel by air."

Flyboy stared at me incredulously.

"We really *should* get going," I insisted. "Loren and I want to catch the Bop Hope show at Camp Eagle, and maybe grab a little breakfast at the mess hall beforehand, if possible. I'm thinking we should stay away from the Ho Chi Minh Trail. It's going to be a long thin parking lot at this time of the night. You can probably follow Highway One most of the way up, and if you have to, turn out over the South China Sea, if it's too congested. This aircraft *is* certified for over-water flights, isn't it?"

The pilot nodded in the affirmative.

"Good. Good. Now, assuming the wind speed remains below 15 knots, and you're comfortable with a slight crosswind landing, I would request runway 35 right, and a straight-in approach to Da Nang, if there's not a lot of traffic in the pattern and the overnight controller will go along with it. Sometimes, I've heard, he can be a prick about these things. He has an obsession with contra-rotating circuit airport patterns so you may have to schmooze him a bit. I heard he drinks *Chivas Regal*, if that's any help. So, what do you say we kick the tires, light the fires, and grab some altitude?"

As the pilot and copilot stared at me with a look of utter bemusement, Loren and I boarded the aircraft by means of a long ramp that folded down below the upturned tail. It happened that we were to share the flight with a group of Vietnamese refugees, including their animals. The flight sergeant, who was dressed in a Santa Claus costume, was not happy about this fact.

"If that pig shits in my airplane," he barked, "there's going to be a price to pay!"

As it turned out, the pig shit all over his airplane, and we never got our in-flight movie, which was a bummer. I really had my heart set on seeing *Butch Cassidy and the Sundance Kid*.

The *Caribou* was a S.T.O.L. aircraft, meaning it was designed to take off from an unimproved field in 460 feet, clearing a 50-foot obstacle at the end of the runway. Evidently, the tree at the end of our runway was 51 feet tall. After landing in Da Nang, Loren and I left Santa the flight sergeant, the pilot and copilot, as they struggled to remove a good-sized tree branch from the nose wheel assembly.

"Why don't you just hang some colored lights and ornaments on it," I suggested.

Following the MPs' directions, we found our way to the *Eagle Entertainment Bowl*. It was a huge stadium that held over 16,000 people. Because we were just a couple of grunts from the bush, our seats were way in the back. High-ranking officers and other VIPs had the good reserved seats up front, with the exception of a few wounded guys in blue pajamas they put in row one for the benefit of the TV audience. We were handed a box lunch as we entered.

"You know, I've got a Silver Star," I tried to convince a Marine MP to give us better seats.

"And I've got a tattoo on my ass. Now, keep moving!"

"If you were in a firefight, and needed support," Loren quizzed me, "who would you rather have? An Army grunt, Superman, or highly intelligent Marine."

"The Army grunt, silly. There's no such thing as Superman or a highly intelligent Marine."

We climbed and climbed.

"I think I'm getting altitude sickness," Loren complained.

"Me, too. Had I known where we'd be sitting, I would have brought some portable oxygen from the plane."

"Move over," I ordered a couple of airmen who were taking up more bleacher space than was necessary.

"Who the hell do you think you are, buddy?"

"Just do as you're told, and I won't be obliged to have my friend Loren here kick the shit out of you."

Deferring to our tattered, faded clothing, (an indication that we were in the heart of the fighting . . . or homeless) they slid over. Loren and I took our seats. From the crowd sprouted a miscellany of hand-painted signs expressing a variety of viewpoints on various subjects and political points of view:

BLACK POWER!

JESUS IS COMING. QUICK, LOOK BUSY.
NIXON! PULL OUT. LIKE YOUR FATHER SHOULD HAVE DONE.
IS THIS WAR REALLY NECESSARY?

THE CONFEDERACY FOREVER!
WHERE IS LEE HARVEY OSWALD NOW THAT WE REALLY NEED HIM?
THIS WAR WILL RETURN AFTER A SHORT COMMERCIAL BREAK.
IF WAR IS THE ANSWER, WE'RE ASKING THE WRONG QUESTION.
SINCE I GAVE UP HOPE, I FEEL MUCH BETTER.
PERHAPS THIS IS ANOTHER PLANET'S HELL.
ZEN IS NOT WHAT YOU THINK!
BLACK IS BEAUTIFUL!
IF GOD IS YOUR CO-PILOT, SWAP SEATS.

"Do you want to split a blunt?" I asked Loren as we settled in.

"Or I've got some *Big Chief* if you prefer."

"Yeah. Let's do *that*. I haven't ingested any psychoactive alkaloids since that *Buckinghams* concert in 1967."

"What! You did mescaline at a *Buckinghams* concert?"

"I know. I thoroughly humiliated myself, dancing around in front of the stage as if I were at a *Grateful Dead* concert. I was entirely out of sync with my fellow concertgoers."

"I really wish you hadn't told me that, Bruce."

"I'm not proud of it."

"You should be *ashamed* of yourself."

"I am. It was *kind of a drag*."

We chewed a dozen buttons of bitter mescaline between the two of us.

"Mmm. Yummy."

"Is this the same stuff that Shoshoka, the company armorer, sells?"

"Yeah. I understand that he belongs to the *Native American Church of Oklahoma* and practices Peyotism. His mother sends him the stuff so he can commune with the spirit world."

"Far out. He has a cool mom."

Our view of the stage was mostly blocked by the scaffolding that was erected for the exclusive benefit of the television cameras and sound equipment. We were told, however, that Astronaut Neil Armstrong was with the show, although Loren and I were only slightly closer to him than we were on the day he was the first white man to take a leak on the moon. Miss World was also somewhere down there on the stage, our program stated.

"If this is Miss World," I asked Loren, "what celestial body did the woman who beat her out for Miss Universe come from?"

"I remember reading that she's from some quaint planet in the Andromeda galaxy," Loren answered, "but that she's studying computational and systems biology at U.C.L.A., and championing women's health issues."

"I like healthy women."

"Me too."

Also entertaining us was Connie Stevens (I had a vague idea she was some sort of female vocalist), Rachel Welch of grape jelly fame, Les Brown and his Band of Renown, plus The Gold Diggers whom I had never heard of before that day, and even after seeing them perform, I still have no idea what they do. The important thing for the audience was that they did it in mini-skirts and go-go boots.

"Bob Hope, Camp Eagle, take one," some television director wearing headphones started the show. The band began to play but after only a few seconds the director commenced waving his arms frantically. Evidently, there was something not to his satisfaction with some of the recording equipment. "Cut! Cut! Cut!"

There was a long conversation between Bob Hope and some of his technical crew. Even from our distant seats, it was obvious that Bob was quite agitated. Technicians ran a series of sound checks while he paced the stage. Eventually everyone returned to their places. "Bob Hope, Camp Eagle, take two."

Inside a couple of minutes Bob threw his golf club in a display of temper, and the director once again yelled, "Cut!" This went on for two more aborted takes. It was getting very hot out there in the Southeast Asian sun. Some of the crowd started hissing and moaning loudly. An angry Bob Hope warned us that we were going to keep doing this until we got it right, even if it took all (expletive-deleted) day.

"This Bob Hope guy is a real asshole," Loren observed.

"He sure is," I agreed. "Do you think that those are really wounded guys down there in the first row or just audience plants?"

"I don't know, but if there's a magician with the show and they saw one of those guys in half, then you can bet that they're plants."

"Or if one of those Gold Digger chicks calls one of them up on the stage and publicly molests him."

"Oh, for sure, then he's a plant."

"Bob Hope. Camp Eagle. Take seven," the director announced.

It was intended that the Bob Hope Christmas show would lift our spirits and boost morale, which it actually did. After sitting in the hot sun, for what seemed an eternity, looking at the back of a cameraman's head, and straining to hear Neil Armstrong talk about going on a rocket ship to the moon over a faulty sound system, I couldn't wait to get back into combat. There, if someone was this annoying, at least you could shoot him.

"Have you noticed, since we did that mescaline, how much closer the stage is now?" Loren asked.

I agreed. It *was* closer, plus one of the Gold Diggers was communicating with me telepathically. From what I could understand, she wanted to meet me behind the ammo dump for sex. At least I *thought* it was one of the Gold Diggers. Upon further investigation, it turned out to be, awkwardly, a male nurse from the *Third Surgical Hospital* in Bien Thuy. He had been on the same flight to Da Nang with us.

When the show was at long last over, after all the cuts and retakes and a half dozen more temper tantrums by Bob Hope, the crowd sprinted for the exits. There was a genuine concern that one of those guys in the blue pajamas would yell "encore," and we'd be stuck there for another two hours.

We found our plane and its crew where we had left them. Because of the problem with the tree branch, they were unable to see the USO show.

"Let me tell ya," Loren assured the pilot. "You didn't miss anything, but I brought something you might enjoy chewing on."

"Do you think that's wise?" I asked Loren. "He's got to fly this thing."

"Don't worry about it. I only gave him one button . . . just enough to enhance his flying finesse, not impair it."

"Still. I'm thinking this may not be one of your most inspired ideas."

Next to us, a big *C-130 Hercules* was being loaded with equipment, wardrobe, and props from the show.

"Look! There's Neil Armstrong," I alerted our boy pilot, who grabbed his logbook and sprinted to the C-130. When he returned, I asked him if he had gotten Neil's autograph.

"You bet I did," he answered excitedly, "and Rachel Welch's too."

He was aggressively chewing the peyote as he spoke.

"You better take it easy with that stuff, pal," I warned him. "You don't want it entering your system all at once. Now, let's 'sky.' Some of us have got a plane to catch, you know."

"Then grab a seat, take a deep breath, and hold on for the ride of your life," the young pilot suggested.

"Fifty bucks says you can't make me toss that box lunch I ate back there," Loren challenged.

"I'll take that bet!"

"This can't be good," I warned Loren, as we boarded the aircraft. "What in the world are you thinking?"

CHAPTER TEN

China Beach

Excited, Loren burst into our hooch.

"Hey Bruce! Did you hear the news? Ho Chi Minh died. Perhaps this will finally mean the end of the war."

"Don't hold your breath. Last I heard, Nixon's still alive. Did one of our guys get him?"

"No. *Stars and Stripes* says he died from old age. He was born in 1890."

"Not a bad life span for a guy who fought indefatigably for his country's independence from the Japanese, French, and Americans . . . all ruthless and cold-blooded adversaries."

"Yeah. Well he probably ate a lot of fiber and exercised. What's the matter? You look bummed," Loren observed. "Did you receive some bad news in that letter you're reading?"

"Yeah, I did. My girlfriend, Toni, is dumping me for another guy. It turns out she's taken up with the fellow who owns the Polaroid . . . the guy who's been taking all those naked pictures of her. Can you believe that crap?"

"That's terrible. But really, Bruce. You're saying that you never saw this coming?"

"No! It caught me totally by surprise."

"I bet it makes you feel like a dick."

"No, thanks. I think I'll soldier on with vaginas for the foreseeable future."

"I meant to say it must make you feel like a chump."

"It does! What I really could use is some sort of distraction to help me stop thinking about her. I'm obsessing over this."

"Well, if this war is not enough of a distraction for you . . ."

"No. No. I'm not complaining that this is some second rate war. For what they've got to work with, our leaders in Washington and the military/industrial complex have gone above and beyond. Those Airforce guys are using B-52Ds to carpet bomb Haiphong for heaven's sake! It's like killing flies with a shot gun."

Loren put his arm around my shoulder.

"I'm so sorry Bruce. If it's any consolation, I think that I speak for everyone in the company when I say that we really appreciated those photos. She doesn't have a slut little sister by chance, does she?"

"No. She's an only child. I was so looking forward to seeing her again. She really broke my heart. I'm devastated, I'm telling you, devastated."

"Falling in love is very like falling into a punji trap."

"Only when you fall in love you're not impaled on sharpened bamboo sticks tipped with feces."

"Granted. But other than that, it's quite similar. Tell you what. Let's get stoned."

"Getting stoned is always the answer for you, isn't it?"

"That depends on the question. For some interrogatives, getting drunk may be the more appropriate response, but in this particular case, I think I was correct in my original discernment of getting stoned."

"So what would you do if we came under rocket attack right now?"

"Get stoned."

"What if your orders to go home came in?"

"Get stoned."

"How about you win the Irish Sweepstakes?"

"Get stoned."

"What if Johnny Cash showed up right here in Bong Son, with June Carter at his side? What if they did a performance of *Jackson* for us over at the enlisted men's club and then took suggestions from the audience?"

"Would he sing that *Boy Named Sue* song?"

"If you requested it. Sure!"

"Get drunk."

. . . in the mud and the blood and the beer.

"Okay. Let's get stoned. By the way, there was some mail for you today."

"Where?"

"I put it over there on your cot."

Loren walked over to his bed, picked up the letter I had placed there, and sat down on the edge of his bunk to read it. A puzzled look formed on his face.

"What's up?" I asked.

"It seems that I've been preapproved for a *Diner's Club* card. They just need a little more information."

"Cool. You should go ahead and sign up for one. That way, when you go into town to get a little stinky on your dinky, you can charge it on your credit card."

"You're contemptible. I've never set foot in one of those unsavory places, and for you to suggest . . ."

"Nor have I. But now that I no longer have a girlfriend, and you're getting a credit card, it will be like we have the key to the city. How much for a massage, you ask? Fifty dong? No problem. Just put it on my good friend Loren's *Diner's Club* card along with a couple of sloe gin fizzes, mixed from your finest top-shelf sloe gin."

"There's no way I'm letting you charge on my credit card."

"Why not?"

"Well first of all, I don't know why you can't drink the house brand sloe gin, and secondly, what if I survive this tour? Did you ever think about that? Then I'd have to pay off my credit card debt when I get home. If I wanted debt, I could have gone to college, earned a degree, and procured a student deferment to boot."

"But really, Loren. Let's be realistic. What are the chances of you surviving this war? I mean, there are some 50 million people in this county, and like 49 million of them want to off you . . . and when one of the few who doesn't, wants to varnish your cane, what are you supposed to do? Tell the poor girl, 'No thank you, Miss' I don't want to run up my credit card?' Now that would be a really shitty thing to do. It would break the poor girl's heart. Dinks have feelings too, you know. You need to be pragmatic about this, Loren. I mean, look at me. I'm just taking it one day at a time, and so should you. Now let's fill this thing out, and get it mailed back as soon as possible. Okay, what do we have here? Let's see. Name? Social Security number, occupation. Hmmm. Occupation. This is going to be tricky. You surely don't want to tell them that you're an airborne ranger or combat infantryman."

"No?"

"No! That would never get you a credit card."

"Then what do I say my occupation is?"

"How about *Government/Foreign Service*?"

"Like a diplomat, you mean?"

"Yeah. Like a diplomat."

"And what do I say I do as a diplomat?"

"You tell them you promote peace, support prosperity, and protect American citizens while fostering U.S. interests abroad, of course."

"But isn't that the exact *opposite* of what I do?"

"Well sure! We all know that, but you want to get a *Diner's Club Card* don't you?"

"I guess so."

"Okay, next question . . ."

Just then, Sergeant Washington knocked on the doorframe of our hooch. We didn't actually have a door per se, just a doorframe.

"Come on in, Sarge," Loren called to him.

"What are *you* boys up to?"

"Loren's applying for a credit card, and I'm helping him," I answered excitedly.

"Good. Good. It's not a bad idea to start building your credit now, while you're young. The only reason I've been in this man's Army since Jesus was a corporal, is because my credit stinks, which makes it virtually impossible to function in civilian life."

"Is that because you're delinquent on an installment loan, or you defaulted on your mortgage?"

"No. It's because I'm black."

"That's terrible!"

"That I'm black?"

"No. Black goes well on you. It's terrible that they would base your credit on your ethnic origin."

"Once, when I wanted to buy a house, the bank pre-denied my mortgage."

"Are you shittin' me?"

"No. I swear before God Almighty."

"Tell me this, Sarge. You didn't by chance fall for that old 'America, the great melting pot' line, did you?"

An acutely curious and at once perplexed expression manifested on his face.

"Oh no Sarge! I'm *so* sorry. That was never meant to include citizens whose ancestors arrived on our shores in the holds of slave ships . . . or indigenous peoples."

"No?"

"No. Didn't your mother ever explain that to you? That melting pot thing is all about *immigrants* . . . Like the Irish and Italians, and Eastern Europeans and the like. People whose ancestors came through Ellis Island. I'm surprised I have to break it to you. I've always looked up to you as a fountain of knowledge and wisdom."

Sergeant Washington looked dejected.

"While we're at it, should we tell him that other thing, Loren?"

"Yeah. You might as well."

"Okay Sarge. Listen up. Now you know when a white guy has some-thing to say on the subject of race, and he prefaces it by saying *I don't care if you're black, white, or purple?*"

"Yes?"

"Then that guy is like an absolute seething bigot . . . even worse than the KKK."

Sergeant Washington's eyes bugged out and his gold teeth shown.

"Den iffin I dun run up again one uf dos folks, uh bitter hod uner de baid."

Loren shot a puzzled glance my way.

"Are you okay Sarge? You're not having a stroke now are you."

"No boys. I was just joshin' with you."

"Well don't do that again. It made me feel extremely uncomfortable."

"Talking about uncomfortable, Sarge," Loren intervened. "You look like you would do well to take a load off your feet. Don't be shy," he motioned with a wave. "Have a seat."

Sergeant Washington sat on the edge of my cot.

"What may we do for you? I hope you didn't come to procure a loan, because both Loren and I are having an out of money experience right now."

Sergeant Washington smiled while looking discriminatingly around the place.

"I don't mean to offend you boys or seem rude, but you two live in a pigsty."

"Well, if you had given us some notice that you'd be stopping by, we would have tidied up and, perhaps, put out some fresh-cut flowers. Did you notice, by the way, how we rearranged our cots in relationship to our foot lockers?"

"Indeed, that's very creative. Most soldiers place their foot lockers at the *foot* of their cot . . . hence the name *foot locker.*"

"Well, not us," Loren explained. "Bruce was reading an article in *Architectural Digest* on *Feng Shui*, and we've been doing a little experi-mentation. What do you think of what we've accomplished so far?"

"Your disambiguation of the space looks to be spot on, but your M-16s leaning in the corner frustrates your attempt at achieving har-mony with the environment."

"We're working on that. Now, what may we do for you, Sergeant?"

"Captain Riley and I were just discussing how horrifying it must have been for you two young men when the Caribou you were flying back from the Bob Hope show overran the runway like it did."

"I know. I hate it when that happens. It's so unprofessional. But, don't worry about it, Sarge. My mantra has always been: *any landing you can walk away from, is a good landing.* I have to say, however, that snap roll, inside loop, and hammerhead stall our pilot performed over the airfield just about brought my lunch back up, and let me tell you, Army cooking is bad enough going down. I take exception to dealing with it twice."

"Yeah, I knew we were in trouble," Loren added, "when I overheard the pilot tell the copilot, *Hey, watch this! When you push on the control wheel, the buildings get bigger. When you pull back on it, they get smaller and when you pull back all the way and hold it there, they get bigger again.*"

"That's always a bad omen. His commanders have no idea what got into him. Up until that unfortunate flight, he had an exemplary flying record. Let me assure you, that young man will never pilot a military aircraft again. I can't speak for the private sector, however. *Northwest Airlines* may very well recruit him. But, that's entirely beside the point. The reason I wanted to speak with you two is because the Captain feels so remorseful about how your trip to Da Nang ended on such a sour note, he insists on making it up to you. That was no way, in his opinion, to treat a Silver Star recipient and his buddy. In recompense, he wants to send you to China Beach for a little R&R."

"What do you say, Loren? Do you want to go to China Beach?" I asked excitedly.

"Sure! Let's do it. I've never been to China before."

"It's not in China, dipshit. It's in Vietnam, near Da Nang."

"It is? Then why don't they call it Vietnam Beach?"

"It's a marketing thing, Madison Avenue fluff, isn't that right, Sarge?"

He seemed to be in a dumbfounded daze.

"Do you copy my transmission? I repeat. Do you copy?"

"Oh. I'm sorry, Bruce. I was still thinking about the melting pot business."

The China Beach R&R Center near Da Nang, much to Loren's and my disappointment, did not include any female guests with whom to mingle.

"This really sucks," Loren commented to me. "What are we going to do now?"

"You could hit on that Marine over there, all oiled-up sunning himself, but I wouldn't get my hopes up. He looks pretty hetero. You never know though. Why don't you go over there and tell him, *me so horny G.I.*"?

"You go first."

"Not me. As I told you before, I really don't go in for that sort of thing. How about, instead, we sign out one of those *Sunfish* sailboats they loan, bear away on that easterly breeze, and steer for San Pablo, in the Philippines? I bet they have some dead-easy women *there* to pop your nut."

"Okay. I suppose it beats cleaning my own rifle. I'll just grab us a couple of beers for the trip."

"I was only joking."

"You were? So we're not going to San Pablo?"

"No. I was just blowing smoke up your ass."

"What are we going to do then?"

"How about we try some surfing?"

"I don't know. Have you ever surfed?"

"I was a lifeguard at the 63rd Street Beach, back in Chicago."

"Yeah, but have you ever surfed?"

"It can't be *that* hard."

"I suppose not. Let's give it a shot."

"Now that's the spirit!"

After splitting a doobie, which we smoked as a prophylactic of glaucoma, Loren and I signed for some surfboards and paddled out about fifty yards, where we floated on our bellies, on the gently rising and ebbing waves while we chatted.

"How do you like free surfing so far, brah?" I asked.

"Gnarly. I'm totally amped."

"Me, too. I'm stoked. I just hope a smacking rogue reef breaker doesn't catch us off guard. I wouldn't want to get crushed in the impact zone, caught in the soup, and carried out on the riptide, to be eaten by a tiger shark."

"That would be a bummer . . . a real hairball."

"We're getting some phat hang-time; wouldn't you say? Do you want to try a takeoff on this next set and hang 10, perhaps?"

"Just stay loose, shubee. You have sand for brains. This is epic. No need to be wiki wiki. We don't want to get caught inside a double overhead and risk a wipeout. This isn't the Triple Crown, after all, dude."

"You're right. It's actually very calming just floating here. As a matter of fact, I'm in Zen mode."

"How'd you get there so fast? You only smoked one *rainy day woman*, and now you're in Zen mode?"

"I did it by not trying. By thinking outside the ammo box."

"Is that supposed to be some sort of a Zen joke or something."

"No. A Zen joke would have no punch line."

"Well, I'm Catholic and our jokes *have* punch lines."

"So, you're Catholic are you? Well, my Karma just ran over your dogma."

"How're you hangin'?"

"Me? I'm thinking about perhaps getting a sponsorship . . . if I ever get out of this place alive."

"Rad."

As we tranquilly floated on boards in the swells, a Huey Slick (evidently returning from a mission) passed only six feet or so over our boards. Thick black smoke poured from the engine.

"If he's headed for the Da Nang Air Base, it's not going to happen," I commented to Loren.

Confirming my conjecture, the helicopter transitioned to a hover, not more than fifty feet from our positions, then plopped into the South China Sea. As the craft settled, listing to the port, the rotors splashed into the water, splintering. I could see the door gunner strip off his flak jacket, and enter the waist-deep surf. He opened the co-pilot's door, and pulled the unconscious occupant from the right-hand seat by the scruff of his neck.

"If I weren't on R&R, I'd paddle over there and help those guys," Loren told me.

"It's not our job anyway," I reminded him. "The Navy has people especially trained in water rescues. They have special certifications . . . and flippers. We wouldn't want to step on their proverbial toes. That would be like, back in Chicago, if a union painter were to do some plumbing. Everybody's got to stick to the job they were trained for."

"What's *our* job, again? Remind me."

"Our job is to go around agitating, frustrating, negating, truncating, checkmating, and, deflating the locals. It's a very important component of our government's strategic mission to achieve peace with honor. We need to stick to what we do best, and let those Navy guys do what they excel at."

"That's just fine and dandy with me."

"That *was* bitchin', the way the pilot put that slick down in the water."

"It was like, *Whoa, man! There's no way we're makin' the airport. So instead, let's ditch this whirly-bird over there by those cool surfer dudes.*"

"We *are* cool aren't we? *Totally!*"

"Check it out, dude. We rule!"

We gave each other "high fives."

"What are we going to tell our buddies if they say something about our being at China Beach while they were up to their proverbial necks in VC back in Bong Son?"

"How about, with tears in our eyes, we sob, '*if you weren't there man, shut up. Cuz if you weren't there, you don't know. You don't know shit. You had to be there.*' How about that?"

"Hey! You're pretty good."

"Thanks. In high school, I played George Gibbs in a highly acclaimed production of Thornton Wilder's allegorical play, *Our Town.*"

"Well good for you."

We drifted on our surf boards in silent bliss as the sun retreated then reemerged from behind one stratocumulus cloud, then another.

"Hey Loren."

"Yes?"

"Are you still thinking about that Marine?"

"A little."

"Yeah. Me too."

CHAPTER ELEVEN

Going Home

At long last, I neared the end of my deluxe, all-inclusive, escorted tour in Vietnam. We used to refer to it, in those days, as being "short."

"I'm *so* short," I bragged to some of the newbies, who were cowering in a corner of the bunker during a pretty routine 82 mm mortar attack, "that I've got to take a piss, but I think I'll just wait until I get home."

As much excitement as I enjoyed in exotic Binh Dinh province, gateway to Gia Lai, and the antipersonnel fragmentation mine capital of Southeast Asia, I made the tough decision not to re-up when invited to do so by Sergeant Washington. He discharged his martial duty, however, and delineated all the compelling reasons why I should consider the Army for a rich and rewarding career.

"Free healthcare," he pointed out. "Look at PFC Crosby, for example. After being shot in the jaw, he's going to be needing tens of thousands of dollars in reconstructive surgery, and good old Uncle Sam will be paying for every dime of it."

"I think I'll just get my health insurance at work," I countered.

"What about retirement?" he asked. "Wouldn't you like to be able to pull a military pension after only 20 years? You'd still be young enough to get another job, and double-dip. Wouldn't you like to double-dip? I understand that back in your home town of Chicago, double dipping is an institution."

"I'm sorry, but I really don't think the Army's for me," I insisted. "I don't care for the unsafe working conditions."

The sergeant persisted. "Okay, I see. That's a very good point. But what about the reenlistment incentive? Re-up today, and the Army will give you a 30-day leave to go home and see your family and that hot little girlfriend whose pictures have been circulating the base. I bet you really miss *her* after 13 months in this unfortunate country."

"I'm going home in two days as it is," I answered incredulously. "For good!"

Sergeant Washington scratched his bald head.

"Okay. Okay. Bear with me here, Johnson. I'm not finished with you yet."

Cupping his right hand to the side of his mouth, he bent forward close to my ear, and whispered, "What about the pot? Don't the drugs in this country kick butt?"

Just as I was about to put my signature on the reenlistment papers, Loren Anderson hollered at me from across the way, "Don't do it Bruce! Don't do it! Our orders are in! We're going home!"

He waved his papers joyously in the air as he yelled this to me. I sprinted over to Company Command, and picked up my paperwork from Ken Quidero. Ken was gay. One of the first clues that I and the other guys had, pointing this to being the case, was his propensity for arousal while showering with other men. For this reason, his moniker around the base was "*Homo erectus.*"

Ken hit on me whenever he drank Harvey Wallbangers at the enlisted men's club. It was cute. He also saw to it that none of my Article Fifteens were typed up and put in my 201 U.S. Army personnel file, as prescribed by the Uniform Code of Military Justice. In appreciation, I said goodbye to him with a big bear hug. He patted my ass.

"Who knows, Ken," I said as we embraced. "*Another time, another place. If it weren't for this insane war. But where I'm going, you can't follow. I'm not good at being noble, but it doesn't take much to see that the problems of two little people don't amount to a hill of beans in this crazy world. Someday, you'll understand that.*"

"And here's looking at *you*, kid," Ken played along.

"We'll always have Paris." I winked.

"Let me know," Captain Riley interjected, "if you guys are going to kiss, and I'll give you some privacy."

"Remember, Bruce," Ken reminded me, "Mardi Gras is February 23rd. I'll be expecting you."

"I'll be there with bells on."

"Ohoo. I'll like *that!*"

"Take care now, Ken."

"You, too. And thanks for the cookies. They were absolutely scrumptious. You'll have to give me the recipe sometime. I love to bake."

"Oh! That reminds me. You can go ahead and put Bill Hasting's KIA notification to his family through now."

"I'll do that. I'm sure they're beginning to wonder why he hasn't been writing."

After saying our goodbyes to the guys in our platoon, Loren and I walked together to the Huey that was waiting with its crew to fly us to Long Binh. Loren Anderson, Bill Hastings, and I had flown into Bong Son on the same helicopter 13 months earlier, and now only Loren and I were flying out together. Back then, our crisp new uniforms betrayed us as "cherries." Now they were faded, tattered, and worn, marking us as battle-hardened bad-asses.

When we first arrived at the sprawling Long Binh base outside Saigon with our orders to go home, we were like a couple of country bumpkins arriving in the big city. An air-conditioned bus with air brakes, driven by a specialist fourth class, transported us from Bien Hoa Air Base to our accommodations.

"Hey, dude," Loren addressed the driver. "What kind of MOS do you need to get a sweet job like this?"

"All passengers will remain behind the white line," the specialist replied. "Distracting conversation with the driver is prohibited."

"But I was just wondering. How did you get a gig like this?"

"Please remain seated while the bus is in motion."

"Were you drafted or did you enlist?" Loren persisted.

Meanwhile, outside the bus, a beautiful African-American Navy medical officer waited to cross the roadway.

"Wait! Stop the bus. Let me off here."

"Passengers may not be disgorged except at designated bus stops," the driver responded, stepping on the gas.

Dispirited, Loren slumped down in his seat with a pout.

"I wasn't looking to get disgorged. I only wanted to see what it's like to *talk* to an American woman again."

"It's just the same as talking to a Vietnamese woman except, with the Vietnamese woman, the reason you can't understand her is because she's speaking a different language."

At our destination, which appeared to be based, architecturally, on the movie set where *Stalag 17* was filmed, we were processed and assigned a place to sleep. Four times each day there was a formation, and the names on the manifest for the next flight out were phlegmatically read. Those not called returned to their barracks to wait in boredom for the next formation. Sometimes we would be awakened in the wee hours of the morning, only to have our hopes cruelly dashed again. It was the military's version of Chinese Water Torture. Subsequently, there was a unsubstantiated rumor going around that some guys in Barracks F were digging a tunnel with spoons they purloined from the mess hall, and the tech-savvy "geek" in the bunk next to me was building a crude crystal radio set from salvaged material he liberated from the trash. It featured an ear plug and an antenna wire with an alligator clip on the end. This he used to attach the unit to his bed springs to improve reception. (He went on, I understand to be one of the founders of a startup computer company in Cupertino, California.) One evening he pulled in the BBC *World News Tonight*, and, on pins and needles, we monitored the Rwandan presidential election results. After a fortnight of this regimen, Loren and I were, at long last, assigned to a flight. When they called my name, I felt as if I had won the lottery. Loren and I congratulated each other, packed up our gear, and reported, as assigned, for drug testing.

"I wonder what kind of drugs they want us to test," I joked with Loren. "I don't want to be doing any of that nasty synthetic crap just before going home."

The special latrine, where they collected our urine, was in the style of a Japanese pagoda. (This is where the *Stalag 17* analogy loses some of its credibility.) A neatly printed sign near the entrance identified it as *The Peehouse of the August Moon*. In a strategically positioned chair, sat a Marine Lance Corporal, whose job it was to ensure that each person was pissing into his own bottle and not someone else's. Failing to piss in one's own bottle was an offence punishable by a court-martial, we were wearily warned. The corporal took his job very seriously. I couldn't help having some fun with him.

"What are you going to tell your grandkids someday," I inquired, "when they ask you what *you* did in the war?"

"Kiss my ass," the corporal replied.

(*Marines are not known to be a particularly articulate lot.*)

"My, my. Aren't *we* touchy."

"Quit bothering the guy," Loren urged me. "He's probably suffering from post-latrine stress disorder. One wrong move, and he could snap."

For 10 Dong apiece, we purchased some fresh urine from a Vietnamese laundress, and turned our specimens over for analysis. The results were ready within 20 minutes.

"Well, the good news," a lab technician informed us, "is that you two passed your drug screenings with flying colors. Curiously, however, you both came back as positive for pregnancy."

"Probably just a false positive," I suggested.

"I'm sure that's all it is," Loren added, "although I have been experiencing a little morning sickness as of late."

"Try eating some saltine crackers before you get up in the morning," the lab tech suggested.

"Thanks. I'll do that."

After our drug tests, a duffle bag drag, and a bowl of grits, we proceeded to the Monkey House, which was named, I presume, for the way it smelled inside. The Monkey House was a warehouse-type building big enough to hold a planeload of men and their bags. I apologize to again be mixing my movie metaphors, but the structure greatly resembled something from the set of *On the Waterfront* starring Marlon Brando. Inside, it was furnished with long benches, about 42 inches high. Each departing soldier had room on this bench to place his gear. We were instructed to open our bags to display the contents, which, we were told, would be thoroughly searched, and subjected to drug-sniffing dogs.

"If there's one thing that *really* pisses me off," the PFC standing next to me commented, "it's drug-sniffing dogs."

"And dogs that sniff your crotch," I added.

"I know where you're coming from! That's where I conceal my stash. Is that where you keep yours too?"

Up front, an Air Force officer stepped up on the podium and blew into the microphone, presumably to see if it was working properly. In response, the speakers belched a horrific, nerve-racking, reverberating screech that caused some of the more shell-shocked in the building to dive for cover. He signaled to an airman who was sitting off to the side at a sound console.

"Testing. Testing. One, two, three, testing. Can you hear me in the back?"

"No. Yes. We can't hear you!" came a host of responses.

In front of the officer stood a large wooden crate, about four feet cubed.

"Hello everyone, and welcome to the Monkey House," he began. "Gentlemen, it's great to be here today with this distinguished group of survivors who, presumably, did not need to learn the hard way that tracers work in both directions. I know that you are all very excited to go home, but perhaps *some* of you may have picked up a *souvenir* while you were in country. If so, I hope that the penicillin the doc gave you will take care of it."

There were a couple of polite chuckles at his attempt of a joke.

"No, seriously," he continued, "There are certain souvenirs that you will *not* be allowed to take home with you. They are, for the record: brass, ammunition, or weapons of *any* type, drugs or drug paraphernalia, and photos of war dead. If you have any of these items with you, you may place them in the amnesty box at the front of the room. If you do *not* place these items in the amnesty box, we *will* find them, and you will *not* be allowed to board your flight, and *you will not be going home today.*"

Slowly, people began to dig stuff from their duffle bags and luggage. A procession moved to the front of the room and the amnesty box. They looked like parishioners going up for Holy Communion.

"Hey!" the Air Force officer continued, tipping the mike towards a soldier. "Where are you from, son?"

"Kentucky," he answered.

"Kentucky! Let's all give a big hand for the moonshine state! Does anyone know what a tornado and a Kentucky divorce have in common?"

He was greeted by a room full of blank expressions.

"In either case, *someone's* going to lose a trailer!"

There were some moans.

"This guy is hilarious," my druggie chum informed me. "I saw him once at the *Purple Onion*. He brought the house down."

"Go ahead and enjoy yourselves boys, but we are not kidding around when it comes to contraband. Do not think that you can get away with any prohibited items in your luggage. There is absolutely no place to hide this stuff that we haven't seen before. We *will* find it, and when we do, you will *not* be going home."

There was a loud thump as someone dropped an M79 grenade launcher into the amnesty box.

"That had to be an Airborne Ranger!" the officer continued. "Boy, you guys have got to have some balls to jump out of airplanes like that."

This got the attention of some fellows with screaming eagle patches on their fatigues.

"If at first, you don't succeed, then being a paratrooper is probably not for you. Hey, look. Here are some brave men from the 101st Airborne! Let's all give them hand."

Nobody did. Even more people made the pilgrimage to the front of the room.

"So, what do you men think about that commander-in-chief of ours? Let me tell you. When I was young, I used to believe that *anyone* could be president. Now I'm certain of it. Just a joke. Just a joke. The problem with political jokes is that they get elected. Look! Over here . . . a Navy Seal. A man who lives by the motto: *when in doubt, empty your magazine.* Is that a fragmentation grenade you just dropped in the box, partner? Just remember, when the pin is pulled, Mr. Hand Grenade is not our friend."

The officer rattled off a few more jokes, crooned a couple verses of *The Way You Look Tonight,* and did a pretty fair impersonation of John Wayne.

"You should see him do Paul Lynde," my new-found friend suggested.

"I'll take a pass."

The amnesty box was nearly full. When the last of the group had returned to their spots, the officer once again took the mike.

"Okay, men. It's been a lot of fun being here tonight. I want to thank the Monkey House staff, our soundman, Billy Millar, (who's celebrating his birthday this evening, by the way) and all of you from the bottom of my heart. Now, before you begin the next leg of your life's journey, let me leave you with this one final thought."

He bowed his head in a long dramatic pause.

"May you have the hindsight to know where you've been, the foresight to know where you are going . . . and the insight to know when you've gone too far. That's it for tonight everyone! Remember, you don't have to go home . . . but you can't stay here. Now close up your bags and follow Sergeant Jones to the transportation outside that will take you to the terminal and that big silver bird of freedom I know you all have been dreaming of."

He snapped a salute.

"Have a good flight back to the world, gentlemen."

Music blared from the sound system:

. . . I'm leavin' on a jet plane.

"Aren't they going to search our bags?" the private who hated drug-sniffing dogs asked a nearby MP who was standing at ease in the corner.

He had made two trips to the amnesty box, each time carrying an armful of plastic-wrapped packages.

"I'm sorry. We don't have the resources for that, soldier."

CHAPTER TWELVE

Freedom Flight

The chartered *American Airlines Boeing 707-320 Intercontinental* touched down at Travis Air Force Base, California on a rain-slicked runway just before dawn. Thrust reversers on the four Pratt & Whitney JT4A-5s hauled the silver bird of freedom down to taxi speed in seconds. A cheer erupted in the cabin. Tears welled up in my eyes. For 13 months I had dreamed nightly of this exact moment, imagining what it would be like to land on U.S. soil . . . *the land of the free, and the home of the brave* . . . sitting in the passenger cabin as opposed to a cargo hold. I looked out the window, straining to see . . . I don't know what. An Air Force Blue *Dodge* pickup truck with a large illuminated flashing sign in the bed that read, *Follow Me*, pulled in front of the aircraft.

We taxied through the predawn darkness following the dauntless little *Dodge* through a maze of airport runway and taxiway lights. The voice of our veteran stewardess (she was the oldest flight attendant I had ever flown with) came over the P.A. system. She had to be at least forty years old!

Gentlemen. On behalf of Captain Sellers, myself, and all the crew of Military Charter Flight 312, we wish to welcome you to the United States of America. More cheering ensued. *We know that you didn't personally choose us as your air carrier today, but we want you to know that we are proud to have been the crew who flew the last leg of your journey this morning, and we hope you will consider American Airlines as your choice for air travel in the future.*

Captain Sellers' gruff voice followed.

And if any of you grunts ever happen to find yourself to be in Krum Texas (God forbid) look me up and I'll be proud to buy you an authentic Texas Barbeque at the Rusty Nail Café. Welcome home, men!

After deplaning and gathering our gear, a convoy of olive drab busses took us on an anticlimactic drive to the south and west. For some inexplicable reason, the busses had heavy-gauge steel mesh over the windows . . . like prison buses. I dozed off for I don't know how long, but awakened as we arrived at a military installation somewhere. To the east, the just emerging sun staged a stunning spectacle of pink, orange and purple.

"Hey man, where are we?" I asked my seatmate.

"I don't know, but I've been seeing a lot more hippies than usual. I think we must be pretty close to San Francisco."

The bus door scissored open and we were herded into a red brick building where a dozen or so personnel of various military branches and ranks (enlisted and officers) stared at us curiously, while sipping coffee, as we clumsily assembled. It was very much the same atmosphere that had existed on our arrival for basic training 24 months earlier.

A Marine Staff Sergeant greeted us.

"Everyone grab your gear and move along to the blood draw."

There was only one person drawing blood, we discovered, (a Navy corpsman) and there had to be close to 150 people on the flight.

"Does anyone here know how to draw blood?" the corpsman broadcast.

Two combat medics stepped forward.

"Anyone else know how to draw blood?"

There was a long silence.

"Anyone want to learn?"

A few more people stepped up.

I approached a master sergeant, who watched the commotion from a corner of the room, seemingly amused.

"Look Sarge, I was really hoping that if I needed to have my blood drawn, it would be by a qualified phlebotomist."

"You say you need to have your blood drawn?" he looked at me incredulously.

"Don't I?"

"I don't know. Do you?"

"Not for any reason that I can think of."

"Well then. I don't know what you're standing in *this* line for. It would seem to me that if I had just spent the last year or so in Viet fucking Nam, I would be eager to get home to see my family . . . but, then again, that's just me."

A little confused, I moved on toward the next station. The sergeant called after me.

"And by the way, sorry about the band."

"The band?"

"Yeah. They had a late gig last night, so we let them sleep in. I hope you don't mind."

"No. Not at all."

When 30 of us (plus or minus) had accumulated at the next station, we were ushered into a classroom of sorts. Many of the men were desperately holding blood-soaked wads of cotton to their forearms. Even before we had all found our seats, a sergeant put down the book he was reading and began speaking with no intonation whatsoever and like twice as fast as a normal person would talk.

"Good morning gentlemen my name is Sergeant Quandt and I'm here today to talk to you about adjusting to civilian life after spending the last year as a highly trained lean green mean killing machine but I suspect that nobody wants to hear me go on and on about shell shock battle fatigue combat stress reaction or post-traumatic stress syndrome but if I'm wrong and you do want to hear my excellent 30 minute presentation on chronic fatigue slow reaction times indecision disconnection with one's surroundings and an inability to prioritize raise your hands I don't see any hands you're excused."

He resumed intently reading his book, *The Electric Kool-Aid Acid Test*. We shuffled on to the tailor shop area to be fitted for our dress uniforms, a little bedazzled.

"Next," a Geppetto-like gentleman gestured to me.

He had a cloth tape-measure around his neck and straight pins in his mouth.

"Okay. Specialist Forth Class, right?"

"Right."

"And what outfit are you with, son?"

He measured my inseam as he spoke, which always makes me feel uncomfortable.

"173rd Airborne."

"Let me see . . . "

He searched through stacks of unit patches.

"It seems we're clean out of 173rd Airborne. Evidently, a lot more of you guys have been surviving your tours than command had anticipated. What's your second choice? It can be anything you want so long as it doesn't require a security clearance."

"Excuse me?"

"All this uniform has to do is get you home, kid, and then you can burn it for all we care."

"How about the 1ˢᵗ Aviation Brigade? I always thought it would be cool to be a *Cobra* pilot."

"Oh. I'm sorry, but to do that, I'd have to make you a Warrant Officer, and as a civilian contractor, I'm not authorized to promote soldiers . . . just fit them for uniforms. Let's see. . . I can make you a tank driver, if that sounds appealing to you."

"A tank driver?"

"I could put you in the 11ᵗʰ Armored Cavalry."

"But wasn't it like being baked in an oven inside those things?"

"I'm sure it was, but I bet shooting stuff with that big cannon is pretty cool."

"Well, nonetheless, I don't want to be that. Don't you have anything less claustrophobic where I would have been working in an air-conditioned environment, perhaps?"

"An air-conditioned environment, you say? You mean like on one of those refrigerated provisions barges?"

"Yeah. Like that! What outfit would that be?"

"Frankly, I don't really know. Could it be the 1ˢᵗ Logistical Command, perhaps? I have plenty of those patches."

"Sure. Put me in the 1ˢᵗ Logistical. That would be great!"

"Is that it, then?" I asked the tailor as I pulled up the trousers of my ill-fitting uniform.

One pant leg, it appeared, was about three inches longer than the other.

"Am I ready to go home?"

"Just throw your jungle fatigues in that bin over there. Did you see the doc yet for your shots?"

"My shots?"

"Yeah. In that passport-like book you've got there. Do you have your shot stamps yet?"

"No. It's not stamped."

"Well then, you're going to have to go down this hall here to see the doc. Just follow the blue line. It will take you there."

"Great. Thanks."

"Remember. The blue line. Do *not*, under *any* circumstances, follow the red line."

"No?"

"No. It will lead you to the Psychological Evaluation department. If you wander in there, you may never see home again."

I followed the blue line as instructed, and received directions by some more coffee-sipping spectators, who lined the hallway, to the office of a large-eared Army medical officer with a receding hairline.

"I'm Doctor Kevorkian," he introduced himself, sporting a sinister smile. "Let me see your book."

I handed it to him. Fumbling, he found the vaccinations page.

"Now, did you want some shots today, or just the stamps in your book?"

"I can do that? I can get *just* the book stamped?"

"Of course you can . . . unless you enjoy getting poked with needles or something. I mean if you're into that sort of thing . . . or if you think you may have been exposed to the Bubonic Plague. Then I'd suggest getting the shots."

"I'll just take the stamps, thanks."

"And if you like, I also have some colorful *Disney* character stickers. Would you like one of those in your book, too?"

"Cool! Whom do you have?"

"Let's see. I have Goofy, (my personal favorite) Donald Duck, Jiminy Cricket, and of course, Mickey Mouse."

"I'll take the cricket, thanks."

"Really? Most soldiers go with Mickey . . . or no sticker at all. So, Jiminy Cricket it shall be. I began my medical career in Korea, you may be interested to know, back in 1953 treating shell-shocked and otherwise maimed troopers. Wretched stuff. But, I can tell you with confidence that *Disney* character preferences are much like a *Rorschach* test. They tell us a lot. Jiminy Cricket, besides being a minced oath for 'Jesus Christ,' represents conscience. I suspect your conscience is bothering you, Son. You will need to address that . . . the sooner the better. If it's acute, after I finish with you here, you can choose to follow the red line down the hall."

"Thanks, but I think I'll be going home to Chicago."

"I *do* make house calls, if you're ever interested."

He stamped my book and pointed me to the last station where I received my separation papers, my travel orders, and a check for travel expenses. Within 45 minutes of my arrival at the processing facility, I was already on an *AC Transit* bus #73. I asked the driver if he stopped at Oakland International Airport, and he told me that it was none of my business. I walked to the back of the bus and found an empty seat. Along the way, I received innumerable icy cold sideways glances from my fellow passengers and whispers. The fellow I sat next to, however, greeted me warmly.

"Ah. Don't pay them any heed. They're just ignorant. You *do* need to ditch that uniform just as soon as possible, however."

At once, an Asian woman, seated directly across the aisle and cradling an infant, sprang from her seat and scurried to the front of the bus as if I had Smallpox.

"Where I just came from, we used to shoot those things like rats," I called after her.

"You really shouldn't say things like that," my seatmate advised confidentially. "It isn't politic."

He examined the patch on my uniform curiously.

"1st Logistical Command! What do you know. That was my unit back in 1948 during the Berlin Crisis."

He shook my hand. His was hard and calloused.

"It's a real pleasure to meet someone from my old outfit. What did you do with the First?"

He caught me off guard. I tried to think of something a logistics specialist might do.

"I drove a forklift," was the first thing to come to my mind.

"A forklift, you say? An *Allis Chalmers?*"

"Yeah. An *Allis Chalmers* . . . with dual machine guns. My tailor wanted me to be a tank driver at first, but I figured it would be too blessed hot in one of those things. I really wanted to be a *Cobra* pilot, but he would have to make me a Warrant Officer to do that, so I decided to drive a forklift."

"Your tailor, you say?"

"Oh, never mind. It's a long story."

"Well, nonetheless I'm pleased to meet you, young man. Just remember. This is going to be a big adjustment for you back to civilian life after a combat tour in Southeast Asia. Don't underestimate that. It might be rough going for a while. You'll need to watch your drinking and recreational drug use. It can be a slippery slope. In fact, you'll need to watch *all* your habits, as they are what determine your character, and it's your character that will decide your destiny. I just hope the military gave you all of the tools you're going to need to be successful in your acclamation back into society."

I thought about Sergeant Quant's talk back at the separation center.

"It's very important that you heed their advice, and seek professional help if you perceive your life to be spiraling out of control," my new friend continued. "There may be times when you'll experience inexplicable rage, or you'll find your behavior to be extremely self-destructive, anti-social, or inappropriate. Be careful. You don't want to become one of those crazy, unemployed, Vietnam vets who grows his beard and hair, wears a tattered field jacket and boonie hat year round, no matter the weather, hugs other sobbing crazy Vietnam vets he meets, and calls them 'Bro,' do you?"

"No. I don't want to end up like that. That would be pitiful."

"Good. Because it's just a matter of time before guys like that end up in some sort of a police standoff, you know. It's inevitable. So, forgive my presumptuousness, but nonetheless, let me give you *one* piece of advice, if I may."

"Go ahead."

"If the psychological burdens from the war ever become more than you can bear, and you feel as if you are about to lose your sanity, instead of grabbing a gun, and a dozen magazines of ammo, then going out and shooting people indiscriminately at the bus station, try instead working a jigsaw puzzle, preferably one with kittens as a theme. When you've finished, I'm confident that, not only will you feel a great sense of accomplishment, but that your pent-up rage will have, surprisingly, melted away."

I looked at my seatmate incredulously. This guy was annoying!

"Why don't you go bother someone else, you dumbass," I suggested.

My Homecoming

I sprinted through Oakland International Airport, Terminal One, to Gate 48, eschewing the moving sidewalk. I had heard creditable tales of those things malfunctioning, coming to a standstill, and stranding people for hours. I had no intention of missing my flight home to Chicago due to a lack of preventive maintenance. Out of breath, I presented my travel papers to the agent.

"Going home, soldier?"

I only nodded in reply. My freshly issued dress uniform should have made it pretty obvious to this clown. I couldn't wait to shed this monkey suit and get into some civvies.

"Looks like you'll be flying first class today, soldier."

"Pardon me? And please, stop calling me soldier."

"Sorry, but that red, white and blue ribbon on your chest tells me you're a Silver Star recipient. I know because my brother earned one of those at the Battle of Okinawa. Lost his right leg below the knee."

Like I really cared to hear about "Sherlock's" brother losing his leg.

"I'll be sure to let the captain know he's got a Silver Star soldier on board. I'm guessing he'll want to invite you up to the cockpit for a look around and shake your hand."

"If it's all just the same to you," I countered, "I'd be more comfortable if the captain kept his hands on the control yoke while I take a nap in the cabin, secure in the knowledge that someone is steering the aircraft."

"You're the customer. Whatever you like, sir."

"Then you should know I like my fillets medium rare with a pink center, my vodka martinis extra dry with an olive, and my stewardesses sexy, sassy, and skirted. Now, are you going to stamp my ticket and board me in time to enjoy a pre-pushback cocktail, or am I going to be obliged to fill out one of those customer satisfaction surveys with a host of disgruntled responses."

Actually, I was raised far better than that, but having just spent the last thirteen months in "Funny Country," I had this uncharacteristic problem with my attitude. Everybody and everything, for some reason, pissed me off.

I boarded the plane and found my seat, shoving some lummox (who was blocking the aisle while trying to stuff his overcoat into the overhead) out of my way, and buckled up.

"Looks like we're going to have good flying weather," my seatmate tried to make conversation.

"Look. If you need someone to talk to, get an analyst."

"I *am* an analyst!"

"Oh, great . . . Oh, stewardess . . . may I change seats?"

"I'm a *stock* analyst. I analyze the stock market."

"Oh, shit. That's even worse! Ah, stewardess."

"Yes sir. May I help you?"

"Yeah. Could you move this bozo next to someone who's looking for some conversation . . . or market advice?"

"I'm afraid that will be impossible, sir. The flight's completely full. In fact, we're overbooked."

"How about that blond over there with the short skirt and kicky heels? Can't he switch seats with her? And, if we're overbooked, she can sit on my lap."

"I'm sorry, but she's flying with her spouse."

"How about you just remove this guy from the aircraft, then."

"On what grounds?"

"Interfering with a flight crew. Being disruptive and unruly."

"But he's perfectly placid."

"That's because you haven't tried to remove him yet. Grab him by the arm and order him off the plane. I bet *that* will really get him agitated. He won't be so easygoing then."

With a nod, the stewardess signaled her partner, who picked up the intercom phone and spoke into it. Within seconds, the first officer arrived at my seat.

"Oh great! I've got a problem with my seatmate, and they send me *Sky King.*"

"Sir. If you don't settle down, I will have no choice but to call Airport Police, and have them forcibly remove you from the aircraft."

"Me? Did you know that this joker here is a market analyst? For all we know, he could be holding a short position on your airline's stock. Do you really want a fellow like that on the aircraft?"

"Please, sir. Why don't I have Judy, here, bring you a nice relaxing drink, and perhaps you can nap during the flight. And, by the way, did you realize that one of your pant legs is like three inches longer than the other?"

I uttered some profanities having to do with autoerotic sex, and then settled into my seat, reclining it into the lap of the fellow behind me.

"Would you care for that cocktail now, sir?" The stewardess offered.

"Sure. I'll have whatever they're drinking up in the cockpit."

"I'm sorry, but FAA regulations prohibit the consumption of alcoholic beverages by members of the flight crew."

"What airline is this, again?"

"*United*. Why do you ask?"

"Oh. I was confused. I was thinking that this was *Northwest Airlines*."

"That's quite understandable, sir. It happens all the time."

"It may sound like fuzzy logic, but actually, I prefer flying *Northwest* inasmuch as your average hijacker would be reluctant, for safety reasons, to fly with them."

As I enjoyed my drink, then another, we just sat at the gate for over 20 minutes. I rang for the stewardess again.

"May I help you sir? Would you like another drink?"

"Well that too, but I was wondering how come we're not moving."

"Well, evidently, while performing his obligatory preflight check, our first officer detected a minor issue with the aircraft's number two engine that gave him pause."

"So, are we waiting for a mechanic?"

"No, we're waiting for a replacement first officer."

The cabin crew had been benevolently furnishing me with dozens of miniature bottles of spirits, so I was pretty buzzed as we arrived in Chicago's O'Hare Airport controlled airspace just as the sun was rising over Lake Michigan. I could pick out Gary Indiana at the bottom of the lake from the blanket of smoke generated by the steel mills.

"People are always harping about air pollution," my seatmate commented, "but it sure makes for the prettiest sunrises."

I said nothing in reply, but gave "Mr. Silver Lining" a contemptuous look. A little burp brought the taste of gin up my esophagus into my mouth.

The *DC-8 Mainliner* banked lazily to our port as we lined up on runway 14 left. Our approach brought us in over the northwest suburbs and *Arlington Park* racecourse. Evidently, the pilot found the resolve to contain his excitement about having a Silver Star recipient as a passenger long enough to bring the aircraft in for a safe landing. While taxiing, the stewardess moved me up to the seat closest to the exit explaining to me that some right wing, Goldwater supporting, war mongering, fascist pig had generously offered to exchange seats with me.

"He saw your Silver Star service ribbon," she informed me. "He wants to be sure that you're the first one off the aircraft."

"Those two chumps probably deserve each other." I agreed to the switch.

My parents were waiting at the gate as I emerged from the jetway. Dad was holding a hand-printed sign that read: *Bruce.*

"People only do that," I explained to him, "when they don't know the person they're meeting."

"You never wrote," he countered. "I was afraid that you forgot who your parents were."

My mom attempted to plant a kiss on me right there in front of everyone at the gate. I succeeded in deflecting it. Dad shook my hand.

"So, you were able to catch an early flight. Well, good for you. I know you're going to want to get out there, find a job and get a place of your own. You know what they say . . . the early bird gets the worm."

My father was a master of the cliché.

"Actually, Dad, I was planning on using the G.I. Bill to go to college."

"College! What do you need college for? I never went to college and I did pretty well for myself, didn't I?"

Dad worked at the Ford plant on Torrence Avenue.

"What you need to do is get a good union job. A job would be the best thing for you. My god, Son. You're nearly twenty years old now. It's time you started taking life seriously."

"And it might also be time you find a *nice* girl and get married," my mother piped in. "To tell you the truth, I never *did* like that Toni girl you were seeing. She seemed so, so, how can I say this without hurting your feelings? Slutty. Those see-through blouses and short skirts she wore left nothing to the imagination. And all of that eye makeup! I have to tell you, Son, I'm positive that some of the neighbors thought you were dating an underage prostitute. I was so embarrassed. I couldn't even look them in the eye. I just *know* they were talking behind our backs."

I now remembered why I had volunteered for the draft just as soon as I graduated from Brother Rice High School in 1968. These couldn't possibly be my *real* parents, I used to think. I must be adopted.

"You must be famished," my mother jabbered on as we drove down the Kennedy Expressway. "Feel free to make a sandwich when we get home . . . if you're hungry. You're welcome to eat anything you find in the kitchen, until you get a chance to do some shopping for yourself. Just don't eat the pastrami. I bought that especially for your dad. I'll make some room in the refrigerator this afternoon so you can have your own special section. The Putnums, next door, sold their house and moved to Dunedin, Florida. That's such a funny name for a town, don't you think? It sounds like *done eatin'*. The new people who moved in are from Detroit, but they're not Negros, thank God. They have two young boys with the blondest hair you ever saw, and a Border Terrier that likes to hump the mailman's leg . . . "

Dad pulled down the alley, and expertly swung the 19 foot long *Ford LTD Brougham* into the garage of the house I grew up in on the 5100 block of South Laramie Avenue. After shutting down the engine, he pulled a notepad and pencil from the glove box and did some quick arithmetic.

"Let me see. That's fifty-four miles round trip at, say, twelve miles to the gallon. We just burned two bucks in gas picking you up from the airport this morning, Son."

I grabbed my duffle bag from the trunk, entered the house by way of the back door, and headed through the kitchen to my bedroom.

"Mom! Where's my bed?"

"Oh, your father converted that room into a studio for my sewing. Because we never heard from you, we naturally assumed that you had been taken a prisoner of war or that perhaps you had located, and made contact with, your biological parents."

"My biological parents?"

"I'm sorry we never told you this before, but it seemed that the older you got, the more awkward it became."

"I'm *adopted*?"

"Didn't you ever suspect?"

"What the hell, Mom."

"We just sort of assumed, all along, that you had figured it out for yourself. You don't look all that Swedish, after all. Anyhow, it just didn't make sense to us, heating an unused space like that. You may put your things in the basement until you find a place of your own. Feel free to move your father's bowling bag if it's in your way. It will be more private down there anyhow. You know. In case you want to bring a girl over."

"Thanks, Mom. That's very thoughtful of you. And I'll try not to bring any of those slutty bimbos back from the bar to bang in your basement."

"Oh! The way you talk. I can tell that being in the army has been a bad influence on you."

"She's right, Son. You never talked to your mother like that before you went in the service," my dad added.

"And come to think of it, I never killed anyone before I went in, either. I guess I'm just a different person now."

CHAPTER FOURTEEN

Buying a New Car

That first night home, sleeping fretfully in my parent's basement, I dreamed I was back in Southeast Asia locked, once again, in mortal combat near Kampong Cham, Cambodia. For some crazy reason, Paul McCartney was my fireteam partner.

"I'm leaving the *Beatles*," he shouted over the blaring battle.

"What?" I yelled back.

"I'm leaving the *Beatles*."

"I don't believe it. When did you decide this?"

"*Yesterday.*"

"You should release a solo album."

"Thanks. I think I'll do that."

Paul then stood up, and with his M-16 blazing, charged headlong into withering enemy fire. *Maybe I'm Amazed.*

I awoke at 5:30 that morning, soaked in sweat, and reached for my M-16 only to realize I was back home in Chicago, *hog butcher to the world, tool maker, stacker of wheat; player with railroads, and the nation's freight handler; stormy, husky, brawling, city of big shoulders.* I didn't have an M-16 anymore. In Chicago, only gang members sport assault rifles . . . and the mentally ill, of course. Emerging from the basement, I was met by the aroma of fried bacon permeating the kitchen. My mother was already up and about. She was packing my father's lunch and had brewed some coffee. I helped myself to a cup. It was bitter, vile, and just awful.

"When did *you* start drinking coffee?" Mom asked.

I gave the question considerable thought, then remembered, I didn't drink coffee . . . never did. Dumping it in the sink, I walked over to the back door and studied the key organizer I had made in eighth grade shop class. It was a pretty good key organizer with a half dozen little hooks to hang the keys on. As I recall, I received a B plus on it. I lost half a grade due to the fact that is was supposed to be a boot scraper.

"What are you looking for, Dear?" Mom queried.

"My car keys."

"You don't have a car, Son. There are no keys there of yours."

I shook the fog from my brain and thought about it. She was absolutely correct. I sold my 1963 ½ *Ford Falcon Sprint* when I went into the Army. I didn't own a car any longer, but for certain, I would be needing one . . . wouldn't I? Rubbing my eyes, I headed for the percolator.

"I need some coffee."

"I thought you didn't like my coffee."

"I never said I didn't like your coffee, Mom."

"You dumped it in the sink. You poured a cup, took one sip, then poured it down the drain. Why else would you *do* that?"

"Because you reminded me, I don't drink coffee."

Dad trudged into the kitchen then and sat down at the white porcelain table with chrome legs and a green *fleur-de-lis* at each corner.

20 years of schoolin' and they put you on the day shift.

On que, Mom cracked three eggs into the hot bacon grease causing quite a spatter.

"I decided to go out this morning and procure for myself a good practical car," I told my father. "I'm thinking that a Grabber Orange *Boss 429 Mustang* with a four-speed and *Hurst* shifter would fit the bill perfectly."

"I'm pleased you're considering a solid, union-built, *Ford Motor Company* product," he commented, "but that doesn't sound like a very *practical* car to me."

"Sure it is," I insisted. "It will blow the doors off *practically* any other car on the road."

"Well, no matter what you purchase, Son, just don't get talked into one of those extended warranties dealers always try to sell you. They're a rip off, and just another way to line the dealer's pockets."

"I'll try to remember that, Dad," I reassured him, as I headed to the only bathroom in the house to shower and shave.

Looking in the mirror, I studied my reflected image intently. My quasi-regulation U.S. Army coiffure was pathetically out of fashion. I decided to grow my hair out to perhaps shoulder length, nurture a droopy mustache, and cultivate some pork chop sideburns. To this day, I am horrified by a particular 35 millimeter slide image of myself as delineated while wearing plaid 27 inch bell-bottomed pants, a wide white belt, white platform shoes, and a paisley shirt with puffy long sleeves and a colossal collar. The inexplicable thing is that I actually went out on dates looking like that, and in more than one instance, went out on a second date with the same girl.

I felt peculiarly lonely during my first solo shower in over eighteen months. After drying off, I descended back down to the furnace room to get dressed and plan my day. The hot water heater was still earnestly cooking away from my recent shower. It sounded as if it were getting ready to blow. I turned the volume up on my dad's *Zenith Royal 500* seven transistor radio to better hear Simon and Garfunkel's *Bridge over Troubled Water*. At five minutes in length, it was a pretty long song, I thought, to be played on AM radio. Notwithstanding, Larry Lujack, WLS's morning show host, explained that it was barely enough time to cover his trip to the men's room, and that he regretted not having played Bob Dylan's *Like a Rolling Stone* instead.

My mother cheerfully descended the basement stairs with a basket of laundry, humming the hymn *Morning Has Broken*.

"Do you have room for my sweat shirt, Mom?"

"It depends on the washing machine setting it requires."

"How do I know what that is?"

"What does it say on your sweat shirt?"

"*Chicago Bulls*."

"Sure. Give it to me. I'll wash it with the coloreds."

"Great! I'm pleased to hear that you're at long last consorting with people of other cultures. I believe it will broaden your viewpoint. Hey Mom."

"Yes, Son?"

"In spite of all the tedious housework you do, you always seem so upbeat. Do you really enjoy doing laundry *that* much?"

"Loads."

While Mom pre-spotted my dad's work clothes with her trusty bar of *Fels-Naptha* laundry soap, singing all the while like a demented Brown-headed Cowbird, I went back upstairs and rummaged through the pile of *Chicago Tribunes* my parents were amassing for the Cub Scout's annual paper drive in May. I was looking for some auto dealer ads to peruse and do some research before I went car shopping. Instead I got lost in an article I stumbled onto reporting President Nixon's latest new clever idea . . . an armed incursion into Cambodia. Mind you, this was not to expand the war, per se, but to *win the peace*. This guy Nixon was not only a military, but a public relations genius! All the while, our generals had been trying to figure out how to win a hopeless and divisive war, when they ought to have been campaigning to win a decisive peace. It was a far more positive message. This was just what the draft card burners, college campus protesters and the like were advocating. Peace!

"Are you going out?" my mother asked, as she reemerged from the basement, lugging a hulking basket of wet clothes.

She still hung her laundry out to dry on the clothesline that stretched from the house to the corner of the garage. A well-weathered five foot piece of scrap one by two spruce with a "V" notch at one end supported the line at its halfway point.

"I'm going out to buy a car."

"You should eat breakfast first. You know what they say. One should never shop on an empty stomach."

"I think they mean *grocery shop*, Mom."

"Whatever, Mr. Smarty Pants. But, just remember, breakfast is the most important meal of the day."

"And that finding was based on peer-reviewed research that was experimentally duplicated?"

"No. Your grandmother told me that when *I* was growing up."

"Then it's lucky I'm headed out to buy a car and not going swimming, or I'd have to wait an hour after eating, least I get cramps and drown."

"Your grandmother was a very wise woman! At least, take a banana with you in case you change your mind."

I declined.

"Do you have your bus fare?"

"Yes, mother."

"You should probably use the bathroom before you go. It could be a long wait at the bus stop."

"I'm leaving now, Mom. See you later."

"You should also wear a heavier jacket than that thin nylon thing you've got on. It's cold out there. You'll freeze to death. And where are your gloves? You should be wearing gloves."

"Goodbye, Mother."

"And one more thing, Son."

"What is it, Mom?"

"Pay heed to your father, and don't get suckered into one of those extended warranties. He knows what he's talking about, you know. He's a wise man."

There was a *Ford* dealer over on Cicero Avenue I intended to visit. It was an easy, albeit cold, walk from my parents' house to Cicero, where

I would be able to catch the number 54B bus. An icy wind blew from the north.

At the bus stop, I stepped into the street, and stretched my neck, searching for a bus on the horizon. It had to be over three quarters of an hour that I stood in the damp Chicago cold, waiting for the south Cicero bus. I was starting to wish that I had used the bathroom before I left the house. Every few minutes, an aircraft on final approach to Midway Airport popped out of the overcast sky and scraped over my head. They were so low, I could have picked up a stone, thrown it, and hit one. As a matter of fact, that's exactly what I was about to do, when my bus at long last arrived in a convoy of two others, all bannered *No. 54B south Cicero*. The doors scissored open with a hiss. I stepped onboard, and fed the coins I was holding into the fare box. My fingers were so numb, I dropped one to the floor of the bus.

"How come you don't space the buses out better?" I asked the driver as I stooped down to retrieve my quarter. "I just about froze to death waiting there, and then three of you come all at once."

"It's a long-standing tradition we have here at the *Chicago Transit Authority*. How come you're not wearing gloves?"

Anticipating the green light by a few seconds, the driver swung the steering wheel, and pulled away from the curb and into traffic. The revving engine in the rear of the vehicle sounded oddly disembodied from the bus itself. I made my way to a seat, grabbing the seat backs for balance in the swaying vehicle. About halfway back, I spied a familiar face.

"Hey, Toni!" I greeted my former girlfriend, and took the seat beside her. "I see they'll let just about anybody with forty-five cents on these buses nowadays."

"Are you still bitter about me taking up with that photographer fellow?"

"Well, yeah. I thought we had something between us."

"You mean like ten thousand miles?"

"You could have waited. What did that guy have that I didn't?"

"What can I say? He had a bigger camera, a Polaroid Model 3000 *Big Swinger*, to be exact. Not like that little *Kodak Instamatic* of yours."

"We *are* talking about *cameras* here aren't we?"

"Of course . . . metaphorically speaking."

I slumped in my seat, dejected.

"But, Bruce. You never wrote! Not even to tell me you enjoyed my pictures. What did you expect? Maybe if you wrote once in a while, things would be different. Was that too much to ask? How much effort does it take to write a letter?"

"I'm sorry. You're right. I should have written . . . and I did enjoy the photos. Thanks."

"Where are you headed?"

"I'm going to purchase a car."

"How nice. You're going to need a car, now that you're back. My cousin just bought a new car . . . a *Firebird Trans Am.*"

"I'm leaning towards *Ford* product. As you know, my dad works for the company."

"Just starting out, as you are, it should be affordable."

"I never heard of a *Ford Ibble.* Are you sure you don't mean a *Torino*?"

"No. I mean something that you can manage financially, and for sure, don't get talked into purchasing one of those extended warranties, now. My uncle is a car salesman, and he tells me that he feels almost like a bandit every time he sells one of those policies."

"Didn't I meet him at one of your family functions? His nickname is *Jessie James*, isn't it?"

"That's him. He's my mother's brother. My father likes to say that he holds folks up with a ballpoint pen. This is my stop up ahead. It was nice seeing you again, Bruce. I'm glad you made it home alive and in one piece. I really am. See you around."

She kissed my cheek and left me with a sleeping, snoring drunk, a woman gripping a wheeled wire cart, apparently containing all of her worldly possessions, and a young mother with the ugliest baby I'd ever seen, amongst my fellow passengers.

The bus worked its way leisurely south down Cicero Avenue, picking up and discharging passengers as it progressed. A trio of gang-bangers boarded the bus at 73rd Street, robbed a businessman at gunpoint, and took a lady's purse, before getting off at the Saint Laurence/Queen of Peace High School bus stop. They didn't appear to be students however . . . dropouts I inferred. One of them was silent, but the two who *did* speak used very poor grammar. The quiet one took an elderly nun courteously by the arm, and assisted her off the bus, which I thought to be antithetic, until he knocked her to the ground and kicked her brutally in the side.

"Take this, you fucking penguin." (thud) "And this, Sister Mary Vicious." (thud) "And this, you sadistic old hag." (thud)

"Aren't you going to help?" the young mother asked me.

"No. Those three guys seem to have everything well under control," I replied.

Having attended parochial school myself, and as a regular victim of nuns' physical and psychological abuse, I understood the assailant's thrashing of the wicked sister perfectly. Besides, beating up a nun was probably a sin that I'd be obligated to confess, be repentant for, have to do a penance, and be absolved of. It seemed like a lot of trouble for the small amount of satisfaction it would afford. After a few more blocks, I spied the blue oval sign of the *Ford* dealership ahead. I tugged the overhead cord signaling the driver that this was my stop coming up.

The bus pulled off, leaving me standing on the curb, choking on a cloud of diesel exhaust, in the shadow of a forty-foot tall, inflated gorilla that was kept erect with the aid of a large fan. Tethered to a guardrail, this big ape swayed in the chilly breeze, leering at me lecherously. I have to say, even though it was just a silly prop, it made me feel extremely uncomfortable. I considered going over to the Chevy dealer across the way, and buying a Camaro, but in the end, walked towards the showroom, a multitude of rainbow-colored plastic pennants snapping in the wind over my head. My family had always driven *Fords*, and it would be tantamount to renouncing my Catholic faith, and becoming a Jehovah's Witness, if I were to purchase a *General Motors* product.

"What's with the inflated balloon outside?" I asked a salesman, who was leaning on the hood of a bright gold metallic, *Torino GT*. "Does it imply that you have inflated prices or something?"

"No! Just the opposite. He's there to convey that we have monster deals."

"But he's not a monster. He's a gorilla. Wouldn't that be more likely to convey the impression that you *monkey* around?"

"Little kids love that big ape."

"How many little kids shop for cars?"

"Look. It's there to attract attention to our dealership. It was the owner's idea, not mine. It was also his ludicrous idea to appear in his own television commercials. Is there something I can help you with?"

"There is. I'd like a four-speed, *Boss 429 Mustang* in Grabber Orange, please."

"Okay. Let's see. I'll just pull one out of my ass."

I gave him a perturbed look.

"Look buddy, that's strictly a special order car you're talking about. We don't stock them. Nobody does. It will take six to eight weeks to build one for you."

"I really wanted to drive out of here today with a new car. The thought of going home on the bus is really disagreeable to me. Did you know I witnessed an armed robbery on the way here?"

"No. How terrible. You should report it to the police so that they can add it to their database. If the statistics show an abnormal rise in crime in a certain area, they will often consider beefing up their patrols, as a counter-measure."

"They also beat the snot out of a nun."

"*That* I would have like to have seen. She probably had it coming. Now, about that car. How about if I were able to get you into a new *Mustang Mach I* today? I've got six of those in inventory. Or how about a late model guaranteed used *Mustang*? That could save you a little money."

"What kind of guarantee are you talking here?"

"Like I said, it's guaranteed to be used."

"Do any of those new ones come equipped with the *351 Cleveland* engine and a *Holley* four-barrel?"

"Absolutely! And you'll love the way she snarls when the secondaries kick in."

"Do you have one with a four-speed manual?"

"Two. One in Dark Metallic Ivy Green, and one painted Wimbledon White."

"Let's see the green one."

"I'm Joe Delong, by the way," he said, extending his right hand.

When I dismissed shaking it, he reached into his shirt pocket, and produced a business card that seemed to confirm that, indeed, he *was* Joe Delong.

"Let's look at the vehicle and then see if we could put a deal together today."

The car he showed me was parked back in the service bay. He pushed open a door that displayed a sign warning, *Employees only. Insurance regulations prohibit customers beyond this point.* I was overwhelmed by a wave of paranoia. Everyone started looking like undercover insurance investigators to me. We were greeted by the staccato of pneumatic wrenches. They had the same tempo and meter as an M-16 on full auto. It brought back sickening memories. A sense of acute anxiety now welled up inside of me. I felt like I wanted to bolt for an exit but there was a suspicious person, smoking a cigarette, and appearing to guard the door. Also, I was pretty sure I saw him speaking into the cuff of his shirt sleeve.

"Here she is," Joe walked me to the car.

It had a mean and sexy stance with its "shaker" hood scoop, rear deck spoiler, dual accent paint stripes, and styled steel wheels. The window sticker also informed me that it was equipped with quick ratio steering, extra cooling package, heavy-duty battery, front disc brakes, and traction lock differential.

"I like it."

"Of course you do. Did you want to take it for a test ride?"

The air guns continued their insufferable chatter. The guy by the door crushed out his cigarette.

"No," I answered nervously. "I'll buy it. Let's just get the hell out of here."

At his desk (which was no bigger than a little kiddy's desk) Joe produced a form that he needed to fill out . . . "just to get a little information." Forty-five minutes later, after giving him more personal data than the FBI would require for a top security clearance, he spun the paper around and showed me where I was to sign.

"What's this?" I inquired.

"Oh, it's just to show the boss that you're serious so that he can give you his best price. You want our best price, don't you?"

"Oh, yes," I replied, and signed the paper.

After all, I wanted to get the best deal possible. I was also eager to be out of there and get some food in me. Having not eaten breakfast, my stomach was growling audibly. I probably would have bought a *Ford Maverick Grabber*, if that's all they had in stock, just to drive out of there and have something to eat.

"Congratulations," Joe said, successfully shaking my hand this time. "I'll have them bring the vehicle over to the wash stand. It'll be cleaned up and ready for you by the time you finish with the finance manager."

Grabbing the paper, I had just signed, but had yet to read, he led me to an office occupied by a large bald man in a wrinkled white dress shirt, with a big smile on his face.

"Wayne, this is Mr. Johnson. Mr. Johnson, this is Wayne, our finance manager."

I sat down in the chair indicated. It was very low. I felt like I was sitting in a hole. Leaning forward, my chin barely extended above the top of Wayne's desk.

"Well now, did you want to finance this vehicle today?" Wayne asked, looking down his nose at me.

"Yes, please."

"Good, good. Now, who's your employer?"

"I don't actually have a job right now."

"You don't have a job?"

"No. I just got out of the Army *yesterday*."

"Vietnam?"

"Yes."

"Well, you're going to *get* a job then, right?"

"No. Actually, I was going to use the GI Bill and go to school."

"Hmm. This could be a problem."

"I have a Silver Star, if that makes any difference."

"A Silver Star! You bet it does, young man. The owner of this dealership is a World War II vet. He was one of the first to land on Omaha Beach. I will lose my job if you don't drive out of here in a new car today."

After running a credit check on me, (which suggested I didn't exist) Wayne fed some forms into a special machine that mechanically filled in all of the blanks.

"We're just going to finance this car in-house, since you really don't have any credit history," he explained. "We can do that because you're a good-looking white guy who lives in a sanctioned zip code."

When the machine had finished its intended task, Wayne lined up the papers in front of me on the desk, side by side. He pointed several times, saying, "Sign here, and here, and here."

As an astute consumer, I insisted that he explain the papers to me.

"This is a standard hold-harmless agreement whereby you absolve our dealership of all liability, and this is a simple waiver of your rights as a consumer under Illinois law, and this paper here says that you decline any and all rebates, cash-back offers, or promotional monies, and assign them to the dealer."

"Why would I want to do that?" I asked.

"So that we can give you the best price of course," he answered. "Now that will be $4,451.16, that you'll be financing, at eight and one half percent interest."

"That sounds like a lot of money."

"That's *out the door,* Mr. Johnson," Wayne assured me. "Title, tax, doc fee, dealer preparation costs, appraisal charges, credit check, gasoline surcharge, quick delivery premium, handling charge, advertising fee . . . everything's included!"

"It still seems like a lot of money," I insisted.

"Not when you consider that it also includes the *Ford Protect* five-year extended warranty."

CHAPTER FIFTEEN

Scouting Colleges

Miss Wilson, the admissions counselor at *Chester A. Arthur College*, explained to me that the school was named after the 21st President of the United States.

"Is that so?" I pretended to be interested. This was my third, and last, college visit.

"We currently have a number of students who are attending *Arthur College* on the G.I. Bill. We want to assure you that not only do we welcome Vietnam Veterans on our campus, but that we also offer no-cost counseling to them with our staff psychologist. As a matter of fact, it's mandatory."

"Mandatory counseling. What's that all about?"

"It's in case of your having a, well, you know . . ."

"No, I don't know. In case of my having what?"

"Like flashbacks or something. Now, if you will just fill out both sides of this questionnaire on your life's experiences, we will be able to possibly apply them to . . ."

"I think I'm having one," I interrupted.

"I beg your pardon, but you think you're having what?"

"A flashback. I think I'm having a flashback."

Apparently unnerved by my remark, and my most menacing madman's mien, Miss Wilson picked up the phone in a panic, asked the switchboard for security, and without taking her eyes off me, returned the phone to its cradle so slowly and gently that you'd think it was rigged to some sort of hair-triggered explosive device. I reciprocated her stare lasciviously, without speaking a word. Within minutes, a pair of panting campus patrol police were in the room, guns drawn.

"Sir! What are your intensions?" one of the officers demanded.

"Oh. I'm okay now."

"Sir. Are you holding Miss Wilson hostage, or is she free to leave the room?"

"I'm very sorry, gentlemen, for the misunderstanding. You see, I thought I was having a flashback, but then I burped, and it turned out to be nothing more than the gyros sandwich I ate for lunch."

"Gyros, you say. You didn't, by chance, eat at the *Pylos Restaurant* over on Titman Street, did you?"

"Yes! As a matter of fact, I did . . . although I'm more of a leg man, myself."

"That's *so* odd! I had a parallel experience eating there once."

"Really?"

"Yeah. Only instead of a flashback, I thought that I was having a painful outbreak of genital herpes."

"That sounds terrible!"

"Yeah. As it turned out, however, the waiter had dropped some flaming saganaki in my lap."

"Bummer. I hope you took that into consideration when you calculated the tip."

"Oh, believe me. I did."

"Tell me. Is that a *Smith and Wesson Model 66*, thirty-eight special you're packing, by chance?"

"Actually, it's a .357 Magnum, *Model 67*. They look quite alike."

"Do you mind?"

"I'm sorry, but it would be against campus police policy to hand over my weapon to a suspected hostage-taker. I think you can understand."

"Sure, but *you* need to understand that I'm recently, and honorably, discharged from the military . . . 173rd Airborne. I've been fully qualified for everything from a *Model 1911* to a fifty caliber M-60."

"I'm still reluctant."

"I have a Silver Star."

He handed me the gun.

"Why didn't you say so, buddy?"

"Nice balance. Good feel. How much recoil are we talking about here?"

"Some, but not as bad as you'd expect. I've gotten some pretty accurate follow-up shots at the range. It's all a matter of proper grip and stance."

I squinted, looking down the gun's sights, aiming the pistol at the portrait of Chester A. Arthur himself, hanging prominently on the wall over Miss Wilson's head. He was a dignified gentleman sporting long hair, and a full mustache that merged with his "pork chop" sideburns. Evidently, the 21st President of the United States was a hippy! Miss Wilson dropped to the floor and exited the room on her hands and knees.

"She's got a nice ass," the officer observed.

"As I told you earlier, I'm a leg man."

"Well, she has nice legs, too. I think you better give me the gun back, however. We don't want to go around scaring the secretarial staff silly."

"Oh. I'm so sorry. Here you go."

Too shaken to carry on with the interview, the traumatized Miss Wilson refused to reenter the office, so her supervisor, the Dean of Admissions, provided me the life experiences questionnaire. He explained how it would be used to potentially give me college credit. I filled out the form meticulously, including the section on military experience. After completing the survey, I affixed my signature, asserting that my statements were true and accurate, under penalty of law.

"I see here that you were in an airmobile unit," the dean remarked as he perused my responses. "Can you fly a helicopter?"

"I don't know. I never tried."

"You also indicate that you're a Silver Star recipient. That, along with your impressive test score results, will just about take care of your entire freshman year academic requirements. Come to think of it, we currently have an opening for a paid position as an advisor to our R.O.T.C. program. You may be just the person we've been searching for, having been awarded a medal for valor and all. Would you be interested in something like that?"

"I don't know. What would the job entail, exactly?"

"Marching, for one thing. You could teach our cadets to march."

"We actually didn't do a lot of marching in Vietnam. There wasn't much call for it."

"Well, let me think then . . ."

"How about cowering? I have plenty of experience along those lines, while under rocket or mortar attack . . . and trembling. I'm not proud of it, but I did a lot of cowering and trembling back then."

"No. No. We really want to downplay the combat aspect of the military and accentuate the ceremonial. I'm afraid it would hurt our recruitment program if the R.O.T.C. candidates thought that one of the consequences of joining up would be getting shot at. They very much prefer parades and the like. Parades with marching bands especially, and baton twirlers in skimpy outfits with little white boots. Are you sure about that marching thing? Our R.O.T.C. leaders are quite keen on marching, after all."

"So, let me ask you. It's just like walking, except with a regular measured tread?"

"Exactly!"

"And the baton twirlers?"

"We recruit the best in the land."

"I suppose I could do that."

"Great. Between your payments from the G.I. Bill, and the advisor position's remuneration, which includes housing and free tuition, you might just be able to graduate in three years' time, and with a nice little nest egg to boot. That's better than thousands of dollars in student loans, don't you think? I can present your life's experience recommendations to the various department heads and have the human resources people draw up an employment offer for the advisor's position this very afternoon. Now, do you have any questions that I may answer for you about *Arthur College* before we process your paperwork?"

"Yes. As a matter of fact, there is *one.*"

"Yes?"

"This isn't a Christian college, is it? I mean you don't teach creationism or have mandatory morning chapel, do you?"

"Absolutely not! At *Chester A. Arthur College*, you will receive a quality secular education unencumbered by the influences, prejudices or practices of any religious persuasion. Why do you ask? Do you have issues with Jesus?"

"No. Not at all. I'm fine with Jesus. It's his followers, for the most part, whom I find altogether intolerable."

"I understand perfectly. They tend, on average, to be an obnoxiously self-righteous, mean-spirited, and sanctimonious bunch. In the spirit of full disclosure, however, there is *one* disadvantage a secular school, such as ours, has over your faith-based institutions."

"Oh? What could that be?"

"Well, when you die, you'll go straight to Hell, of course."

"But I'm a Catholic."

"Oh. In that case, you'll need to serve your obligatory stint in purgatory first, and *then* you'll go to Hell."

"With all due respect, I just spent the last thirteen months in Hell, and found it to be, altogether, disagreeable."

I rolled up my sleeve and showed him my tattoo:
If I had a house in Hell
And farm in Vietnam
I'd sell the farm and go home

"Perhaps your tour in Vietnam will count as 'time served.' I can't say. It's really not my area of expertise. If this sort of thing is important to you, you might want to research *Oral Roberts University*, but then, as a pre-med student, they may not be exactly right for you either."

"How's that?"

"I'm not positive, but I'm pretty sure they believe in 'faith healing' over there in that part of Oklahoma.

"Faith healing. What's that?"

"Like when someone has a burst appendix or something, they form a circle around the patient, hold hands, and pray."

"Really?"

"I'm fairly certain that's how they do it."

"Praying, you say? I tried praying for my buddy Bill Hastings, when he was shot in the gut while on a long range patrol one time."

"How did *that* work out for you?"

"Not well . . . and even worse for him. He suffered an agonizingly painful and protracted death."

"No. I'm afraid that Oral Roberts wouldn't be the school for you, although, some people do claim to have witnessed miracles in answer to such appeals."

"And some people profess to having been abducted by aliens, too. Frankly, I've become quite disillusioned with prayer."

"I empathize with you. I myself was an infantryman in the big war, and once you've looked into the blank, glassy eyes of a soldier dying on the field of battle, you gain an entirely different perspective on these matters. I can't imagine what those imbeciles in Washington D.C. were thinking when they got us entangled in Vietnam."

He stood to shake my hand.

"Will we be seeing you in the fall, then?"

"Will I still be required to participate in psychotherapeutic counseling?"

"I'm afraid so. But, it's more along the line of group therapy. You'll be meeting with other war veterans in a relaxed and supportive environment that will serve to remove your sense of isolation. It will be the group leader's aim to validate your wartime experiences and raise your self-esteem."

"How very thoughtful. My self-esteem, you say?"

"Yes. In the realm of contemporary psychology, self-esteem seems to command a disproportionate emphasis, when compared to those

qualities that, common sense will tell you, *really* count, such as character and integrity."

"I don't know about this."

"Just go along with the scheme. Our board of regents put a lot of
energy into their veterans initiative. Humor them."

CHAPTER SIXTEEN

The Watering Hole

Logging 11 miles to the gallon of 102 octane gasoline, I piloted my spanking new *Mustang Mach I* on a magical mystery tour/road trip down Illinois Route One, and on to New Orleans, where I hooked up with my old Army buddy, Ken Quidero. He had received his discharge papers not long after Loren and me. As the company clerk, he simply typed them up himself, and put them in a pile of documents for Captain Riley to sign.

"I don't know why I didn't think of that sooner," he told me. "I also promoted myself to Staff Sergeant and put in for a Bronze Star . . . just because I could."

Ken lived in the Garden District, above the head shop he co-owned with his partner, Jeremy. He answered the door wearing short shorts and cowboy boots, shirtless, with a double gold chain around his neck, and caressing a furless Sphynx cat. I suggested that he go back in the closet.

"I would," Ken explained, "but my mother would be devastated."

After I obdurately rejected Jeremy's suggestion of a threesome, Ken was hospitable to show me around his hometown, then took me fishing down by Port Barre in Saint Landry Parish where we dressed in style, went hog wild, and ate some of that jambalaya, crawfish pie, and fillet gumbo. After we caught all the fish in the bayou, Ken then joined me on the next leg of my impromptu peregrination, with a spontaneous visit to Key West, Florida, where we drank margaritas until they asked us to leave the island. I dropped Ken off at his sister's place in Boca Raton, and then deadheaded back to Chicago playing Rod Stewart on the cassette player until the tape broke and splayed out on the floor of my *Mustang* like spaghetti. I arrived back in *Chitown* with a quarter tank of gas and six dollars in my pocket.

"I'm concerned about you, Son," my father remarked as we sat in the living room, in front of the television, as a family, eating our *Swanson* dinners from atop TV trays, while watching The Flip Wilson Show on Dad's new Zenith *Chromacolor* set with *Space Command* remote. "You don't seem to have any direction or motivation since you got back from the war. Look! Look! Flip Wilson is doing that Geraldine Jones character again. That Geraldine absolutely cracks me up. How about you? Don't you just love her?"

"Not really," I answered frankly.

I never could grasp the entertainment value of a man dressing up as a woman. It always makes me feel awkwardly uncomfortable.

"I'm going down to the Park District tomorrow to see if I can get my old summer job back as a lifeguard at the 63rd Street Beach," I replied.

"And until then?"

"I think they'll let me paint, do maintenance on the boats, and organize the lifesaving equipment until the beaches open."

"Well, Son," my mother interjected, "Your father and I are just concerned that you don't seem to have a realistic plan for the future. We're just not sure about this rash idea you have of going to college. It seems like such a scatterbrained notion to us, that's all."

"Mom, lots of people go to college. Most of my friends from high school are already in their second year."

"And if most of your friends jumped in the Chicago River, would you jump in the river, too?"

"Your mother's right, Son. That river is full of sewage and, God only knows, what other industrial pollutants may be in there. The company I work for indiscriminately dumps toxic paint sludge containing lead and arsenic. You shouldn't be jumping in the river, Boy"

"Dad. I wasn't going to jump in the river."

"Well, you should tell your friends from high school not to jump in the river then."

"Which friends from high school?"

"The ones you say are all going to college. That's one thing they don't teach you in school . . . common sense. Do you think Flip Wilson ever went to college? Hell no, and he probably makes more money than the President of the United States. I'm willing to bet Flip Wilson never jumped in the Chicago River when he played The Regal Theater over there in Jew Town. No way! Do you know why? Because he has more presence of mind than that. If you don't believe me, just listen to his monologue sometime. He's a comedic genius! That Negro has more common sense in his big toe than the entire student body over there at the University of Chicago have in all their big toes put together."

A really odd image popped into my head.

"I can't listen to this. I'm going out for a beer."

"You didn't tell me what you think of our new TV."

"It's a fine TV, Dad, and I like how you can change the channels without getting out of your *Barcalounger*."

"Isn't that something? The chassis is handcrafted you know."

"No. I didn't know that."

"And look at that color! Did you ever see a picture so bright, so sharp, and with so much contrast?"

"I can't say that I have."

"It's the standard of excellence in color TV."

"I'm staggered."

"The *Chromacolor* system is so revolutionary, it's patented."

"Wow. Patented, you say. Then it *must* be good."

"Good? The salesman over there at *Polk Brothers* told me it's *totally advanced*."

"I'm happy to hear that, Father. We wouldn't want the word getting out, after all, that you've been watching The Flip Wilson Show on a television that was only partially advanced, now would we? What would the neighbors think?"

"Don't mock your father, Son," my mother piped up.

I took my empty frozen dinner aluminum tray into the kitchen for my mother to wash. She had a stack of them a foot and a half high. In an era before recycling, I had no idea what she was going to do with them, and neither did she.

"During the big war, they would have collected these to melt down and build big *Boeing B-29* bombers," she once informed me. "That's how we civilians were able to do our part to incinerate the citizens of Tokyo and Osaka, and the like."

"Well good for you, Mom. That's something to be proud of. I'm going out for that beer now. Don't wait up for me."

Stepping out the front door, I paused to wait for the sprinkler my father had set out, to clear the front walk. Dad's eight-foot square patch of bent grass lawn was his pride and joy. Every two days he would clip it to a uniform three quarters of an inch with his *Craftsman* push-style reel mower, and catch the clippings in a basket that hung on its chassis. Guarding this oasis of green was a sort of dwarfish ceramic figurine that appeared to be a cross between a gnome and a leprechaun. Now, on my way *to* the bar, it looked more like a gnome, but from experience, I knew that it would, disconcertingly, be a leprechaun when I returned home later in the evening, with a few beers under my belt.

Because every bungalow on the block was basically identical, that gnome/leprechaun hybrid lawn ornament served the very practical purpose of personalizing the property. Pretty much, every neighbor had *something* out front to identify their home, and to discourage others from unintentionally walking into the wrong house. As I strolled down Laramie Avenue, I passed a Virgin Mary, a black jockey holding a lantern, a pink flamingo, a little cupid boy peeing in a fountain, a Buda, and a variety of differently colored glass gazing balls, plus saints Frances, Joseph, Christopher, and one apparently generic saint of unknown genesis.

The bell over the front door jingled as I walked into MacHeath's Shark's Tooth Pub, and was greeted by MacHeath himself, who was tending the bar. His trademark fancy gloves lay on the back bar, next to a sign that read: *Those Drinking To Forget, Please Pay In Advance*, but his jackknife, he kept out of site.

"There's our Silver Star hero," he announced. "What are you drinking tonight, Bruce?"

"Well, I only have six bucks," I replied, placing the cash on the bar.

"You can put that six dollars back in your pocket. Your money is no good in here. Silver Star recipients will always drink for free as long as my name is on the sign out front."

"In that case then, I'll have a bottle of *1787 Chateau Lafite*, please."

"Oh. I'm so sorry," Mac replied sarcastically. "I just poured the last one I had. How about a *Blue Ribbon* instead?"

"Sure . . . as my dad would say, 'I'd rather have a bottle in front of me than a frontal lobotomy' . . . and a bag of helicopter flavored potato chips, please."

"Sorry. All I got are plain."

"Yeah. Give me some of those then."

"You went to school with Jim Ketch, didn't you Bruce?"

I nodded in the affirmative.

"Well, you might be interested to know, he finally proposed to his high school sweetheart in here last night."

"Really? Janette Lane?"

"Yep. It was very romantic. After four Martinis, he got *up* on one knee and asked her to marry him."

"What was her answer?"

"She told him, no . . . that her salary wouldn't support the two of them."

Lighting a cigarette, I glanced around the smoky barroom. It was fairly busy for a Thursday night.

"Hey kid," a fellow collecting drinks for his table addressed me. "Those things will kill you."

"My great-grandfather lived to be ninety-five," I replied in rebuttal.

"And did he smoke?"

"No. He minded his own business."

At a table seated near me were a middle-aged couple, clearly married. The man was facing, and was mesmerized by, the television in the corner. The woman had her back to it. There was no conversation whatsoever between them.

"How about another shot and a beer before it starts, Axel?" Mac asked the man, who nodded affirmatively, accepting the offer.

"Sure. It may be slow poison, but I'm in no hurry."

Mac delivered the drinks to the table, then returned to his place behind the bar.

"She hates the sight of him when he's drunk, and he hates the sight of *her* when he's sober," he confided in me. "Those two have been squabbling for so many years now, it's become a family tradition."

I sipped my *Pabst Blue Ribbon*. The brew conferred a sharp texture and flowing sweetness, evident at the first sip. A slowly increasing hoppiness added to the interplay of ingredients, while the texture smoothed out by mid-bottle. The clear, pale-gold brew was light and fizzy. Medium-bodied, it finished with a dusting of malts and hops.

"Tell me, Mac. I'm planning on entering the premed program over at Arthur College, but my parents think it's a dumb idea. What do you think?"

"Go to school. Get an education. That's what I did. I went to bartending school and have never regretted it. I didn't want to follow in my father's footsteps and crew on a tugboat all my life . . . down by the river, don't-cha know. The man worked like a horse . . . never took a vacation. Not me! I just got back from a week in Las Vegas, as a matter of fact."

"Did you win?"

"Big time!"

"Well Macky, now that you're back in town, flush with cash and spending like a sailor, I was wondering if you will ever give any consideration to expanding that tiny restroom of yours. There's always a line forming over there on the right, just to use the can."

"I've considered it, but I don't want to do anything rash. It's going to start any time now," Mac addressed the man at the table behind me . . . the one sitting with his stoic wife. "Do you want another round before it does?"

Again, Axel accepted.

"But no more for my wife. I can always tell when she's had enough. Her face gets blurred."

Suddenly there was a loud thump as a patron fell off his bar stool. He laid on the floor motionless.

"That's one thing about Kenny," his not so far behind buddy explained to Mac, "he knows when to quit. You can always tell when he's been drinking. He leaves his clothes on the floor . . . with him still in them. When he read about the evils of drinking, he quit reading."

"It's guys like you two that give drinking a bad name," Mac replied.

"Actually I don't care all that much for drinking, but it gives me something to do while I'm getting drunk. I always take life with a grain of salt, plus a slice of lemon, and a shot of tequila."

"I know what you're talking about," a middle-aged woman interjected. "Part of me says that I've had enough to drink tonight, and the other part tells me not to listen to her because she's drunk. A helpful lesson I learned from drinking is that it's best to go Christmas caroling with a group . . . preferably in mid-December."

Having thoroughly enjoyed my first beer, I gestured for another. Just as Mac slid my second round before me, the front door jingled and a fellow walked into the bar with his pet monkey. Immediately, I recognized that I was, doubtless, party to an unfolding and amusing anecdote, and this was the prototypical set-up. I began to chuckle in anticipation, as I pondered the potentialities for the pinnacled punch line. A burley man on the next barstool noticed my titter, glanced first at me, and then caught sight of the gentleman and his pet monkey. He too realized the comic constituent of the circumstance and began laughing aloud. The two of us were having quite a hoot.

A third patron of the bar, whom as chance would have it, happened to be a theoretical physicist from the University of Chicago, took note of the ruckus, and concluded, right off, that he too was the beholder of a droll anecdote. From similar anecdotes, (one of those involving a guy in the movies with a duck in his pants) he quickly deduced the presence of levity in the scenario, but asserted it to be, "too trivial a corollary to be significant, much less funny."

"That's a perfect case for getting a good liberal arts education," MacHeath furthered his argument for me to go to college. "So you can understand more jokes."

"It's just about to start, Mac," the man facing the television announced. "Let me have another shot and a beer. My father once told me that alcohol may not be the answer, but it helps you to forget the question."

His wife suddenly and sharply broke her silence. "So! You're going to get bent again tonight are you? Well that's just great! You'll stagger home, flop down on the couch, and fall asleep while I . . ."

"There, it started," Mac whispered to me as an aside, his cupped hand over his mouth.

The bell on the entrance jingled once again. Next in the door of the bar walked a fellow who clearly had a good head start on his evening's drinking. His coiffure looked like a dead seagull on top his head.

"Never give yourself a haircut after four martinis," he answered the bar patron's curious stares.

Though he was not fully coherent, we were able to decipher that he had been in court that afternoon, over on South California Avenue. His public defender, apparently, proved to be a grand disappointment.

"All lawyers are assholes," he announced as he stumbled up to the bar.

"I take offence at that," a customer at one of the tables protested.

He was dressed in a conservative gray Brooks Brothers suit, custom-made white starched shirt, and power tie.

"Why? Are you a lawyer?" the drunk asked with belligerence.

"No, I'm an asshole."

"Is that so? Well what do you know? I *thought* you looked like an asshole the second I walked in the door, but I didn't say anything because I thought you might be sensitive about it. What are you drinking there pal? Let me buy you a another."

"*Schweppes Bitter Lime.*"

"Just plain old *Schweppes*? This is a tavern my friend. You know . . . a gin mill."

"I don't drink hard stuff. *Schweppes* suites me just fine, thanks."

"Well personally, I don't drink anything stronger than pop, and my pop drinks 114 proof *Plymouth Navy-Strength* gin. You don't by chance happen to be associated with that *Alcoholics Anonymous* group do ya?"

"No. Why? Are you looking to join?"

"No. I'm looking to resign."

"Alcohol isn't going to solve your problems, pal. In fact, it is likely *responsible* for your problems."

"Tell that to the fuckin' judge," the drunk rejoined belligerently. "He asserts that I'm responsible for my own problems. What a crock that is. You know, it isn't easy being the town drunk in a town as big as Chicago."

A young man wearing a number 14 Ernie Banks *Chicago Cubs* jersey, and sitting nearby, attempted to calm the inebriate down. His effort was greeted with hostility.

"You know, I did your mother last night," the trouble-maker loudly sassed, "and you know what? She was a real screamer!"

The Cubs fan just shook his head in abhorrent frustration.

"And besides that, afterwards, your mom told me that I was the best lover she ever had."

"Look, why don't you just get your coat and I'll take you home, Dad," the Cubs fan pleaded. "You're making a complete fool of yourself."

Officer Halvorson, of the Chicago Police "Farce," was the next person in the door. (At this point, I was half expecting a Catholic priest, a rabbi, and a Presbyterian minister.) He looked very dapper in his dress blues and *Corfam* shoes.

"Chicago's finest!" MacHeath called to the copper. "What brings you in here . . . as if I didn't already know."

With his left and right index fingers, Mac pushed down simultaneously on two keys of the cash register, causing the money drawer to pop open with a ding.

"I'm here to shake you down," Halvorson responded. "Who's the guy with the ugly baby?"

"It's a monkey."

"I was going to say. By the way. Did you hear about Louie Miller? He disappeared last night after drawin' out all his hard-earned cash."

"No, I didn't hear that. By the way, that reminds me, Jenny Diver was in here yesterday, and she was asking about you."

"Oh, really. How is the old gal? She still hanging out with that little blue-eyed blonde? What's her name?"

"Sukey Tawdry."

"Yeah. That's the one. Now there's a woman who knows where her husband is every night . . . unlike the spouses of the better part of your upstanding clientele here, Macky."

"Oh. One of those hey?"

"Yeah. She's a widow."

MacHeath removed a twenty-dollar bill from the machine and held it out to the officer.

"Sure. Jenny, Sukey, and Lucy Brown come in here after work a couple nights a week. They're all hairdressers over at Miss Lotte Lenya's place, *Scarlett Billows.*"

"Well, say hi to the girls when you see them next. I'll have to stop by their place of business sometime to see if they want to procure any police protection. By the way, it's going to be an extra five bucks for you tonight, on account of you've got an underage drinker at your bar," Halvorson insisted, nodding towards me.

I kept a straight face and muttered, "Huh?"

"But he's a Silver Star recipient," Mac argued while he removed a five-spot from the drawer.

Halvorson waved the five dollars off. "Buy the kid a couple rounds of a nice import with that."

"You look fatigued tonight," Mac observed, "but I suppose it's pretty hard work extorting folks."

"Don't even joke like that. It's not funny . . . unless of course you're talking about shaking down the clown school over on Halstead Street. Then it can be downright hilarious, but generally it's a tough job. I just came from the *Knights of Columbus* club before here."

"Are you a member?" I asked. "My dad's a knight."

"No. I'm just the one who collects the bribe money for the police to look the other way on that gambling operation they've got set up there. It would be *unethical* for me to be a member. Conflict of interest, you see. I'm sure you can understand."

"I do."

"So, what other illegal activity you got going on here, MacHeath? Any drug dealing going on in that backroom of yours? Or what about prostitution? There any hookers in your place tonight?"

"I'm a hooker," a young woman at the bar spoke up. "What are you looking for?"

"I don't really want to discuss this here, in front of all of these nice people. It wouldn't be professional. Perhaps we could go out to my squad car, where we'll have more privacy, so I can, uh, arrest and handcuff you."

"What would your wife have to say about this?" Mac asked. "Or is she still not speaking to you from that last time you patted down a hooker?"

"She hasn't uttered a word to me for over a week now . . . and I'm not about to interrupt her."

Halvorson and the harlot left by way of the front door. The bell jingled again.

"Teacher says, *every time a bell rings an angel gets his wings,*" uttered a drunk at the end of the bar.

"Good. I'm glad he's gone," Mac commented. "At least now we don't have to listen to him go on insufferably about his hemorrhoids as usual. Hey! You! I thought I told you that there's no soliciting allowed in here."

He was addressing a middle-aged woman who was peddling counterfeit *eau de cologne* to the patrons.

"How about a little something for your wife for Mother's Day," she suggested as she spritzed the fellow in the power tie and Brooks Brothers Suit with her pungent fragrance.

"Get away from me with that crap," he protested. "My wife will think I smell like I've been inside a whorehouse."

The woman looked aghast.

"You can squirt some of that stuff on me," the theoretical physicist announced. "My wife has no idea what the inside of a whorehouse smells like."

"Hey Mac!" an obviously long-time customer greeted MacHeath as he bellied up to the bar.

"Good afternoon, Mr. Dollinger. Come for some of your special reserve *Don Felipe*?"

Mac kept the customer's personal bottle of tequila in a special locked cabinet, along with some expensive brandies for some other valued habitués.

"You read my mind."

After receiving his drink, Mr. Dollinger spied the fellow with the pet monkey and approached him.

"Hey, guy! We don't get many organ grinders in here these days."

"At these prices, I'm not surprised."

"I'll tell you what. Mac keeps some private reserve tequila behind the bar for me. May I offer you a taste?"

"Oh, I'm sorry. I can't drink tequila. It doesn't agree with me."

"This is *Don Felipe*, pal. It's incredibly smooth. I think you'll like it."

"No, no. The last time I drank tequila, I ended up doing the old *psychedelic yawn*, if you get my drift."

"They don't charge a small fortune for this stuff for nothing. It drinks like a fine cognac . . . with a nice numbing sensation of the alcohol at the finish. You really *must* try it. It's not like those other tequilas Mac pours."

"No, I was in Mexico once, and I had some of what, the bartender told me, was *his* best. It even had a worm in it. I spent the rest of the evening on my knees in a disgusting toilet stall praying to the proverbial porcelain god."

"I'm telling you, this won't do that. It has the depth of a fine brandy or a barrel-aged whiskey. It goes down like silk."

"And I'm telling *you*. I appreciate the gesture but I'm taking a pass on this one. The last time I drank tequila I ended up *blowing chunks*."

"But this is Don Felipe, my friend. It's perfectly smooth from start to finish. If anything, it will just give you a nice glow."

"Look. I don't think you understand what I'm saying here. *Chunks* is my monkey."

At about 2 a.m., I switched from beer to wine, a *Stags' Leap Cabernet Sauvignon, 1966*. It made me feel very "sophisticated," although I couldn't say it. That didn't stop me from repeatedly trying, however.

"Yes, Bruce," Mac replied condescendingly, "You're very *phosisticated* . . . and also, quite the cosmopolite."

I wasn't sure if that was a good thing, or a bad thing, or even if there was such a thing. I requested another pour of the wine I was drinking and contemplated. Now, there's something about the consumption of alcohol that makes *some* people think that their former girlfriend is sentimentally nostalgic to hear their voice at two o'clock in the morning. I climbed down from my bar stool, feeling around with my right foot for the floor, wobbled across the room, put a dime in the pay-phone next to the men's room, and maladroitly dialed Toni's number. It was difficult reading the numbers on the phone's dial. I had, earlier that evening, walked into Mac's place optimistically, but now I was misty optically. After about 15 to 20 rings, Toni's mother groggily answered the phone in a husky voice.

"Hello! Is Toni home?" I loudly, nearly yelling, spoke into the mouthpiece. There is also something about the consumption of alcohol that causes some people to mistakenly think they are using their "inside voice," when indeed, they are in "cheering for the Bears against the Packers" amplitude.

"She's out on a date," I was informed.

Disheartened, I apologized, hung up, and decided to head home. After all, for the last hour or so, I had been just sitting at the bar with a silly smile on my face because I had no idea what was going on. I bid everyone a cordial goodbye, left by way of the front door, and walked unsteadily to the bus stop at the corner. I was lucky to catch the last N4 Cottage Grove "Night Owl" service of the evening. Staggering down the bus's aisle, I took a seat next to an elderly lady who was earnestly reading her *King James* bible. I could have sat anywhere. She was the only other person on the bus, but I was looking for a little light conversation on the ride home. One last thing about the consumption of alcohol, then I promise, that's it: *A sober man's thoughts are a drunk man's words.*

"I've got news for you, young man," the bible reader scathingly responded after listening to me crack priest/altar boy jokes for about five minutes. "God is watching!"

"Then the least we can do is be entertaining."

"I don't know if you realize it, but you're going straight to hell mister. Do you know that?"

I jumped out of my seat.

"Jesus Christ! I'm on the wrong bus!"

CHAPTER SEVENTEEN

63rd Street Beach

The forecast called for temperatures to be in the mid-nineties, under a cloudless sky. I was expecting an enormous crowd at the 63rd Street Beach, much as we had experienced the previous two similar days. Gathering my gear in the lifeguards' station, located in the elegant Classical Revival style beach house, I completed my morning paperwork.

"Good morning, Bruce," I was greeted by Nell Bruck, one of my deeply tanned, hard-bodied, fellow guards. "Are you ready for another day of unmitigated chaos?"

"As ready as I'll ever be. Yesterday I initiated two rescues, responded to four medical emergencies, and had to break up a couple trying to copulate in the water."

"Isn't that something? I don't know how many times I've had to tell people, 'I don't swim in your bedroom, so don't have sex on my beach,' but for some reason, it still seems to be one of the more popular lakefront activities."

"Didn't you and I have sex on the beach one time?" I offered.

"Well, yeah, but that was different. First of all, it was after hours, and secondly, we're professionals, duly certified by the *American Red Cross*."

"As I recall, that was some of the best CPR I ever received."

"Really? Well, thank you. Since then, you might be interested to know, I've been certified as an *Advanced* Open Water Lifeguard."

"You're killing me. Did you see that guy, yesterday, who put a potato inside his trunks trying to attract girls? It was disgusting! I had to tell him, 'Dude, the potato goes in the front!' And, if I *never* see another middle-aged man in a *Speedo*, it will be fine with me. Sometimes I have nightmares about some of the beach attire I witness here."

"I see you're in the boat this rotation," Nell read from a mimeographed page, clip- boarded and hanging from a nail in the wall. "I'll be in the south chair."

"See you later, then. You know, I was just thinking. This evening, after the beach closes, you wouldn't by chance want to. . ."

"I'm engaged to be married now. But thanks for asking."

"Just a thought."

We went our separate ways. I walked over to, and unlocked the steel cable from my guard boat, and pushed it into the lake. When I was in deep enough water to accommodate the draft of the craft, I jumped in, seized the oars, and rowed into position, just beyond the beach's outer marker buoys. Setting the oars, I drifted, gently rising and sinking on the passing two-foot waves. Sailboats blossomed on the horizon, but my attention was focused in the opposite direction. My whistle shrieked as I blew hard into the mouthpiece. A kid, floating on an inflated truck inner tube, was drifting too far from the shore.

"Stay inside the buoys," I yelled.

I blew my whistle again to gain the attention of a fellow munching a Chicago-style hotdog with sport peppers and fries.

"No eating in the water."

When a speedboat, carrying four well-tanned "pretty boys," and christened the *Wet Dream*, ventured too close to my swimmers, I grabbed my bullhorn and warned them away. They responded with catcalls and mocking gestures as the craft's engine throttled up and they sped off. It was my secret wish that they would run out of gas, drift onto, and break up on the rocks over by *McCormick Place*. Contrary to my lifeguard ethos, it was also my desire that they would all drown.

About halfway through my rotation in the lifeguard boat, my attention was drawn to an unnatural engine sound of an aircraft taking off to the south from *Meigs Field*. Looking towards the source, I spied a twin engine *Cessna 310*, obviously in distress. The pilot was fighting a losing battle to gain some altitude. The aircraft sank lower and lower, its wings tipping side to side. Then, not more than 50 yards from my location, a wingtip contacted the water, spinning the plane one hundred eighty degrees as it splashed into the lake. I broadcast a succinct distress call on my waterproof VHF radio, then grabbed the oars and began to row frantically to the slowly sinking aircraft.

As I approached, I could see the pilot (the sole occupant of the plane) to be hunched over, apparently unconscious. I stepped out, onto the port wing, and struggled with the buckled door. It wouldn't budge. I grabbed the mooring rope of my boat and pulled the drifting craft closer, hooking a loose loop over one of the plane's prop blades. Then, removing an oar from the boat, I used the unwieldy tool to pry open the aircraft door. By this time the *Victor L. Schlaeger*, a Chicago Fire Department boat, was approaching from the south at full steam. When within 50 feet or so, the boat's captain cut power and came hard to port. Two rescue divers entered the water, swam to the plane, and instructed me to get back in my boat and return to lifeguard duties, helping to evacuate all swimmers from the water, while they completed the rescue. I happily complied.

The beach was closed for the balance of the day due to aviation fuel in the water. Nell and I teamed up to patrol the shoreline, blowing our whistles and warning people not to venture into the lake. Television news crews from WGN, WBBM, WLS, and WMAQ aimed cameras at Nell and me as we talked.

"So, whom are you engaged to?" I asked Nell.

"Nobody you know. Just someone I met at school."

"I'm starting school in the fall, myself."

"Oh, yeah. Where are you going?"

"Arthur College, in Michigan."

"I'm happy for you."

"Yeah. My parents want me to get a job at the *Ford* plant where my dad works. They can't understand my wanting to go to school."

A reporter from the *Chicago Tribune* interrupted our conversation.

"Sir! You were the first on the scene when the aircraft went down into the water. Can you describe for our readers what you found?"

"I'm sorry, but I'm on duty now. I can't speak with you."

"He's a Silver Star recipient," Nell spoke up. "Just got back from Vietnam in March."

"Why'd you tell him that? It has nothing to do with what happened here today."

"Well, you know how you veterans are always getting a bad rap in the press. Like 'Vietnam vet snaps, and drives his car into a crowd of Christmas shoppers,' or something like that."

"You know. It's interesting that you used that particular example. I get the urge to do that kind of thing every time I'm behind the wheel, and for some enigmatic reason, I especially have an almost ungovernable impulse to kill Christmas shoppers."

"Really?"

"No. I'm just kidding."

"So then, you don't have any psychological issues from the war?"

"No. Other than my misanthropy . . . and the night sweats, I'm fine. I really am, and the panic attacks, of course. But, except for the flashbacks, melancholy, and occasional fits of rage, I'm doing pretty well in that department. Thank you for asking."

"Good. Good. I was a little concerned."

"And the persistent, incessant, anxiety."

"You're sure you're alright?"

"No. No, I'm fine. I just don't take rejection very well, that's all. Other than that, I'm good."

"Look. I told you I was engaged. If I weren't, I'd be more than pleased to have sex with you after the beach closes."

"I understand perfectly. Just keep in mind, that if you intend to be a true and faithful wife to this fellow . . ."

"Darrel."

"Darrel?"

"That's his name. Darrel."

"Sure. Now as I was saying, if you're truly intending to be faithful in your upcoming marriage to Darrel, you really need to get all of your unchastely urges out of your system now, before you tie the proverbial knot."

"It's terribly thoughtful of you to care so much about the success of my marriage, Bruce, but the answer is still no."

"Well, if you ever change your mind, just let me know."

"I'll do that."

"I saw you on the news!" my mother excitedly announced as I walked in the door. "And, to my surprise, you weren't being ushered into a courtroom shackled and wearing an orange jumpsuit."

"So they got some footage of the aircraft ditching in the lake and my 'heroic' response? That's cool, but remember, in all modesty, I'm a highly inculcated professional lifesaver, so I only reacted as I was trained to behave in a crisis situation."

"No. You appeared to be propositioning some attractive young woman, and I have to say, it looked like she shut you down cold."

"That was on the news?"

"It sure was, and let me tell you, Son. You shouldn't come across as being so desperate. You need to let the woman think it's *her* idea."

"What exactly did they put on the TV?"

"Well, let's just say that they didn't show you on your knees, begging for sex. You can at least be thankful for that."

"Mom! We were just walking and talking, and these news crews wouldn't leave us alone."

"I understand, but from your gestures, facial expressions, and body language, it was pretty obvious what the two of you were talking about."

"I can't believe this."

"Now let me give you some advice, Son. When your father is feeling, how shall we say, a little frisky, what he does is . . ."

"I don't want to hear this!"

"Why? You can learn a lot from your father, you know. He's quite the lover."

"I'm getting some frightening images as it is, Mom. Please! Drop the subject."

Just then, my father walked in the door, and kissed my mother.

"What's for dinner, my little fox?" he asked.

"Pot roast," my mother replied.

"And what's for *dessert*?"

He put his hand on her behind, and rubbed it in a circular motion.

"Are you eating with us this evening, Son?" my father asked.

"No. I'm feeling a little nauseous tonight."

"Too much sun?"

"Something like that. I think I'll just take a relaxing drive in my *Mustang* and see if I can find a crowd of Christmas shoppers."

"I don't know what you're thinking, Son," my mother responded. "It's July. People don't Christmas shop in July. Bruce was on the news this afternoon," she addressed my father now.

"Really? Did the judge release you on your own recognizance?"

"No. I saved a man's life."

"Well, good. But, isn't that what they pay you to do down there at the *63rd Street Beach?*"

As I closed the screened door behind me, and stepped outside to the porch, I could hear my father ask of my mom, "What's up with him?"

"Oh, I just don't know," my mother replied. "One would think that going to war would have matured him, but I swear, he's more eccentric and idiosyncratic than he was as a teenager."

"As a young Marine," my father explained, "I saw some horrific action in the Battle for Henderson Field on Guadalcanal, and also at Okinawa, in what we called the typhoon of steel. To this day, I can't begin to comprehend the savagery I experienced as a 17 year-old, but I *can* tell you this much, Dorothy: If the gods of war don't take your life . . . they will steal your soul."

This was the first, last, and only time I ever heard my father mention his service in World War II. Years later, two weeks after retiring from the *Ford Motor Company,* a neighbor found him slumped over inside his idling *LTD Crown Victoria,* in his closed garage, asphyxiated. Since he never left a suicide note, my mother went to her grave, unwaveringly believing her husband's death to be an accident. I knew better, however, understood perfectly, and never held his taking his own life against him.

CHAPTER EIGHTEEN

Starting School

"You must be Phil," I introduced myself to my new roommate. "I'm Bruce."

Phil was college-aged with two eyes, and a nose just below in the middle of his face, his mouth just below that. A pair of ears protruded from either side of his head which was capped with hair.

"Good to meet you."

"Pretty nice room."

"The rooms in this section are all reserved for student employees. They're extra spacious and have these modest little dens."

He showed me a sunny eight-foot by eight-foot space with windows on three sides, furnished with a Chippendale writing desk on which a *New American Standard Bible* was lying, open to *Proverbs*.

"Are you a *Christian*?" I asked apprehensively.

"No. I'm not 'afflicted' with any organized religion, but this girl I've been dating is an *Evangelical Methodist*. I've been trying to determine some biblical justification for her to engage in fellatio with me."

"I'm no biblical scholar, but you might try *Geneses 2:24* or *First Corinthians 7:3-4*."

"Thanks!"

"Not that I've ever resorted to any such underhanded deception, or duplicity, mind you."

"Of course not. I'm sure you haven't. But, thanks nonetheless. I appreciate it."

"No problem. Actually, you can use the bible to further just about any point of view you wish to advance."

"Really?"

"Sure. For example, slavery: *Slaves, obey your earthly masters with fear and trembling,* or, *tell slaves to be submissive to their masters and to give satisfaction in every respect.*"

"That's in the bible?"

"You bet it is. So why settle for five minutes of oral sodomy when, with the right bible verses, you can have your own harem of devoted, Evangelical Methodist, bible-based, bondwomen."

"You mean like Charles Manson?"

"Now, I'd have to say that would be taking it to the extreme. Perhaps you could find a happy medium between that and sitting home alone on a Saturday night, tweaking your *Twinkie*. So, what do *you* do here at Arthur College?" I asked.

"As a grad student, I conduct research on the peripheral nervous system. I'm also Executive Director of the *Young Republicans* club here on campus."

"You don't say! Then I bet the U.S. involvement in Vietnam makes a lot of sense to you . . . if only Washington would let the military do their job."

Phil gave me an incredulous look.

"And, correct me if I'm wrong here," I continued, "but I bet some of your best friends are black. Right?"

"Actually, not."

"What about moral fiber?"

"What about it?"

"Well, it's a pretty damn important attribute, wouldn't you say? That, along with family values."

"Where do you come up with these partisan stereotypes?"

"The liberal media. You know, like Walter Cronkite and Charles Kuralt."

"What do you do here?"

"I'm the new advisor to the R.O.T.C. program."

"Well good for you."

"And, I'm contemplating setting up a chapter of *Vietnam Veterans Against the War.*"

"We already have one of those."

"You do? Do they meet here on campus?"

"Negatory. They muster in the boonies, blue legs. Three klicks to the November whiskey."

"I have no idea what you just said."

"Excuse me. I guess I just got carried away. I've been preoccupied lately; still can't get over that *League of Nations* business. You know, I often wondered. Perhaps you can tell me. Why do those R.O.T.C. cadets always refer to themselves in the third person?"

"*Sir. This roommate does not understand that question, sir.*"

"Yeah. Like that. Exactly!"

"It's odd, isn't it?"

"It certainly is."

"You know what? That's going to be one of my first orders of business as R.O.T.C. advisor."

"Getting them to speak in the first person?"

"Well, not all at once. I think I'll start with the second person, then see how it goes from there."

"Good idea. So, where do you call home?"

"Chicago. South side. And you?"

"Ypsilanti, here in Michigan."

"*Ford* country, hey. My dad works at the Torrence Avenue *Ford* Plant in Chicago, and I drive a *Mustang*. We're a *Ford* family, you might say."

"Sure. They build the *Galaxy 500, LTD*, and *Mercury Marquis* there."

"You bet! My father actually worked on the very car he drives. He hung the front bumper on it. Dad likes to brag that no bumper has ever spontaneously fallen off any car he's had a hand in assembling."

"That's good to hear."

"He even has a little U.A.W. lapel pin that he proudly wears, proclaiming *zero defects*."

"I don't mean to diminish, in any way, your father's penchant for quality, but my family has always driven *General Motors* products, and we never had a bumper fall off either."

"Well. There you go. Now you know why they say, 'what's good for *General Motors* is good for the country.' Just imagine what our roads would be like if they were littered with defective bumpers. But keep in mind, however, the primary reason those *GM* bumpers need to be so substantial is to provide some purchase for the hook on the back of the *Ford* tow truck."

"Well, personally, I'd rather push a *Chevy* than drive a *Ford*."

"Yeah? Is that so? Because, if you own a *Chevy*, you'll likely be doing a lot of pushing. And, let me tell you, my *Mach I Mustang* requires more torque to tighten the lug nuts than a *Z-28 Camaro's* engine produces at 3400 RPMs."

"I read somewhere that 80 percent of all *Fords* are still on the road."

"I'm not surprised."

"The other 20 percent made it to their destination."

"Enough of this banter."

"I agree," Phil changed the subject. "What do you do in your spare time? Do you play sports or a musical instrument?"

"Actually, I've been thinking about writing a fictionalized account of my war experiences, and the subsequent transition back to civilian life."

Phil nervously shifted his weight from one foot to the other. I watched him curiously.

"Do you need to use the bathroom or something?"

"No. It's just something characters occasionally do in novels."

"Well, don't do it again. I don't like it, nor do I want any of that kind of animation in *my* book. So, what's the food like in the cafeteria?"

"It's just about time for them to begin serving. Why don't we go down, and you can find out for yourself?"

Phil and I walked across the quad to the cafeteria. There was a short line forming outside the still closed doors.

"What's on the menu today?" Phil asked a couple of coeds in line ahead of us.

"Mystery meat, of course," one of them answered. "We have that for dinner every evening. Today, the menu asserts it to be broiled and served with brown mushroom gravy."

"Mmmm. Yummy."

"Then there's vegetable medley, whipped potatoes, and a pudding-like substance for dessert."

"Does the vegetable medley include peas?"

"Yes," the girls answered in unison, like the *Doublemint* twins.

"Then forget it."

"They're not bad, actually."

"I hate peas."

"Look. All we are saying, is *give peas a chance*."

"Do you eat peas?"

"Of course! I'm a vegetarian."

"What about your friend here? Is she a vegetarian as well?"

"Oh, no," she answered for herself, "I'm a humanitarian."

"So then you'll be having the . . ."

"Baked *beings*, of course."

"I bet you humanitarians, (cannibals, if I may) get asked this all of the time, and it may be politically incorrect, but, is it true? Do clowns really taste funny?"

"Not if you marinade them well for two to three hours before cooking. I like to use the juice from two limes, balsamic vinegar, extra virgin olive oil, garlic, cumin, kosher salt, freshly ground black pepper, and finely chopped fresh cilantro leaves."

"What about the cafeteria's beverage selection?"

"Oh, the usual. Coffee, tea, milk, *Alka-Seltzer, Pepto-Bismol . . .*"

"I'm glad I brought my appetite," I commented. "Are you girls freshmen?"

"I am, but Kathy here is a sophomore. I'm Piper, by the way."

"Nice to meet you, Kathy and Piper."

Phil started up with that confounding shifting of his weight from foot to foot again. Piper gave him a curious look.

"Is your friend alright?"

"I thought I asked you not to do that anymore," I addressed Phil. "If you're going to exhibit annoying body tic idiosyncrasies at the expense of my book audience, at least have some creativity."

Phil's eyes darted duplicitously.

"Is he having a seizure," Kathy asked. "Should we give him something to bite down on?"

Now I was really annoyed.

"Okay, Phil. That's it!"

"Very well then!" Phil ejaculated.

"What did you just do?"

"I ejaculated. As in to say something quickly and suddenly. Look it up in the dictionary. It's in there. You can use it in your book."

"I don't *care* if it's in the dictionary. You're not going to interject any of that kind of smutty talk in my novel."

"Too late!" he ejaculated again.

The doors opened, and the line began to move. After our meal tickets were punched, we grabbed our still wet trays and utensils and proceeded through the serving line. Not seeing anything that appealed to my palate, I asked to speak with the chef. She emerged from the kitchen, wiping her hands on a white cotton towel.

"May I help you?" she asked.

"Yes. I really don't have an appetite for anything I see here," I explained. "Would it be a terrible inconvenience if I were to order *off menu*?"

"Of course you may," she replied.

I sensed a hint of sarcasm in her response.

"Very well, then. In that case, I believe I'll start with Duck *Foie Gras*, hot, with roasted apple wedges, honey, apple cider *jus*, and celery root. Then, I think, some mushroom '*cappuccino*' soup, would be pleasant, with curry and pistachio *biscotti* . . ."

The chef stared at me blankly.

"Are you getting this?" I asked. "Perhaps you should be writing it down."

"Forget it, Bruce," Phil insisted. "The *Foie Gras* here is consistently greasy with a bile-like aftertaste. You won't care for it very much."

"In that case, then," I addressed the chef, "I'll just dine from the buffet selections. But, thank you so very much. I'm sorry to be a trouble. I hope I haven't inconvenienced you too terribly."

"You may be interested to know that this woman is a world renowned chef," Piper informed me.

"Oh really? Did you cook for the Queen, or President or something like that?"

"No. Actually, I'm the creator of *Cheez Whiz*."

"*Cheez* Whiz? I *love* that stuff! It's like a staple for me when I've been smoking pot. I should have guessed such, just as soon as I saw your pudding concoction."

After getting her autographs (one for me, plus one for my mother) and our drinks, Phil and I found a table and set our trays down. We took our seats. Kathy and Piper waved and smiled at us from across the room.

"They seem like very nice girls," Phil observed. "We should have sex with them sometime."

"I'm pretty busy getting settled in right now. It would have to be just a *quickie*."

"Of course. Have you met your cadets yet?" Phil asked.

"Not until after the holiday. I have their files and I'm supposed to be studying them."

"Anything interesting so far?"

"No. This group, it seems, sets a new benchmark for mediocrity."

"So, you were in Vietnam?"

"Look, I'm not particularly proud of it, you understand? I pretty much got hoodwinked by my recruiter. He told me that if I volunteered for the draft, rather than *wait* to be drafted, I would most likely be sent to Germany."

"You didn't know that recruiters lie? I mean, didn't you notice his lips moving?"

"No. I trusted him. He even served me an ice-cold *Mountain Dew* and showed a remarkable 20-minute *Kodachrome* slide presentation of Bavarian Castles, some of them more than one thousand years old."

"I'm so sorry you had to find out the hard way. I, on the other hand, had a friend in high school whose uncle was a Marine recruiter. In order to qualify for the job, I learned, he had to fail a polygraph test. This was in spite of the fact that he had two convictions for perjury listed on his résumé."

"People have been known to lie on their résumés, you *do* know. In this case, however, his being up front about those perjury convictions, likely counted against him."

"I suppose you have a good point there. I bet you were pretty pissed-off at that recruiter fellow when you found yourself in Vietnam."

"Not as pissed-off as I was when I found myself in a firefight with a boatload of Viet Cong who were, in turn, pretty pissed off themselves that I was over there harassing them, I have to tell you. When you're low on everything except the enemy, that's when you know you're in combat."

"Wouldn't you be perturbed, if you were them?"

"Of course."

"Well, there you go. Did you ever go back to complain to that recruiter and give him a piece of your mind?"

"No. That would be futile and unproductive."

"So you did nothing?"

"Oh no! I didn't say *that*. I slit the tires on his *Plymouth Barracuda*, put sugar in the gas tank, and gouged a six-foot long scratch in his paint job with a can opener."

"Well, that's good to hear. So often, nowadays, people don't want to take a stand on important issues. We live in an age of apathy. But you! Now *you* stood up and took charge. Good for you. We need more Americans like that. I'm proud to be your roommate. They should award you a Silver Star for your moxie."

"It's funny you should say that. I was, indeed, decorated a Silver Star."

"See. Now, had you only known where the Secretary of Defense parked his *Cadillac Fleetwood Seventy-Five Limousine*, you could have received the Congressional Medal of Honor. You going to eat your pudding?"

"I'm a pretty gutsy guy, but not *that* brave. I think I'll take a pass."

"I was just going to say, if you're not going to eat it, the stuff makes for a pretty good product to pack your wheel bearings with."

"I'll try to remember that."

"It will outperform anything they sell at the auto parts store."

CHAPTER NINETEEN

Hell Week

My company of R.O.T.C. cadets were lined up in formation on the athletic field behind the P.E. building. They were dressed in full combat regalia, including M-14 rifles, but with empty magazines. In fact, per school policy, cadets were not allowed access to live ammunition whatsoever. We didn't even keep any in the armory, or anywhere else on campus, for that matter. This policy was judiciously established, years earlier, to avert accidental shootings. In the event that it actually became *necessary* to shoot any protesting or marauding student demonstrators for antiwar activities, or other subversive exercise of the First Amendment, the plan was to call in the National Guard, who were especially trained in this discipline and had the appropriate and corresponding qualifying badges.

Nearby, the cheerleading squad practiced their routines, and the girls' tennis team played sets on the courts behind the formation. Other students splayed out on the grass of the baseball field to enjoy the warm, late-summer sun while studying. One coed brought a blanket and "study partner." They were on third base. The spectacle proved to be a formidable distraction for my cadets.

"This is Mr. Johnson," the company commander introduced me. "He has just returned from a combat tour in Vietnam where he earned a Silver Star for heroism and gallantry under fire. He is a civilian, and no longer wears the uniform, but you will, nonetheless, always address him as 'sir.' You shall not, however, under any circumstances, salute him. Mr. Johnson is the soldier you will aspire to be. You will be humbled in his presence. You will follow his lead. You will learn from his example. Mr. Johnson."

He stepped back, leaving me standing alone in front of the pathetic assemblage. They stared at me with looks of anxious anticipation on their faces. I needed to come up with something tough, but inspirational, to say. Sadly, these men looked to me as a role model.

"Good morning, gentlemen."

I clasped my hands behind my back and paced dramatically, while looking at the ground.

"Welcome to *hell week*. During the next seven days, we are going to push you harder, drive you further, and, and," (I tried to think on my feet) "we're going to do jumping-jacks; lots and lots of jumping-jacks and pushups and stuff like that. And besides that, you are going to be doing a lot of running. You are going to run everywhere you go. There will be absolutely no walking permitted. If you get caught walking, you'll do pushups, and while you're doing pushups, I'm going to stand over you and hurl insults at the top of my lungs; like I'll call you a momma's boy or something disparaging along that line; something really demeaning. And you'll be thinking to yourself, while doing pushups under the hot sun and being verbally debased, 'Who the hell is *this* prick?' and I'm going to be reading your mind and answer, 'I'm your worst nightmare, you little piece of monkey shit.' And then I'm going to make you do jumping-jacks until your jumping up and down on the earth threatens to change the orbit of our planet around the sun (which we don't want to do) so then I'll make you do that thing where you lie on the ground with your hands clasped behind your head, and you arch your back and rock back and forth on your belly. You know the exercise I'm talking about. I can't think of its name right off the top of my head, but it's really quite disagreeable and you won't like it very much at all."

Looking up at the cadets, I was greeted by forty-eight blank, bewildered and bemused faces.

"A pint of sweat will save a gallon of blood," I tried.

Still, just a bunch of curious looks.

"The difference between the courageous and the coward is an eyelash."

Nothing.

"Follow me if I advance. Kill me if I retreat. Revenge me if I die!"

No reaction. It was like I was talking to a brick wall.

"Look. Why don't you all just take the rest of the afternoon off and relax," I suggested, "inasmuch as this is going to be hell week and all. You're going to need to be well rested."

The company commander stepped forward and, in a loud voice announced, "Company...dis...missed."

"Sir," one of the cadets piped up.

"Yes, Cadet."

"Did you really mean for us to *run* back to the armory, with all of this heavy gear on, to return our weapons?"

I thought contemplatively about his question for a few seconds.

"We'll make an exception, just this one time," I answered. "You're going to need to conserve all of your energy for what's yet to come. This hell week is going to be . . .uh . . .hell, you know. Did I mention that we're going to be separating the men from the boys? I don't think so, but that's what we're going to be doing. You're going to want to be well rested for *that*. You might want to also consider getting to bed early tonight. Morning formation will be exactly sometime between zero eight hundred hours, a.m. and eleven hundred hours in the morning or nine o'clock, to nine thirty sharp, Zulu time, plus or minus. You don't want to be more than a few minutes late for the last call to formation or you'll be given a stern warning, and then after that, if you're persistently late, severely disciplined."

"Pushups or jumping-jacks?"

"Pardon me."

"What will the punishment be? Pushups or jumping-jacks?"

"Both! This is *hell week* you know. We're not messing around here."

I watched as the cadets slowly dispersed and headed leisurely towards the armory, grumbling. I never knew, before that afternoon, that I had such a knack for being a hard-ass. Before the semester is done, I thought, these men are going to hate my guts with every bone in their body. Their blood is going to boil at the very sight of me. It was my job to determine who had the intestinal fortitude to be officers and who didn't. Then it dawned on me. I needed to get to my three o'clock anatomy lab.

I raced over to the Science and Medicine Building, passing some of my cadets along the way. They smiled and gave me a friendly wave. I didn't want to be late for my lab. Ever since that earthworm in the eighth grade, I have been enthralled with dissecting organisms. Then there was the frog in freshman biology, and the cat in advanced biology class. To my parent's exasperation, none of our family pets escaped my scalpel when they expired. I was obsessively engrossed with anatomy. Even my first sexual experience went badly because of this pathological fascination. Parked along the lakefront with Darlene Hood, (watching the submarine races) I became distracted, during foreplay, trying to locate and identify the perineum, preputium clitoridis, and labia minora with a small flashlight I kept in my glove box.

Due to this morphological passion of mine, I actually enlisted to be a medic, when I joined the Army, but ended up in the infantry due to a transposed numeric code on my DD Form 4/3. That's how I ended up in

Vietnam where I witnessed a lot of blood and guts. As horrific as it was, however, when Bill Hastings got shot in the belly that day over in Phu Yen Province, and his intestines spilled out as they did, I have to confess that I was just a wee bit curious to see where the transverse colon was connected to the small intestine. That's how goofy about this shit I am!

I was originally enrolled in Arthur College's excellent pre-med program, but ultimately switched to a biology major when I found myself struggling with organic chemistry. When I asked my faculty advisor what type of career a biology degree would qualify me for, she thought about it for 15 or 20 seconds, with a puzzled look on her face, then answered, "I suppose that you could always sell annuities."

That day, we were going to do a little spelunking in our cadaver's vena cava. (A small example of anatomy lab humor.) First we needed to free the heart from the pericardial sac. I deferred to one of the nursing students to do the removal of the organ, as I had previously dissected many a four-chambered heart in my day.

"I saw you with the R.O.T.C. cadets just now," one of my female lab partners commented. "But you don't dress like one of them."

"Oh," I explained. "I'm not a cadet. I'm a paid advisor to the R.O.T.C. program here at Arthur College."

"An advisor? How did you qualify to get a job like that?"

"I never said anything about being qualified."

"But you got the job."

"I know. It's silly, but I was offered the position because I received a Silver Star while I was in the Army."

"A Silver Star! One of my sorority sisters writes for the school paper, *The Arthur*."

"You mean she's an author for the *Arthur*?"

"Yes. She should arrange to interview you. Would you mind if I gave her your phone number?"

"Well, this is a little embarrassing, but you see, there has been some speculation that the medal wasn't actually intended for me, but rather a buddy of mine who was killed in combat."

"Speculation? By whom?"

"Guys in my platoon who knew me, and my propensity for exceptional cowardliness under fire."

"I just *know* that's not true. May I have her call you? Could you write down your phone number?"

"I don't know about this."

"Please."

"Well, I suppose so."

I scribbled on a scrap of paper.

"Thanks! Her name is Maria. She's studying art and sociology. You'll like her. She's nice."

The nursing student lifted the heart out of our cadaver and placed it in a stainless steel pan.

"Okay!" I announced. "Now let's have some fun."

CHAPTER TWENTY

The Interview

With grave misgivings, I agreed to meet Maria at 7 p.m. in front of the neoclassical, Romanesque library building, crowned with a statue of Athena, the goddess of wisdom and courage. How ironic. The prospect of my being interviewed by some naive 18-year-old child, about my most personal and intimate war experiences, was not my idea of an entertaining evening. It was my plan, therefore, to act as if I were some sort of crazy, deranged, and psychologically damaged Vietnam vet who was on the verge of snapping. This was a handy tactic that I had frequently employed since being discharged from the service. It encouraged people to be respectful of my "personal space."

I had a few creative ideas of how I could mess with her head and dissuade her from ever troubling me like this again. Earlier in the day, I had done some intense roll preparation, as a paranoid schizophrenic, in front of the mirror in my dorm room.

"Just because I'm paranoid," I snarled at my own reflection, "it doesn't mean they're not after me."

"What the hell are you doing?" asked my roommate, Phil.

"I'm practicing acting crazy."

"And here I was always under the impression that it came quite naturally for you."

"Joke if you must, but the reason I'm so convincing is because I avoid using cheesy clichés and florid eyebrow acting."

"The reason you're so convincing is because you're certifiably nuts!"

"Look here. I've got to scare away this Maria chick by making her believe that I have Post Traumatic Stress Disorder."

"Don't you?"

"That's beside the point."

"Do you know Maria's last name?"

"Maciel, or something like that. Why do you ask?"

"Because if it's the same Maria Maciel I'm thinking of, you may not want to be scaring her off, like you're planning on doing."

"What do you mean?"

"I mean that she's just about the most stunningly beautiful, bright-eyed female specimen you'll ever likely meet. She was in a couple of my art classes I audited, and I have to tell you, I couldn't keep my eyes off of her."

"I could care less about that sort of thing. Beautiful women don't faze me in the least. As a matter of fact, I've been considering becoming a homosexual."

"A homosexual! Since when?"

"Since I saw you soaping up in the shower the other day."

"Hey, man. You're creeping me out now. I really, really don't want to be listening to this."

"Why? Are you homophobic?"

"Honestly, I have to tell you that, at this very moment, I feel myself leaning in that direction."

"I didn't say that I *was* gay. I only said that I was considering it."

"You can't just decide to be gay, you dumb ass. You've got to be born that way. Homosexuality isn't a decision, it's a realization. I'm a *Young Republican*, and still, even I know that."

"Well, I just realized that it's my decision to choose my sexual orientation. It's all in the Bible. Look it up sometime."

"It's in the Bible?"

"Sure it is. I spent twelve years in Catholic school, remember. But then again, it's also in the Bible that one is forbidden (Leviticus 19:19) from wearing clothes woven from different fabrics . . . like a plaid polyester sport jacket with a purple cotton shirt, acetate slacks, and a paisley silk tie."

"Now, *that* would be gay."

"The bottom line here is that I don't want to be discussing my wartime experiences with this Maria, or anyone else for that matter. Not even you."

"Okay. I'll respect that, but tell me. You don't seriously watch me when I'm showering now, do you?"

"Do I *seriously* watch you? No. I'm sorry, but it would be quite impossible to be *serious*, after seeing you naked."

Maria waited for me, on the steps of the library, at the appointed time. I knew it was her because she fit Phil's description to a 'T.' She was the most stunningly beautiful, bright-eyed female specimen I had ever laid my eyes on, instantly changing my mind about becoming a homosexual.

"You must be Maria."

"And you're Bruce, I presume."

She offered her right hand, which I took with both of mine. I didn't want to let go, and, indeed, didn't until a glimmer of concern shown in her eyes.

"Sorry. I don't know what came over me. I've never had that happen to me before."

"It's quite all right. It happens to me all the time. Do you care to go inside? I reserved a conference room for us."

"Yeah. Sure. I'm not gay you know."

"Is that so?"

"Yep. As a matter of fact, I'm straight as an arrow."

"Super. Is there some reason you're telling me this?"

"No. I'm just saying. Like when my roommate, Phil, is showering, I just look the other way."

"How considerate."

I let Maria lead the way, partly because it seemed the gentlemanly thing to do, but mostly because I wanted to hang back a step and check out her gorgeous shapely legs. They were smooth, clean-limbed, and attractive. Her dark brown, nearly black, shoulder-length hair shimmered in the incandescent light.

"Here we are."

Maria paused outside a conference room door that had a card affixed:

RESERVED

MARIA MACIEL

7:00 P.M.

"You have very beautiful hair," I stupidly blurted out.

"Thank you. Shall we go in?"

"Phil tells me that you're studying studio art. What medium do you work in?"

"Mostly I paint, mainly pastels, sometimes in oil."

We entered the small room, which was furnished with a partners' desk, an Arts & Crafts table lamp, plus two library chairs, and took our respective seats.

"Do you mind if I tape record our conversation?"

"So long as you Mirandize me first," I joked.

"Okay. You have the right to remain silent, but then that wouldn't make for much of an interview, would it?"

"I could blink my eyes in Morse code. You know, spelling out something like: T-O-R-T-U-R-E."

"That would only work if I were filming you. I'm just taping, you understand, as in *audio*."

She had a good point there, and a pretty, toothy smile, and firm sinewed arms, and glowing bronze skin . . .

"Were you ever wounded in the war? Did you receive a Purple Heart?"

"Yes. I was indeed slightly wounded once, but because it was from 'friendly fire' I didn't qualify for a Purple Heart."

"What happened?"

"I caught a small piece of shrapnel in my left lingering."

"So, you sustained a lingering injury then?"

"Precisely."

"Were you a prisoner of war?"

"No, but I've watched a fair number of episodes of *Hogan's Heroes* on CBS, so I have a pretty good feel for what it would be like."

"How very interesting. May we get started?"

"Of course."

"You do realize it's a farce, don't you?"

"Our country's involvement in Vietnam? Of course I know that. I was there remember."

"No. I was referring to the television show. The premise is farcical. There was no such *Stalag 13* where the POWs actually used the camp as a base of operations for espionage and sabotage against the Nazis."

"Now you've gone and spoiled it all for me. Why'd you do that?"

"I'm very sorry."

"So, you're saying there was no Colonel Klink in real life?"

"No."

"And Hans Schultz?"

"Just a preposterous character in a television sitcom comedy."

"Gosh. They sure are convincing."

"Just clever writing and talented actors."

"Now I'm feeling hoodwinked, and frankly, a little credulous and naïve. But, go ahead and ask your questions. I'll do my best to answer them candidly and without perjury."

"Very well, then. Specifically. What were your actions on the battle-field that accounted for your being awarded a Silver Star?"

"Now, there you go. You see, that's where the dilemma lies. There was a lot of confusion that day, what with all of the shooting and such. A firefight can be a very disconcerting environment. In all of the mayhem, they apparently got me mixed up with someone else. The Army dressed us all alike, you understand."

"With whom did they mix you up?"

"Like someone doing something courageous or heroic. Someone like Bill Hastings, for example."

"Tell me about this Hastings fellow, then."

"He was my best friend and a great guy. We went through basic and AIT together. He was killed on an LRP . . ."

"LRP?"

"Long range patrol."

"And you were with him when he died?"

"Yes. Yes, I was. He was shot in the gut. He literally died in my arms. Jim Mullen was there, too. Jim threw up. We had just Zippo raided a small hamlet and were preparing to move out when all hell broke loose. The V.C. hit us with everything they had."

"What did you expect after you had just burned their homes to the ground?"

"I don't know. I think it was intended that they would set up some sort of a democratic political system model, and vote for candidates endorsed, backed, and underwritten by the U.S. government."

"In practice, that sort of logic never works. Did you honestly think it would?"

"No. I suppose you're right, but I'm confident that we, as a nation, have learned a valuable lesson from the war, and our citizens will never allow our elected officials to try to impose our values or political system on other nations again."

"I'm sure you're right. Now, may we get back to the subject of you being awarded a Silver Star?"

"Look, this is terribly embarrassing."

I was feeling an imminent panic attack burgeoning.

"I have to go. I'm not the right person to interview. You need to talk to someone else. This Silver Star business was just a huge, bureaucratic boondoggle."

"I'm so sorry."

"Don't be. It has nothing to do with you. It's me. I'm just a fraud. I did nothing heroic in the service. Heroism's not even in my nature. I couldn't even help Bill that day when he begged, with his glazed-over eyes, for me to do something. I need to go. You're absolutely talking to the wrong person."

She stood as I opened the door to leave.

"I'm really sorry. I am. I had no intentions of upsetting you. Please forgive me."

" . . . and Fraulein Hilda?" I blubbered.

"If it makes you feel any better, I think I remember reading somewhere that her character was based on an actual person."

CHAPTER TWENTY-ONE

The Date

The next evening, I sat in my room, drinking excessively, (which was becoming a new hobby of mine) and drafting an excellent paper for my physics class, purporting a grand unified theory of the universe, eliminating all the disparities between relativity and quantum theory, when the phone rang.

"Can you answer that?" I asked Phil. "I think I'm really onto something of momentous consequence here, and I don't want to break my train of thought."

"You always think that when you drink. Last week, as I recall, you were convinced that you had cracked the secret recipe for *Coca Cola*."

"The elusive flavor of the nutmeg oil confounded me. Now please, just pick up the phone."

"Hello. Yes. May I say who's calling? One moment, please."

Phil put his hand over the receiver.

"Hey, Bruce. It's Maria. She wants to talk to you."

"Tell her I'm busy."

"I'm sorry. He's writing a paper right now, and can't be disturbed, lest he lose his concentration. May I take a message? Sure. I can do that. Absolutely! I'm sure he'll be delighted. No problem. That sounds wonderful. It's my pleasure. Goodbye."

"What did she want?"

"She called to ask you out on a date. I told her you'd go."

"When?"

"Saturday night."

"I'll need to buy some rubbers then. Be sure to remind me when we go to town."

"It's not that kind of a date."

"What do you mean, it's not that kind of a date? Just exactly what kind of a date is it?"

"You're going miniature golfing."

"You set me up on a date to go pee wee golfing? What the hell were you thinking, Phil?"

"I was thinking that perhaps, on the last hole, if you got your ball past the blades of the windmill, and scored a hole-in-one, you could win a free game."

"Well, in the future, I'll make my own dates, if it's all just the same to you."

"She's picking you up at seven. Try to be civil with her now. Promise me. She's a nice girl."

"And, if I'm a real good boy, and act like I'm having fun, and accurately record all of my strokes on my scorecard with that stubby little pencil, do you think I'll get a little something special at the end of the evening?"

"Sure! If you do all that, plus compliment her on whatever she's wearing, I'm confident she'll treat you to an ice cream cone."

"An ice cream cone? Perhaps you're being facetious, but I do enjoy ice cream very much. Do you think I could get a double scoop?"

"I wouldn't push it. Not on the first date."

I waited outside my dorm, leaning against a big terracotta planter containing stiff ornamental grasses, colorful annual-blooming flowers, and cascading ornamental potato plant vines. It was a very attractive ensemble that smokers used to crush out their cigarettes, before entering the building. As the clock in the tower of the auditorium played its Westminster chime, announcing seven o'clock, a Donnybrooke Green, *1970 LT-1 Corvette* pulled up with Maria looking alluring behind the wheel.

"Hey. Nice car!" I complimented her, as I opened the passenger door and got in.

"Thanks. It was my high school graduation present from my dad."

"Cool dad!"

She slipped the M22 heavy-duty "rock crusher" close ratio 4-speed into first gear and released the clutch. Even at considerably less than full throttle, my body was pressed, firmly, back into the seat.

"This car rocks," I told her.

"It has gobs of torque. Do you want to drive?"

"No. No, I'm fine," I lied.

After driving about 15 minutes, we pulled into the parking lot of the golf center. There was also a lighted driving range on the property.

"I hope you like miniature golf. I think it's fun."

"Oh. Me, too. I love pee wee golf," I perjured myself again.

Like most of my relationships with young women, this one was starting out with the customary pack of lies.

"Great! I had a feeling you would."

Great! She had a feeling I would.

We walked toward the concession stand where the money was exchanged and the golf balls and clubs were issued.

"Hi," I greeted the high school-aged boy behind the counter. "I believe we have a seven-thirty tee time this evening, and we'll carry our own clubs, thank you."

I reached for my wallet. Maria stopped me.

"No. This is my treat," she insisted. "I asked *you* out. Remember?"

"Oh, of course. That *is*, after all, why we're miniature golfing, now, isn't it?"

"I thought it would be fun."

"I'm sure it will be a barrel of monkeys."

"Are you being sarcastic?"

"No. Not at all. I'm enjoying myself. Really. I like you."

"It didn't seem so the other night."

"I didn't know you drove an *LT-1 Corvette* back then."

She knelt to tie her shoe as she spoke.

"Well, I hope you're different from most guys, and you're not just going out with me because you want to get into the driver's seat of my Corvette."

"No. That's not the *only* reason," I assured her, as I took the opportunity to look down her blouse.

We putted our way around the course, laughing and talking.

"So, where do you live?" I asked.

"We have a house on Geneva Lake, in Wisconsin. I live with my father. My mother died when I was quite young. How about you?"

"I grew up near Midway Airport in Chicago, just off the end of runway 13 Left/31 Right. As a kid, I just loved seeing those big planes drop out of the clouds over our house. I was infatuated with the dream of becoming a pilot someday."

"Why didn't you?"

"Conscription, and now school. But I'm still going to fly, believe me. After I finish school. After I settle into a career."

On the eighth hole, I received an excited hug from Maria when she evaded a water hazard and scored a hole-in-one. It made me wish she were a better golfer. On the last hole, our balls disappeared permanently down the bottomless tube, and back, I presume, to the concession stand to be rented again.

"May I buy you an ice cream cone?" Maria asked.

"Well," I pretended to cogitate, "I know this *is* our first date, but, do you think I could get a double scoop?"

"You can have a *triple* scoop, if you wish, so long as you don't drop it in your lap and make a mess in my car."

CHAPTER TWENTY-TWO

Mandatory Counseling

I showed up for my initial mandatory psychotherapy session with a closed mind and bad attitude. The room felt joyless. Thirteen assembled veterans stared into space, stony-eyed and unsmiling. Undoubtedly, the majority of the group suffered from PTSD, however, I detected glimmers of Schizoaffective Disorder, OCD, Dissociative disorders, and Psychosis. Apparently, *Chester A. Arthur College* had been doing some aggressive recruiting of the Psych Ward patients at *Walter Reed Hospital.*

I took a seat next to a trembling fellow who was wringing his hands obsessively.

"Hi." I greeted him. "I hope you remembered to unplug your iron before you came here."

He got up and bolted out the door.

With the exit of "OCD Dudley" we were left with 12 Vietnam veterans in the room (which begged the question as to how many of us it would take to screw in a light bulb) and the group leader, who identified herself as Mindy, a psychology grad student and qualified psychodramatist.

"There's no such thing as a psychodramatist. You just made that word up," I taunted her.

"There is *too* such a thing. I'm certified by the *American Board of Examiners* in *Psychodrama, Sociometry,* and *Group Psychotherapy.*"

"Show me in a dictionary where there's such a thing as psychodrama, or sociometry, for that matter," I insisted.

"This evening," she deflected my challenge, "we're going to introduce ourselves and do a little role-playing."

"Goodie," I piped up sarcastically. "I want to play an alto cheese Danish."

She shot me a cold glance that told me she wouldn't be asking me out any time soon. That was a shame. At about five foot eight, with long, nylon-clad legs, she was as tall as me, in her black loafer pumps with two and one half inch stacked heels. She was dressed like a lawyer or a CPA . . . very professional. Her button front navy blue pencil skirt matched her crosshatch tweed jacket, which she wore over a classic white roll sleeve blouse. Her shoulder-length hair was dark auburn, her eyes hazel. She had a high forehead and wore glasses, giving her an intelligent appearance.

"The voices in my head may not be real, but they have some pretty darn good ideas," one of the vets offered.

"I hope one of those ideas," I suggested, "is to transfer to a different school."

Another vet chimed in, "Whenever I think about the past, it brings back a lot of memories."

These guys were enthusiastic!

"Yeah. Life would be a lot more comprehensible," another added, "if it weren't for the fact that it's composed of both real and imaginary elements. It makes things so confusing."

"Those are some good observations. You're going to be a great group! Now, let's introduce ourselves," Mindy proposed. "Starting on my right, I'd like to go around the circle, with each of you telling the group three distinct things about yourself, two that are true, and one lie. The others will then try to guess the lie."

She received some skeptical looks, including mine.

"Try it! It's a fun way to get to know each other," she insisted.

"Okay. Okay. Let me think," started the veteran to her right. "My name is Brad, I'm from Williamsport Pennsylvania, and I once had sex with a captured Viet Cong woman, and then afterwards, I killed her, making me a *double veteran*."

"Oh my! That's some tale, Brad . . ."

"It's John."

"Pardon me?"

"My name. It's John."

"But you just said that your name was Brad."

"Yeah. And you just said that we were supposed to tell you two things that are true, and one lie."

"Oh, my God! How ghastly."

"She was my first, you know."

"Your first enemy kill?"

"No. I lost my virginity with her."

"I'm not liking the tenor of this conversation!" I protested. "We need to change the subject. This is insane."

"Well, isn't that why we're here, after all? For Mindy to make us whole again? Of all the things I lost in the war, it's my mind that I miss the most."

"Under the circumstances, perhaps we should try something different to introduce ourselves to the group," Mindy suggested.

"Are you shittin' me?" another vet piped up. "This is great entertainment."

A second veteran jumped in. "I want to go next. I've got a good one."

"No, I don't think so," Mindy insisted.

"This is bogus! Brad got to do his three things . . ."

"It's John."

"Pardon me."

"My name is John. 'Brad' was my lie . . . and Jesus loves me."

"Well, whatever your name is, Jesus may love you, but the rest of us think you're an asshole. Did you know that? Has anyone ever told you that before?"

"Not anyone who lived to tell about it."

"Now, now boys," Mindy tried to calm things down.

"Boys? Do you see any boys in this room? I don't see any boys. You see a boy, point him out to me and I'll kick his sorry ass and send him home to his mommy."

"Please. Please," Mindy pleaded.

"Are we role-playing now?" I asked. "Because I'm feeling a little uncomfortable with the verisimilitude of this exercise."

"Yeah. Aren't you supposed to be presiding over and managing the tenor of this session? Isn't that *your* role?"

"I am," Mindy replied.

"Well, if you don't mind my telling you this, you're doing a pretty piss-poor job of it. I think you may need to be decertified."

"Are we going to do some of that 'free association' business?" a group member asked.

Mindy shot him an annoyed glance and answered, "Later."

"Earlier," he snapped back.

Obviously frustrated, Mindy pleaded, "Please."

"Thank you."

"Stop!"

"Light."

"My girlfriend gave me one of those mood rings for Christmas," a tattooed ex-Marine piped up. "When I'm in a good mood, it turns green.

When the aftermath from the war is getting to me, and I'm drunk, it leaves a big red mark on her forehead. She hates it when I drink, but my dog finds me to be quite amusing after a few shots of *Old Grand-Dad*."

"I wrote a poem," an African-American vet, who had been sitting silently, up until that point, spoke up. He unfolded a sheet of lined yellow legal-sized paper and began to read:

I got drafted and shafted then put in the Army
Shipped to Kentucky and trained
Shipped to Fort Benning, Georgia and trained some more
Learned to fire a machine gun, toss a grenade and dig a foxhole.
There were some other things we were taught to do there too
Things that would get civilian folks detested or arrested, or both
And in some states, executed and in some of those, electrocuted
But that's what we learned to do
So, that's what we did...ten thousand miles away
Because it's always better to do that sort of stuff...
Ten thousand miles away...from your mother
And they gave us medals
Commendation medals, Bronze Stars, Silver Stars and Purple Hearts
Air medals, and Distinguished Flying Crosses
Posthumously, and some while we were pretty much still alive
But sometimes missing a leg or an arm or part of a brain
That's what the Purple Hearts were for
And burned too
Was one of my worst fears...burning up
Had nightmares about it
Still do
See a Doc about it when I can
Take the pills she prescribes...most of the time...when I remember
Take a drink or two or three when I don't
Take the pills with a few drinks when it gets real bad
It's been getting bad more often lately
But I've got my Purple Heart for comfort
Ruined a good thirty-five dollar Elgin watch with a Twist-O-Flex
band getting' that Purple Heart

"That sounds to be a very heartfelt poem," Mindy observed. "Thank you for sharing it with us . . ."

"Maurice," the vet offered his name, for which she was hunting.

"Well, thank you Maurice, for sharing that with the group. Does anyone want to comment on Maurice's poem?"

"That poem's bullshit," John interjected. "What is that? Free verse? Who do you think you are? Bob Dylan? Well, your poem sucks, man."

"And I suppose you can do better?"

"Sure, I can."

"So, let's hear it."

"Okay. Here's a limerick for you to chew on:"

> *There once was a guy named Maurice*
> *Whose burden was Vietnamese*
> *So when he got home*
> *He wrote a dumb poem*
> *About his breach of the peace*

There was an audible reaction to the limerick, mostly negative, I conjectured, sort of like the reaction one would expect had the group just been informed that they'd all be receiving rectal exams that evening.

"I've got a haiku, if anyone's interested," I offered.

"Sure. Let's hear it," Mindy responded with way more enthusiasm than would be befitting the quality of the verse thus far.

> *I cleared my throat.*
> *The war's objective*
> *Peace with honor?*
> *Silly me.*

"I can see that we have an exceptionally creative group here," Mindy observed. "Does anyone else have something you wrote that you'd like to share?"

"I have a manifesto," one of the vets offered.

"A manifesto. How delightful."

"I was going to save it for a special occasion . . ."

"Like when you're in a police standoff and holding bank customers hostage," I suggested. "You could demand it be published prominently on the front page of the *Washington Post* in exchange for your releasing the bank manager who's conspicuously in distress and in need of insulin therapy."

"Yeah. That's what I was thinking. Something along that line."

"Well, just don't buckle in to them talking you into releasing the pretty teller with the short skirt and nice legs. That 'capture-bonding syndrome' is for real, man. All of her sobbing may simply be in response to how much her heart aches for you. It could be an epic love story for all time . . . like Bonnie and Clyde. You don't want to blow something like that. It's like once in a lifetime."

"No?"

"No. Not so much as they offer you pizzas in exchange for her release. Don't do it! I mean, as a rule, women find a man with explosives strapped to his chest hard to resist."

"You *do* realize," suggested a group member, "that you guys are only *reinforcing* the negative stereotypes people entertain of Vietnam War veterans."

"You're absolutely right. I certainly didn't participate in all of those '*Zippo* raids,' search and destroy missions, and special Psy Ops only to have people form negative stereotypical opinions of me. I've got a Silver Star after all, damn it!"

One of the vets, who I just then noticed was missing both legs above the knees, spoke up.

"Shit. I'm in this wheelchair for life, and all I got was a Purple Heart. What the hell did you do to warrant a Silver Star, Jack?"

I was overwhelmed by an irrepressible wave of shame. I couldn't answer his question. There was no good answer. I couldn't even look him in the eye, and for sure, I couldn't look at the stumps where his legs once were. I had no idea why this guy was here, tormenting me, and not tucked away in some VA hospital somewhere, safely out of the public's view.

"This is bullshit," I addressed the group as a whole. "I'm out of here."

And with that, I exited the building, stepping into crisp late October night air. A whiff of burning leaves evoked memories of the previous Saturday evening's miniature golfing date with Maria. What a nice time we had . . . probably, the most fun I had *ever* had with a fully clothed female. I decided to give her a call, just as soon as I got back to my dorm room.

CHAPTER TWENTY-THREE

Mr. Maciel

"I told my father, when I was home last weekend, that you received a Silver Star when you were in the Army," Maria informed me as we were fooling around, late one night, on the sofa in the parlor of her sorority house, pretending to be watching television. "Now he wants to drive down on Saturday to meet you."

Since my pee wee golfing adventure with Maria, we had been seeing each other regularly now for over two months. As it turned out, she was indeed a very special person, and good medicine for my asocial (pronounced *ass hole*) behavior. When I was with her, all . . . well some . . . of my hostility and anxiety from the war melted away. I could recognize that there was virtue in the world. I appreciated each day of my life. Most importantly, I liked the person she brought out in me far better than the old post-Vietnam Bruce . . . the bitter, cynical, miscreant. (Now, I was at worst, a bitter, cynical, putz.)

"He wants to meet me because I received a Silver Star?"

"Well that, and also because I told him that you had deflowered me."

"You're kidding me, right?"

"No. I'm serious. My father and I are very forthright with one another . . . possibly because my mother died when I was very young. I share most everything with him."

"But Maria . . ."

"Don't worry. I told him we use condoms."

I slapped my forehead with the heal of my hand.

"Maria, I would really prefer that some parts of our relationship remain just between you and me. I hope you can understand this."

"Of course. I never tell him how, occasionally, you have performance issues, or how you can't talk about sex, or . . ."

"Stop!"

"See. You can't talk about it."

"Sometimes, Maria, there's nothing to talk about."

"Yeah. Exactly. Those are the times I'm referring to."

I found our conversation exasperating.

"I can't do this Maria."

"That's okay. We can just cuddle."

As we lay there entwined on the sofa, Maria's soft breath in my ear, I blissfully dozed.

"So, tell me," Maria whispered, "that we're sleeping together because you love me. That *is* the reason, isn't it?"

"Maria," I groggily answered. "I'm very sorry to burst your bubble, but I can't deceive you any longer. The truth is, I'm sleeping with you because I love tongue tacos, and your father is widely known as the taco king of North America. If that's a problem for you, then we need to break this thing off right now."

"Well, it *is* a problem for me and I'm afraid I *will* be breaking it off, but not just right now, however. I mean, don't you want a little something to remember me by?"

She pulled me close by the collar.

"Now that you mention it, I do." I pressed my forehead to hers. "You don't happen to have any more of those *buy two tacos, get one free* coupons, do you?"

Maria's father, I had learned, immigrated to the United States from Mexico as a young man. His first job was as a busboy in a Mexican restaurant in Chicago's Little Village neighborhood. By the time he turned thirty, he owned the place. He was now opening something like 40 restaurants a year, and his franchises were ranked by *Enterprise Magazine* as one of the top 10 small business opportunities of 1970.

Maria and I stood outside the library, waiting hand in hand, in the brisk December cold. A foot or so of fresh snow had fallen overnight. Maria's father emerged from his Ivy Bronze Metallic *Lincoln Mark III* with dark green leather interior, wearing a gunmetal gray wool overcoat, white scarf, and a Dobbs fedora. His shoes were cap toe Balmorals by Berluti.

"So *that's* your father?" I asked Maria as we watched him approach the library, where we had arranged to meet him. "He's very distinguished looking."

"Why? What did you expect?"

"I don't know. I guess I sort of thought that he'd be driving a customized pickup truck, with tassels on the windshield, wearing a big sombrero and pointy alligator hide cowboy boots."

Maria punched my shoulder. "Are you disappointed?"

"Yeah. Just a little."

"Well, you know, growing up in the Mexican community, we have *our* stereotypes too."

"Like?"

"For one, I was indoctrinated to believe that white people smell funny."

"Really?"

"Yes."

"Like the smell of liver and onions cooking?"

"Exactly."

"Damn! That explains *so* much."

"What's that?"

"Ever since I was old enough to remember, I always wondered what that curious odor was."

"See. Now you know. It was *you* all along."

Maria and her father embraced, then greeted one another in Spanish. After their salutations, he turned in my direction, and looked me discriminatingly up and down. It was uncomfortable.

"Nice to meet you, young man," he shook my hand, then crinkled his nose and sniffed. "Hmm. They must be cooking liver and onions in the cafeteria today. Maria has told me a lot about you."

"So I understand," I replied.

"Tell me. Are you a hard or soft man?"

"I beg your pardon, sir."

"Maria tells me you like tongue tacos. Hard shell or soft?"

"Hard," I answered.

"Well, now I see what you and Maria have in common. Lately, I understand, she likes them hard, too, but that sometimes, if that's all there is, she'll settle for soft."

Beads of sweat were forming on my forehead.

"Dad. I'm sure Bruce doesn't want to talk about food."

"Who's talking about food?"

"Dad! Please. I'm sorry, Bruce. Father takes sadistic enjoyment from trying to make my male friends feel uncomfortable."

"Well, you're doing an excellent job of it, sir."

"May I see it?"

"Excuse me."

"Your Silver Star. May I see it? I never saw one in person before."

"I'm sorry, but I don't have it with me right now. It's not actually something one wears like a wristwatch."

"Well, let me see *that* then."

"My wristwatch?"

"Yes. Let me see *that*. I'd like to know just what kind of a watch a Silver Star recipient wears."

"It's just a self-winding *Timex* auto date."

"A *Timex*! That's a fine watch for the average schmuck on the street, but a Silver Star recipient should be wearing a *Breitling*. Here, take mine, son. My gift to you."

He removed his watch and held it out to me. I hesitated.

"You better take it," Maria spoke up. "You don't want to refuse my father."

"Thank you, sir. That's very generous."

"Generosity runs in our family. In fact, Maria tells me that she's been decidedly generous with you lately."

He put his arm around my shoulder and squeezed hard.

"I hope you *appreciate* that, son."

"Oh, I do. Very much so."

"Good. Good. Have Maria tell you, sometime, about what happened to the boy who stood her up for that *Heart Hop* dance her sophomore year in high school."

"She already did."

"Let's just say that it was not a good day for Anglo/Latino relations. But, enough of this talk. Let's get something to eat."

We lunched in the College's *President's Club*. The walls sported quarter-sawn oak, there was an abundance of burgundy leather, and a student cellist played Mozart.

"I never even knew this place existed," I commented as the waiter poured me a glass of *Chateau Du Cedre*.

It made me feel very sophisticated.

"I always eat in the cafeteria. There, instead of a maitre d', we have a grey-haired lady with a nickel-plated *Sportline 385* mechanical counter, who clicks it each time a student takes a tray and gets in line for food."

"Next time, try thinking of her as *une personne qui compete*. Things always sound more cultured and elegant in French."

"Really?"

"Yes, indeed. For example, that wine you're drinking . . ."

"Which is exquisite, by the way."

"Well, there are dozens of domestic, unvinted wines for half the price that will hold their own against what you're drinking. However, the label, being in French, makes you feel very sophisticated, I imagine."

"You're absolutely right!"

"See! I learned that little trick from being in the restaurant business for thirty years."

"But you sell 69-cent tacos."

"And if I were to call them *farcie coquilles a tacos*, put the waiter in a vest and bow tie, they'd be $5 tacos."

"You're kidding! That would be the only difference between a 69-cent taco and a $5 one?"

"Well, I suppose the cook would also want to drizzle something over them. It's very trendy right now, you know."

"Like a black truffle and olive oil puree?"

"No. Like taco sauce."

"This is very nice, and so much more relaxing than the cafeteria."

"From here on out, I want you to know that you are welcome to eat in this dining room any time you are so inclined, and I insist on it whenever you're dining with my Maria here. Just tell the club manager to charge your meal to *me*. I give this school an obscene amount of financial support each year, so don't feel bashful to take advantage of the food here. I'm confident it's far better than anything you can find in the cafeteria, with the possible exception of the onion rings they serve down there. I have to tell you, those are some of the best onion rings in the Midwest, if not the country. I don't know how they do it. I've been trying for years to duplicate them in our research kitchens."

At this point, he and Maria commenced speaking in Spanish. They carried on for some time. Being mono-lingual, I looked uncomfortably around the room, wiped my mouth with the napkin, and glanced at my newly acquired chronograph-style watch. It looked like a miniaturized instrument panel from a *P-51 Mustang*. Just watching Maria's joy of being with her father lightened my heart. She was better medicine than any antipsychotic drug or psychoanalytical intervention. I couldn't recall a time in my life when I was happier.

"I apologize, son. Maria was just telling me that the two of you have talked about getting married upon graduation."

"Yes sir. We have. Maria is a special person."

"Well, I don't know if you've given any consideration to working in the food services industry or not, but I want you to know that your

Silver Star, and my daughter's love for you, are credentials enough for me to hire you for a well-paying position with my company. I expect you to graduate first, of course, but then I will be proud to have you as part of our team."

"Well, thank you, sir. That's a very generous offer. I had been planning on becoming an M.D., but I've been struggling with organic chemistry as of late, giving me some pause."

"Well, that's perfect then. There's virtually nothing organic on our menu, so you won't be needing any of that. And, you can thank me by always being true to my Maria. Please, don't feel that you need to give me your answer now. I realize it's a major decision. Take your time, and by all means, talk it over with Maria. Do you have any questions?"

"Just one," I replied timidly.

"Go ahead. Shoot! Don't be bashful."

"Well, sir, I was just wondering. Are you a hard or a soft man?"

He slapped me on the back.

"To be perfectly honest with you, son, I rarely eat Mexican food. It gives me indigestion."

CHAPTER TWENTY-FOUR

Maria

One of the many things I liked about Maria; she possessed a keen sense of humor. That is to say, she laughed at all my jokes. While Maria maintained her perennially upbeat and playful personality, I on the other hand, found myself declining into a blur of alcohol consumption, my moods swinging like a wrecking ball from walking on air one day, to lying on the sofa staring blankly at the ceiling the next. Unfortunately, that's how Maria found me one Saturday, in Phil's and my apartment, an empty Vodka bottle nearby on the floor, an ashtray overflowing with reeking cigarette butts, and my *Notice of Academic Probation* letter on my chest.

"It's past noon," Maria chastised me. "What in the world are you doing?"

"I'm contemplating the ceiling," I responded. "I find it to be, at once, meditative and enthralling."

"You do, do you?"

"Indeed. You might say, I've become an avid ceiling fan."

"Any self-respecting ceiling fan would generate a refreshing breeze. You, on the other hand Bruce, are excreting a skanky odor. This whole room stinks."

"That's what I've been trying to tell him," Phil chimed in. "The air in here is *toxic*. My house plants are dying."

Maria snatched the official-looking correspondence from the Dean of Students off my chest.

"What is this?"

"Oh, that? I meant to mention it to you. I'm flunking out of school."

"Is it due to your attendance?"

"Actually, it's more due to my *lack* of attendance."

"We need to talk!"

"Okay. You're not pregnant, are you?"

"Absolutely not . . . and we'll talk after you *shower*."

"Do you want to come with?"

"No. Now, get in there!"

I looked at Phil.

"Me neither. Maria and I showered together just before you woke up."

I pulled myself to my feet, then shuffled to the bathroom. My mouth was dry and my head throbbed. I felt sluggish and queasy. My shower, however, invigorated me. Phil and Maria were right. I was overdue. The soapy water swirling down the drain had a cappuccino appearance to it. If I were Phil, I wouldn't want to be the next person to use the facility. After drying off, I wrapped my towel around my waist, brushed my teeth (causing my gums to bleed) and stepped back into our living area.

"There. Better?"

"I'm worried about you, Bruce," Maria sobbed.

"*I'm* worried about myself. I'm not sure, but I think I may have PTSD. Either that, or demonic possession. Maybe I need an exorcism . . . or a Bloody Mary."

I could see that Maria was not amused. Even Phil remained stoic.

"Bruce. Maria is right. You need to square yourself away."

He was dead serious.

"Okay, okay you two. It's clear you guys are earnest, and you're right. So, I'll tell you what. I promise. I'll regularly attend classes, study diligently, graduate, and build my fortune the old fashioned way."

"How's that? With hard work and determination?"

"Actually, I thought, if Maria will still have me, I'd marry into money."

"I don't know what you see in him," Phil addressed Maria.

"I see a wounded veteran."

"How do you know for sure he's not just an irremediable asshole?"

"I don't. That's what worries me . . . more than anything else."

I more or less kept my word. It alarmed me to see the other side of Maria. Until that minor incident, she never exhibited any moodiness or ill temper. She was, however, known to cry effusively at times, like when Olga Korbut scored a 9.8 at the 1972 Olympics on the uneven parallel bars, Marvin Gaye sang the *National Anthem,* and any performance of *A Day's Long Journey into Night.* She was commendably solicitous for the welfare of animals and small children. To her further credit, Maria was also deeply concerned with those in society who were less fortunate than she, and thanks to her father, that was like 99 percent of the population. I admired the work she did in the Mexican community, helping recent immigrants establish themselves without falling prey to those who would exploit them. Of all her attributes and qualities, beyond her bubbly personality, intellect, and kindness, I think what attracted me most to Maria, however, was her smoking-hot body.

As I rounded the informational kiosk at the center of the quad, and turned down the path towards the *Jose Antonio Maciel-Iglesias Performing Arts Building* (which was named for Maria's father), I spied my fiancée sitting on the chair-height limestone-capped brick retaining wall. In her short plaid skirt and low-cut sweater, I could see that she was attracting quite a bit of attention. Her sitting there, legs crossed as her long, raven-black hair danced in the spring breeze, inspired one guy to stop and tie his shoe. A male professor put down his attaché case, pushed up his sleeve to read his watch, and pretended to be waiting for someone. More than a few male students decided that this would be a fine place to get in a little last-minute reading before their next class, and one coed, wearing *Birkenstock* sandals, walking shorts, and a folksy print top, stopped, ostensibly, to ask Maria for directions.

When Maria spied me, she jumped to her feet and ran excitedly into my embrace. The professor picked up his case and proceeded on his way. Books snapped shut as the area was quickly evacuated. The butch chick thanked Maria for the directions, then with a wave, continued on her way.

"Oh, Bruce. Look! She's going the wrong direction," Maria exclaimed.

"Don't worry about her," I reassured my naive little valentine. "She knows where she's going."

"How do you know that?"

"Because I recognize her from the front desk at the administration building. She works there giving people directions. She's one of the girls who hands out those little maps of the campus with the visitor's destination circled in red."

Maria looked confused.

"I'll explain it to you someday," I told her.

Taking my arm, Maria peered at me lovingly with her big brown eyes, wearing a toothy smile, as we strolled the sinuous paths of the campus, ending up at the duck pond. We sat on the bench and shared some bean dip and chips that she brought, as we chatted.

"This dip is a prototype for a new product my father intends to test-market in Texas," Maria explained. "What do you think of it? They have been working on it in the test kitchen now for over a month."

"It's good. It tastes almost as if someone blended refried beans, picante sauce, shredded *Monterey Jack* cheese, and chili powder, together and baked it in a 350 degree oven until hot and bubbly, stirring frequently."

"It also has cream cheese and a touch of cumin. I'll tell him you like it. It will mean a lot to him. He also wanted me to ask if you could put your hands on that Silver Star. He's decorating the office that will be yours, and thinks it will look good in a shadowbox of some sort, on your credenza. He wants to send it off to the framing gallery he uses for his personal art collection."

"I think it's in my parent's basement. I'll check next time I go home."

"Talking about home, are you ever going to take me with you to Chicago and introduce me to your parents, or are you *that* ashamed of me?"

"Oh, Maria. With the exception your of keenness for the *Bee Gees*, I'm not ashamed of you, and you know it."

And how can you mend a broken heart?
How can you stop the rain from falling down?
How can you stop the sun from shining?

"I want to show you off to the entire world . . . just not my parents, right now."

"But why? Why can't I go home with you next time you visit?"

"Well, first of all, my parent's house is very small. It's your quintessential Chicago bungalow. I actually sleep in the basement next to the furnace when I'm home. It has an electronic ignition and makes a hideous clicking sound before cycling on with a loud woof. Believe me. My parent's house is nothing like your fathers palatial property in Wisconsin, on Geneva Lake."

"I don't care. I want to see where you grew up. I want to meet your family. I want to see where you went to high school . . . where you hung out."

"It's just a mundane working-class neighborhood. It's not at all like what *you're* used to," I argued. "And there's one other thing you need to know, Maria. I don't *have* the same kind of close, open relationship with my parents that you have with your father. Not all people are like that."

"Are you saying that your folks don't know you're engaged?"

"Well, not exactly. Actually, what I'm trying to say, Maria, is that my parents don't know I'm engaged to a *Mexican* girl."

Maria looked at me with shock. "Are your parents prejudiced? Is that what you're trying to tell me?"

"I don't know if *prejudiced* would be exactly the word I'd use, although I suppose it *could* describe them. I'm thinking, however, brazenly *bigoted* would more accurately define how they view Mexicans."

"So why do you think your parents are that way? Do you think that they're afraid for you to marry a Mexican girl?"

"No. I don't honestly think that's it. I think what they'd be more afraid of is that if I *do* marry a Latina, we might move into the neighborhood and have kids. They don't like Mexicans very much in that part of the city. They prefer that 'wetbacks' stay in the Little Village district."

"Your parents sound very narrow-minded."

"I'm adopted, you know. Thank God. It's my only solace."

"No. I didn't know that."

"I always suspected it, but they never told me . . . at least not until I was almost 20 years old."

"I wonder why they waited so long."

"I don't know. Perhaps they were deferring until they were sure they wanted to keep me. Tell me more about *your* family."

"Well, as you know, my mother died when I was quite young. I have only the vaguest memories of her. I was raised solely by my father. He didn't even hire a nanny or an *au pair* to help out, or anything like that, although he could well have afforded it. I grew up in the business, playing in his office, and helping in the research kitchen. He's a wonderful father. Once a year, we travel to his hometown in Michoacán, Mexico to visit family. He's like a celebrity down there. With his own money, he has built and staffed a health clinic, put an addition on the school, and constructed a rectory for the church."

"And, don't forget. He also bought you a *Corvette*."

"Well, yeah. That, too. It's one of only 25 1970 *LT-1s* built with the special purpose *ZR-1* option, you might be interested to know."

"So what does *that* do for you?"

"The *ZR-1*? Well, let's just say that in a dual, your Mach I Mustang would eat my dust, while on the other hand, I would have a difficult time keeping up with a *Phantom Jet* . . . if he lit up the afterburners."

CHAPTER TWENTY-FIVE

Vista Lago

After a pleasant lunch at *Charly O's* with Sunita, one of Maria's sparklingly sprightly sorority sisters, who was in town for our wedding, Maria and I stood, hand in hand, on the Williams Bay Municipal Pier at the appointed time. Her father insisted on providing water taxi service to us as an excuse to pilot his 40 foot, 1948, *Chris Craft* enclosed bridge, aft cabin, cruiser. This was the boat's first summer on the water after a comprehensive two and one-half year restoration at *Gage Marine*. The gratifying outcome was a 25-year-old yacht, as pristine as the day she was launched, and rechristened *Fantasma Del Lago*, a great improvement over the original *Buoy, Oh Buoy*.

Two blasts of the cruiser's horn announced its arrival as Mr. Maciel expertly swung the craft's stern to port, then reversed the engines at precisely the perfect instant, so that the boat merely kissed the rubber bumpers on the dock. This skilled maneuver, and the subsequent application of power and reverse power, precluded the necessity of mooring the boat while Maria and I boarded. (It reminded me of a hovering Huey helicopter.) We merely stepped from the dock onto the stern spar deck and then down into the aft well deck, which afforded us comfortable, elegantly sophisticated upholstered seating and a well-stocked bar, of which I availed myself.

My immoderate and problematic drinking persisted, despite the fairy-tale life I enjoyed.

As Mr. Maciel pushed the twin chrome-plated throttles forward, he called over his shoulder to us, "I trust you're both wearing deck shoes."

He obsessed about proper footwear on his unblemished boat.

"Yes, Father," Maria assured him. "I am, but Bruce insisted on wearing his golf shoes."

Although I'm certain he knew she was kidding, I *did* notice him glancing up into the boat's panoramic rear-view mirror, his stern eyes meeting mine.

With the application of more power to the two *Pirkins Sabre 225TI* diesel engines, the perfectly trimmed vintage cruiser rose on the water to planing speed. The skipper of a sleek *Bayliner* ski boat, bobbing in the bay, gave us a big smile and a thumbs-up as we passed. I'm not sure if it was our pristine classic *Chris Craft* that impressed him most, or if it was Maria, who was in the process of striping off her swim wrap to reveal her California sweetheart bikini and perfect dark-skinned body. I'm guessing he liked the total package. I know I did. I sipped my martini and sat back for the ride.

It was an unusually warm autumn day, perfect for being on the water. Seagulls followed our steady progress across the lake. The sails of sloops and dinghies and ketches billowed in the southerly breeze. In the distance, a bright yellow, vintage bi wing, cabin series, *Waco* floatplane skimmed across the surface, then lifted gracefully into the sky. The pilot tipped her wings as she passed over us, in deference to another art deco relic from the past, preserved. Maria and I waved, each with both of our arms, crossing them high over our heads. The plane circled for another low pass.

"I'm going to learn to fly one of those things someday," I told Maria.

"You'll need to cut back on your drinking to do that."

"Well then, maybe not."

Sitting back down, the two of us cuddled, exchanging a few kisses along the way. It may sound cliché, but it felt as if I didn't have a care in the world. Life on the lake seemed like that. Back on Chicago's south side, where I grew up, opening a fire hydrant on a hot summer's day served as our idea of recreation.

The boat's engines changed pitch, and we settled a foot or so deeper in the water, as Maria's dad throttled back for our approach to pier 585, *Vista Lago*, (the Maciel's year-round lake home). I could see an army of workers preparing for the 24 guests the house would accommodate over the weekend of our wedding. There were landscapers and painters, carpenters and masons.

The structure itself stood as a wood-framed, three-story Victorian with a four-story tower. Built in 1888, the house sat high upon a point of land jutting into the lake, offering expansive views from the broad porch that entirely wrapped the mansion. On this weekend, the 12 bedrooms, living spaces, and kitchen would be attended to by the addition of four agency workers, but normally managed competently, including the grounds, by Pilar and her husband Jorge, who resided in a quaint and cozy cottage on the property. They also tended the expansive vegetable garden and henhouse. Mr. Maciel liked his eggs fresh.

Jorge waited for us on the pier as Mr. Maciel docked the boat. I threw him the bow line, which he lashed loosely to a pile. After Maria next tossed him the stern line, Jorge then made fast the craft with the exact amount of latitude prescribed by the finicky skipper.

"*Buen trabajo, Jorge,*" Mr. Maciel complimented the groundskeeper, then cut the engines, jumped to the pier, and scrambled up the 130 stairs to the house. He maintained a home office and was always eager to get back to business.

Jorge greeted Maria with a long hug before reluctantly shaking my hand.

"*Buenos dias, Señor Bruce.*"

"*Buenos dias, Jorge,*" I replied.

Jorge and I were known to banter with one another from time to time. I don't believe he cared very much for me.

"I just saw four Mexicans out on the lake in a two-man dingy," I informed him.

He stared at me with a confused look on his face.

"You don't understand? Let me see. How do I say this in Spanish?" I pretended to be thinking. "Oh, I know! I know . . . *Cuatro* sink-o."

Jorge frowned.

"What do you use for birth control, Mister Bruce? Your sense of humor?"

"So, you don't think I'm funny, hey?"

"Nope. I think you're a typical, Chicago south-sider, and I'm surprised that Señor Maciel would accede to you marrying his precious daughter."

"Do you know how many Mexicans it takes to screw in a light bulb?"

"No. Do you know how many entitled white guys it takes to screw in a light bulb?"

"Personally, I'd just hire a Mexican to do it."

"I heard that you missed your eighth-grade graduation because you had jury duty. Is that true?"

"Well, when I was in the *sixth* grade . . ."

"Now, I suppose you're going to tell me a sob story about how those were the toughest three years of your life."

"No. What I was about to say is that when I was in the sixth grade, the Mexican kid down the block got *my* bicycle for Christmas."

"Boys. Boys." Maria came between us. "Enough is enough."

"Do you know you're marrying a bigot, Miss Maria? You should marry a nice successful Mexican man."

"Oh, yeah," I offered. "Like one who has his own lawnmower?"

"Please!" Maria raised her voice to me. Jorge walked away with a smirk on his face as he started to climb the stairs.

"He may act as if he's only joking," I told Maria, "but I say that man truly doesn't approve of me."

"Oh, don't pay any heed to him. He's my godfather, but he thinks he's my guardian angel. Jorge's just afraid that you'll talk me into engaging in some lowbrow, white trash activity."

"White trash activity? Like what?"

"Like having sex while going through the carwash or something sick and perverted like that."

"It never crossed my mind."

"See."

"Until now, that is."

"Bruce!"

"Well, you're the one who brought it up."

"Forget it! Just forget it."

"How can I forget it *now*? You planted the idea in my psyche."

"I'm warning you, Bruce."

"I actually worked at a carwash when I was in high school, you know."

"You never told me that before."

"Sure. It was my responsibility to wipe the vehicles completely dry after they emerged from the 'hurricane' blower. Of all the positions at the *Super Wash*, mine was the choice job, because it was where the tips were conferred."

"So, did you make pretty good money then?"

"Not bad. The average tip was a buck. Some folks tipped more; others tipped less. Born-again Christians often handed to me, in lieu of cash, a thoughtful little note printed on business card stock: *Best tip yet . . . Accept Jesus Christ as your savior.*"

"I'm sure they meant well though."

"Probably, but we car wash workers all pretty much thought of them as assholes. For quite a few of my coworkers, it inspired them to become steadfast agnostics, and one, Joe Shimkus, after being stiffed like that a few too many times, went on to reject his devout Presbyterian upbringing and join the Church of Scientology."

From the first landing of the stairway leading to the house, Jorge yelled, "He's only after your father's money. Before he met you, his greatest ambition was to own a fireworks stand."

How Jorge knew about the fireworks stand thing, I can't tell you.

"One more word, Jorge," Maria sternly warned, "and you'll be walking down the service drive with one month's severance pay in your pocket." She turned to me, "And as for you, Bruce. Any more racist jokes and you'll be playing a flute solo on our wedding night, if you get my drift."

"Yes, ma'am."

"So, we understand each other perfectly, then?"

"Absolutely."

"And you have nothing more to say for yourself?"

"Well, I'm still thinking about that carwash thing. You don't suppose you'd reconsider? They have the brushless wash, rain-water rinse, and hurricane dryer, you know, plus for only an extra 25 cents, the special hot wax application."

"No! And don't ever bring it up again."

CHAPTER TWENTY-SIX

Our Wedding

So, there I stood, in my rented, baby-blue tuxedo from *Genghis*, and union made patent leather shoes by *Florsheim*, looking swank, standing sanguinely in front of two hundred or so well-wishers, my best man Phil Hadley, similarly attired with rings in hand, reassuringly at my side. I felt a little apprehensive when the organist began to play the "Bridle Chorus" from the opera *Lohengrin*. Accompanied by viola, a somber soprano, standing stoically in a strapless chiffon shift sang:

> *Wie Gott euch selig weihte, zu Freude weihn euch wir.*
> *In Liebesglücks Geleite denkt lang' der Stunde hier!*

I know. I know. You really had to be there. It's my understanding, from musical experts who dissect and scrutinize such things, that Wagner's music is far better than it sounds. Why else do brides everywhere continue to be presented to their guests accompanied by a wedding march from the pen of Adolf Hitler's favorite composer and incandescent beacon of German National Socialism?

Anyhow, I was lost in thought, contemplating the opera's curious premise, trying to imagine just what a knight transported in a swan-drawn watercraft might look like, and how you'd ever waterski behind one of those things. At that moment, my heart skipped a beat or two as I glanced up to glimpse, gliding down the aisle, an angelically alluring and beautiful woman, befittingly, as winsome and magical as a Rhine maiden. She was Maria's maid of honor, Robin Fox. This was unfortunate. I shouldn't have to explain that to you unless you're a dunce. Universal justice, if such a notion even exists, would have demanded that, in the very least, my eyes be burned out with a red-hot fireplace poker . . . but that would have been entirely another opera altogether (*Samson and Delilah*) and, in deference to my sophomore year English teacher, Mrs. Carlson, who once cited me for doing conspicuous damage to the English language, and who, brandishing a red marker, slashed away with vigor at my convoluted run-on sentences, awarding me a

D-minus, I don't want to risk mixing my musical metaphors. (*Try diagraming that sentence on the blackboard, you old hag!*)

Just for the record, I'm blaming PTSD for everything from my malapropos behavior at the bachelor party, (and by the way, if you're straight, never leave it to a gay groomsman to plan this sort of event, however, if you're gay, by all means do) to my arrest and incarceration on our honeymoon.

The bridesmaid dresses Maria had chosen, charitably exposed generous cleavage, and I was mesmerized watching Robin's chest heave, ever so subtly, in and out as she breathed. Father Bob, I could tell, had also taken notice of Robin's nice bazongas, but carried on commendably with his priestly duties.

Now, I bet you thought I was going to insert a sick and inappropriate altar boy joke here, but, even with my exceptionally low standards, I can't come up with a good one just now that doesn't include a nun, a lawyer or a Rabbi.

After the photos there at the church, we drove to the reception in Ronnie Hines's ground pounding, Hemi-powered, nitromethane fueled, supercharged Road Runner. He had the slicks on, the headers wide open, and we turned in an elapsed quarter mile time of 10.9 seconds at 126 miles per hour. Subsequently, as prescribed by Einstein's theory of special relativity, we arrived at the club a couple of nanoseconds into the other guests' future. Despite a few intrinsic problems with the slight time dilation, once there, we all had great time acting like your prototypical congregation of witless chowderheads.

Our wedding party started out with four ushers, a best man, a maid of honor, and six groomsmen; one for each bridesmaid. (After hours of heavy drinking, however, the evening ended up with six groomsmen for one bridesmaid and none for the rest.)

Ann Dunning wore one of her short skirts, so Mike Jozik and a few of the other guys who were sitting around her kept dropping their napkins on the floor, and there was a five-piece band that played, for some inexplicable reason, *Proud Mary.* We also did the *Hokey-Pokey*—puttin' our left foot in and puttin' our left foot out--and then, after we turned ourselves about, we all wondered why, but by that time it was too late to salvage any self-respect.

The photographer snapped some pictures of Maria tossing her bouquet to the single girls. He then passed out his business cards and offered "modeling opportunities" to the more attractive ones.

We proceeded to observe most of the time-honored rules of wedding reception protocol, without ever letting such stuff as decorum or dignity get in the way of our fun. Jeff Jens and Lynn Erickson regularly popped outside to her *Pinto* to smoke a joint, and before the evening concluded, the two of them had eaten most of the wedding cake. There were girls dancing together, girls dancing alone in their stocking feet, guys in tuxedos on their hands and knees, puking their guts out in the club's parking lot.

Our wedding reception was held at the *Shore Club* in Lake Geneva. A little drunk, Phil was still at the microphone blabbering on with his toast, " *. . . and love does not consist of standing around idly gazing at one another, but looking outward . . ."*

No one was listening. In fact, the band had impatiently begun to play, and wedding guests were already dancing. It was loud and boisterous. My parents cowered in a corner, uncomfortably clasping their drinks tightly to their chests. There were 250 guests, and it appeared as though 248 of them were Mexicans, the males wearing bolo ties, and the females, implausibly short backless dresses with plunging necklines. Virtually all the ballroom staff were also Mexican.

"Look at them! This has got to be like their worst nightmare," I nearly shouted, close to Maria's ear, for her to hear me over the pandemonium, as we danced to the mariachi band. If our wedding reception had a theme, it would have been *Mexican cliché.*

"I feel sorry for them, nonetheless," Maria countered.

"Don't. They did this to themselves . . . with their narrow minds. Did you do as I asked?"

"Yes, but I think it's cruel."

"Good. So then, you instructed the wait staff to communicate in only Spanish when addressing my folks?"

"I did. How do you think your father ended up with that rhubarb margarita? I bet it's just awful."

"He's drinking it!"

"Indeed, he is. He has no alternative. And, I told the bartender that for his next drink, no matter what he tries to order, your dad is to be served a fuzzy navel."

"And if he drinks that?"

"A slippery nipple."

"Maria. You're terrible! I never saw this side of you before. What else don't I know about you?"

"Keep those martinis coming and you might just find out."

Maria's cousin cut in, leaving me, momentarily, without a dance partner. One of her uncles approached me and shook my hand with zeal.

"I know it sounds hackneyed, but you are a lucky man. Maria is one-in-a-million."

"Oh, I know it, sir. You don't need to convince *me*."

"Hey, Bruce!" came a familiar female voice from my past. "Great party."

"Toni. What the hell are you doing here?"

"I'm crashing your wedding reception. What did you think?"

"I'm thinking that it may not be terribly appropriate for you to be here, in-as-much as you're an old girlfriend. I don't think I really would want to be meeting any of *Maria's* former beaus here tonight, and you know what they say . . . what's good for the goose, is good for the gander."

"Oh, don't worry. I'm not here to make trouble. Believe it or not, I'm dating your photographer. I came with him."

"Too much information."

"No. No. I *came* with him as in I traveled here with him . . . in his car. How have you been, Bruce? It's been awhile."

"Fine. I've been just fine. How about you?"

"Oh. I'm fine, too. I think about you, though."

"You do?"

"Yeah. I do. Let me ask you, Bruce. Do you still have any of the photos I sent you while you were in Vietnam? Did you keep any of them?"

"I'm sorry, Toni. I hope you won't be offended, but I sold them, and I have to say, I got a pretty penny for them, too."

"You sold them?"

"Yeah. To a lonely Master Sergeant over in the second brigade. I have to tell you, he seemed to really appreciate them, especially the one of you on the swing."

"The one of me on the swing? You know, it's hard to take action shots with a *Polaroid*. Too slow a shutter speed or something like that. We went through two 100-Series film packs to get that shot just right."

"Well, the textural feel of the photo's composition was terrific, while your photographer's use of lighting heightened the contrast between the background and your image, helping to give more presence to your excellent form."

"How did you feel about the interplay of sunlight and shadow?"

"Oh, it was great! And I liked the toning. It was simple but effective."

"Was that your favorite photo?"

"No. Actually, I most enjoyed the one of you standing in front of the Christmas tree, with a pout; as if you didn't get what you wanted for Christmas."

"I don't remember that one. What was I wearing?"

"That was it. Just a pout."

"Did you, at least, keep that one . . . since it was your favorite?"

"Nope. I'm sorry to confess I sold it too, but I got an extra fifty cents for it, inasmuch as it had a touching holiday motif. In fact, you were the subject of that Master Sergeant's personalized Christmas cards that next holiday season. Everyone on his list received a copy of your image."

"You know, you're a real jerk, Bruce."

"That's what a lot of people have said. But, that was before Maria. I'm a changed man now, since I met her. I'm a different person. Look, my parents are over there in the corner. I'm sure they would be thrilled to visit with you."

"Yeah. That might be a good idea. I always liked your mom. She's so sweet."

"And she was always equally . . . how should we say . . . *impressed* by you."

Toni took off in the direction of my folks. I called after her.

"Just a small piece of advice."

She turned.

"What is it?"

"Any time you find yourself at a wedding reception with piñatas, and a dozen guys named Jose, all of whom have shotguns in their pickup trucks . . . don't stay 'til the very end."

"Thanks. I'll remember that."

I joined my best man, Phil, who was now at the bar.

"How's it going, guy?"

"Great. Just great."

"Thanks for standing up for me today."

"It's *my* honor, friend. Thanks for asking me. I have to tell you. That was quite an interesting bachelor party the other night."

"It was, wasn't it?"

"Who's that?"

"Where?"

"Over there with your parents . . . that girl dressed like a hooker."

"Oh. Just an old girlfriend. She used to write to me when I was in Vietnam."

"Well, she and your mom really seem to be hitting it off. Would you mind if I asked her to dance?"

"My mom?"

"No. Your ex-girlfriend."

"Go ahead. Knock yourself out. She's nothing to me. I've got Maria now. Maria's all I could ask for."

"Your marriage will be better off for it."

Phil excused himself and approached my parents.

"Hello, Mr. and Mrs. Johnson. Swell reception, isn't it?"

My folks agreed, unconvincingly.

"What's that concoction you're drinking, Mr. Johnson? It looks quite unusual."

"I'm not sure. I ordered a Manhattan but got this instead. Nobody seems to speak English around here. You can't communicate with them. This is America! These people should learn to speak American."

"They do speak American . . . *Central* American."

"Very funny."

My father took a sip of his cocktail.

"Yuck. This drink is awful! What the hell is this?"

"Looks like you've got a slippery nipple there, Mr. Johnson," Toni suggested.

"I beg your pardon."

"Your drink. It looks like a slippery nipple."

"Look here, young lady," my mother cut in. "We'll have none of that smutty talk from you. Not with *my* husband, you little slut."

"So, you're Toni?" Phil asked. "Bruce told me that you used to write to him while he was in the service. I'm Phil . . . Bruce's best man."

"Nice to meet you, Phil."

Toni eyed Phil up and down, lasciviously.

"It's true, you know," she sensually murmured as she pulled him close by his cummerbund.

"What's true?"

"I *am* a little slut . . . and there's something about weddings that gets my motor running. Do you want to dance?"

Phil gasped, choking on the garnish in his drink. Toni was aghast.

"Are you okay? Do you need the Heimlich maneuver?"

"No. No. I'm all right."

"Thank God. I was afraid that you were going to croak before I had the chance to jump your bones."

Once again Phil commenced retching. The expression on Toni's face conveyed a real sense of concern.

"You know, I'm not sure if I should be feeling insulted here or what?"

"I'm so very sorry. I apologize. Yes. Let's dance. I would very much enjoy dancing with you."

The band played *Smoke Gets In Your Eyes* as Phil and Toni swayed imperceptivity on the dance floor, her head on his shoulder, his mouth close to her ear.

Meanwhile, I ordered another vodka martini and watched Maria as she danced with her father. She looked so beautiful and happy. I could hardly fathom how fortunate I was to be married to this woman, and to think, it all came about because of my Silver Star and her newspaper article.

Phil rejoined me at the bar after his very intimate dance with Toni, walking stiffly, like a robot. He looked drained.

"Seems like you could use a cold shower, my friend," I observed.

"I'm afraid it's too late for *that*," Phil responded.

"Oh. I'm very sorry. Remember, that's a rented tuxedo you're wearing. I hope it's not premature to say that."

"Look, Bruce. I just wanted to warn you that you might want to keep an eye on your father. I think he may be getting pretty drunk."

"What makes you think that?"

"He just came back from the bar with a 64 ounce strawberry sriracha margarita. The thing's the size of a frigging fish bowl!"

By midnight, the reception was slowly winding down. My Grandpa Johnson was leaving with his arm around the shoulder of one of the waitresses, and the phone number for the club's fetching events manager in his pocket. Some of the club's staff were already beginning to clear the tables and clean up. The sounds of dishes clanking, and Spanish conversation emanated from the kitchen. The banquette room was a haze of stale smoke. Most of the guests had, long ago, expressed their good wishes and left the party. The exceptions were some of my friends from the Army and a few budding romances indefatigably slow dancing to the band's now lethargic melodies.

"Why don't you lose the wife, and come with us to *White Castle* for some sliders?" Loren Anderson suggested, punching my shoulder. "You never know when you're going to see your old Army buddies again."

"I can't say exactly why," I reluctantly answered, "but my intuition tells me that it probably wouldn't be a good idea tonight. Maria's been acting a little testy today for some reason."

Loren shook his head and pursed his lips. "Women! You better get used to it my friend. They ain't going to change."

CHAPTER TWENTY-SEVEN

Our Honeymoon

Maria was still sound asleep when I awoke to the first rays of a rising sun and the calls of seagulls outside our open window. A cool October breeze, blowing off Geneva Lake, induced the sheers, hanging over our balcony door, to a billowy ballet. As stealthily as possible, I slipped out from under the covers and tiptoed to my travel bag, unzipping it virtually one zipper tooth at a time so as not to disturb my slumbering bride. With equal furtiveness, I slipped into my casual clothes and strapped on my wristwatch. It was five minutes after six.

"Hey, Maria," I announced. "I'm going downstairs to grab a cup of coffee and enjoy it by the lake. Did you want me to bring a cup back for you when I return?"

I saw the blankets move as Maria rolled onto her side, away from me. Only her beautiful dark-brown hair protruded from under the bedclothes.

"What time is it?" she mumbled, her voice muffled by the sheets. I think she may have been just a little hung-over from the reception.

"It's a few minutes past six. Did you want anything?"

"Yeah. I want you to get out of here and let me sleep another hour or so."

"They start serving breakfast at 7:30. You *do* want breakfast, don't you? It comes with our package."

"Where are my shoes?"

"Which ones? The ones you wore last night, or your walking shoes?"

"I don't care. Any shoe I can throw at you that will make you leave."

"Okay. I'm going. I'm going. I'll be down on the pier if you're looking for me."

"I won't be looking for you, so don't fall in the water."

I let myself out, testing the door to ensure it was locked, and hung the *do not disturb* sign on the doorknob. It was emblazoned with the image of a winking chambermaid holding her index finger to her lips. The implication seemed to be that the occupants were busy having sex in the room, and that the maid was cool with it. That made me think. This was, after all, our honeymoon. Perhaps Maria craved some tender early morning love-making, while I like a dunce, searched moronically for some strong coffee. Maybe that's why she was cranky. I inserted my key and pushed the door back open about 12 inches.

"Maria."

"Hmm."

"I was just wondering . . ."

Her shoe ricocheted off the door jamb missing my nose by less than an inch. *So much for that, brainchild.*

"Good morning, sir," a worker greeted me, turning off his vacuum cleaner and flipping the cord aside so that I wouldn't trip on it. Somehow, I managed to, nonetheless.

"I'm so very sorry, sir," he apologized profusely in a Mexican accent. "How clumsy of me."

That's what he said. What he was thinking, I'm confident, was something altogether antithetical to that, but tempered by the probable fact that he really needed this job.

"Good morning to you. Is there coffee somewhere?"

"Yes, sir. Just outside the main dining room, in the Vista Bar, we are currently serving a continental breakfast. Both a full menu breakfast and breakfast buffet, including an omelet station, will be available in the main dining room from 7:30 until 9:30."

"Thank you."

"You're welcome, sir."

I made my way to the Vista Bar. In the adjacent dining room, wait staff were industriously setting the tables for breakfast. I poured my coffee and took it outside with me. It was a brisk October morning, with just a few wispy cirrus clouds in the sky. Only a single motorized rowboat plied the glassy still waters of Geneva Lake, leaving a long V-shaped wave in its wake. I found a bench at the end of the pier and wiped the dew from the seat with my handkerchief before sitting down. A fisherman near me, his bait container and tackle box at his feet, cast his line with a whirr and a plop.

"Any luck?" I asked, because that's what I've always understood to be the customary way one greets a fisherman. My grandfather used to take me fishing when I was young, but I never grasped appeal of it.

"Two Large Mouths and a Catfish," he replied, pulling his stringer of fish from the water and holding it up, just in case I didn't want to take the word of a stranger. "There's a fine line between fishing and standing on the shore looking like an idiot. Do you fish?"

"No. I'm not a sportsman, but if I were, I think I'd like to shoot something with a high-powered rifle . . . like a mountain lion, for example."

"Hunting's okay, but I prefer fishing. Have you ever fired a gun?"

"A couple of times."

"Ever killed another living creature with one?"

"You know. Perhaps you're right. Maybe fishing *would* be a better sport . . . should I ever decide to become an outdoorsman, that is."

"It's relaxing. Fishing puts a person into a better frame of mind."

"What are you using for bait?"

Again, I knew from observation that this was another of those obligatory things one asks a fisherman.

"Mealworms."

I had no idea what those might be. I was sure, however, that they were manifestly disgusting and not something a non-fisherman would want to discover a colony of residing in his or her box of *Malt-O-Meal*.

"Do you live near here?"

"Over by Slades Corners. I work at the *River Valley Ranch* mushroom farm."

"So you're a mushroom farmer, then?"

"Yep."

"I don't think I ever met a mushroom farmer before."

"Many people don't realize it, but less than one percent of Americans are mushroom farmers."

"Is that so? I never imagined. So, you must be a 'fun guy' then."

"That's a stale old joke, but some people *do* find me fun to be around."

"Well, you haven't convinced *me* yet. Look. You're fishing after all."

"Well, I guess I am."

He offered his hand.

"By the way, I'm Gus."

I shot him a skeptical look.

"Fun Gus?"

"The one and only. Fun Gus the mushroom farmer. What do you do, besides annoy the local fishermen?"

"I just graduated from college in June . . . got married yesterday. I start my new job a week from Monday."

"Where's your bride?"

"She's still in bed . . . a little cranky this morning. I got pretty drunk last night, and things didn't go so well in the old wedding bed."

"Really?"

"And this morning, she tried to throw a shoe at me."

"Well, at least it wasn't her wedding ring. You better watch your Ps and Qs young man, or you'll wind up like me . . . baiting your own hook. One of the advantages of marriage is that you get to have sex whenever she wants. I think it was Ben Franklin who said 'Keep your eyes wide open before the wedding, half shut afterwards.' What line of work you going into?"

"Fast food."

"And, you needed a college degree for *that*?"

"I'm going to be the vice-president in charge of franchises," I replied with pride.

"You seem a little young and inexperienced to be a vice-president."

"It's my father-in-law's business."

"I see. I see. They call that nepotism, you *do* know. So you married the boss's daughter, hey?"

"Well, yeah, but it's supposed to be a good job . . . and I'll have a secretary."

The fisherman reeled in his line, which had drifted too close to shore, and recast it into open water.

"Hmm. A secretary, you say. I guess that will make you a pretty important person then. Are you going to have her place your phone calls?"

"I suppose so."

"And bring you your coffee?"

"Sure. And, I'll buzz her on my intercom when I want her to take dictation."

"You should have her keep one of those scheduling calendars for you with all of your appointments and planned activities diligently delineated, and deep in detail."

"I never thought of that."

"It's a good idea. She could plan your day to the tiniest particular . . . accounting for every minute of the workday . . . so that none of your valuable time is wasted."

"I like that idea!"

"And then you can buzz her on your trusty *Dictograph*, and say, *Miss. Jones. Clear my calendar. I'm going fishing today.*"

"I'm glad I ran into you. You're very astute."

"As a rule, mushroom farmers tend to be."

"Too bad you constitute less than one percent of the population."

"It would do away with a lot of horseshit if there were more of us."

"And turn it into compost for the garden!"

"Now you're getting it! And, there would be no more wars. Did you know that no armed conflict, in recorded history, has ever been initiated by a mushroom farmer?"

"No. I didn't realize that. Is it really true?"

"I can't think of any. Can you?"

"Now that you mention it, no. But, then again, you guys make up just one percent of the population, after all."

"Not unless you want to count the Crimean War of 1854."

"The Crimean War?"

"Yes. It's a little-known fact that Nicolas the First enjoyed harvesting mushrooms from the forests around Saint Petersburg."

"But that's not actually *farming* them."

"No. Not at all."

"So, as I was saying, statistically, you would expect one percent of wars to be started by mushroom farmers, but they aren't."

"They're started by politicians!"

"Exactly! Politicians who, like mushroom farmers, account for less than one percent of the general population."

"So, then there *is* a solution to the age-long quest for peace!"

"It's been right under our noses all of this time, my friend."

"How did you acquire all of this wonderful insight?"

"The hard way, I'm afraid. I was with the 1ˢᵗ Marine Division at the battle of Chosin Reservoir during the Korean War."

"I'm so sorry."

"Yeah. Me, too. Listen kid, and believe me when I tell you this. You don't ever want to see combat, no matter how noble you may think the cause. War is the last resort of fools."

Our Honeymoon Package

When making our *Shore Club* reservations, I naively opted for the all-inclusive "Honeymoon Package." Had I known how unfortunately things were going to turn out, however, and had I met my angler buddy sooner, I would have elected, instead, the three-day fishing deal that included a 16-foot aluminum boat with an *Evinrude Aquasonic* 7.5 horsepower motor, and a contour map of the lake.

Our honeymoon deal came with an expansive breakfast buffet, a sack lunch, (to take with us while hiking the shore path) and dinner, at the same table, with the same waiter, each night in the main dining room where dozens of other happy newlyweds toasted their futures together, giddy and in love. Unlike us, though, I suspect they were having sex.

There were, however, abundant alternative opportunities for recreation that Maria and I took full advantage of. We were less than 48 hours into our marriage, and Maria persisted in taking harsh exception to my "emotional numbness," and my alcohol consumption, and my indecisiveness, and my lack of focus and . . .

"Don't forget my inability to maintain personal relationships," I reminded her. "That's pretty profound too."

So, we kept active water skiing, playing tennis, shooting trap, and horseback riding. One afternoon, we climbed to the top of a 150-foot tall observation tower. (After we did, we both wondered why, but by then it was too late.) We also rented a canoe. This escapade nearly ended our already imperiled marriage because Maria couldn't seem to grasp the concept of coordinating our efforts and paddling on a prescribed course. She also stubbornly refused to abide by my helpful suggestions on proper "canoemenship." I knew right then and there that I would never consider hanging wallpaper with this woman. On the last day of our honeymoon, Maria went to the spa while I, for some inexplicable reason, used our discount and went golfing at the *Lake Geneva Playboy Club*.

If you think that having a cross bride can sap the fun out of a good honeymoon, try playing some golf. Golfing was the worst time I ever had while trying to have fun. Eighteen holes of golf were about as excit-ing as a Gordon Lightfoot concert and only marginally more entertain-ing than a colonoscopy.

At the last tee, I positioned the ball just inside my left heel, thank-ing God that this pathetic game was nearly over. Just nine or ten more strokes, I estimated, and I would be in the clubhouse merrily drinking vodka martinis. I chose a closed stance, in order to hold the beer I was drinking between my knees while I addressed the ball. Knowing that the kinetic energy transferred from my club to the ball is proportional to the mass of the club head and the square of its velocity, I took a mighty swing. If the smoke from the cigar I was gripping in my teeth hadn't gotten in my eyes, I doubt I would have sliced the ball as badly as I did, knocking a lady off her golf cart. It was just one of those unfortunate things.

This immediately got the attention of the eagle-eyed golf ranger. After performing CPR on the woman I beaned, he jumped into his ranger cart and came speeding after me. Instinctively, I made a run for it. The high-speed pursuit that ensued took us on a wild ride across the green, down the fairway, and into the rough. My driving was, admit-tedly, erratic. I was slightly impaired by the six-pack of *Heileman's Special Export* I had recently consumed. It was not a good situation. If caught, I would be looking at a minimum two-stroke penalty, perhaps three, I feared, if the woman, whom I beaned in the head, died.

My best chance was to out-maneuver him in the dogleg. There was no way I could prevail on the straightaway. My 50cc two-cycle *Suzuki*-powered cart was far outclassed by his specially equipped, police inter-ceptor *Kohler* engine. I tore through some flowerbeds, knocking over a purple martin house, and across the practice green. Blasting through a sand trap like a dune buggy, I neglected to rake the bunker. This, I later learned, was in violation of acceptable golf etiquette.

I was accustomed to driving a 300 horsepower *Mach I Mustang* with the special heavy-duty suspension. In contrast, my underpowered cart exhibited excessive body roll, a fair amount of oversteer, poor braking power, and a lack of body stiffness. This made it difficult for me to prop-erly compensate for my slip angles in the turns. I was, therefore, appre-hended after I lost control on some wet grass at the eighteenth green, (guarded by a pair of bunkers and some water, the pin placement was challenging, down and away near the far edge) and drove into a shallow pond just south of the clubhouse.

The Ranger approached me as I waded to shore. He had a shaved head and wore mirrored aviation-style sunglasses.

"Let me see your green fee ticket," he requested.

I fumbled for my billfold.

"Take it out of your wallet," he commanded, but in a firm but commendably tactful and non-threatening manner, as he was probably trained to do in ranger school.

I handed him the soggy slip of paper.

"Do you know why I pulled you over?" he asked.

I had a fair idea that it was for violating a litany of *United States Golf Association* rules or regulations, but I didn't want to incriminate myself. (RE: Miranda v. Arizona, 1966)

"No," I answered innocently.

"I very much suspect that you're drunk, Sir."

"Well, that explains it! I thought that my cart's steering was malfunctioning. I intended to report it to the golf cart attendant when I returned the machine. I feared perhaps it needed new tie rod ends, idler arm bushings, lower ball joints, and a front-end alignment."

The ranger turned and walked back to his cart, I presumed to get his copy of the rulebook. Meanwhile, all of the beer I had consumed was about to burst my bladder, so I snuggled up to a European larch that I calculated would nicely shield the restaurant diners' view of me. I couldn't have held it for another second.

At the end of the day, I was prohibited from further play on the course, and all public courses licensed by the state of Wisconsin, for a period of ninety-nine years. This was for the consumption of alcohol in public areas, disturbing and distracting other players, failure to prevent unnecessary damage, and gross disregard for the spirit of the game of golf. The only *criminal* act that I was charged with was public urination.

A deputy sheriff was dispatched to transport me, dripping wet and in handcuffs, to the Walworth County courthouse. Once there, I was arraigned by a judge whom they brought in special for my case. He had been at his daughter's house, celebrating his grandkid's second birthday when he received the phone call. The judge made a special point of telling me that.

Evidently, my pissing on a larch tree was the biggest crime they had had for some time in that part of southeast Wisconsin. The courtroom was packed with a team of three prosecutors, a court stenographer, a bailiff, a gaggle of newspaper reporters with accompanying photographers, and a gallery full of spectators. You might have thought that this was the Scopes Monkey Trial, or a scene from *To Kill A Mockingbird.*

In a blur of incomprehensible jurisprudent jargon, courtroom protocol, and legal maneuvering, it was determined the case would be held over until the next day so the judge could get back to the party in time for ice cream and cake. Since I had no permanent local domicile, or ties to the community, it was decided I would spend the night in jail, pending trial.

Pleading for mercy, I explained to the bench that spending the night in jail would pose an undue hardship, as I was on my honeymoon. (I didn't tell him how badly that was going.) The judge expressed his sympathy, and in consideration of the exceptional circumstances, graciously offered to arrange a conjugal visit. I sincerely thanked him but asked (jokingly) if it would be okay for me to see a photo of the woman first.

He looked straight at me with an unnerving twinkle in his eye.

"Who said anything about a *woman*?" he responded, nodding at the bailiff to take me to my cell.

Marriage Counseling

Admittedly, due entirely to my deplorable behavior, excessive alcohol consumption, flashbacks, and emotional numbing, it became necessary to procure guidance from a licensed professional counselor.

"You've been married for less than a month, and already you're in counseling?" Phil questioned me. "That's got to be some sort of a record."

"Maria's been going around telling our friends that I'm an alcoholic," I lamented.

"I didn't know it was supposed to be a secret."

"Well, I'm not. I may be a drunk, but I'm not an *alcoholic*."

"I fail to grasp the difference."

"I don't have to go to those goddamn meetings."

"How'd she get you into counseling anyhow? After your regrettable experience with 'mandatory' counseling in college, you told me you'd never participate in something like that again."

"Well, I have to tell you, Maria and I had quite a heated discussion on the subject. She was insistent, but in the end, I had the last word. I *always* do."

"What was that?"

"*Yes Maria.*"

"Just don't screw this one up, Bruce. Maria's your best shot for a wholesome future, and you're already on shaky ground."

As it turned out, the marriage and family therapist Maria and I procured for guidance was a worthless quack. She caught me looking down her blouse, interrupted my innocent curiosity as "emotional infidelity," and implored Maria to get out of the marriage just as soon as possible.

"Hey," I protested. "Aren't you supposed to help *salvage* our marriage by giving us advice on how to jazz up our sex life and such?"

She turned to Maria with a horrified look.

"You're not having sex with this creep, are you?"

Maria reassuringly shook her head to the contrary, mouthing the word "no."

"Thank God you had the good sense to not indulge in *that*! It's a filthy, perverted act invented by Satan to spread disease and corrupt society."

"Wait a minute! Just exactly what kind of marriage counselor are you anyhow?" I protested.

"A God-fearing *Pentecostal Christian* marriage counselor," she answered, "and I beseech you to get down on your knees this very instant and invite the Holy Spirit to enter your hardened heart."

"What?"

"You need to reject your polyamorous ways and accept the gift of salvation. I implore you to follow the Lord and put your trust in Him."

"Look. I'll be the first to admit that I'm not a perfect husband. I mean before we were married, I never knew there was a wrong way to unload the dishwasher or that my lack of fashion sense . . ."

At this point in our session, our counselor, incredibly, went into some sort of a trance. Her eyeballs bugged out of their sockets and she began to tremble. As she tensed, I could see the veins in her neck bulging. Her tremors became convulsions and sweat poured from her brow. Maria and I looked at each other incredulously. The woman crumpled to the floor and, lying on her back, her arms stiffly at her sides, began flopping around on the carpet like a fish on the boardwalk. It was a very awkward exhibition to witness, and it made me extremely uncomfortable. I wondered if I should call 911 or an exorcist or someone.

"What if she swallows her tongue?" I asked Maria.

"Stick your wallet between her teeth," she suggested.

"No way! You stick your clutch purse in her mouth."

"It's an *Yves Saint Laurent*."

"What else do you have? Anything from *J. C. Penney*?"

A surprisingly composed Maria, spurning the commotion, picked up a *People* magazine featuring the 25 most intriguing individuals of 1973, and calmly thumbed through it, totally ignoring the peculiar situation unfolding in front of us. Taking my cue from her, I pushed my chair back, and got up to examine the numerous framed certificates on the wall. I was impressed. Not only was this woman a certified *Transformational* leader, but she was also, I learned, the March *Charismatic* counselor of the month. There was also a photo of her riding a camel with the Pyramids of Giza looming in the background.

"We should go to Egypt sometime," I suggested to Maria.

"They frown on alcohol consumption there. It's a predominately *Muslim* state. It probably wouldn't be for you."

In the interval, a calm came over the crazed charismatic counselor on the carpet. She shook her head as if to clear her mind, as she pulled herself to a standing position, while studying her watch. She vocalized but it was just a jumble of syllables with no discernable syntactical structure. I'm not one hundred percent positive, but I'm fairly certain she was now speaking in tongues . . . either that or Swahili.

"I believe this will be our last visit, thank you," Maria told the therapist.

She took my arm and guided me towards the exit.

"Boy, that was some crazy counseling session," I commented to my bride on our way out to the car. "I wonder how she explains those carpet burns to her husband?"

"You know, Bruce, there are varying degrees of psychological dysfunction, and I just now realized that you are a modest example. I need to better appreciate that."

"And I need to retract my resistance to counseling. You were absolutely right. It *does* work!"

Kissing her deeply while I opened the car door, I pushed her down on the front seat and started to unfasten the buttons on her fur-trimmed puffer jacket from *Marshall Fields*.

"Stop, Bruce. When we get home."

CHAPTER THIRTY

Starting Work

In my new office, on the wall behind my desk, hung a large black and white line map of the United States. Color-coded stickpins represented our restaurant locations: red for franchisees and blue for company-owned stores. There was also a single yellow pin denoting Dinwiddle, Indiana, for which I have no explanation. My father-in-law, as threatened, had my Silver Star framed in a shadowbox decorated with molded brass bunting. It sat prominently on my new walnut credenza.

"Good morning, Son. Are you settling in all right?" Mr. Maciel asked as he entered my office. "You saw that you've got your own private lavatory with a shower, didn't you? I thought that you'd like that."

"Yes. Very much, sir. Thank you."

"I have one in my office, and I have to tell you, I use it more often than I would have ever guessed."

"The shower?"

"No. The toilet. Prostate issues. Not uncommon at my age. I don't think I've *ever* used the shower. I can't figure out what the hell prompted them to put *that* in there. And how about the car we leased for you? Is it satisfactory?"

"Yes. Very much so."

"It's American made, you realize. Not one of those supercilious German sports sedans that people purchase to stroke their egos. You don't need your ego stroked, do you? Because, if you do, or if you're distraught over the size of your penis, I could have the finance department lease a BMW for you."

"Oh, no, sir. It's a fine vehicle. I like it very much. I don't need an ostentatious car to build my self-esteem."

"I didn't think so. You've got a Silver Star, after all. What more do you have to prove? Well, I'm pleased you like the car. It was assembled at the Baldwin Avenue plant in Pontiac Michigan. You should know we have a company-owned restaurant nearby, and the factory workers account for the lion's share of our sales."

"Yes. I saw the stickpin in my map."

"They buy our Tacos, the least we can do is purchase one of their cars."

"Of course."

"And did you meet Ms. Dorsey, your secretary?"

"Yes, I did. She seems very pleasant."

"Ms. Dorsey has been with us from just about the beginning. She will be able to help you get oriented. I'll leave the two of you alone now to get acquainted. We'll have lunch in the test kitchen at noon. I want you to try out a couple of new menu ideas I have."

My father-in-law signaled Ms. Dorsey with a nod as he exited, and she entered my office carrying a steno pad.

"Please, take a seat," I offered.

My secretary looked to be in her middle fifties, about the same age as my mother. She was fit and smartly dressed in a jacket, white blouse, A-line skirt falling just above the knee, black opaque hose, and pumps .

"Did you want me to take some dictation?"

"Oh, no. Actually, I was just wondering if you had any ideas as to what I'm to do."

"You're the vice president of franchising."

"That's what I've been told, but what are my duties exactly?"

"You meet with prospective franchisees, travel to established stores, promote goodwill, endorse contracts . . ."

"I don't have to play golf, do I?"

"No. Mr. Maciel is strictly business. He has no tolerance for games."

"Thank God. I *hate* golf."

"I should *think* so."

"What do you mean by *that*?"

"Well, I just heard, through the grapevine as the say, that you recently played an unfortunate round at the Playboy Cub, whereby you shanked the ball on the 18th, causing some subsequent inconvenience."

"Yeah. And on top of that, the greens were perturbingly fast."

"Do you want to go over the itinerary for your upcoming trip?"

"Tennis is all right."

"Pardon me?"

"I'd play tennis if I *had* to, but just not golf."

"Fine. But we don't play tennis around here, either. Now, as I was saying, on Monday you're booked for an 8 a.m. flight out of O'Hare. A car will pick you up at your home at . . ."

"I *do* like to ski."

"Good. Skiing is a wonderful recreation. We have franchises in Salt Lake City and Denver. Perhaps we can plan your visits there to coincide with the ski season. May I continue with your itinerary?"

"Please. By all means."

"You will be picked up at your residence, at 5:45 . . ."

"I'm not one of those obnoxious 'hot dog' skiers, you understand. I just like to get back on some of the more remote runs and enjoy nature."

"*So*, you like nature. Good for you. However, I really *do* want to go over this itinerary with you, if you don't mind."

"I'm very sorry. Please. Go ahead."

It took Ms. Dorsey close to 10 minutes to go over my travel plans in minute detail. From what I could extract, from all the flight numbers, airlines, and hotels that she rattled off, it seemed that I would be going on a trip somewhere, in the near future.

"I'll have all of the paperwork and promotional material you'll need prepared by this afternoon. You can review it during the flight. Mr. Maciel has packed a lot into this trip. It may require a bit of multitasking.

"Multitasking! Nobody ever said anything about multitasking when I signed up for this position."

"You don't multitask?"

"No. Never. Not in my entire life. The whole concept sounds so, so, schizophrenic."

"This could be problematic. So, you have never performed more than one task at a time, then?"

"If it's any help, I did ride on a train once, while reading the newspaper."

"I'm going to need to think about this one for a while."

"Tell me, this multitasking, it isn't something one can fake his way through, is it?"

"I don't think so. But you might try acting as if you're full of yourself."

"Full of myself?"

"Yes. It's been my experience that people who multitask tend to extract some sort of self-worth from the activity."

"Is that so."

"Absolutely. They're quite like vegetarians in that respect."

"Vegetarians?"

"Never mind. I was off on a tangent. I'm sorry."

"What's this about vegetarians now? I want to know."

"Well, we have quite a problem with these people in our business . . . especially the animal rights activists who believe it's unethical to eat meat."

"If you don't eat it, it's just going to go bad in the refrigerator."

"I know, but try to explain that to them. There's a lot of misinformation out there. It's tough for those of us in the ethnological cuisine business. Did you know that there are some people who believe that we serve donkey meat in our restaurants?"

"Really? And here I always thought it was more of the equine genus. Did you know that animals in different countries make different sounds?"

"No. I didn't."

"Sure. In Vietnam, for example, the cats made a sizzling sound."

"Don't even joke like that. This is a subject that Mr. Maciel is very sensitive about."

"I'll try to remember. So, he's not a cat person then?"

"Please. Let's not discuss this any further. Is there anything else I can do for you?"

"Well, perhaps. You *did* say you take dictation, didn't you?"

"Yes, I do. Did you want to dictate something?"

"And you use those little scribbles and lines and dots?"

"Yes. That's the customary practice."

"That is so cool. Please, then, take this down. Are you ready?"

Ms. Dorsey shifted in her chair, switched her crossed legs, opened her steno pad, and rested it on her left knee.

"Yes. Go ahead."

"Dear Maria, (Maria's my wife)"

"I know. I attended your wedding."

"I am dictating this letter to you. Ms. Dorsey is taking it down employing *Gregg* shorthand. My new office has a private restroom with a shower and a telephone. Your father leased a Copper Metallic *Pontiac Grand Prix SJ* with Sandlewood leather interior for me. It has a 455 cubic inch engine with a *Rochester Quadrajet* four-barrel carburetor. If you need me to pick up a gallon of milk on the way home, it should have plenty of power. I'm expecting the gas mileage to be somewhat better than a *Boeing 747* executing a full-rated take off. Evidently, I'll be going on a business trip in the near future, and Ms. Dorsey wants me to multitask on the airplane. I suspect, however, that there may be some sort of an FAA regulation prohibiting the activity while in United States airspace. What makes me think that is . . . it just popped into my brain. I'm going to have our legal department research it. I positioned our wedding photo on my desk where I can view it while being a vice president and making executive decisions. You're my inspiration. Love, Bruce."

"Will that be all?" Ms. Dorsey asked.

"Yes. Thank you. Now if you could type that up, with a carbon copy for me, and get it out in today's mail, I would appreciate it. Or, better yet, send it as a Telex message."

"Very well. Does your wife have a Telex machine?"

"Well, just mail it then. And hold my calls. I want to do a little thinking outside the box."

"Okay."

"I need to get the complete picture, now that I'm going to be swimming with the sharks."

"Whatever you say, Mr. Johnson."

"If I'm going to drink the *Kool-Aid*, I want to be firing on all cylinders, after all. I don't want to be left at the altar for not eating my own dog food."

"I really have no idea what you're talking about, sir."

"It's *business-speak*. It's the jargon we businessmen use when talking shop."

"Oh. I see. How very interesting."

CHAPTER THIRTY-ONE

How My Grandfather Died

It was at about this time that my hard-living, heavy-drinking, philandering Grandpa Johnson, regrettably, began indulging in hallucinogens, setting in motion the unfortunate series of events leading ultimately to untimely his death in 1976. Gramps was an unabashedly corrupt, union boss. It was at Maria's and my wedding that he was introduced to one of my old Army buddies, Shoshoka Dekowta. Shoshoka had been our company armorer when I was with the 173rd Airborne Brigade. He was very proud of his Native American heritage, and possessed an expansive repertoire of "Custer jokes" . . . probably the most comprehensive body of work on the subject of "Little Bighorn humor" in existence at that time. For example:

Question: What kind of a shirt did Custer wear?

Answer: An *Arrow* shirt.

At the wedding, Gramps and Shoshoka got along swimmingly. Grandpa Johnson was fascinated to learn about Shoshoka's religion, which was Peyotism.

"So, you're telling me that it's absolutely legal to use peyote, sacramentally, so long as you are a member of the *Native American Church*?" my grandfather asked.

"It's our constitutional right," replied Shoshoka, "to worship in a manner the spirit moves us."

By the time Maria and I returned from our honeymoon, Grandpa Johnson had erected a sweat lodge in his yard and was in the process of converting the ladies from the *Lake Forest Garden Club* to his new religion. My father was beside himself and lit a candle at church after cocktails with Father Maher. His concern was that this new faith had somehow hijacked the Gramps we all knew and loved.

"I'm at my wit's end," my father told our empathetic priest. "My dad is on some crazy kick; abstaining from alcohol, deviate sexual activity, prideful behavior and married women."

"I had no idea it was that serious," Father Maher replied. "Perhaps we should consider an intervention."

Meanwhile, the Federal Express driver (completely oblivious to the fact that he was Gramps' drug dealer) made weekly deliveries of organically grown, seed raised, fresh cactus to my grandfather's house, while agents from the DEA were anchored on a 19-foot Cuddy Cabin about one hundred yards offshore of Gramps' 250 feet of Lake Michigan shoreline. Concomitantly, he was under surveillance by agents of the house subcommittee on organized crime for racketeering, so there was also a perennial *Illinois Bell* telephone van parked at the curb of his house.

Meanwhile, Grandpa became obsessively immersed in Indian culture, reading all he could on the subject. He took to carrying a suspicious medicine bag on his belt, owned a special ceremonial rattle and started referring to my youngest female cousin as "Little Paleface."

Peyote, my grandfather discovered, gave one a powerful and vivid sensation of flight. That's when he came up with the bright idea to incorporate his ingestion of the hallucinogenic with his hobby of hang gliding. He speculated that there would be a thrilling synergy from the combination.

"What do you think?" he asked me about the idea.

After some pensive contemplation, I told Gramps that I couldn't think of any drawbacks with his plan, so long as he made sure that his leg straps were secure and harness lines weren't twisted. So, in 1976, my Grandpa Johnson bit the dust; literally. He died, at the base of Camelback Mountain in Paradise Valley near Phoenix, while hang gliding. An officer from the Aviation Section of the Arizona Highway Patrol told my father that Gramps was probably doing close to 140 miles per hour when he hit the desert floor. In aviation terms, it's known as *landing hot*, but in this incident, it was a dry heat.

"People tend not to survive impacts like that," he explained.

Grandpa's tragic death, as is often the case in mishaps like this, was the result of a series of events. Any one of these, taken by itself, would be innocuous enough, but in *just* the right combination, the result was disaster.

First of all, my grandfather was 69 years old when he launched from the mountaintop that morning. Although he was in great shape for his age, Gramps *was*, admittedly, approaching his geriatric limits. Secondly, it was reported that there were some anomalous thermals and dangerous downdrafts on and around Camelback Mountain that day, which the Highway Patrol investigators point to as a contributing factor in his crash. Lastly, my Grandfather was flying, while stoned out of his mind, on mescaline.

Per his wish, Grandpa's burial ceremony was in accordance with the traditions of *both* the Catholic faith and that of the *Oklevueha Native American Church.* This basically meant that, after the customary Requiem Mass and celebration of the Eucharist, the somber congregation filed solemnly outside to the churchyard and participated in a Ghost Dance. The vivid mental picture of that haunting ritual will remain with me all my living days. Performed amid the shadows of a setting sun, it was poignant and inspirational; stirring and heart-rending. I would very much like to recount it here today, but, unfortunately, the English language is a woefully inadequate tool for the task. This curious spectacle brought a whole new dimension to the ageless issue of white people dancing. (Think Sonny Bono or John Denver here.)

After Grandpa Johnson's spirit had been blessed, consecrated, sanctified and ceremonially released, I'm a little concerned if they knew what to do with it in the next world. (A priest, a rabbi and an Ojibwa medicine man show up at heaven's gate. Saint Peter asks: *What is this . . . some sort of a politically incorrect joke?*) Even after six years of catechism classes, I'm not clear whether *all* souls become angels or if just certain ones are selected for the job based on their education and previous experience. If the latter is the case, then I think his résumé would dictate a different, less cherubic role for Gramps in heaven. I just can't imagine him as an angel, and certainly not one in the angelic choir. *He* would be the one shooting spitballs at the chorus director. (In that same vain, Gramps would make a very unlikely candidate for attendant at God's throne.)

I suppose my grandfather *could* be one of God's messengers to mankind, or perhaps a *guardian* angel, but, in those cases, I would caution against assigning him to any attractive young female subjects, as he will undoubtedly have some difficulty keeping it strictly professional. Especially in light of today's litigious environment, it would be lamentable if Gramps were the basis for a malevolent lawsuit against heaven, its officers and board of directors. It could be quite a pickle for them up there in heaven, as there wouldn't likely be any suitable attorneys in residence to defend it.

The other thing I wonder about is if Gramps was reunited with my Grandma Johnson when he arrived. (I don't know how these things work.) Assuming that she had been looking down from heaven on her husband's antics all of these years, I'm afraid she may have welcomed him to paradise with a swift kick in the nuts. My memory of her is that of a feisty woman who didn't take any crap. I've been told that, when young, Grandma was a "flapper" girl who wore her hair and dresses short, danced in a sexually suggestive manner, drank, smoked and attended "petting parties." She was pregnant with my father at age fifteen, (I think it may have had something to do with one of those petting parties.) and, hence, always cautioned me to use "protection." As I was only eight years old when she died, you can imagine how this constantly repeated piece of advice left me perplexed.

At his wake, a lot of people, who knew my Grandpa Johnson well, told me that I'm his "spittin' image." From photos of him when he was my age, we *do* look to be cut from the same proverbial cloth. My Aunt Mary often referred to us as Tweedledum and Tweedledee. Gramps, in turn, used to insist that she was Tweedledimwitted. My mother worried that Gramps was a bad influence on me growing up. When I was 12, he took me skiing in Stowe, Vermont. It was a fun trip. We redefined "freestyle" skiing, received three warnings from the ski patrol for horseplay, and on our last day, had our lift tickets revoked for skiing off the trail.

Even though Gramps and I were skiing together, he insisted on getting in the "singles" line for the chairlift.

"Next to being a ski instructor," he explained, "It's the best way on the slopes to meet women."

While he rode up the mountain with a charming redhead, I ended up sharing my chair with some creepy middle-age guy who asked me if I enjoyed masturbating.

After that run, I went into the lodge to warm up and give Gramps a chance to ski a Black Diamond. While I was sipping my hot chocolate, my grandfather was able to do some extreme carving down the zipper line of a mogul field, caught some big air, met a lady from France, and received a stern warning about the seriousness of impersonating a purple merit star ski patrol.

In the evenings, we skiers gathered in the lodge by an enormous stone fireplace with a crackling fire. For entertainment, there were young women in stretch pants and a guy who played a guitar while singing Irish protest songs. He looked very serious. His unnatural brogue, however, had some people thinking he was from Australia, so he received more than one request to play that *Tie Me Kangaroo Down* song. This, I could tell, really pissed him off. Worried that he might be concealing a homemade bomb in his guitar case, I retired to our chalet while Gramps entertained two tipsy sisters he met at the bar. They were chicly dressed in the latest ski fashions, which was a clear indication they weren't skiers. They were locals looking for some New York type to buy them drinks. Grandpa seemed quite fond of them. He called them his "double-mint twins."

When my grandfather died, my father had the post office forward Gramps's mail from his Lake Forest house to the Laramie Avenue address where I had grown up. Eventually, the only mail of my grandfather's that my parents were getting at their house was the balance of a two-year subscription to *High Times Magazine*. I thought it was hilarious. My mother, on the other hand, was gravely concerned about, and embarrassed by, what the mailman would think.

"Oh. Don't you worry about that Mrs. Johnson," he reassured her. "That's nothing compared to some of the stuff I deliver to the parish house over at Saint Symphorosa's Church."

CHAPTER THIRTY-TWO

My Club Membership

For me to attain membership in the Tower Club, the bylaws required that a Legacy member, such as Mr. Maciel, submit the obligatory recommendation letter to the membership committee. He, however, elected to entrust Maria to draft the document.

"For God's sake! The man's got a Silver Star," he argued. "If that's not enough for those arrogant snobs, I don't know what more I can say."

The committee chairman's greatest concern, it seemed, was that I clearly understood jackets and ties were required in the main dining room at all times. Maria assured him that I owned not only a handsome Scottish tweed shooting jacket with genuine leather buttons, but a nice single-breasted business suit, with two pairs of trousers, from *J.C. Penney* as well.

To complete my application, I needed, in addition to a letter from the proposer, two additional letters, one from a seconder and one collateral letter of support. That was the hardest part of the application process.

"Your friends are all a bunch of losers," observed Maria as we racked our brains, trying to think of someone who could testify that my character was such that it would not bring dishonor or shame to the club, and thereby its membership, all the while employing letter-perfect spelling, cohesive sentence structure, and good grammar. What sealed the deal was a masterfully concocted, eloquent, and downright counterfeit testimonial from Hubert Horatio Humphrey, who praised my integrity and assured the membership committee that my character was beyond reproach. He went on to elaborate about the lively discussions we had (over brandy and cigars) on morality, integrity, and justice, plus "walking into the sunshine of human rights." He also thanked me for my generous contribution to the LBJ presidential library.

Maria gave me a stern warning against using the forged letter.

"It could backfire on you," she cautioned. "You *do* realize that virtually the entire membership committee are Republicans."

After being initiated, the Tower Club became my home away from home . . . a good place to meet friends, socialize, and expand my cultural horizons. Few of my fellow club members (captains of industry) would have much to do socially with me (taco boy), however.

I did, nonetheless, get along splendidly with the elderly Mr. Howard L. Franklin III, who suffered from post-stroke vascular dementia. His wife dropped him off at the club a couple of days a week so that she could go over to his law office to do the billings. Mrs. Franklin counted on me to be around, to look after Howard, and keep him out of mischief. It's hard to imagine what she was thinking. Sometimes Howard and I would go down to the billiards room to smoke Cuban cigars and drink brandy. Other times we'd go into the kitchen and bother the cooks by pretending to speak Chinese. We also liked to stop by the barbershop for a shave or enjoy additional club amenities including a well-stocked library, an art gallery, and an excellent pool, which for reasons I don't want to expatiate here, we were politely asked not to use in the future. (Just for the record though, it was Howard, not me.)

There are 6 bars conveniently located throughout the clubhouse. Howard and I liked the one on the 12th floor because Rudy, the bartender there, made the driest vodka martinis. Next to Howard, Rudy was one of my dearest friends. In fact, I was friends with most of the club's staff. Bernie, the elevator operator, and I had gone to a number of Cubs games together, and the bell captain invited me to both of his children's weddings. I was also very close to Berta, an attractive young waitress in the Walnut Room, until Maria, thoughtfully, found her a well-paying job with a law firm across town.

"Mr. Johnson," Berta thanked me with her cute Mexico City accent, "you have such a very nice wife. You are so lucky."

I was lucky. Lucky that Maria got rid of Berta and not me.

There are four restaurants at my club, so I never got bored by eating lunch in the same place every day. There are also three dining rooms available for private affairs. Howard and I rented one of these once to throw a party for Licky when he retired. Licky ran the corner newsstand at Madison Street and the river on the plaza of the Art Deco *Daily News* building. All of his friends, family and many of his customers showed up for this retirement bash. Licky was beside himself. At times, you could detect tears welling up in his eyes.

In order to retain some vestige of a dress code at our party, the club dispensed all of their loaner jackets and ties, plus they had to send a runner over to *Marshall Field's* for more. Our group also depleted the entire supply of toiletries in the men's lounge. The dining room we rented reeked from the blended smell of mouthwash and after-shave, while everybody's hair glistened with tonic. It was a fun party.

Leon, the homeless fellow who plays the saxophone down by Grant Park, entertained us with some old-school smooth jazz. Some of the membership, however, were visibly appalled by his presence in the clubhouse. Although the club has no specific rule prohibiting them, you virtually never see homeless people inside the place. It wasn't that any of the members had a personal grudge against Leon. To the contrary, most of them liked him, enjoyed his talent, and generously threw dollar bills into his coffee can when they cut through the plaza on their way to work. Their biggest concern about having him in the clubhouse, they seemed to concur, was the precedent it set.

My club, I'm proud to say, has some of the finest accommodations of any in Chicago. We also reciprocate with over 150 other clubs around the country, all of which restricted Howard and me from using their swimming pools as well. I never traveled without first obtaining (or forging) a letter of introduction from our club manager. This, along with my *Allstate Motor Club* card was better than having a key to the city. It's like I didn't even need money.

The Tower Club is my proverbial home away from home. In fact, there are 56 well-appointed sleeping rooms for members to use when they happen to be stuck in the loop overnight. These are quiet, very comfortable, and as nice as any in a fine hotel. I know this because I was, in fact, stuck downtown for a number of nights myself after Maria received the billing for Licky's retirement party.

My drink of choice is an extra dry vodka martini, straight up, with an olive. From time to time though, I, like anyone else, appreciate a change. It's pleasant to have a little variety in life. So, if I've been drinking martinis at my club's main bar on the mezzanine level in the morning, I'll sometimes go up to the Terrace Tap on the 12th floor to drink tequila in the afternoon.

"Number 12, Mr. Johnson?" the elevator operator asked.

"Thanks Bernie. Any good-looking women on 12 today?"

"A few, Mr. Johnson, but none as attractive as your wife."

Per my standing request, Bernie stopped the car in such a fashion that we experienced a couple of seconds of weightlessness at the pinnacle of our assent.

"Hey Rudy!" I greeted the Terrace Tap bartender as I stepped off the elevator while Bernie held the door open. A pleasant breeze was coming off the lake, and a number of people were on the terrace enjoying the fresh air.

"Good afternoon Mr. Johnson. Come for some of your special reserve Partida Reposado?"

Rudy keeps my personal bottle of tequila in a locked cabinet, along with some expensive brandies for some of the other club members.

"You read my mind," I replied noticing an attractive and vaguely familiar woman enjoying her drink alone at a small round table by the railing.

"I'm *still* reading your mind," Rudy offered, "and if she looks familiar it's because she's a friend of your wife."

"Thanks for the heads up."

"You're welcome, Mr. Johnson."

"Rudy here has a gift for knowing what other people are thinking," I explained to an attractive mature woman seated at the bar next to me. "Don't you, Rudy?"

"What am I thinking then?" she tested him teasingly.

"You're thinking that Mr. Johnson here, who is one of our distinguished members," (he wore a smirk on his face) "Might do well to spend a little less time at the club, and a little more time at the office."

Insulted, I took my drink and turned, scouting the room, for a familiar face, and one who wasn't, preferably, one of my wife's acquaintances or, as it turned out, a board member of my father-in-law's company.

"Hey Marta," I called to one of the housekeeping staff. "You're from Mexico, aren't you? How about a tequila?"

"Oh. I'm sorry Mr. Johnson, but I'm from Mexico so it's time for my siesta."

"Okay. Perhaps some other time then."

"She's being sarcastic," Rudy advised me. "You probably don't realize that."

"Is that what your extra-sensory perception told you?" I asked Rudy. "Can you tell me what Marta's thinking . . . even if she's thinking it in *Spanish*?"

"No, Mr. Johnson. I can't tell you what Marta's thinking. I do, however indeed *know* what she's thinking . . . I just can't tell you."

"With an attitude like that, you must not care very much about those Cubs tickets I get for you each season."

"Oh. You mean the ones in left field, behind the post? The ones with the obstructed views? Did you know they mounted a television monitor there now so even if you're over five feet tall, one can still enjoy the game?"

"Do people often advise you to be less insolent, Rudy?"

"Do people often advise you to drink less, Mr. Johnson?"

It's hard to tell sometimes, but Rudy and I are actually good friends.

"Why do you insist on answering my questions with another question?"

"Do you consider that to be insolence?"

"I do, and I'm not above discussing it with the club manager. She'll likely have a conversation with you about this."

"I know you're not above that, Mr. Johnson, and actually she'll send another memo around to all of the staff imploring us to please be on our condescending best behavior whenever you're on the premises."

"It must suck to be a service employee."

"With all due respect, Mr. Johnson, I can read your mind, and I happen to know that you think it would suck to be encumbered by any type honest employment whatsoever."

At a table in the corner I spied one of our octogenarian club members. He was Emmett Braxton Greenberg, one of the keenest intellectual property jurists in the country.

"Do you mind if I join you?" I asked him. "I've been having a little difficulty with Rudy and some of the ladies this afternoon."

He offered no objection, so I pulled up a chair and sat down. He was reading the *Wall Street Journal.*

"How about that stock market," I offered. "It's crazy isn't it? Do you know the definition of a bull market? It's a random market movement making the investor think of himself as a financial genius. That's what it is. Not me though. I'm not trusting my money to some stock broker. You know why they call them brokers don't you? Didn't you ever wonder about that? It's because they take your money and make you broker . . . that's why. My priest told me once that God created market analysts to make weather forecasters look good . . . that's because market analysts are wrong so often, get it? If you're looking for a recession-proof stock, I say put your money in *Tootsie Roll Industries*. Think about it. No matter what the economy does, people are still going to eat *Tootsie Rolls*, don't you think? Did you know that Rudy can read people's minds? Hey Rudy! Read Mr. Greenberg's mind. Show him how you can tell what he's thinking."

Rudy furrowed his eyebrows and concentrated for a moment. "My God, Mr. Johnson. He's dead!"

I sprang to my feet, stepping back, and knocking my chair over in the process.

"Holy shit! I thought he was just hard to amuse."

While Rudy dialed security, I took my drink and joined some stranger at a table as far from Mr. Greenberg as I could get.

"Tell me you've got a pulse," I insisted before I sat down. "I need some company that's a little more animated than that guy."

"Just promise me you didn't bore him to death," the stranger requested.

"I hope not. That was some of my best material."

"Are you a member?"

"Does that surprise you?"

"We don't get many comedians as members."

"Oh. I'm not a professional."

"Obviously."

"I work for *Tasty Taco*."

"We don't get many fast-food workers as members either."

"I'm the vice president of franchising."

"Are you publicly traded?"

"No. We're privately held. Why do you ask?"

"Having met you, I thought that a person could make a little money going short on your company's stock."

"That would be insider trading. Besides, I'm actually very successful at selling franchises."

"Really? Give me your sales pitch . . . your spiel"

"Pardon me?"

"So, tell me why I should invest with you."

I proceeded to launch into our standard patter while Rudy kept the liquor flowing.

" . . . we operate and franchise restaurants in 36 states. Last year our franchise sales were $6,626,000 or 41 stores. Annual gross sales have increased consistently in the 9 to 12 percent range over the past

10 years. Franchised margin dollars represented about 70% of the combined restaurant margins in 1970, 1971 and 1972 . . ."

"Very impressive numbers. But, how about you? What about your character? How do I know you are a man of integrity?"

"Well, I have a Silver Star, if that means anything," I let slip, due to the booze.

"Son, that's all I need to know," he replied, putting his hand on my shoulder and giving it a gentle tender squeeze.

Over the next 9 years, he purchased 16 restaurants.

CHAPTER THIRTY-THREE

Mr. Cunningham

"So, this is it . . . your Silver Star," the gentleman sitting across from me at my desk inquired; the same fellow I had met earlier at the club.

He cocked his head slightly to get a better look.

Mr. Cunningham, it turned out, was an already established and singularly successful restauranteur in the Chicagoland area. He had been scrutinizing our franchise opportunities since our encounter at the club and was here today to pick up the indentures for three southern California locations where he was expanding.

"Actually, there's a story behind this medal," I tried to confess.

"I would imagine so. This is the third-highest combat military decoration that can be awarded for valor in the face of the enemy. You are in an elite coterie, my friend. Omar Bradley, James Doolittle, Lyndon Johnson, Chuck Yeager, John McCain, George Patton, Richard Bong . . ."

"Thanks, but actually, this Silver Star should have gone to a buddy of mine, Bill Hastings. Unfortunately, however, he was killed on a long range patrol in Phu Yen province. It was somehow subsequently consigned to me through some sort of bureaucratic bungle. Frankly, I'm kind of embarrassed to flaunt this undue decoration in such a manner, but my father-in-law insisted on displaying it prominently here in my office, and one doesn't argue with Mr. Maciel."

"I know how it is with you guys. You don't fool me. The *real* heroes always deny being such."

"Trust me, I'm no hero."

"Yeah, yeah, yeah," he responded, shaking his head.

"Now, I'm sure you'll want to have your attorney look this contract over," I suggested.

"Is it okay? Is it what we discussed?"

"Yes. Of course it is. I spelled out the general agreement, our in-house counsel meticulously drafted the document, and Ms. Dorsey prepared it. But, never-the-less, you should have your legal people look at it."

"Not necessary! I have the word of a Silver Star recipient. That's good enough for me. Now call your secretary in here so she can witness my signature."

I buzzed Ms. Dorsey.

"Yes?" her voice crackled from the intercom accompanied by a loud hiss.

"Ms. Dorsey. Would you please summon Sally and Shauna, and come in here to witness Mr. Cunningham's signature on the contract you prepared this morning?"

"Why'd you do that?" Mr. Cunningham asked.

"Do what?"

"Speak to your secretary on that antiquated electronic contraption when she's sitting but five feet away; just outside your office door; within easy earshot."

"Oh. He just loves playing with that thing," Ms. Dorsey answered for me. "Sometimes he'll request landing instructions on it, sometimes he'll order a missile launch, and once he broadcast an all-points bulletin via that machine warning that the perpetrators should be considered *armed and dangerous*. He has a very active imagination."

"Really?"

"Indeed! He's even been known to purport being a Vice President in the company, with the authority to endorse contracts on its behalf."

Mr. Cunningham gave me a curious look.

"She's only saying that to get even because I didn't purchase any of her granddaughter's *Girl Scout* cookies."

"That's terrible!" Mr. Cunningham accused. "*I'll* certainly buy some, Ms. Dorsey. What are my choices? Can I get some of those *Thin Mints*? My wife is quite partial to them."

"Absolutely!" Ms. Dorsey replied. "I have some order sheets at my desk. Come this way."

The two of them were having quite an animated conversation there, discussing the merits of different varieties of cookies while Mr. Cunningham diligently filled out the order sheet. Mr. Maciel happened to be passing by my office just then, saw Mr. Cunningham hunched over Ms. Dorsey's desk, and signaled to me to step out in the hall.

"Don't tell me Cunningham's signing the deal right here and now. *Good* job, Son."

"Thanks, but actually, he's ordering *Girl Scout* cookies right now. However, he told me he intended to go ahead and close on the deal today."

"*Girl Scout* cookies! Who's got *Girl Scout* cookies?"

"Ms. Dorsey. She's selling them for her granddaughter."

"I'll buy some of those."

He stepped into the outer office.

"Ms. Dorsey. Let me have one of those order sheets."

He turned to Mr. Cunningham, extending his right hand.

"I'm Mr. Maciel, by the way."

"Nice to meet you. Have you ever tried the Trefoils?"

"Yes. They're very good. They're *all* good! You can't go wrong with *any* of them. They're *Girl Scout* cookies, for heaven's sake."

Sally and Shauna arrived as requested.

"You needed us to witness a signature?" Sally asked.

"Well, yes, but they're all preoccupied with *Girl Scout* cookies at the moment."

"Cookies! I could use some cookies. Where do I sign up?"

"Me too," Shauna added. "I used to always buy them from my niece, but she quit scouting when her pregnancy began to show."

The two of them dove into the fray. Ms. Dorsey took a blank order sheet to the duplicating room to make additional copies. More cookie customers wandered in. As the proverbial *odd man out*, I dejectedly walked down the hall to the men's room, pushed open the door, and stepped inside.

"What are you doing in here?" one of our staff asked me as he dried his hands with a paper towel. "I thought you had a private washroom in your office."

"I do, but my space is evidently *Girl Scout* cookie central right now.

"Cookies! Do they take checks?"

"I think so; if it's drawn on a local bank."

He balled up his paper towel, poised himself as if he were on the basketball court, shot, and missed the overflowing waste can by more than a foot.

"Got to go get me some peanut butter *Savannahs*."

We eventually got around to endorsing the franchise contract a little after four that afternoon. Trying not to seem too adrenalized, our small group huddled around Mr. Cunningham as he sat, hunched over the contract, fountain pen in hand.

"There we go," he announced as he executed the document and then slid a cashier's check across the table. "If these three restaurants do as well as I anticipate, you can expect me back here a year from now for another signing ceremony. It's an honor doing business with you, Bruce."

I stood to shake his hand. Instead of taking it, however, he rose from his chair, and snapped to attention.

"Thank you," I told him.

"No. Thank *you!*" he countered, then crisply saluted me. Spinning on his heels, he turned and walked briskly out the door to the elevator.

"That was strange," Ms. Dorsey commented incredulously. "I wonder what *that* was all about."

I waved the cashier's check in her face. "That, Ms. Dorsey, was all about three hundred and thirty thousand dollars. Make no mistake about it!"

I turned up the volume on our *Muzak* sound system, broke out the Tequila, and led a conga line, with the three ladies, around my office. We danced and drank shots raucously, in spite of the fact that this type of behavior tended to be quite unsettling for the accounting people, whose offices were just down the hall.

My father-in-law cut into his salmon. We were seated at his regular table at the club, overlooking Lake Michigan.

"So, Bruce, tell me. How did you reel in Mr. Cunningham? We've been courting him for some time now."

"I don't know. He just came around."

"It seems that a lot of new franchisees have been *just coming around* since you took that position. Not only am I pleased with your performance, I'm very proud of you, Son."

"Thank you."

"I did, however, receive another remonstrative intra-office memorandum from our comptroller. It seems that he's very concerned about some of the unprofessional behavior in our franchising department. What do you think we should do about it?"

"Does he have an employment contract?"

"No."

"Then I say, *fire* him."

"Fine. I'll do it first thing in the morning."

"And what about that accounts receivable manager who douses himself in *Old Spice*? I always feel like I'm being tear-gassed when he enters my office to gripe insistently about past due accounts."

"He's a remarkable employee you *do* realize. On a good day he can complete eight hours equivalent of work before lunch."

"On a bad day, however, he returns from his two-hour lunch drunk, and tries to recruit the attractive young office girls to join his mixed singles bowling league. Yesterday was the third day this week it happened . . . but then, it was only Wednesday."

"I'll let him go, too. Anyone else you'd like to get rid of while we're at it?"

"No. I think that will be enough to send a stern message to the accounting department."

We returned to the business of eating our meals.

"The halibut is very good today," I commented. "How's your salmon?"

"It's excellent, as usual. You *do* know that there will be a considerable bonus for you, having landed *that* deal."

Thanking him again, I excused myself from the table and proceeded to the men's lounge. I had a little business to take care of . . . literally.

"Hey, Mr. Johnson! What's happening?" the washroom attendant greeted me with a soul handshake that I flubbed my end of.

"You look like a *dork subculture affiliate* when you soul shake, Mr. Johnson. Why is this so perplexing to you white dudes?"

"I'd answer that except I don't want to insult a prospective customer. Tell me, Malcolm. When are we going to put together a deal for you to franchise one of our restaurants?"

"Well, assuming that Mr. Shonkwiler doesn't miraculously recover from his irritable bowel syndrome, and my daughter won't need braces, I think I'll be handing over a check to you about *one* year from now . . . plus or minus."

"Great! It will be the best investment you'll ever make. You just let me know when you're ready."

"It's always business with you, isn't it, Mr. Johnson?"[2]

He turned on the water for me and tested the temperature with two fingers.

"It can't be anything else, Malcolm. Didn't you read the club manager's daily memo to staff? You see, I'm now a *Legacy* club member."

---

2. Even though Malcolm and I were "tight," *Tower Club* rules required that he always address me as *Mr. Johnson* while inside the club. Outside the club, however, it was a different story. There, Malcolm was free to address me as *Mr. Bruce* or even *Bruce.*

"So?"

"So, you're the washroom attendant."

"And you, Mr. Johnson, have managed to embody virtually every hallmark I hate about white people. Are you still coming to my daughter's recital, or is that out now too, inasmuch as you're a *Legacy* club member, and I'm merely the perennially deferential and obsequious washroom attendant?"

"You know I wouldn't miss it," I answered while scrubbing my hands. "You're one of my best friends."

"Now that's sad. That's really sad."

"You just keep saving those tips, Bro. I'm counting on you to help me set a new, all-time sales record for 1974."

"Anything I can do to help an already prosperous white guy out to make even more money gladdens my heart."

I gave him a critical look.

"Are you going to hand me that towel you're holding, or not?"

"Yes sir, Mr. Johnson. Here ya go, Mr. Johnson."

CHAPTER THIRTY-FOUR

Our New Home

"So this is your new place, is it?" my mother commented as I opened the craftsman-style mahogany front door. "Now that you're living like a swell, I suppose you don't have much desire to come back to the old neighborhood, and your blue-collared, Democratic working-class roots."

Mom could be snarky when she put her mind to it.

"Are you inviting Maria and me? Because, I have to tell you Mom, you and Dad have not made us feel as if we were very welcome south of Roosevelt Road."

"So you want an invitation? Is that what it is? Oh *my*, Son. You don't need an invitation! Just phone us first to let us know when you're coming by to get those unsettling radioactive boxes of yours out of our attic."

She was referring to the crates that contained the residuum from my infamous high school science fair project.

When I learned, in fourth-period physics class, my junior year, that a number of select radioactive isotopes will sustain a chain reaction when bombarded with neutrons, I knew exactly what my science-fair project was going to be. Energy availability, I was confident, would be a critical factor in the future, and I could foresee the need for small, portable, personal nuclear reactors; something that could fit into a suitcase. For my partner, I recruited Jimmy Shanks, the smartest kid in our class.

Our formidable challenge was to build a neutron gun. To my knowledge, this was something that had never been done at the high-school science-fair level before. It was not, however, impossible.

With a little research, we learned that the radioactive isotope *americium-241* was commonly used in some medical diagnostic equipment. Armed with this knowledge, we proceeded to engage in a little creative flirting with some members of the school's *Future Nurses* club. It didn't take long before we were able to identify one who worked as a volunteer in the nuclear medicine department at *Michael Reese Hospital*. Jim started putting the moves on her, and before long, they became quite serious, romantically. Being a typical guy, Jim pulled the old "if you *really* love me you'll prove it by getting me some radioactive isotope" line, and before we knew it, she was furnishing him with all the *americium-241* that a young man could dream of.

By packing this stuff into a lead pipe with a 1/64th inch hole carefully drilled in the side, alpha rays beamed out on our target of simple aluminum foil. Now I don't want to get too technical here (I know some readers were on the wrestling team) but the alpha rays were absorbed by the aluminum, and consequently expelled neutrons. The result was a primitive neutron gun. All we needed now was to isolate some *thorium-232* from gas lantern mantles, which we simply purchased at the local hardware store, and refined by using the lithium, reduced to its metallic form, from some depleted flashlight batteries. The resultant purified thorium, when bombarded with our improvised neutron gun, successfully produced fissionable *uranium-233*. We had built a simple nuclear reactor!

Miss Greene, our science-club coach, was confounded by our accomplishment. She never realized the level of scientific sagacity that existed right under her nose. I think she was pretty much expecting us to be crossing different varieties of peas and studying the relationships between dominant and recessive phenotypes.

"Yes Mom. I'll get those boxes out of your attic, but trust me. The radiation that you and Dad are exposed to by having them there is no more than you would receive from a simple chest X-ray."

Maria took my parent's coats. As she was hanging them up, I escorted Mom and Dad into our living room.

"That's so sweet of her," my father commented. "Do people often mistake your wife to be the housemaid? I bet they do . . . living in a snazzy place like this, and her being Mexican."

I told him that he was being insensible. This was in spite of the fact that, last Halloween, I had actually suggested to Maria that she retain her sexy medieval parlor maid costume (that she had worn to the YMCA Halloween party) when we retired to the bedroom. With absolutely no hesitation, she invitingly flopped down backwards on the bed, so dressed. I was staggered and should have gone for it right then and there. My big mistake was asking her if she wouldn't mind getting down on her hands and knees and pretend to be scrubbing the floor.

We had been in our new home for a few months now. After first considering Chicago's northern suburbs, we ended up in Glen Ellyn, which was *west* of the city, and an easier commute for me to the office. Our

Keck & Keck, prewar contemporary sat atop a glacial moraine, overlooking a small lake and park. The room we presently occupied appeared to be cantilevered over the hill's crest, although it was, indeed, discretely buttressed by a pair of sturdy steel stringers. On this January evening, the sweeping view from our expansive window-wall included ice skaters. A fire crackled in the common brick fireplace.

"May I fix you a *Manhattan*, Dad?" I offered.

"That would be fine."

"And Mom. Are you still partial to *High Balls*?"

"Thank you, Son."

I mixed Maria a *Margarita* and myself a *Martini.*

"That's a pretty fancy set up you have there," my father observed as I mixed the drinks. He was referring to the 1930s, art deco, radio/phonograph console that we had a cabinetmaker transmogrify into a bar.

"It was such a beautiful piece of furniture," I answered, "but the electronics were shot, so Maria came up with the idea of converting it."

"I had an old RCA like that before you were born."

My father stirred his drink, and then took a sip.

"Had I known that some hoity-toity might want it, to accessorize his 'architecturally significant' house, I wouldn't have put it out for the trash man when the turntable stopped working, and your mother couldn't play her Lawrence Welk records anymore."

"I remember seeing it in some old photos of you and Mom."

"Yeah. Back in those days, just after the war, we didn't take our old junk and reuse it. We had our fill of *that* during the Great Depression. If something broke, we tossed it out and bought a new one. It's what kept the economy rolling after war production ceased. It was the patriotic thing to do. It created jobs."

"And landfills," I argued.

"Look, Son. Do you think I could have afforded that comfortable house you grew up in, or for you to attend parochial school, if people fixed up their old vehicles, for example, and drove them forever? You may not realize this, but we actually build cars, nowadays, from a remarkable AISI-SAE, resulfurized/rephosphorized, plain carbon alloy. It was especially developed by the metallurgists over at *U.S. Steel*, in liaison with the *UAW*, to rust through after a predetermined number of years, so as to encourage people to trade in their old corroded cars for shiny new ones."

"That doesn't seem to me to be a sound business model," I argued.

"What it is, Son, it is good old American ingenuity and enterprise. This is why those Japanese automakers will never make a dent in U.S auto sales with their little imported rice-burners. They don't know how to innovate."

Maria tried to lighten up the conversation. I had earlier explained to her how my father had been a Marine during the war, and fought in the Pacific, so she knew full well how he felt about the Japanese.

"So, Mrs. Johnson, Bruce tells me that you are quite the gardener. Perhaps you can help me choose some indigenous plants that will naturalize well with our surroundings here this spring. I know next to nothing about horticulture."

"Oh, my dear child. I just assumed that, being Mexican, you'd have a natural gift for landscaping."

"It's not genetic, Mom," I interrupted.

"No. Of course not. I'd be pleased to help you. And Frank, here, is a wiz with the electric hedge trimmers. He could teach Bruce how to clip your shrubs into attractive pom-poms and such."

Maria cringed. I stood and motioned to my father.

"We'll leave you ladies alone to plan the garden while Dad and I go pick up the food. We ordered some Chinese from *Chin's* to be ready at seven o'clock."

My father followed my lead, and also rose.

"I was wondering, when we walked in the door, and I didn't smell anything cooking, what we were going to eat. What's the matter? Don't you cook, gal? Dorothy and I have been married for over 25 years now, and she's put a meal on the table virtually every night."

"It was a toss-up between Chinese carry-out, and *Hamburger Helper*," Maria quipped, "and I decided to go with the Chinese. I hope you're comfortable with that. I ordered yours with extra MSG. Just like Bruce told me you like it."

My father looked at me with distress in his eyes.

"She's joking, Dad," I reassured him.

I backed my 1973 *Pontiac Grand Prix SJ* out of the garage, into the turnaround, and pulled out onto Crescent Boulevard, driving west towards town. WBBM, the all-news radio station I had been last listening to when I parked the car, was enumerating the headline stories of the day.

"What do you think about OPEC doubling the price of crude oil?" I asked my father, trying to make conversation.

I had an idea that he might have an opinion on the subject.

"Do you think that it will hurt the sales of those full-sized cars you build at the plant?"

"Americans will never give up the safety, comfort, and ride of a *Mercury Marquis* or *Ford Galaxie*," my father answered, "for a few extra miles per gallon. Gasoline would have to top a dollar a gallon before *that* would ever happen, and I can't conceive of something like that ever occurring."

"Nor can I. That would be crazy . . . a dollar per gallon!"

"I'm confident that before gasoline would ever hit a dollar per gallon, we'll be driving vehicles propelled by hydrogen fuel cells or batteries recharged by solar panels on the roof."

"Or compressed natural gas."

"Yeah. America would never allow herself to be held hostage by those OPEC bastards or big oil companies. Presidents in the future will be elected based on their willingness to stand up to *Big Oil*."

"Right on!"

It was the first time I can remember my father and I ever agreeing on anything. I found a parking spot in front of Chin's, ran in, and picked up our food. I handed the steaming bags to my father.

"Did you get fortune cookies?" he inquired.

"I'm sure. They always include them here."

"Good. Because the last fortune cookie I opened read, *The fortune you seek is in a different cookie.*"

"Well, I guess then, today is going to be your day."

"By the way, son, there's something about your adoption I want to set straight. Your mother and I have not been totally forthcoming with you about that."

"You mean like waiting until I was 20 years old before telling me?"

"Well, besides that. You see, it's true. I adopted you, however, your mother is indeed your biological parent. She was a 15-year-old single mom when you were born. In those days, it was quite a scandal. I adopted you when your mother and I married."

We drove in silence for a block and a half, while I digested this revelation.

"Dad"

"Yes, Son."

"What ever happened to my real, uh, I mean, biological father?"

"Oh, him? They reassigned him to Saint Thomas the Apostle."

Back at the house, Maria had set the table with plates and utensils, and made some *Da Hong Pao* tea. At $12.00 an ounce, it smelled like musk oil, tasted like brake fluid, and purportedly palliated prostate problems. I stuck with the *Martinis*. We opened the food cartons and placed them in the center of the dining room table, pushing a big serving spoon into each container.

"Why don't we all try using the chopsticks?" Maria suggested. "I think it would be fun."

After experimenting with numerous creative and divergent chopstick techniques, (during which my father nearly lost an eye) we all, pretty much, gave up and used our forks.

"Chopsticks are just another good example of why those Japs lost the war," Dad announced.

"Well, I, for *one*, thought that dinner was good," I commented to keep the conversation light. "Does anyone need some more tea?"

There were no takers.

"My prostate is just fine," my father alibied.

"I don't even have one of those," my mother added.

"Dad! Why don't you open your fortune cookie and read it to us?" I encouraged.

He grumbled something unintelligible.

"Go ahead, dear. Read it to us," my mother insisted.

"See what it says, Dad," I added.

"Yes, Mr. Johnson," Maria joined our petitions. "Read it to us."

My father pulled the thin strip of paper from the remnants of the cookie shell.

"What does it say?" Maria offered her encouragement.

Dad put on his reading glasses from *Walgreens*, cleared his throat, and read, "*You will be hungry again in one hour.*"

CHAPTER THIRTY-FIVE

The Granite Care Kit

A few months after we moved into our lovely new home, Maria concluded that our master bathroom needed to be remodeled.

"Why?" I asked, agog.

"Because it's dated."

"Of course, it's dated," I countered. "Our house is an authentic *Keck and Keck* designed historical landmark. That's the allure. Didn't you ever notice the plaque from the *Glen Ellyn Historical Commission* on the front door?"

"Regardless. I can't contend with the *Cusheen* vinyl countertops nor the pink four-inch square bath tiles any longer. I want granite. Steve and Doris have granite, and it's gorgeous."

Steve and Doris were our attractive next-door neighbors to the east. They had hired a *Certified Residential Interior Designer* named Morgan to redecorate their house. For six months, it seemed, all I heard Doris talk about was Morgan. *Morgan wants to do this and Morgan thinks that and Morgan says such and such will really make it pop.* When the job was at long last complete, Steve told me, they had but $125 left in their *Glen Ellyn Savings and Loan* money market account, and that was only because Morgan didn't know about it.

So, naturally, when Maria wanted Morgan to do *our* design, I balked. I don't remember exactly what argument I gave her, but it had to do with something I claimed to have read about Morgan in the *Glen Ellyn News* "Police Roundup" column. Incredibly, she believed me. That unsavory invented tidbit successfully convinced Maria to instead visit *Hines Lumber* in Downers Grove.

"That's just appalling," Maria bemoaned. "I wonder if Steve and Doris have any idea of what kind of abhorrent woman they were inviting into their house."

"I wouldn't tell them now," I suggested.

"But how can a woman who possesses the proficiency to plan a powder room that *pops* also be involved in such a reprehensible activity?"

"I can't answer that. Perhaps it's something as simple as her color choice for the guest towels."

At *Hines*, an accommodating middle-aged man, with a pocket protector in his shirt pocket and a tape measure clipped on his belt, helped us select a lovely vanity and new toilet. He also referred us to Andy, a contractor who specialized in kitchens and baths, and his brother-in-law to boot. Andy, in turn, assured us that he was fully insured, had decades of experience bastardizing historic architecture, and owned a *Paslode* GN-212 nail gun.

"My specialty is building soffits (and plenty of them) as well as sunken tubs. Have you given any thought to a sunken tub?"

Maria and I both indicated that we hadn't, but somehow ended up with one, regardless. On learning this, Doris informed us that Morgan thought sunken tubs were passé.

When the time came to select the most crucial element of all (Maria's coveted granite), we drove to an industrial park in Elk Grove Village where, armed with templates of our bathroom fixtures and samples of our flooring choice, we spent the better part of a Saturday afternoon walking through a sweltering 150,000 square foot warehouse. A sturdy steel structure supporting the threshold lights of O'Hare Airport's runway 10 Left stood in the parking lot of the *Stone Center*. Every minute or so, a huge jetliner popped out of the clouds just over our heads. It was awesome.

"Would you mind if I stayed out here and watched the planes?" I asked Maria before we went in.

That not being an option acceptable to her, we instead viewed and evaluated slabs of stone, the select of which were destined to become our vanity top and shower surround. We even picked out our headstones while there, which I didn't even know we could do.

The next six weeks were a nightmare of chaos, plaster dust, and construction debris, exacerbated by the interminable pandemonium of Andy's nail gun and compressor. When the remodeling job was at longlast complete, Maria and I celebrated together with a bubble-bath in our new sunken tub, sipping wine, burning scented candles, and listening to Puccini's *La bohème* on WFMT radio 98.7. After Mimi tragically died of the Consumption, and having finished off the bottle of *Stags' Leap Cabernet Sauvignon*, slippery, wet, and naked, Maria and I struggled and squirmed striving to extricate ourselves from our new death-trap tub.

In due course, after quite some time floundering about, steamy, sultry and slinky, it eventually occurred to us that there existed a certain sensuality in the activity. To this day, Maria is convinced that our daughter Yazmin was conceived that evening.

"Well, that was interesting," I commented after we were eventually on dry ground once more. "We should do that again, sometime."

"Then I think I'm going to need to put some more *Neutrogena* body oil on my shopping list; perhaps the 32-ounce economy size next time."

While drying off, my lovely wife presented me with a thoughtful gift that she had stashed under the sink in the vanity.

"What's this?" I inquired.

"Just a little something for you to do when you have some time on your hands; a little project, if you will."

She handed me the "care kit" that she had optimistically purchased to prolong the useful life of the abundant granite in our bathroom. It was suggested to me that sealing granite might be a worthwhile and esteem-building project for me to undertake while she went to *Oakbrook Mall* and *Marshall Field's*, the following day, to shop for bathroom linens.

"But I don't *do* projects," I protested, to no avail. "You know that."

Admittedly, it had been some time since I took that class in geology to meet a lab science graduation requirement, but as I recalled, granite is an igneous rock, something like 25 million years old (more than twice as old as your typical Formica countertop installation) demonstrating to me that granite possesses a *natural* longevity. The idea of spending my Saturday applying some sort of a chemical sealant, that might add an extra six to eight months of useful service, 10 or 15 million years after I'm dead, didn't reconcile with me. I did, however, wistfully respect my wife's wishes.

"If you ever want another bubble bath, you'll humor me," Maria insisted. "You *do* want another bubble bath, don't you?"

I told her that I did. That much was true. I didn't tell her, however, that I was also thinking how it would be twice the fun if Doris from next door could join us. I knew better than that.

"Bruce," Maria spoke shyly.

"Yes, Maria."

"I'm not actually suggesting it, but I was just thinking, how it would be twice the fun if Steve from next door could join us next time."

"You're sick, Maria! You're really sick."

The next morning, after Maria had left to go shopping, I carefully and dutifully read a fair portion of the care kit instructions. They were informative. Bottle A, I learned, contained a special cleaning compound, which was to be applied with a clean dry soft cloth using a circular motion, in a well-vented area, being careful not to breathe the fumes. Bottle B was a sealant, which was to be applied with a special foam applicator. I was to let this stuff dry for 5 to 10 minutes until a slight haze formed. (It was a little confusing to me how a slight haze was going to form if I was being so careful not to breathe the fumes.) Next, the surface was to be buffed to a glaze with a second clean dry soft cloth. The instructions also cautioned me to do only a small area at a time (one or two square feet) so as not to get so far ahead of the game that the stuff hardened up like an epoxy. That certainly sounded like good advice and something that I didn't want to try to explain to Maria when she arrived home.

After rereading a good portion of the instructions to ensure I understood them somewhat, I poured about three-quarters of each bottle down the drain, but not before *first* cleverly soaking a rag with the more astringent smelling of the two products. Wedging it between the toilet tank and the wall, I then spent the balance of my day happily drinking vodka martinis to moderate excess and enjoying Puccini's *Tosca* on the stereo. The more I drank, the sadder the music became. I was a blubbering basket case by the time Maria arrived home from shopping late that afternoon.

When my dear spouse walked in the door, after her day selecting bath accessories, she predictably went straight to the master bathroom to see how the project turned out, smelled the tang of petroleum distillates, and showered me with compliments as to what a wonderful husband I was.

Now any time that Maria caught herself showering me with compliments for being a great husband, a little bell . . . or maybe it was a buzzer . . . I'm not sure, but some type of warning device went off in her brain. She became suspicious. She picked up the granite care kit, looked at the instructions on the backside, and began cross-examining me as she read.

"Did you use bottle A first?" she began the interrogation.

You have to keep in mind that I had consumed somewhere between three to six martinis that afternoon.

"With a clean, dry soft cloth," I replied sprightly.

But I wasn't off the hook yet.

"Did you open a window?"

That was nice. She worried about my health.

"I turned on the exhaust fan."

The inquisition continued.

"How long did you let the sealant dry?"

I instantly answered, "Five minutes. Until it formed a slight haze, and I only did approximately two square feet at a time."

I have to tell you, my granite-sealing lie had some endurance.

Maria seemed almost pleased as she continued to read further. This concerned me. I hadn't read the instructions beyond this point, and she was still going strong. A curious look formed on her face, which evolved into a frown as she shook first one, and then the other bottle close to her ear.

"You dunderhead!" she exclaimed. "There was supposed to be enough product here to do 15 hundred square feet. You shouldn't have used more than a quarter of each bottle, and there's got to be seventy-five percent gone!"

I said something like, "Dah, uh, um."

"That's so typical of you. If a little is good, you think that more is better. I can't trust you to do anything around this house if I'm not here to supervise. You must have spent the whole day wasting your time, and wasting what should have been a two-years' supply of cleaner and sealer."

"Let's eat dinner before it dries out," I suggested as a distraction, and on the way to the dining room, I stealthily popped into the kitchen to put the empty food containers from *Boston Market* at the bottom of the recycling bin.

"This is good," Maria commented as she cut a second bite of braised chicken. "Is it one of the recipes from that cookbook I gave you for Christmas?"

By this time, I was in so deep I figured I had nothing to lose, so I nodded my head in the affirmative. As I poured a glass of wine for my wife, I told her about the invigorating shower I took just before she arrived home.

"You should see how the water beads right up," I proudly commented.

Glaring at me, she shook her head.

"So, now you're telling me that you didn't wait the required 24 hours before using the shower after sealing it?"

I just sat there with, I'm pretty sure, a stupid look on my face.

CHAPTER THIRTY-SIX

My First Business Trip to Kentucky

We were bringing a new restaurant online in Henderson, Kentucky. In those days, Mexican cuisine was fairly new to the commonwealth, and Kentuckians who ate burritos were thought, by their fellow citizens, to be *avant-garde*. Some of them, to impress their dates, even attempted to order in "traveler's" Spanish. Nurturing the practice was discouraged, however, as a matter of company policy. This was because none of our order-takers spoke the language. Not Billy Bob, not Cooter, not Magnolia, and not Zadie.

I was excited about my upcoming trip for the requisite grand opening ceremony. All of the essential local politicians had been lined up for the ceremony, including one, whom I was told, actually had his own personal pair of giant ribbon-cutting scissors as well as a chrome-plated, short-handled, round-point shovel for ground breaking ceremonies. I knew the type and delighted in the fact that I needn't bring my company issued, three-foot long scissors with me on this trip. They tended to cause considerable consternation at airport security checkpoints.

The only time previously I had been to Kentucky was when I was 12. It was to visit *Mammoth Caves National Park* on one of our family's annual, dysfunctional family camping trips. From what I remember, the subterranean labyrinths of the caverns proved to be too claustrophobic for my mother. She curled up in the fetal position, while on the *Violet City Lantern Tour*, and refused to proceed further with the group. It took two park rangers and a 10 mg *Valium* to coax her back to the surface.

Ms. Dorsey procured for me an official state highway map of Kentucky so that I could familiarize myself with the geography. From what I could determine from the map's text, (in a greeting from their governor) Kentucky was divided into four major regions, three of which, apparently, boasted numerous paved roadways.

"Where is Dry Ridge, Kentucky," I asked as I spread out the map on the conference table. "Is it anywhere near Henderson?"

"Why do you ask?" Ms. Dorsey responded.

"I had an army buddy from Dry Ridge. Jim Mullen was his name. If it's close enough, I'd like to look him up and see how that rural electrification program has been working out for him."

Ms. Dorsey looked up *Dry Ridge* on the index of towns and cities, noted the map coordinates, and with her two index fingers, traced them until her fingers converged.

"Here we go. Dry Ridge. It's southeast of where you'll be staying."

I leaned back in my chair and meshed my fingers behind my head.

"Jim Mullen. It might be interesting to see him again. I wonder what he's been up to."

"I'll see if the telephone company has a record of him," Ms. Dorsey offered. "It will just take a few minutes."

While she was back at her desk, I tried, unsuccessfully, to locate Mammoth Caves on my map. Perhaps, I speculated, they were a casualty of the recent recession. I imagined a padlocked gate at the entrance sporting a bullet-perforated *closed* sign.

"I have his number," Ms. Dorsey announced. "Shall I attempt to get him on the line?"

"No. I'll dial it myself, thank you. You may, however, ask the switchboard for a WATS line, if you will."

"I'll do that and let me fold that map back up for you. You're doing it all wrong."

Matching my scribbles on the scrap of paper I held as I drove, to the address on the mailbox, I swung the *Oldsmobile Cutlass Supreme Brougham* I had rented, down the long driveway to the farmette where Jim Mullen resided. A big yellow dog of dubious breeding ran alongside my car, barking. Jim emerged from one of the outbuildings, wiping his hands with an oily rag.

"Bruce! Good to see you."

"Good to see you, too." I punched his shoulder. "How've you been?"

"Fine. Until you showed up just now and punched me."

"I'm sorry. It was meant as a gesture of conviviality."

"Hitting someone? Well, I'm not familiar with your customs up there in Chicago, but down in these parts, when you punch someone, it has an entirely different connotation than camaraderie. How should I have interpreted it if you had pulled out a knife and stabbed me? That we're like soul mates?"

"I'm very sorry."

"You should be. I'm just thankful you're not gay, with a fervent lust for me. What would you have done then? Pumped three rounds from your *Ruger 380* into my gut? Nice car, by the way."

"Yeah. It's got the 403 *Oldsmobile 'Rocket'* engine."

"Pop the hood. Let's see."

I did as he requested.

"What does she take? Premium or regular gas?"

"I don't know, actually. I just assumed it burned rocket fuel."

As Jim and I admired the power plant, we talked about old times and a little about what we'd been doing since we last saw each other. He told me that he had been having a rough go at it, what with the recession and all.

"With all due respect," I asked looking around, "how, exactly, do you know when there's a recession in Kentucky?"

"It's very subtle, but there are indicators. Now! I've got some genuine whole-corn Kentucky white-lightning moonshine in the house that you may find to be amusing. What do you say we go in and have a taste?"

"Yeah. Sure. You can't drink all day if you don't start in the morning."

Sitting at his kitchen table, we continued our conversation while throwing back shots of what smelled and tasted very much like isopropanol.

"Is this stuff safe?" I asked.

"No."

"No!"

"Well, it is so long as you keep it away from an open flame, and you don't take it internally."

"But I *have* been taking it internally. This is my fourth shot!"

"Oh, don't worry about that. In a little while from now, you'll vomit most of it right back up. It's your body's natural response, designed to expel toxic substances that may find their way into one's stomach."

"Do you remember Bill Hastings? He was from Kentucky too, wasn't he?"

"He sure was. Beaver Lick."

"Pardon me?"

"That's where he was from. Beaver Lick, Kentucky."

"That's a very unusual name for a town."

"Sure is. There's also *Big Bone Lick State Park* over by Union, Kentucky. They do a brisk business in tee-shirt sales at their gift shop."

"Where is Beaver Lick from here?"

"It's not far. I've got a cousin over that way. She tells me Bill's father is the pastor at *Beaver Lick Baptist Church*. His whole family still lives in the area. I thought about driving down there and looking them up, but I was afraid I wouldn't know what to say to them."

"It could be uncomfortable, but do you suppose they would ever like to talk with one of us who were close to him when he died?"

"I don't know. Perhaps they just want to forget it. I know I do."

"Well, not this trip, but maybe sometime in the future, I'll look his folks up. You *do* remember that there was a lot of speculation that the Silver Star I received should have gone to *him*."

"I can't say if it should have gone to him or not, but one thing I know for certain; it sure as hell shouldn't have gone to *you!*"

"Thanks a lot."

"I'm just being frank. You, my friend, pushed the envelope and redefined the concept of lily-livered, chicken-hearted, yellow-bellied cowardliness."

"Come on, now."

"Come on now? What about the time you promised that farm boy from Iowa . . . Halvorson . . . you'd pay him 25 bucks to walk point for you. He consequently lost his left leg below the knee, and then you stiffed him for the cash!"

"Well, how was I to know that he'd be leaving the outfit before pay-day? I was going to pay him. I was going to pay him when *I got paid.*"

"He left the outfit because he had his leg blown off by a bobby trap! And what about the time you were supposed to be guarding the ammo dump?"

"Now that's unfair; bringing that up."

"Well, I say it's indicative of your injudicious decision-making virtuosity."

"Nobody was killed."

"Is that how you appraise the outcome of your exploits? If someone gets killed or not?"

"Well, this trip, I'm pretty booked, but maybe the next time I'm in Kentucky, I'll look the Hastings up. You say his dad's a Baptist minister, though?"

"That's what I'm told."

"So then he's probably of the persuasion that when Bill got himself killed that day, in Phu Yen province, it was because God was calling him home."

"More than likely. God harvests the good ones for heaven, you know," Jim added sarcastically.

"It was probably God's will then, that he got shot, and not because we were laying waste to the countryside; those people's home."

"For sure. One never knows His ways. The Lord gives, and the Lord takes away. Ashes to ashes, dust to dust."

"God must have had a special plan for him; a special burden to bear."

"That's for sure, but he's in a better place now."

"He's at peace."

"Well, like I said, Bill's folks live over in Beaver Lick if you want to visit them. It's easy to remember. It's like . . ."

"Yeah, yeah. I get it. Just leave me alone. I'm feeling sick."

I stumbled into the bathroom.

"All right, then. I put some coffee on the stove. After you're through driving the porcelain bus in there, you may want to have a cup or two."

I said something in reply after that, but I don't really know how to spell it, nor does the spell check on my computer. Something like "Ahhhhhhh."

CHAPTER THIRTY-SEVEN

Baby Yazmin

A Lot of people like to make a big deal out of childbirth, especially women, but even the fathers, nowadays, seem to want to participate vicariously, and experience labor. Actually, I've been told by a reliable source (my mother) that it's highly overrated.

"I just wish they had some of the pharmaceuticals that are available now, back when I was pregnant with you," she confessed to me once after a couple glasses of wine.

Alcohol, for my mother, was like truth serum.

"Like better pain control?" I suggested.

"No. Like better birth control."

To be well prepared for the birthing journey, some dangerously left-wing conspiratorial organizations even offer classes on the subject for prospective parents, then give it a pretentious French-sounding name. It sounds silly to me, but then, I suppose, it would be more useful, than say, a Political Science degree.

Personally, I get a big kick out of the way old Hollywood movies used to portray the father's role to be a bumbling basket case, running around the house in a panic, when his spouse informs him it's time to drive her to the hospital. Once there, he invariably proceeded to loosen his tie and nervously chain-smoked cigarettes in the waiting room.

That, most assuredly, was not the case when baby Yazmin was born. For starters, due to the number of martinis I had consumed there in the den of our Glen Ellyn home, while enjoying Mozart on my new *Sony HP-188* stereo, it would have been unwise, and downright dangerous for me to drive Maria to the hospital on that particular afternoon. Additionally, already driving on two tickets, I surely didn't want to face a third (which would suspend my driving privileges) speeding my wife to the hospital. And, if that weren't argument enough, what if she had the baby right there in the car? I've heard of that happening. I certainly didn't want an ugly mess like that in my *Grand Prix*.

"I can't believe I've got to drive myself to the hospital because you've had too much to drink," Maria chastised me.

"Sorry, but perhaps you should have given me a little more of a heads up."

"A little more of a heads up! Look at me. I'm as big as a whale! What did you think was going *on* here?"

"Well, I'm afraid you're going to have to move the *Mach I*. It's parked behind the *Suburban* in the driveway. Give it two pumps, and then crank the starter leaving your foot off the accelerator. If it doesn't start on the first try, and you smell gasoline, try holding the pedal to the floor, and crank it again."

Perturbed, Maria grabbed the keys to both vehicles and waddled out the front door, slamming it behind her. I was glad she was finally going to have this baby. Although I would never tell her so to her face, the look on her was not flattering. While I mixed another martini, I could hear the growl of the special low-restriction exhaust on the *Mustang* as it sprang to life. I loved the way that car sounded, especially the loping idle of the radical high-performance camshaft that I had the speed shop install. Next, the garage door rumbled open, and Maria's car backed out of the driveway. Finally, I heard the *Mustang* pull into the garage, shut down, and the garage door close. Pleased that Maria was able to start the engine of my car without flooding it, I savored my martini for three or four minutes, munching on the olive, while enjoying *Mozart's Flute Concerto Number Two, in D major*. (I have two favorite composers. One of them is Mozart; and the other one isn't.) Suddenly, the front door sprang open again, banging into the coat tree.

"Aren't you at least coming with me?" Maria asked.

"Sure," I cheerfully replied. "If you want me to."

Maria was an exemplary wife and I didn't mind it at all; indulging her from time to time.

"Just let me grab a quick shower and I'll be ready to go."

"Now!" she screamed.

Pregnancy, you should know, can play havoc with women's hormones. At times, it requires a lot of patience and understanding on the part of their spouses.

"Okay. Okay. I'm coming."

Because she needed to put the seat back so far, to fit her big belly behind the steering wheel, Maria could barely reach the pedals of the *Chevy Suburban*. She looked quite awkward driving. Every couple of minutes or so, she would also grimace as her contractions became more acute.

"I think you're supposed to breathe when that happens," I suggested. "Either that or you're supposed to *hold* your breath."

Although I hadn't eaten any lunch, and suffered a major attack of the "munchies," in route, Maria refused to stop for doughnuts. She drove directly to the hospital. Fortunately, they provided valet parking for the maternity ward patrons. Otherwise, it would have been a long walk for Maria from the parking garage after she dropped me off at the hospital entrance.

"I think my wife is going to have a baby," I announced to the admissions clerk. Maria was still well behind me. She had had some trouble with her suitcase in the revolving door.

"Oh. And what makes you think *that*?" the clerk asked.

"Well, I wouldn't want to tell you this if she were in earshot, but she's been very irritable."

We were quickly processed and escorted to the labor room where Maria exchanged her street clothes for a hospital gown. It was a very nice and comfortable space. They had, it seemed, thought of everything. There was even some refreshing oxygen available to breathe through a little hose with two jets that fit into one's nostrils.

"This is nice," I told the nurse, as I inhaled deeply. "Could we also get some nitrous oxide pumped in here?"

Not that I really wanted to anyway, but it wasn't allowed that I go into the delivery room with Maria when her time came. Evidently, the hospital had some sort of a regulation restricting disruptive drunks and young children from certain sensitive areas of the facility. They *were* kind enough, however, to provide me with a jovial uniformed security guard to keep me company in the waiting room while baby Yazmin was being delivered. His name was Joe.

Joe and I had a swell time telling jokes, watching the television monitor that was thoughtfully installed for our entertainment, and trying to guess the puzzles on *Wheel of Fortune.*

"Buy a vowel! Buy a vowel!" I shouted at the TV.

"We had a kid born here last week that was *so* ugly," Joe jested, "that they threw away the baby and kept the afterbirth."

"That's an old joke," I reminded him. "If you're going to work the maternity ward on a regular basis, you're going to need some fresh material. How about this one? The husband of a pregnant woman wants to ask the doctor a personal question, but he's a little embarrassed, so the doctor interrupts him and tells the husband that he gets asked that question all the time. He goes on to explain that it's perfectly fine for the wife to continue having sex until quite late in the pregnancy, but then the husband tells him that he was actually wondering if she can still mow the lawn."

"That's funny," the guard replied, chuckling. "Where did you hear that joke?"

"Oh. That's not a joke," I had to explain. "That actually happened."

I could have really gone for a cup of coffee from the hospital cafeteria about then, but on closer observation, it seemed that my left wrist was handcuffed to the arm of the chair in which I sat. Other people in the room were giving me a lot of strange looks, and those with young children, held on to them tightly. Looking around, I was, apparently, the only person there in the maternity ward waiting room that afternoon wearing handcuffs.

Maria told me later, in no uncertain terms, that she was totally humiliated by my behavior that day, which I thought was ironic. Here *she* was the one, wearing no makeup, dripping with sweat, her legs spread wide in front of a bunch of absolute strangers while the muscular wall of her uterus contracted and her cervix expanded and relaxed and then her sac burst, releasing amniotic fluid . . . and she was humiliated by my exchanging a few good-natured jokes with the hospital security guard? I just sloughed it off as a common case of the postpartum baby blues. Based on my own personal experiences with the amazing advances in modern pharmaceuticals, I was confident that the doctors would be able to give her something for it. As a matter of fact, when I asked the obstetrician that very question, the next day, she told me that, indeed, there was something I could give Maria that would have a profound effect on her postpartum depression.

"As long as it's legal," I insisted.

"Oh, it's legal," the doctor replied. "You could give her a divorce."

Postscript to Chapter Thirty-Seven

On a "Zippo Raid" patrol in October of 1969, I and our platoon shouted, in crude Vietnamese, orders to evacuate a small hamlet in the Central Highlands that we were about to torch, all the while firing our weapons exuberantly in the air.

"Mau. Mau. Di ra. Di ra."

Out filed the "straw hats," terrified, weeping and wailing, and a few, audibly cursing us. It was a pretty typical campaign, as these things go, intended to persuade the locals to reconsider their political affiliations. When we had successfully congregated the villagers at a safe distance, we lit their thatched structures ablaze. They burned ferociously. One self-proclaimed and heavily tattooed white supremacist in the platoon seemed to delight in watching the conflagration; however, most of us just executed our grim orders mindlessly. This whole dog and pony show seemed, even to the most calloused amongst us, to be . . . well . . . mean-spirited. I sincerely hoped that I would never be taken a prisoner of war someday, and subject to the retributive justice I surely had coming.

As we somberly packed up our gear and began to hike out, proud to be Americans, I reached for my cigarettes and realized that I had lost them somewhere in the hamlet. I ducked back to retrieve my smokes. Retracing my tracks, I turned a corner. That's when I saw it. Just out of the corner of my eye, at first. Oh, my God! I wish I hadn't; but I did. All for a pack of cigarettes. In the smoldering debris, I was horrified to discern the charred corpse of a woman, frozen in mid-delivery of her child, like one of those immutable denizens of Pompeii caught in the eruption of Mount Vesuvius.

I could never have been with Maria to witness the birth of Yazmin. Not with that hideous image seared into my soul. I just couldn't.

CHAPTER THIRTY-EIGHT

The Reporter from the Glen Ellyn News

"Someone's at the door," Maria called from the den, where she was having far more fun than befitting, playing a fatuous game of peekaboo with two-month-old Yazmin.

"It's for me," I hollered back. "I'll get it."

I had an appointment this Saturday morning with a reporter from the *Glen Ellyn News*. He had phoned me earlier in the week. It was his ambition to interview me for the special Veterans Day issue, regarding my Silver Star. I had different ideas, however. I decided it would be amusing to have some good-natured fun with him.

"You're not planning to bamboozle him like you did me when I interviewed you back in college, are you?" Maria asked. "Remember what happened then."

"Oh yeah. That's right. We ended up becoming sexually intimate. No. Don't worry. I'm not planning anything like that."

"Remember, Bruce, some of our friends and neighbors read that paper."

After fumbling with the sticky deadbolt, which always gave me difficulty, I finally hit on right combination twists, bumps, and curses opening the front door to my guest.

"Come on in," I welcomed the young man, doing a pretty fair Bruce Dern impersonation. "I'll need to squirt some *WD-40* on that lock sometime."

I doubt that he was any older than 20; 19 would be a good guess.

"Oh, they sent a 'cub' reporter," I observed. "I'm so glad that you stayed on the path. I wouldn't want you to have fallen into one of the spike trap pits I dug."

"You have booby traps on the property?"

"Oh, yes. They're out there, you know."

"Who?"

"The VC. They're out there waiting." (I made my best "crazy eyes" while telling him this.)

"Waiting for what?"

"Their chance. They're waiting for their chance to overthrow our democratic system of government and replace it with their tyrannical, oppressive, and despotic form of communism."

I led the now visibly apprehensive reporter to the library and offered him a seat in my burgundy leather club chair. I remained standing throughout the interview, however, glancing nervously out the window.

"We're on our second mailman now," I informed the young man. "The first one tried to take a shortcut to the next-door neighbor. They're not supposed to do that, you know."

"No. I didn't know that."

"Yeah. It's a postal regulation. Look it up sometime."

"I'll do that."

"I have both volumes of the *Code of Federal Postal Regulations* on my nightstand."

"Sounds like stimulating reading."

"You'd be appalled at some of the conspiratorial stuff in there, and it's all right under our noses. Your paper should do an investigation. All of that Watergate business, and the President's recent resignation; that's just a distraction to divert the public's attention away from the *real* issues. I've read it all, so I know. That's why I've set up a defensive perimeter around our place. Plus, I own an AR-15 with a 30-round banana clip. I had you in my sights all the way up the driveway."

"With all due respect, how in the world would someone like you come into possession of an assault rifle?"

"Easy! I just went to the gun show at the fairgrounds and bought one. It's my Second Amendment right you know. A lot of people naïvely believe that our right to own guns is limited to sporting pursuits and self-defense, but no! We have the right to offensive weapons too. I'm looking to purchase a shoulder-fired surface to air missile next."

"But . . ."

"Second Amendment!"

"Only when the constitution was drafted, they had in mind muzzleloaders."

"Bah. That's an originalist interpretation of the constitution, and a minority view, by the way. The original intent theory holds that interpretation of our constitution should be consistent with what was meant by those who drafted and ratified it. I, on the other hand, subscribe to a revisionist interpretation of the constitution whereby the Supreme Court must succumb to the social, political, and financial pressures of the *National Rifle Association*."

"But what might you do with an AR-15?"

"For one thing, I shot my neighbor's dog last week when he wandered onto my property. Never liked that dog. Used to bark all night."

"You shot your neighbor's dog?"

"Yep. Clean shot to the heart. I located his carcass, cut off his penis and stuck it in his mouth."

"This is all very interesting, however, I have to be somewhere at noon. May we get started with the interview?"

"By all means."

By this time, I was imagining a headline in the *Glen Ellyn News* reading:

LUNATIC VETERAN LIVES IN OUR MIDST

"Very well then," my disquieted guest began, "can you elucidate the circumstances under which the honor of a Silver Star was bestowed on you?"

He was stiltedly reading from notes neatly printed on 3" by 5" cards.

"Actually, I'm unclear on that. It's all pretty murky."

"As in the fog of battle."

"No. As in the fog of narcotized euphoria."

"Excuse me?"

"I had been doing drugs all morning trying to efface the memory of the February 28th long range patrol and was too stoned to walk point on this one."

"Which one?"

"The March 2nd L.R.P. The one for which I received the Silver Star."

"I don't understand."

"Bill Hastings took the point in my place that day."

"Bill Hastings?"

"Yeah. He was the guy who saved my life on the February 28th L.R.P."

"He saved your life?"

The reporter was frantically taking notes.

"Mine and about six other guys."

"But that was on the February 28th L.R.P., you say. What about the March 2nd L.R.P.? The one for which you were awarded the Silver Star?"

"Oh. That's the one where Hastings 'entered upon the eternal Sabbath of rest,' so, I guess his Silver Star somehow devolved to me. Don't ask me how that happened. It just did. It's like if you save someone's life, then that makes you responsible for everything that person does after that. Like, for example, if he robs a bank someday, and shoots the guard, then it's your fault, or if that person finds a cure for pancreatic cancer, it's because you saved him."

"I'm not sure I'm following you."

"Watch the movie *It's a Wonderful Life* sometime, and it may be clearer to you. I just *love* that movie. I've seen it a dozen times."

"A dozen times?"

"Yeah. And that was just in one sitting."

The reporter made some mad scribbles in his note pad. I went on.

"Strange, isn't it? Each man's life touches so many other lives. When he isn't around he leaves an awful hole, doesn't he?"

"So, you're saying that Bill Hastings was killed on the March 2nd L.R.P. because he saved your life on the February 28th L.R.P., and then because you were too stoned, he had to walk point in your stead?"

"Pretty much. But then if he *hadn't* saved my life on the February 28th L.R.P., I would have been too dead to walk point on the March 2nd L.R.P., and he would have been killed either way. So, you see, it can't be my fault that he died, even though that's the way it looks on the surface. At least that's the way I view it."

"But! Had Bill Hastings saved your life on the February 28th L.R.P., and you in turn refrained from doing drugs before the March 2nd L.R.P., then he would still be *alive* today."

"Yes. That's true, but then I would have been killed walking point on the March 2nd L.R.P., and that would mean Hastings didn't actually *save* my life on the February 28th L.R.P., but that he only protracted it by three days."

"If you don't mind my asking, all of this has *what* to do with the Silver Star?"

"Look. This Silver Star has been like a lucky charm for me. Every time something wonderful or serendipitous happens in my life, it can be traced back to that confounded medal. It's as if Bill, somehow, saw to it that it was passed on to me when he was killed because by saving my life, he was responsible for me. I bet you could make a good, sappy, made-for-TV movie with this material."

"This is all very interesting, but for the benefit of our readers, could you kindly recall for me the exact circumstance for which you were cited?"

"Okay, how does this sound? I carried my wounded comrades to safety while under heavy enemy fire."

"How many?"

"Comrades?"

"Yes. How many wounded comrades did you carry to safety?"

"Oh, I don't know; some; a half dozen maybe."

"And were you scared?"

"Not as scared as *they* were. In combat, you really don't want your life to be in the hands of some guy who's under the influence of powerful pharmaceuticals that precipitate pluck. I think you can appreciate that."

"So, that's what earned you the medal?"

"Actually, there's more."

"Go ahead."

"You see; I did all of this without regard to my personal safety. That's a very important distinction. If not for that, I would have received a Commendation Medal, or perhaps even a Bronze Star, but certainly not a Silver Star."

"I can only imagine how hard that must have been; disregarding your own safety."

"Actually, it's not hard at all, if you've been doing opiates all morning. My emotions were running pretty flat that afternoon."

"Well, I think I have, at least, a semblance of what happened that day."

"Yeah. You really had to be there."

"Is there anything else? Is there anything more you want to add; about Bill Hastings, perhaps?"

"Do I want to say anything more about Bill Hastings? Yeah, I do. He's the reason you're sitting there, in my comfortable club chair, interviewing me, after all. Let's see, you can say in your article there that he was the best friend a guy could ever ask for. I think about him every single day; from the time I get up in the morning, until I go to sleep at night."

"The two of you weren't lovers, were you?"

"Hell, no! It sounds like it though, doesn't it? We were just the best of friends. I may be a little swishy, but I'm not gay, although I actually thought about it when I was in college."

"You thought you were gay?"

"No. I thought about *becoming* gay, but you see, my roommate, Phil, who was homophobic, freaked out about the prospect, and in deference to him, I married a lovely woman, and had a kid. It all worked out quite well in the long run. I'm very happy with my decision."

"You know you just can't decide to be gay, don't you? You have to be born that way."

"That's *exactly* what Phil told me. You guys think alike. You're not, by chance, homophobic too, are you?"

"No. As a matter of fact, I'm gay."

"Oh, really? What do you think, then, about the colors in this room? My wife picked out the drapes, but we had a hard time deciding if the sofa fabric coordinated well with them."

"I'm also color blind."

"Color blind? That's crazy! Isn't that sort of like Beethoven's being deaf?"

My guest became visibly restless, and started to stand, but I wasn't through messing with him yet.

"Since we're baring our sexual identity souls here, you might also be interested to know that I'm actually a woman trapped in a man's body."

He squirmed uncomfortably.

"Surprisingly it works out very well for our marriage, however, because, as it turns out, I'm a *lesbian* woman trapped inside a man's body! Isn't that crazy?"

"Look. I really need to go."

"I understand. You're on a deadline, right?"

"No. I have a dentist appointment."

I saw him to the door.

"Okay. Nice talking to you. Just walk in the same footprints you made coming up the path and you should be all right."

Standing at the door, I watched him get into his car and drive off.

"How did the interview go?" Maria asked with an affectionate hug.

"I think it went swimmingly. He seemed like a very nice young man."

"I hope you had the good sense not to say anything you wouldn't want to see in print. Remember, that was a newspaper reporter, after all."

"Nothing. Nothing I can think of, but I appreciate your concern."

"What would you do without me?" Maria asked.

"I don't know. Masturbate?"

"That was a rhetorical question."

CHAPTER THIRTY-NINE

Opening Night at the Opera

For people who have never been to one, an opera is very like a play except, for some inexplicable reason, the words are sung and not spoken. Additionally, one of the singers usually succumbs to a tragic and protracted death in the last act, valiantly singing until they draw their last breath. Knowing how I enjoy classical music, Maria presented me with a pair of opera tickets for my 25th birthday. Since she was so thoughtful, I invited her to be my date for the evening. After dinner at the club, we saw Giacomo Puccini's *Madama Butterfly* at the Lyric Opera of Chicago.

All action takes place at the turn of the 20th century, in and about United States Navy Lieutenant Benjamin Franklin Pinkerton's rented house overlooking Nagasaki Harbor, Japan, where he is on temporary assignment. One might reasonably infer that, with some of the characters being Americans and the balance Japanese, there would be a language barrier amongst the principals. This is not an issue however, as apparently, without exception, everyone in Nagasaki, Japan conveniently speaks Italian. As handy as this may be for the cast, it unfortunately leaves non-Italian speaking audience members with the choice of either reading the super-titles projected above the stage or watching the opera.

Act One finds real-estate broker/matrimonial agent and self-important man of many talents, Goro, showing Lieutenant Pinkerton around his newly leased matchbox of a house, teetering on a jetty of granite overlooking Nagasaki Harbor, and the *USS Abraham Lincoln*, (Pinkerton's ship) at anchor below. In lieu of walls, this inexpensively built but ingenious structure boasts *shosi*, or sliding panels, enabling the occupants to modify the configuration or floor plan at will, like the seats of a modern mini-van. Goro is demonstrating the workings of the house and introducing the servants when Sharpless, the U.S. consul, enters. Pinkerton boasts to Sharpless of the swell deal he negotiated. Apparently, Pinkerton has leased the house, complete with an occupant bride for the pittance of one hundred yen, and for a term of nine hundred and 99 years, with the option of canceling the lease and annulling the "marriage" in any given month.

Sharpless is skeptical. He tries to warn Pinkerton of the potential for tragedy in this arrangement, but Pinkerton will hear nothing of it. He rejects the advice of Sharpless because, if he didn't, there wouldn't be an opera. Filling their glasses with whiskey, Pinkerton proposes toasts to, "America forever, the folks at home, and the day when he will enjoy a *real* wedding in *God's country*." Finally, Pinkerton toasts the immediate future in the aria *Amore o grillo,*(I'm Getting Some Tonight). The pair then stands quietly in awe as they gaze out over the fairy-tale setting that surrounds them. (Because opera is "make believe," they are actually gazing out in awe at the audience.)

From below come the angelic voices of young women. Closer and closer, they draw. Louder and louder becomes their song. They sing of the cherry blossoms and the beauty of the day. (I knew this because, as you recall, I was reading the super titles.) The music swells, but above it all soars the crystal voice of Butterfly. They reach the top of the hill and ascend the stairs to the little house's terrace.

Sharpless engages Butterfly in conversation. Her father, he learns, committed *hari-kiri,* thrusting her family into poverty and her into a life as a geisha. Now here's the problem. Not only is Butterfly only fifteen years old, but she turns out to be head over heels in love with this Pinkerton fellow. She has even converted to his Catholic faith, spurning her Shintoism. Butterfly, furthermore, vows, in a sign of humility, to dispense with her few modest possessions should they not complement the décor preferred by Pinkerton, who favored the then emerging arts and crafts movement of William Morris. (Definitely, her porcelain, waving cat would have to go.) Butterfly also vows to be a frugal wife by clipping coupons, and never buying a new kimono until the third markdown.

Wedding guests and relatives arrive by the dozens. The Imperial commissioner performs the wedding ceremony. Photographs are exposed and there is much toasting to the couple as the band plays, *Ancora un passo or via* (Tie a Yellow Ribbon). Saving the situation from further deteriorating, i.e. before they start in with *Bimba dagl' occi pieni dim alia* (The Bunny Hop), Butterfly's Uncle Bonze, a Shinto priest, barges onto the scene. He curses and condemns her for rejecting the faith of her ancestors and threatens eternal punishment not only to her, but all the wedding guests, for marrying outside her religion. He turns out to be the quintessential party-pooper. All of the guests scatter, leaving Butterfly in tears. Pinkerton tries to console her in the love duet *O quant' occhi fisi* (Can't Help Falling in Love with You). It is implied that they subsequently have sex.

In Act Two, it is more than three years later. Pinkerton, as you might have guessed, is long gone, but Butterfly, along with her three-year-old boy, who, for some unexplained reason, is named Trouble, still naively waits for her "husband's" return. Butterfly's faithful servant, Suzuki, reminds her that the bank account is running low, and that if Pinkerton doesn't show up soon, they may need to do something creative to earn a few extra yen. She suggests one possibility could be to convert the garden house out back into a workshop for assembling and selling motorbikes. But, Butterfly's faith in her husband's return is unshaken. In tears, Suzuki prays to Buddha. To comfort her, Butterfly sings *Un bel di verdremo*, (One Fine Day) which was destined to later became an A.M. pop radio hit in the summer of 1963, when it was recorded by The Chiffons, a popular all-girl group of the day.

Some day soon, (shoo bee doo bee doo ooh la la) cannon will boom in the harbor announcing the return of the USS Abraham Lincoln (shoo bee doo bee doo ooh la la). I will see Pinkerton climbing the hill, calling out old names of endearment (shoo bee doo bee doo ooh la la). I will tease him by hiding (shoo bee doo bee doo ooh la la) . . .

Butterfly is swept away by the joy of anticipation of her husband's eventual return. In walks Sharpless. He has a letter from Pinkerton. Before he has a chance to read it, however, Butterfly interrupts. She tells him Pinkerton promised to return in the happy season when the robins nested next. She is confused. In Japan, the robins have nested three times since Pinkerton sailed. She wonders if, perhaps, robins in America nest on a different ornithological cycle. Sharpless shakes his head in disbelief. He can't believe how dense this girl is. Once again, Sharpless tries to read the letter.

Goro, who has been hovering outside, laughs aloud at what he has overheard. He enters and tries to convince Butterfly to take a Japanese husband, and presents Yamadori, a wealthy businessman who claims to be in love with her. Butterfly rejects Yamadori and his wealth. He has been many times divorced, and Butterfly scorns him.

"In America," she professes, "spouses remain faithful to one another."

As Sharpless once again tries to read the letter to Butterfly, he suggests to her that Pinkerton may never return. She fetches Trouble, and argues that when Pinkerton learns of his child, he will surely return.

The boom of a cannon sounds from below. Butterfly runs to a spyglass and reads the name of Pinkerton's ship on its bow as it enters the harbor. Her long wait is over! Her husband has returned! Suzuki and Butterfly rush about, scattering cherry blossom petals around the house. Butterfly changes into her wedding kimono, and dresses Trouble in a cute little sailor's suit, but night is falling. The *Abraham Lincoln* will not be able to anchor until morning. Now comes the haunting vigil scene and its humming chorus. Suzuki and Trouble fall asleep leaving Butterfly alone.

The dawn breaks at the beginning of Act Three. Butterfly has been up all night and Suzuki insists that she rests. Butterfly and Trouble retire to an interior room. Up the path comes Sharpless, Pinkerton and Pinkerton's new American wife, Kate. Now here's where things get a little dicey. (In retrospect, it would have been better if Pinkerton had just left Kate on the boat while he grabbed his things.)

Suzuki warmly greets the two men, then, spying Kate, and realizing who she is, collapses in agony. Only after some persuasion, does Suzuki agree to help break the devastating news to Butterfly. Pinkerton, full of remorse, sadly informs Suzuki that he and Kate have only come to adopt the child, and to pick up his green cardigan sweater, which he left in the foyer closet, along with his bowling shoes. He then intends to sail immediately for America.

Pinkerton exits just as Butterfly bursts in, expecting to greet him. Instead she finds a weeping Suzuki, along with Sharpless and the mysterious Caucasian woman. She comes to realize the awful truth. She asks if Pinkerton is alive. Suzuki answers a feeble "yes," and Butterfly knows she has been spurned.

Kate expresses her sympathy and asks for the child. Butterfly replies that to only Pinkerton himself will she relinquish Trouble. Kate and Sharpless leave. Butterfly orders Suzuki to get the boy ready in a different room. Meanwhile, she retrieves her father's dagger, (the one he killed himself with) and prepares for the *seppuku* ritual, "to die with honor when one can no longer live with honor."

In a last-ditch effort to deter Butterfly, Suzuki pushes the boy into the room. Butterfly covers him with kisses and tells Trouble to look into her face so that he will always remember her. She gives him a doll and an American flag to play with, then blindfolds him. She next steps behind a screen (in deference to the more squeamish audience members) and stabs herself. Staggering out, mortally wounded, she stumbles to the boy and gives him one last embrace. Pinkerton walks in as she draws her last breath (now this is the part where the opera gets a little sad) and finds his son sitting on the floor near the boy's dead mother, playfully waving an American flag.

As we left the opera, Maria's eyes were red and swollen with tears. I was still trying to figure out why Butterfly didn't just marry the rich Japanese businessman, Yamadori, buy a nice house with walls, send the kid off to boarding school, and fire Suzuki for being such a downer all the time.

"How did you find the opera?" asked a tuxedoed man in his mid-70s, as we collected out coats.

He had been lasciviously eyeing my wife all evening long, and was addressing Maria, but I answered.

"Oh. It was easy. From the Eisenhower Expressway, we exited at Racine turned north onto Washington, to Wacker Drive, took a right, and there it was. How about you? How did you find the opera?"

"What I meant to . . . I mean . . . We took a cab."

"You're lucky. Sometimes it can be tough finding a cab on opera nights."

Maria grabbed my arm and ushered me away.

"You can be such an asshole sometimes," she snarled.

CHAPTER FORTY

The Grand Opening

Of all the ribbon-cutting ceremonies I had officiated, this was my proudest. We were on Chicago's southeast side, opening my good friend Malcolm's first, of what later turned out to be 11, restaurants. This being Chicago, of course, it took a sizable donation to the ward alderman's campaign fund to secure the necessary zoning, so we were opening on a proverbial shoestring.

"I'm going to miss you at the club," I advised Malcolm. "The washroom attendant who replaced you just doesn't measure up."

"How's that?"

"He never gets the water temperature just perfect, like you used to do."

"There's a knack to it."

"And when he brushes the lint from my clothing, I often get an uncomfortable feeling. You must agree that there is something phallic about that lint brush."

"That, my friend, is strictly between you and your therapist."

"However, he doesn't giggle like a junior high student when someone farts while using the can, like you used to do."

"I'm so glad to be out of that place."

"I bet you are, and I want to thank you again for choosing one of our franchises as the vehicle to do so."

"I'm going to make a go of this taco stand thing, you know."

"I *know* you are. The location has been well researched, Mr. Maciel's business model is irreproachable, and we've got the whole Chicagoland market saturated with advertising . . . print, television, billboards, radio, and subliminal."

"It sounds like an amusement park when you say that."

"Say what? Subliminal?"

"No. *Chicagoland.*"

"It does, doesn't it? Excuse me for a second. I need to get the giant scissors out of my car's trunk. It's almost time for you and your alderman to cut the infamous ribbon."

I walked over to my 1975 *Grand Prix LJ* that I had recently picked up on a lease from *Roseland Pontiac Auto Sales*. It was my second company car. Parked next to me was a Dodge van belonging to the break-dancers we had hired for the entertainment. They were unloading their sound equipment.

"Excuse me, sir," I addressed one of them. He was built like a gymnast and wore a sleeveless white tee shirt and baggy basketball shorts that reached the middle of his calves. "Did you, by chance, notice any suspicious characters around my car here?"

"That's your car?"

"Yes. Yes, it is."

"There's no wheels on your car, mister."

"How about that! I came to exactly the same conclusion. That's why I was asking if you may have seen any suspicious-looking person or persons in the vicinity of my vehicle in the last half hour or so."

"How would you define suspicious?"

"Like someone carrying a four-way spider-type lug wrench, or pushing a hydraulic floor jack, or something along that line."

"Lots of people carry lug wrenches and push jacks in this neighborhood, Jack. You're going to need to be more specific than that."

"Well, perhaps you may have noticed one of those people removing the wheels from my car."

"Oh, him? Yeah, I saw that guy."

"You saw him stealing my wheels?"

"Absolutely."

"Could you tell me what he looked like?"

"Sure. He looked just like the sort of fellow that would steal the wheels right off a fellow's car, if you turned your back on him for more than 30 seconds."

"What would make you think that?"

"Well, first of all, he was carrying a lug wrench and pushin' a jack."

"A lot of guys carry lug wrenches and push jacks in this neighborhood. Could you describe him in better detail for me?"

"Yeah. He was a big ugly white guy with a shaved head and tattoos. Looked like one of those Hell's Angels dudes."

"Did you see what he was driving?"

"Sure. It was a white van."

"Did you, by chance, notice the make or model?"

"No. Just a nondescript white van. Nothing special about it."

"Are you sure it didn't have any distinguishing markings or features? Did it have any dents or scrapes or a broken headlight or anything like that?"

"Well, let me think. There may be one thing I remember that might help."

"What would that be?"

"On the side of the truck, there was some lettering."

"Lettering? That could be a clue. Do you remember what it said?"

"Let me think . . . Yeah. I remember! It said *Five-Star Discount Auto Parts, 1836 South Western Avenue, (312) 885-2200*. Is that any help?"

"Yes! That's a big help. Thank you so very much."

I shook his hand enthusiastically.

"I appreciate your observations. So many people don't want to get involved nowadays, but you've been most helpful."

"There's a couple more things you may want to know that could be beneficial to you if you really want to go after this guy."

"What would that be?"

"They're open every day but Sunday, and they take all major credit cards."

"Wow! Thanks a lot. You're a veritable eagle-eye."

"In this neighborhood, you need to be. And by the way, to report erratic driving, you should phone (800) 293-7094 and refer to vehicle number 6280-B-4Y."

Popping open the trunk, to retrieve the ceremonial scissors I was seeking, I couldn't help but notice that my spare tire was missing as well. I pushed my way back through the crowd, who were assembling, and found Malcolm speaking to a couple of beat cops. He was busy negotiating the terms, cost, and scope of police protection the restaurant was to receive.

" . . . and, of course," one of the coppers was saying, "by convention, police eat for free."

"Hey, officer," I interrupted. "My car's just been broken into. Somebody took all of my wheels, including the spare."

"So, why are you telling *us* this? Do we look like a couple of insurance adjusters to you?"

"No, but you're in law enforcement, aren't you? The last time I heard, stealing wheels was still against the law."

"And did these 'lawbreakers' spit on the sidewalk, too? Look, buddy, we're trying to conduct business here. If someone leaves a body in the trunk of your car sometime, and then sets it on fire under the 'L' tracks, we'll talk, but right now, you're interfering with the duties of a peace officer, and that's a felony!"

"This is crazy . . . even by Chicago standards."

"Standards? Are you being a smart-ass, Buster?"

"No. I'm being a concerned citizen, and you know what? I'm going to report you to the review board on police ethics. What's you badge number?"

"That's it, buddy! You've crossed the line. Now, put your hands behind your head, and turn away from me."

I did as requested. He roughly grabbed me by the wrists, one at time, and handcuffed them behind my back.

"What are you doing?" I asked as I struggled.

"I'm arresting you, dipshit. What did you think I was doing?"

"Arresting me? I've got a grand opening here to officiate. It's important that I do this thing. I wrote a nice speech and all. Look. There are black folks everywhere around here. Why don't you arrest one of them?"

"I would," answered one of the cops. "But then we'd have to transport him back to the stationhouse, and torture him into a confession. That can take hours, and I'm expected at my inlaws' house for dinner tonight at 5:30 to celebrate my niece's first birthday. They live all the way up by Belmont and Cicero. Sorry, Buddy. Some other time. Today, you're going down."

"But please. Just this once. Can't you, only give me a warning?"

The two officers looked curiously at one another.

"What do you say, Fred? Should we give him a warning?"

"Yeah. He seems cool. Just give him a warning."

The first cop then proceeded to un-holster his service pistol, and jabbed its barrel into my throat under my jaw.

"Don't you ever fuck with me again, you little prick," he warned, then pulled the gun away from my throat and fired a single shot into the air, painfully close to my right ear. A bloody pigeon dropped from the sky and plopped to the ground at my feet. The officer holstered his gun, un-cuffed me, and then gave me a shove into the crowd.

"It takes all types," I heard him comment to Malcolm. "You don't happen to *know* this loser, do you?"

"Just some lackey from the corporate office," Malcolm replied. "I *did* hear, somewhere, however, that he had been awarded a Silver Star for valor while in Vietnam."

"A Silver Star, you say? Surely there had to be some mistake *there*. It's my guess they probably gave it to the wrong guy. It may have been something as simple as a transposed serial number. That sort of stuff sometimes happens all the time in large organizations, you know. I was the 46th District's 'Officer of the Month' for March, after all."

CHAPTER FORTY-ONE

Purchasing a Weekend Home

"The real estate agent you engaged is a ditz," complained Maria. "How did you come to choose her?"

The rationale was simple. A photo of her in the real estate brochure depicted an exceptionally attractive woman wearing a sexy short skirt and heels, arms crossed, leaning confidently up against a sold sign.

"For her tenacity and knowledge of the local market," I answered Maria.

We were hunting for a weekend house on Washington Island, in Door County, Wisconsin, a slow-paced, rural getaway, population 700, accessible only by ferryboat or aircraft. For those very reasons, Maria found it quaintly appealing.

We had our eye on a charming little three bedroom, three bath neo-Victorian farmhouse, sitting neatly on forty acres, of mostly agricultural land with ten acres of woods, a barn and a half dozen assorted ancillary outbuildings. Our plan was to view the place on Sunday. Linda was to meet us up at the Northport pier at 20 past noon. We would take her car on the ferry over to the island. It was a simple enough plan. Just in case there was a last-minute glitch, Linda gave us her car phone number.

Back in those days, plumbers and real estate agents had mobile phones installed in their vehicles. There was some sort of a black-box contraption in their trunk and an antenna on the rear window that allowed them to make and receive phone calls while on the go. It was a technological wonder, so much so, that users felt obligated to announce, at the beginning of each phone call, "I'm talking on my car phone." More often than not, however, it sounded more like "I' . . . t . . . ing on m . . . ar ph . . ." This was usually attributed to being in a tunnel, going under a bridge, or nearing the fringes of the caller's service area. Linda's business card listed her office number, FAX, direct line, home phone, car phone, and pager numbers. This made it confusing and difficult to get a hold of her.

Eking out a living in Door County could be a struggle. To do so, Linda, in addition to being a real estate agent, also served as Harbor

Master, Airport Manager, Bar Tender, lingerie model, and school bus driver. She was quite industrious and active in the local *Rotary Club*.

When we arrived at the Northport pier, Linda was nowhere in sight. I fumbled for some coins to use the payphone. Maria helped me out with a quarter she found in her change purse. The phone booth was splattered with stickers suggesting ways to save money on my call. I could, if I wished, dial 1-(800) SAVE BIG, prior to entering Linda's number, for up to a 70 percent discount on my phone call. Another sticker suggested that I hand my life over to Jesus, and there was also a phone number, scribbled in indelible marker, to call for oral sex. This, as it turned out, was disconcertingly the same as Linda's home phone number.

My first attempt connected me to a squealing FAX machine. The second number I tried put me through to Linda's answering machine.

"I am either away from my desk, out of the office, or showing proper-ties," the message informed me. *"Your call is very important to me. Please leave a detailed message and I will return your call as soon as possible."*

Before I could leave my message, Linda pulled up to the pier in her black *Cadillac Fleetwood Brougham DeElegance*. It was equipped with wire wheels, vinyl top, and *"Astro Roof."* The car took up half the parking area.

"Sorry I'm late," she greeted us. "I thought that you might be hungry, so I picked up a dozen eclairs from the *Door County Bakery*."

They were half gone.

Linda was dressed in a tight, short black skirt, high heels, and a white blouse that revealed more cleavage than my dear wife thought to be professional. She also wore an excess of eye shadow, eyeliner, lipstick, and mascara. Some cream filling from the pastries (I trusted) dribbled from her chin and down her front.

"If we hurry, we can catch the one o'clock ferry," she informed us.

She stuffed another eclair in her mouth.

"These are good. You should try one."

We boarded the ferry, leaving it to the ferryboat company's car-jock to drive the *Caddy* onto the boat. After witnessing Linda's parking skills, I was pretty sure that this was a sound idea. The ferry listed past thirty degrees as the four thousand pound car was driven onto the car deck. The starboard propeller lifted entirely out of the water. Panicking passengers ran for their life jackets.

"This is just like the Titanic," Maria observed as people clawed their way to the high side of the vessel.

"Except the Titanic had a band," I reminded her.

A fifty-two-passenger motor-coach, carrying a load of senior citizens from Iowa, next drove on the ferry, counterbalancing the *Cadillac* perfectly. After a leisurely ferryboat ride to the island, during which Linda pitched *Avon* products to Maria, we drove to the prospective property. From the road, it appeared to be just the place we were looking for. A tour of the interior and grounds confirmed this. The secluded acreage held an abundance of flora, dominated by pitch pines, scrub oak, and blackjack oak. A plethora of wildflowers substituted for what would be a lawn. While walking down by the pond, Linda lost one of her shoes in the muck. We found a long stick and recovered it.

"This reminds me of my mud-wrestling days," Linda observed.

Maria and I found a private spot to discuss the property.

"It's just what I had in mind," she informed me. "Let's buy it."

"This property won't last long," Linda called over to us. "If you're interested, we better make an offer today."

"Okay," Maria spoke up after a little more discussion with me. "We'll make an offer."

Linda suggested, to ensure that our offer was seriously entertained, that we come in at 10 percent over the asking price and with no contingencies.

"Sounds reasonable to me," I replied.

Maria glared at me.

"Let me do the negotiating."

After agreeing on a more realistic price for the offer, we sat down at the kitchen table to write a contract. Both Maria and I signed in the designated places. Next, we went back out to the Fleetwood so that Linda could phone the offer to the sellers and their agent. When she told them our offering price, I could hear a lot of whooping and hollering from the other end of the line. They seemed to be very excited.

"I understand," Linda spoke into the phone. "Okay. Okay. I'll tell them." Turning to us with a somber look on her face she said, "They're counter-offering at three hundred and seventy-five thousand. If you really want the place, I suggest that you meet their price. There has been quite a bit of interest in this property."

"But that's more than fifteen percent above the listing price," I argued.

Linda patted the dashboard of the Fleetwood with her free hand and replied, "I don't know any other way that you're going to get back to the mainland today. It can get pretty cold out here at night."

CHAPTER FORTY-TWO

On Stage at the Opera

After holding season tickets at the *Lyric Opera* for a couple of years, and a few martinis, I came up with the idea of auditioning with them as a supernumerary (or additional cast member). It's very like being an extra in the movies. Maria was supportive. Even after all of her disappointments, she was still hoping I would find an activity outside of work that would keep me out of mischief. Although I was competing with over two-dozen hopefuls for nine spots, the audition went well, (I fit the costume) and I felt fortunate to land a part in Verdi's *Rigoletto*.

This opera, I knew, opened with a gratuitous orgy scene, so I "scrutinously" (i.e. lasciviously) looked over the female supers, wondering which one I might be paired with. I finally decided that, although any one of them would be quite satisfactory, my first choice would be the attractive young woman in her mid-twenties with the chestnut-brown hair and perfect body.

Even before the first rehearsal, I excitedly told all my friends at the club that I was going to be in an opera. Many of them went straight out and purchased tickets, as did a couple of our neighbors, some of Maria's friends from church, my mother, and Malcolm. I understood they were all looking forward to seeing me in my stage début, with the exception of Malcolm, who still insisted that he wasn't my friend and was only attending to enjoy, what he considered to be, the first of Verdi's mid to late career operatic masterpieces. There was even an announcement of my landing a part at the Lyric published in my alumni magazine. To say I was excited would be a grand understatement.

I arrived punctually at the stage door for rehearsal number one. Checking in with security, I was issued my photo I.D., and escorted to rehearsal room 200, a large space with high ceilings and mirrored walls. Components of the set we would be using on stage were set up and carts loaded with props lined the walls. Stagehands stood at the ready. A somber-looking group of individuals sat at a folding table strewn with direction notes and reams of music. The director, a flamboyant man in his mid-sixties, dressed in a pink shirt with billowy sleeves, and skin-tight jeans tucked into his engineer boots, introduced himself. Although I had never heard of him, one of the assistant stage directors told me that he was, indeed, renowned . . . the Hank Aaron of opera.

Looking over the supers who had been selected for this production, the director commented that he could always count on the *Lyric* for the "loveliest supernumeraries in the business." One by one, he grasped them from behind by the shoulders and steered them to their marks, giving each a pat on the rear when they reached their position.

"I can't wait to see you in costume and makeup," he proclaimed. "You're all so beautiful! Now, who am I missing?"

"Mr. Johnson and Mr. Wright," the assistant director answered.

"Oh. Mr. Wright. My goodness. For sure, send him over."

The director tilted his head one way, then the other as he inspected the young super.

"Ahh, Mr. Wright. I've been looking for you my entire life," he stated, pinching the man's cheek. "Have you done *Rigoletto* before?"

"No. This is my first time."

"How wonderful! And a *Rigoletto* virgin to boot."

Now alone, I stood at stage left, eagerly waiting to see where he would put *me*. I wondered if I would be in a prominent spot on stage when my "fans" came to see my *Lyric Opera* début. It would be a shame if, after all my hype about being in *Rigoletto*, I were relegated to 30 seconds of stage time in some obscure corner of the set.

"Don't worry Mr. Johnson," the director reassured me, "I have a very special role for you, but we won't be rehearsing it tonight."

He turned to the assistant director and informed her I was released.

"Mr. Johnson, you're released for this evening," announced the A.D. "Back here at 6 p.m. tomorrow night."

It was the same story for rehearsal number two. I was released shortly after I arrived.

Meanwhile, it seemed everyone I knew was interested in how my new career at the *Lyric* was going. I became weary of explaining to them that I still didn't know what I would be doing in this production, but that the director had promised a very special role for me. Although Malcolm was still unimpressed, this pronouncement sold another dozen tickets as curious friends phoned the box office to see if seats were still available. It seemed as if I was going to single-handedly sell out the show.

Rehearsals numbers three and four still left me as a nonparticipant. It wasn't until halfway through the first stage rehearsal that I was finally called upon.

"Where's Mr. Johnson?" the director, speaking into a chrome microphone, inquired.

He was seated in a glass room at the rear of the auditorium. His greatly amplified voice was like one would imagine when God spoke with Moses.

"Right here!" I hollered from my seat in the darkened house. I jumped to my feet.

"Get up on stage," the director's divine voice commanded.

I trotted up the temporary steps built for that purpose and into the bright lights. Squinting, I took a quick look around. The set depicted a magnificent hall in the Ducal palace. Down-stage center was a five-foot long velvet-covered daybed on which I was directed to recline. I did as requested.

After consulting with the A.D., the director asked the chorus master if he was ready. The chorus master indicated with a nod that he was.

"Okay," the assistant director addressed the pianist, "rehearsal five, page sixty-six, bar eleven."

The pianist found her place and began to play. From one of the many doors entered two tenors (the Duke of Mantua and Borsa) who commenced a singing conversation in Italian. All around me, supernumeraries, plus chorus men and women were industriously engaged in your customary orgy activity. A female super went to her knees before a chorus man and began unbuttoning his fly. The attractive young woman, who had caught my attention at rehearsal number one, was pinned up against a pillar, passionately kissing her stage lover. He held her crooked, stocking-clad leg by the thigh while thrusting his pelvis into her. Half-naked couples chased about the stage. On the carpet sprawled a male super, his arms spread like Jesus on the cross, while a bouncing, bare-breasted chorus woman straddled him. I, meanwhile, was still lying on my back on the daybed, wondering how I would be participating in the orgy scene, and trying to guess with which woman (or better yet, *women*). I was also thinking about all of those people who would be coming especially to see me on opening night. I worried just a little, however, that Maria might be just a wee bit jealous to witness me with another lover, even if only acting.

Mentally, I prepared myself for my anticipated role. I wanted to be emotionally one with my character for this, my big stage début. I was determined to be the best damn Act One, Scene One, "orgyist" since *Rigoletto's* premier performance in 1851.

"Now, Mr. Johnson," the director's voice boomed over the loud-speaker system.

Every muscle in my body tensed spontaneously.

"I want you to simulate masturbation."

Even though he still insisted that we were not friends, Malcolm told me that he very much enjoyed my compelling performance.

"The only thing I don't understand," he remarked, "is why were you the only guy on stage without a sex partner?"

"After the bel canto opera movement of the early 19th century," I held forth, "Verdi spearheaded a more forthright and assertive style, blurring the distinction between the aria and recitative as never before. In this context, my part in *Rigoletto* is at once demanding and exposi-tory. Not all actors have the prowess and dexterity for such a complex and nuanced role."

"I have to say," Malcom agreed. "You certainly are dexterous. I just never presumed that a talent like that could land you such a prominent role in Italian Grand Opera."

CHAPTER FORTY-THREE

Anticipating My Second Visit to Kentucky

Maria and I held hands as we walked with little Yazmin around Lake Ellyn. The Redbuds were in full bloom and a balmy breeze blew from the southwest, kicking up little whitecaps that gently lapped the shore. When she spied the playground, Yazmin raced ahead and climbed the slide apparatus. With a wave from the summit, she called, "Hey, Mom! Watch this," and then she launched herself through the twisting tube. Maria and I took our regular Saturday morning seats on the park bench and chatted while we kept a watchful eye over Yazmin's frenetic activities.

"See, Bruce," Maria explained, snuggling up to me on the bench. "It *is* possible to give Yazmin memories she won't need to repress."

She was right. My life felt so perfect, it actually made me a bit uneasy; a little anxious.

"Are you still going to Kentucky on Monday?" Maria inquired.

"Yes. I'll be going into the office first and leave from there. It's open-ended when I'll be returning; probably Thursday or Friday."

"Did you want me to pack your suitcase?"

"No, thanks. I can do it."

"You're so pensive when you travel to Kentucky. Is it because you're still contemplating a visit to the family of that army buddy of yours; the one who was killed?"

"Maria, how do you know me so well?"

"You talk in your sleep."

"You're pulling my leg now, aren't you?"

"No."

"Yes you are."

"Who's Marge?"

"That's totally unfair!"

"Who is she?"

"She's just a waitress at the club."

"A waitress at the club, you say? Do you want my advice?"

"Sure."

"Ask Rafael to reassign Marge to a station that does not include your table, apologize to me over dinner at the *Cape Cod Room*, and go see them."

"Whom?"

"The Hastings. This thing has been nagging at you ever since you opened that restaurant in Henderson. I think it will lift a burden from your soul, and although I could only imagine what it would be like to lose a son like that, my guess is that his parents would be gratified to hear from you."

"But what do I say to them? That I knew Bill? That I was with him when he died? What if they ask me if he died quickly or painlessly? What do I say then? Do I lie to them, or do I tell his parents how he laid fully conscious in the mud for forty-five minutes, with his intestines spilled out through his stomach wound, begging for someone to do something?"

"I don't think I'd tell them that."

"Do something! What the hell was I supposed to do? Try to shove his guts back in his abdomen? Put a bullet in the base of his head? Damn, Maria! I was just a 19-year-old kid. Nothing had ever prepared me for that type of shit!"

"Settle down, Bruce. Settle down." Maria encouraged me in a soothing voice. "I can see how upsetting this is for you, but I still think you should visit them. I really do."

Ms. Dorsey handed me the file she had put together in preparation for my trip.

"Everything we discussed is in there," she advised me. "Since you're driving yourself to the airport, you'll need to be getting on the road soon to allow time for parking. I suggest you use the main parking garage. The outbound Kennedy, I-290 circle to O'Hare is running 34 minutes. Do you have your extra set of car keys in your briefcase?"

"Yes. Thank you, Ms. Dorsey. You're the best."

"Good. We don't want a repeat of that incident when you returned from San Francisco now, do we?"

"No, Ms. Dorsey."

I put the file I had been handed into my attaché case, along with a copy of *Zen and the Art of Motorcycle Maintenance,* then sat back in my chair, and took in a long view of my office. On the wall I faced hung an

Erte print, *L'Oriental.* Below it, and to the right, perched on an onyx pedestal, a Demetre Chiparus sculpture pleased my eye. Other original art, that my father-in-law had acquired to decorate my office, included works by Armand Godard and Bruno Zach. Even my paperweight was *Victoire* by Lalique.

As I rose to fetch my hat and coat, one last object caught my eye. It was the shadowbox housing my Silver Star. I paused to pick it up. I examined the gold, five-pointed star with a laurel wreath, encircling rays emanating from the smaller silver star in the center. Looking at it brought back memories. They weren't memories I cared to visit just now. I started to replace it on my credenza, but changed my mind mid-action, and tucked it, instead, into my case.

"I'm off!" I bid goodbye to my secretary. "See you on Monday. I'll phone in regularly. I promise."

"Have a good trip and save your receipts."

"I will."

"And take your vitamins every day. Just because I'm not there to remind you doesn't mean that you can skip them."

"Yes, Ms. Dorsey."

"And when you land, be sure to . . ."

"I'm getting in the elevator now. Goodbye."

On the third floor, I was joined in the elevator by Li Wang, our chief chef in the test kitchens.

"Good afternoon, Mr. Johnson."

"Good afternoon, Li. Any exciting new authentic Mexican menu ideas I should know about?"

"I've come up with a couple of proposals to tweak our new breakfast offerings."

"Good. Good. I'll be looking forward to sampling them when I return from my trip."

"May I ask you a personal question, Mr. Johnson?"

"I'm not sure. Just how personal, exactly, are you talking?"

"I was wondering about your relationship with your wife. When she attends company functions, the two of you always seem so happy together; so much in love. How do you maintain that spark?"

Messing with her, I replied with my old joke, "Well, don't let this get around, but I'm actually a woman trapped inside a man's body."

"I know. I read it in the *Glen Ellyn News.*"

"Oh, yeah. I forgot about that. Maria was horrified by that article. Why are you asking me all of this?"

"Because I became engaged over the weekend."

She held out her left hand to display her ring.

"That's a pretty small diamond you've got there."

"It is, and my fiancé is considerably embarrassed by that fact. It was what he could afford, though. He's a social worker, you see. He works for the *Department of Child Services*."

"Well, in that case then, I retract my previous observation. It's not a small diamond at all, but one that's, how shall we say, differently sized."

"Of course. There's nothing wrong with my diamond. The problem lies with the diamond sizing and grading system."

"Now, you're catching on. You're not *humiliated* by your cheap-ass engagement ring from *J. C. Penny's*; you're *empowered* by it! Right?"

"So then, what you're saying is that all I need to do, to be as fulfilled and happy in my marriage as you and Maria, is to define some sort of a measurable outcome, and do a factual analysis."

"And now you know my secret for a good marriage. Keep your sense of humor."

"Thanks for the advice, Mr. Johnson."

"And there's just one more thing I might suggest, if you really want to have a happy marriage."

"What's that, Mr. Johnson? I'm all ears."

"Are you sure you want to hear it?"

"Please. Go ahead. I have a lot of respect for your wisdom."

"Well, if it's not too late. I mean if you're not pregnant or something, what you should really do is marry someone else, not the social worker fellow who gave you this cheap-ass piece of crap ring."

CHAPTER FORTY-FOUR

My Second Business Trip to Kentucky

Slowly, I drove past the Hastings' place in the *Lincoln Town Car* Ms. Dorsey had reserved for me with the rental company. The one-story, metal-roofed house was sided with tarpaper. A *Maytag* wringer-type washing machine stood on the front porch, and clothes hung on the line, blowing in the warm southerly spring breeze. A woman, who appeared to be in her late fifties, toiled in the half-acre plus vegetable garden. She was, apparently, incorporating hog manure into the soil. I inferred this from the fetor. When she looked up, wiping her brow, I accelerated away and drove immediately back to the car rental kiosk at the airport.

"Yes, sir. May I help you?" the young woman at the counter offered. She was dressed in a uniform very much like an airline stewardess'.

"My secretary made a mistake when she reserved this car," I explained. "I really needed something more pedestrian for this trip."

I laid my paperwork out on the counter.

"May I exchange this car for something smaller perhaps?"

"You say you want a *pedestrian* automobile?"

"Yes."

"Isn't that an oxymoron?"

"I suppose you could look at it that way. You see, what I need is an *unpretentious* car."

"I'm so sorry you found your *Lincoln* to be pretentious. If you were to look in the owner's manual, however, you would find the car's engine requires only 'regular' unleaded gasoline. I don't think that's very ostentatious, quite frankly."

"Nonetheless, I would really prefer something considerably more on the modest end of the spectrum. How about a *Pinto*? Does *Ford* still build *Pintos*?"

"Wow! You weren't kidding when you said you wanted something unpretentious. However, I'm afraid that we don't have a *Pinto* available at this time. Would a *Mercury Bobcat* be satisfactory? It's similar to a *Ford Pinto* only less 'equinesk' and more cat-like."

"You say they're similar, though?"

"Yes. They come down the same assembly line in Edison, New Jersey. The *Mercury* has a slightly modified front grill design, and the tail lights are in a different configuration, but it retains the *Pinto's* lack of an adequate reinforcing structure between the rear panel and the fuel tank."

"What are you saying?"

"The vehicle will likely explode into a big boiling orange ball of flame if rear-ended."

"Holy cow! Does *Ford* know about this defect?"

"They do, but their accountants conducted a cost-benefit analysis and determined that, based on the $11 per car fix, it would be cheaper to pay off the anticipated lawsuit settlements from the resulting deaths."

"Boy, that's scary, but I suppose it makes sense. They need to be accountable to their stockholders, after all. How many people have died like that?"

"Actually, not nearly as many as you would expect. You see, the *Pinto* is also equipped with woefully inadequate four-wheel drum brakes. Overwhelmingly, they are the ones to do the rear-ending, and are rarely rear-ended themselves."

"That's crazy!"

"Now, if all of this makes you reluctant to take a *Bobcat* out into traffic, I also have a *Chevy Vega* available. It too is a very unassuming vehicle."

"No, thank you. I *do* want an unpretentious car for my purposes, but I think a *Vega* would be taking things just a little to the extreme. After all, there's a steep hill I need to climb to get where I'm going."

"Oh, well, then. The *Vega* will never do. At only 70 horsepower, it's more of a city car."

After a few swift strokes on her computer keyboard, the industrious little printer on the back bar inserted the pertinent information on the rental forms, and she tore off my new contract along the perforations. Placing the document in front of me, and reading upside-down, she used her pen to point.

"Just sign here and here. Initial here if you are declining the optional insurance and check this box here."

"What does it *mean* when I check this box."

"You are indicating that you have read the entire contract and agree to all of its terms and conditions."

"But actually, I *haven't* read the entire contract."

"In that case then, you can check this other box here."

"What does it mean when I check that box, then."

"Nothing really. It's just some verbiage our legal people insisted on putting in there. You know how lawyers are. However, if you *do* check that box, we won't be able to rent a car to you today."

I made my marks as requested.

"Good. Good. Someone will bring your vehicle around at once. Do you have the keys to the *Lincoln*?"

"Yes. They're right here." I handed them to her.

"Here. You may want to keep these."

She handed back the keys to my company car, which I forgot I had attached to the key ring of the rental.

"Oh, thanks. I did that in San Francisco once, and boarded my flight without my personal car keys. It was a fiasco when I got back to Chicago."

"It happens all the time."

"Really? You mean I'm not the only one?"

"No. Actually, I've never heard of such a lame-brained stunt before."

"But you said it happens all the time."

"I was just trying to make you feel less stupid. It was like a white lie."

"How do you mean, *white* lie?"

"In customer service training, they teach us to tell white lies if it helps to set the renter at ease."

"So, you're taught to *lie* to the customer?"

"Yes, but only *white* lies."

"I don't understand. What do you mean by white lies?"

"Oh. We use them all the time. For example, did you notice the advertising banner over the counter when you walked up?"

I stepped back and looked upwards.

"You mean $9.99 per day, unlimited mileage, weekend rentals?"

"Yes. Well, you see, that's a white lie; and have you ever heard our motto, *we try harder?*"

"That's a white lie, too?" I asked incredulously.

"I'm sorry to burst your bubble. Don't you ever use white lies in *your* business?"

I considered the question for a few seconds and contemplated the recipe for our *all beef* taco filling.

"I guess, when I really think about it, we do indeed tell white lies from time to time," I answered.

"See, I told you so. Now, is there anything I can do to be of further assistance?"

"No, thank you. You've been a great help."

"In that case then, I want to thank you for choosing us for your car rental needs. It has been a real pleasure serving you today."

I looked her in the eye.

"White lie?"

She shrugged her shoulders.

"Sorry."

I accelerated hard onto Route 212, but for some reason my rental car seemed sluggish. I checked to see if I had left the parking brake on. I hadn't. At once, my entire rearview mirror was filled with the reflection of the grill of a giant semi-truck; a *Peterbilt*, to be exact. I pushed the accelerator to the floor in an attempt to kick in the passing gear of my baby *Mercury*. She downshifted as I had hoped, the engine's RPMs increased to a feverish pitch, but the car went no faster. It just got louder. By the time I pulled into the parking lot of my hotel, I was all too familiar with the sound of car horns, and the Doppler effect they produce when passing.

Still shaking, and drenched in sweat, I inserted the key into the lock of my room and pushed open the door. The temperature inside was about the same as one would adjust his refrigerator to, if he had been having a problem with his beer freezing. I walked over to the combination heating/air conditioning unit below the window, which was earnestly rattling away, blowing the frigid air into the room. Opening the little metal control panel access door, I found a host of choices, selections, and options. There was *heat/cool, high/low, on/off, outside air*, some push-buttons numbered one to four, and a little dial with arching arrows indicating *cooler/warmer*. It appeared that everything the building engineer would need to achieve a comfortable seventy-two degrees was there, if adjusted in just the perfect combination.

I made the appropriate phone call, and in no time at all, the engineer on duty was at my side. The script sewn into his blue work shirt told me his name was Justin, and the patch over his other pocket indicated that he was (comfortingly) a union stationary engineer; something I never would have expected in Kentucky. I apologized for the inconvenience.

"Oh, don't you worry about it in the least. I just happened to have a few minutes between lunch hour and my mandated afternoon coffee break. We'd much prefer that you report this at once, rather than waiting until you suffer from hypothermia. All too often, by the time I get the call, our guest has become disoriented, confused, and combative, exhibiting incoherent and irrational behavior."

"That's all from the cold?"

"And also from being in the *American Legion* . . . and drunk."

"Well, I just wasn't sure how to adjust this thing. To me, it looks very much like the instrument panel of a Boeing 747; less the turn and bank indicator and artificial horizon, of course."

"Basically, it's a lot simpler than it looks," Justin explained to me. "I know that with all of these intimidating controls, it can be a little overwhelming, but when all is said and done, it actually boils down to just two simple choices. Most of these knobs and buttons do absolutely nothing. In fact, they're not even hooked up to anything inside." (I had always suspected this to be the case.)

"So, what are my two choices?" I asked.

"They would be these two buttons over here," he pointed as he spoke.

"Off and On?"

"Yep. If you get too hot, you push the *on* button, and when it gets too cold, like now, you push the *off* button. In the winter, it's the same, only opposite."

CHAPTER FORTY-FIVE

The Hastings

Awakened by the ringing racket of my *Bulova* folding clamshell travel alarm the next morning, I showered, dressed, then grabbed a cup of coffee and a cheese Danish from the hotel's courtesy bar. Today, I had promised myself, would be the day that I visited the Hastings, and I wanted to get a bright and early start; before I changed my ambivalent mind. Holding the gooey pastry in my teeth, while I fumbled for the car keys, I approached my rental. There was a note under the driver's-side windshield wiper. I placed my coffee on the roof, unlocked the door, tossed my attaché case (containing my Silver Star) on the passenger seat, and took the note in hand. Unfolding the paper, I read the succinct message: "Learn to drive, asshole," it charitably suggested.

The drive to Beaver Lick was uneventful, save a close call with an opossum on Dickerson Road, and another with an 18-wheeler, just outside Cincinnati. I also experienced some consternation on a long downhill grade where my brakes exhibited a disconcerting amount of fade as they approached the "knee point" on the temperature-friction curve. Driving a Bobcat in traffic, I soon discovered, tested one's mettle more so than anything I had ever experienced in combat. For my own wellbeing, I considered driving back to the airport to retrieve the *Town Car* I had exchanged.

The racket of Ginny Hens announced my arrival to the Hastings, as I courageously pulled in their driveway. After turning off the ignition, the engine of my rental car continued to diesel for ten to fifteen seconds, shaking the vehicle from side to side and producing an odor of rotten eggs. It was very embarrassing; Detroit's version of farting in public.

"Hello, there! What can we do for you, son?" a slim man in his late fifties greeted me as I exited the car.

"Are you Mr. Hastings?" I inquired.

"I'm *Pastor* Hastings to my flock," he replied.

"My name is Bruce Johnson. If I have the right Pastor Hastings, I was in Vietnam with your son Bill."

There, I did it. There was no turning back *now*.

"Well, you've the right place, boy, and I have to tell you, this is quite a bolt from the blue."

"I'm so sorry, sir. I should have phoned first. You do have telephone service out here, don't you?"

"Yes we do, and it's quite all right. Come inside. I think there's still some coffee left from breakfast."

"Virginia! This young man has come to visit us. He served in Vietnam with Billy."

"I'm Bruce."

I extended my hand to the woman I had seen in the garden the previous day.

"Oh, dear! This is quite a surprise."

"I know. I was just telling Pastor Hastings that it was rude of me not to phone first."

"Oh, don't you worry about *that*. Please sit down. Do you want me to take your case?"

"No, I'll just hold it, thank you."

"So. You were in the war with our son."

"Yes."

"How interesting."

"We were actually pretty good friends."

"He may have mentioned you in his letters. It's been some time. I don't recall right now."

"We also went through Basic and AIT together."

"Oh, sure! Now I remember him mentioning you. Did you want some coffee?"

I spied Bill's photo on the fireplace mantel. A sense of terror suddenly overwhelmed me.

"No, thank you. I really need to go."

My heart was pounding so hard, I swore Bill's folks could hear it beating in my chest. I was having cold sweats and a difficult time breathing.

"I was just in the vicinity, so I thought I'd stop by and say hello."

"But you've only . . ."

Pastor Hastings put his hand up to hush his wife.

"I'm sure Bruce is on a very tight schedule, Mother. If he says he needs to go, we must respect that. Thank you for stopping son. I'll walk you to your car. Perhaps you can come by again someday when you have more time."

We were now at my car, out of earshot of Mrs. Hastings.

"It would mean a lot to my wife and me if you would do that," he spoke now in a low, soft, and soothing voice.

"I'll do that. I'll stop again when I have more time, and I'll phone first. Goodbye. It was nice to meet you."

I squeezed into my tiny rental car and pulled out onto the gravel road. I was shaking so uncontrollably that it was difficult to drive. Just as soon as I was out of sight of the Hastings homestead, I pulled off the road, got out and I kicked a big dent in the driver's door. I walked around the car, with my fists clenched, taking long deep breaths. I kept circling that piece of crap *Mercury Bobcat* until, after a dozen or so orbits, I had calmed down enough to wedge back into the driver's seat and drive to the Greater Cincinnati Airport.

"There's a big dent in the door here," the car rental porter observed.

"Where?"

"Right here. I don't know how you couldn't have noticed it when you got in to drive."

"Oh, that. I guess I must have parked in a bad spot. Have the girl at the front desk put the repair costs on my company credit card."

"Did you file a police report?"

"No, I didn't. Look. Please. I'm in a hurry. Just charge me for the damages. I'm trying to catch an early flight out of here this afternoon. It's very important that I get back to Chicago just as soon as possible. I really need to get home to see my wife."

"I'm sorry, but it's going to be necessary to have someone look at this."

"What's there to look at? It's a dent. Haven't your people ever seen a dent before?"

"Did you sign the damage waiver?"

"I don't know what I signed. I signed where the gal inside told me to."

"Which box did you check?"

"I don't know. Here's my contract. Look for yourself."

I handed my papers to the man.

"This contract is for a *Lincoln Town Car*."

"So?"

"You can't rent a *Town Car* but return a *Bobcat*. You have to return the same car you rented."

"Look. It's been a very stressful day for me. In spite of that, I'm going to very calmly board that shuttle bus over there and take it back to the terminal where I'm going to see if I can procure a seat on the 1:40 flight back to Chicago. Here's your car back. It is *not* a *Lincoln Town Car*. It's a *Mercury Bobcat*. It has a big dent in the door. You have my credit card number. We have nothing further to discuss."

"But . . ."

"No. No. No. No. Don't speak. Do you have a wife? Children . . . people who love and depend on you? Because if you do, it's absolutely critical to them that you unconditionally understand, *unequivocally*, that I am a Vietnam veteran who suffers from Post-Traumatic Combat Stress Disorder. My condition has been in remission more or less for a number of years now; since I first met the woman who is now my loving wife. But! At this very moment, due to circumstances that I do not care to bore you with, the disease, I feel, is percolating to the surface. Trust me when I tell you that you do not want to be an obstacle in my path to boarding that flight this afternoon.

CHAPTER FORTY-SIX

Back Home

I entered the house through the service door from the garage. Maria was in the den, reading her Spanish-language newspaper by the light of the late afternoon sun. I ran to her, grabbed her, and nearly smothered the poor woman with a powerful bear hug that lifted her feet clear off the ground. She made a muffled attempt to speak.

"Oh, Maria! I missed you so much; you and Yazmin."

She broke free enough to reply.

"I'm inferring from your demonstrativeness that you worked up the nerve and visited the Hastings."

"I did and it was awful. Just awful. I don't know what possessed me to do it. What in the world made me think that these people would ever want to see me, and dredge up hard memories of their dead son? It must be one of the most idiotic things I have ever done. You married a fool, Maria."

"I know, but I was in love."

"Thanks."

"I'm *so* sorry that it didn't go well, Bruce. What happened? Did you receive the impression that you were trespassing in their lives? Is that it? Did they resent your visit?"

"No. Not at all. They were quite cordial, actually."

"But, nonetheless, it went badly?"

"Well, for me it did. I think they were fine with my stopping by."

"Don't tell me you freaked!"

"I *absolutely* did. I suffered the mother of all anxiety attacks right there in their living room; cold sweats, nausea, acute anxiety. Like I said, it was just awful!"

"Well, you're home now and Yazmin is at her friend's for a play date. She's having dinner with them. Do you want to have sex? Would that help take the edge off?"

"Let me think about this now. It's *been* awhile, hasn't it?"

"For me it has. On the other hand, I don't know what *you* do for relaxation on those business trips of yours."

"Me? I harass and torment the poor parents of soldiers killed in combat. What did you think? It makes for splendid leisure-time recreation, you know. It's very entertaining. In fact, I think I'll write a book about it someday. That way people far and wide can be vicariously amused by my wacky escapades."

"If this is going to be one of those 'kiss and tell' books, you can forget about that proposition I just made."

"Maria. If I ever write a book about my life, the whole world is going to know what a special person you are."

"Good."

"And all about the steamy sex we have."

"That's it! You lost your opportunity."

"Oh, come on. I was just joking around."

"Forget it!"

"Well, let me tell you. They're going to know about *that,* too."

"Who's going to know about what?"

"My readers. They're going to know how capricious you can be."

"So, this *is* going to be one of those tell-all books, is it?"

"It's my book, so it can be anything I want."

"I know what you're doing, Bruce. You're avoiding the essence of our conversation by talking nonsense. Now, tell me straight up. What did the Hastings have to say?"

"Not much. I wasn't there long. Pastor Hastings *did* say that I should come back again someday when I could stay longer."

"You should do that, then."

"But what if they invite me for dinner?"

"Then you should have dinner with them."

"What if they serve possum?"

"Then, I wouldn't stay for dinner if I were you, and I'd steer away from the raccoon stew too, but that's just me."

"Mr. Hastings is a Baptist minister, you know. What if he wants to make a circle with the chairs and read bible verses? What if he tries to save me?"

"You tell him that you're Catholic."

"But then he might try to convert me."

"I'm pretty sure Baptists view Catholics, along with Scientologists and Theistic Satanists, as lost beyond any plausible hope of salvation."

"Well then, what if I need to use the bathroom, and they tell me it's out back."

"I don't care how many excuses you fabricate, I'm your wife, you asked for my opinion, and I advocate seeing them again; only next time, I suggest making prior arrangements. Send them a note to let them know when you'll be in the area. Let them invite you. If you had an invitation, wouldn't that make you feel more comfortable?"

"Yeah. I suppose so. But Maria, I can't even begin to describe to you how horrific it was for me. There was a graduation photo of Bill on their mantel. His mother still had a shoebox full of his letters that she saved. I had to drive a *Mercury Bobcat* on the four-lane, for heaven's sake!"

"I never heard of a *Mercury Bobcat*."

"It's similar to a *Ford Pinto*, only more cat-like."

"But, I thought Ms. Dorsey always reserved premium rental cars for you."

"She did. She reserved a *Lincoln Town Car* for me, but the Hastings' house had tarpaper for siding so I had to trade it in for a *Bobcat*, and then the car rental girl told me this white lie and made me check a box on the contract against my will so that when I returned a different car than the one I rented, and it had a big dent in the driver's door, the porter started giving me grief, and I almost missed my flight which, if I had, I'm pretty sure it would have gone very badly at the airport, and there would have been a police standoff, and it would have made the five o'clock news in Cincinnati. I would have been identified by some pretty, young, female reporter as a Vietnam veteran who snapped."

"Bruce! What's gotten into you? I've never seen you like this."

"Oh, Maria. I don't want to give up my Silver Star. I'd have nothing, if not for that medal. Nothing! Not you, nor Yazmin, or this house, or my job. I'd be one of those homeless guys living in a cardboard box on Lower Wacker Drive."

"You're scaring me, Bruce. You're really scaring me. Come upstairs and let's lie down together. We don't need to have sex. Let's just hold each other."

Maria took me by the hand and led me to our bedroom where I fell asleep in her arms.

CHAPTER FORTY-SEVEN

My Identity Thief

It was a picture-perfect late spring afternoon. Yazmin was merrily riding her tricycle in the driveway, Maria picked zinnias from the cutting garden, and I was filling sand bags when the mailman, his heavy bag slung over his shoulder, approached, aiming his aerosol can of mace at my face.

"Now Mr. Johnson, I don't want any trouble from you. I just need you to sign for a registered letter from the IRS, and I'll then be on my way."

If you've ever had dealings with the IRS, then I probably don't need to tell you that they can be, well, heavy-handed at times. It seems that, evidently, there were some tax liabilities I incurred (and never paid) when I inherited my grandfather's estate. This got them on a roll. Next, some snot-nosed agent tried telling me there existed some sort of silly rule where you're supposed to withhold taxes on your housekeeper's wages, and send them in on a quarterly basis, plus . . . and you're not going to believe this one . . . according to him, it turned out that I was supposed to be filing annual income tax returns!

So, thanks to the IRS's indefatigable persistence, and also because of some co-pays and deductible items from my health-care provider that somehow were never reconciled, and some overlooked credit card bills, I was receiving dozens of phone calls daily from collection agencies all around the United States, and one in Idaho. Although most of these annoyances could be quite tiresome, there was *one* sexy-voiced collection agent, named Jill, whom I actually *enjoyed* hearing from. She did, however, have a habit of phoning me at the most awkward moments, so, for convenience sake, I convinced Jill to give me her phone number at home. That way, I was able to relax comfortably with a cigar and a brandy, in my tufted leather burgundy club chair next to a cozy crackling fire on the hearth, and chat with her at my leisure. Jill, I learned, was a single mom with two sweet little boys, ages 8 and 10.

"I'm also in the opera." I boasted to her in one flirtatious phone conversation. "I just finished Rigoletto at the Lyric Opera of Chicago."

"How fascinating. I adore opera. Do you sing?"

"Well, no. Actually, I masturbate."

"Oh! My goodness. What kind of phone line did you think this is? Did you think that I was going to talk dirty with you?"

"No. No. Not at all. I don't think you understand. That was my part in *Rigoletto*."

"Of course it was. And I'm lying here buff-naked, sprawled out on my satin sheets, with a vibrator."

"Is that true, or are you just being sarcastic?" I asked sheepishly, but by that time, she had already hung up on me.

I didn't hear from her for a while after that. Meanwhile, due to all the "hate mail" I was receiving from my creditors, Gabriel, our gardener, found it convenient to leave a polyethylene U.S. Mail tote by our front door to accommodate the avalanche of letters I was receiving daily. I gave him my permission to read them when he got bored. Gabe found some of my collection of letters to be quite entertaining.

"Mr. Johnson," Gabriel greeted me one afternoon, "it says here that you have five business days to remit or they're going to cut your electricity off."

"Believe me," I replied, "They've threatened to cut off far worse than that."

"You're the only person I ever knew that has a *negative* credit score. How come you don't pay your bills, Mr. Johnson?"

"I would, Gabriel, I really would, except it's gotten *so* far out of hand now that I wouldn't know where to begin."

Then, a year ago last January, the phone calls abruptly stopped, the collection notices were, all at once, entirely absent from my mail deliveries, and Gabriel found it necessary to take out a subscription to the *Wall Street Journal* for some entertaining and informative substitute reading material. As it turned out, I had become a hapless victim of identity theft!

For the first time in years, I was at peace. No more shady-looking people popping out of the bushes, serving me papers. No more harassing phone calls. No more threatening collection letters. Someone else, it seemed, now possessed my identity, including all the pesky annoyances that went with it. Not only was a heavy burden lifted from my shoulders but I was now also receiving some excellent investment advice from Gabriel. With his help, I was making a killing in the commodities market, buying and selling pork belly futures, of all things . . . tax free!

Meanwhile, six weeks passed before my identity thief inevitably called. It was pretty late in the evening as I remember, an unusual time for my phone to ring, now that the collection agencies had stopped badgering me.

I took the call waiting.

"Mr. Johnson?" came the disheartened voice from the other end of the line. "I want to offer you your identity back. For only one hundred dollars, your life can return to normal."

"Well, you'll need to give me some time to think about *that* one," I replied.

"Look!" he snapped. "You can have it back for free if you want . . . and I'll toss in a list of 10 debit card numbers along with their corresponding pins."

I hung up. This guy sounded, to me, like he might be some sort of a charlatan or a confidence man or something. The next evening I heard from him again.

"Listen buddy. I'm not fooling around here. I know people who can make you rue the day you were born. You take your identity back or else there will be no place on this spinning planet of talking monkeys for you to hide."

I doubted that to be true. I could think of many good hiding places where no one would think to look. For example, what about behind the waterfall at Niagara, New York, or inside Roosevelt's nostril at Mount Rushmore? This guy seemed a bully, so I refused to capitulate to his threats, and indeed, he followed through with his promise by hiring a couple of goons to "rough me up." My tormentor was not one to make idle threats, I quickly learned. Unfortunately for him, however, since he now held my identity, these hired thugs knocked on *his* door instead of mine. When he answered, they dutifully beat the snot out of him, leaving the poor schmuck with a broken nose and two cracked ribs. He phoned me again the next evening, pleading.

"Perhaps if you gave me a little monetary incentive, I would consider it," was my response to his insufferable whimpering.

"What did you have in mind?"

"Pay off my IRS debt and my doctor bills, and I'll take my identity back."

There was a long pause over the phone. In the background I could hear the faint voices of another party's conversation bleeding over to our connection, then my caller's voice back on the line again.

"How about if I pay for the fines, penalties and interest on your IRS obligation, while you pay only the original tax liability?"

"But what about my doctor bills?"

"Okay. I'll agree to pay the outstanding balance for the surgeon and the anesthesiologist but I think it's only fair that you pick up the operating room costs. If you agree, I can have my attorney draw up the papers in the morning."

It sounded to me like a good compromise but I acted as if I was reluctant to agree.

"Okay." I answered after a long hesitation. "You've got a deal then; and by the way, have you by chance received any collection calls from a young woman named Jill?"

"Dude! Are you kiddin' me? Has she got the sexiest telephone voice you have ever heard or what? Where do you think she's from, Kentucky?"

"Bowling Green, to be exact," I answered. She's a single mom with two sweet little boys, ages 8 and 10. I've got her home phone number and address around here somewhere, if you want it."

I fumbled through one of the drawers in my smoking stand.

"Here it is. Do you have something to write it down with?"

"Yeah. I have a nice silver-plated *Parker Premier* fountain pen, as a matter of fact, with the 18-karat gold nib."

"That's a pretty impressive writing instrument you've got there pal."

"Thanks. In all candor, I actually purchased it with your *American Express Gold Card.*"

I read Jill's address and phone number off the scrap of paper.

"Thanks, buddy. I really appreciate that. Are you sure you don't mind if I call her?"

"No. Not at all. I'm a married man, after all. I shouldn't be carrying on with another woman anyhow; even if just chatting on the phone."

"Well, you have a very lucky wife. You're a good person."

"I try to be. I always try. Character counts, you know."

"By the way. There's just one more thing."

"Sure. What is it?" I insisted.

"I'm almost too embarrassed to ask."

"No, really, go ahead. You and I are like confidants. We're pals. You can ask me anything. What is it?"

"You didn't, by chance, also happen to get Jill's Social Security number, did you?"

CHAPTER FORTY-EIGHT

Washington Island

Growing up in suburban Chicago, Yazmin, like me for that matter, had little exposure to rural life. The furthest she had ventured down the food distribution chain was a Jewish delicatessen in West Rogers Park. For her, the four major food groups were, Kosher, Chinese, Italian, and Mexican. Maria wanted Yazmin to be more culinarily well-rounded than that. She wanted her to understand, with the possible exception of sausage, where her meals came from. For some inexplicable reason, Maria wanted Yazmin to milk a cow.

Vern, our next door neighbor on Washington Island, as chance would have it, owned a dairy farm complete with a herd of dairy cows that, twice daily, needed milking. I was told this included Sundays and most holidays. The drive north was picturesque. Along the way, Maria played an entertaining travel game with Yazmin. It was called I spy. Taking turns, one of us would say, for example, "I spy with my little eye something *blue*," and then the others would have to guess what it might be. Maria sure had a knack for entertaining children on long rides. Yazmin, it seemed, loved to play this game, which continued on and on, long after it had ceased to be amusing.

"I spy with my little eye something black and white," she chirped.

"I know that one," I responded excitedly. "It's a Holstein cow."

'No," replied Yazmin. "It's a police car!"

As the stern-faced officer wrote my second ticket in six months, Yazmin, unvexed, continued with the insufferable game. I ultimately had to resort to playing my *Fleetwood Mac* tape at somewhere in the neighborhood of 135 decibels. (For reference, that would be the equivalent of a London air raid siren.)

We docked in Washington Island's Detroit Harbor on the last ferry from the mainland that evening, too late for the afternoon milking. Mrs. Harrison greeted us with hugs.

"Vern is in the main barn over yonder," she indicated a red building with a tall blue silo attached. "He's been looking forward to your arrival all day."

First impressions, they say, are lasting. I have to agree. My first impression of our neighbor Vern is indelible. As we walked into the barn, I was greeted by the sight of the man with his arm, past the elbow, up the rectum of a cow. He was in the process of artificially inseminating the beast. Now if one happens to be the type of person, as am I, who can't manage even a vestigial of conversation with a mother while she is breast-feeding her baby in my presence, multiply that discomfort by 10-fold.

"Hi," greeted Farmer Vern. "I'd shake your hand, but I'm a little busy right now."

I felt like running, but I just stood there, speechless. It was obvious to everyone that I didn't possess the mental maturity necessary to deal with this in an adult manner, so Farmer Vern tried to set me at ease with a little bucolic levity.

"I was just pointing at this here cow when she all-a-sudden backed up on me."

I promised myself, right then and there, that during our entire visit I would only refer to any cow I had occasion to discuss, verbally, and only verbally, such as "That big black and white one over there in the corner." No pointing at them.

"Actually, I caught this cow in standing heat this morning," Farmer Vern continued. "I bred her once before and thought she had settled, but I guess I was wrong. Luckily, I had one last straw of Black Star semen left in the tank. After I'm done here, I need to take a walk down by the dry-cow lot and bring back a couple of the heavy springers. If you're lucky, we might have a calving sometime during your stay."

I was only able to decipher fragment of what he was saying, but it seemed to me that at least one baby cow was due to be born. That sounded exciting. Maria and Yazmin would be able to witness a birth, and they could tell me all about it on the ride home.

On the way to the dry-cow lot, which was about a half mile down the gravel road from the main farmstead, Farmer Vern explained to us all about artificial insemination and its use on the modern dairy farm. There was more, way more in my opinion, discussion of vulvas, cervixes, and uteri than was appropriate for a child of Yazmin's age. *Heck!* I didn't think the discussion was appropriate for me. Although Maria and Yazmin were utterly fascinated, I mostly squirmed and blushed.

"Does your husband ever speak?" Farmer Vern asked Maria.

"Yea, but mostly to inanimate objects, like his banana in the morning. Sometimes he talks on it like it's a telephone. I have to explain to

Yazmin that we should ignore him at times like that. If we don't, it only encourages him. I tell her that he behaves that way because he smoked a lot of pot when he was in the war. As a matter of fact, when admonishing Yazmin to stay clear of drugs, I usually summarize my argument with the question, 'You don't want to turn out like your father, do you?' It makes for a sound argument against recreational drug use."

"I've often contemplated rotating those 40 acres of beans down by the creek into cannabis," mused Farmer Vern, "but a while back Sheriff Jackson got a new helicopter with one of those infra-red cameras. He really enjoys flying around in that thing. The scary part is that he's been known to bring along one of his deputies as a door gunner."

Greeting us on our arrival at the dry cow lot were a lot of dry cows, which didn't surprise me at all, except that one of the animals had two hooves protruding out of her rear just below the tail. It looked as if that calf Farmer Vern was talking about was going to be born sooner rather than later.

"Look at that one, Dad!" exclaimed Yazmin. "Farmer Vern must have pointed at that cow, too."

I agreed with an embarrassed nod. We all helped move the animal into a box stall that was made ready with fresh straw on the floor. It was different than I expected. Farmer Vern didn't load the cow up onto a trailer, as I thought he would, and take her to the animal hospital. Instead, he produced, from a cabinet, a pair of chains that were jumbo-sized versions of a dog's choke collar. Fastening one of these to each of the calf's hooves, he then attached a 10-foot length of rope to them and asked, "Who wants to help pull? This one looks like she's going to need a little help."

"I do! I do! I do!" cried Yazmin and Maria in unison.

I tried to make myself inconspicuous over by the barn-cleaner where I could observe from a safe distance. Let me tell you right up front, there was a lot of slime involved in the whole process. As Yazmin helped Farmer Vern pull, the calf's nose emerged, its tongue limp and hanging out the side of its mouth. The cow moaned in discomfort with each contraction, but not nearly as much as one would expect delivering a 100 lb. plus baby. I was impressed.

Once the calf was out past its shoulders, it slipped quickly to the ground with a thud. Farmer Vern picked up a piece of straw and tickled inside the calf's nose, causing it to sneeze and thus begin breathing. He lifted a rear leg and happily announced we had a heifer calf.

Not taking Uncle Vern at his word, mother cow turned around to inspect things for herself. First, she sniffed the placenta, which was lying on the ground next to the baby. Confirming it was indeed a placenta, and not some sort of embryonic space alien pod, for which it could easily be mistaken, she next inspected her calf and gave it a quick lick with her long tongue. After concluding, evidently, that her calf tasted just fine, she went back to the placenta and proceeded to eat the after-birth.

At this point, I decided that it was a little stuffy in the barn and stepped outside for some fresh air.

CHAPTER FORTY-NINE

Easter Morning

On Easter Sunday morning, Maria, Yazmin, and I dutifully attended church at Saint Petronille's, in downtown Glen Ellyn. A curious statue of God, sitting on his thrown, with an upturned finger graced the church's entrance.

"What the hell," I exclaimed.

"It's his *index* finger," Maria pointed out. "If you study it closely you'd see that. He's beckoning the masses hither"

"Well, if it's his ambition to lure pigeons into his fold, he's achieving great success."

We were welcomed by a friendly greeter, wearing a handsome *Brooks Brothers* suit, starched white shirt, and black wingtips. He handed us two worship bulletins emblazoned with advertisements for a myriad of local attorneys, insurance agents, realtors, dry cleaners, florists, carpet cleaners, and funeral directors. We blessed ourselves with holy water, then stepped into the nave. It was packed.

"Looks like they're sold out," I told Maria. "What do you say we go get ourselves some *Egg McMuffins*?"

An obliging usher, wearing a white carnation in his lapel, detected the distress in Maria's expression.

"You don't want to do that," he advised. "Our communion wafers are far tastier than an *Egg McMuffin*."

He found us some seats in the highly shunned second row, seating me next to an elderly Italian lady who was reverentially praying the Rosary. Her mouth moved as she benevolently fingered the glass beads with her bony fingers, but no sound passed her lips. The indications of extreme religious devotion, and dementia, I thought to myself, are virtually indistinguishable.

I glanced over to Maria and smiled. She looked so alluring, dressed in her Easter finest. Maria smiled back, then bashfully lowered her eyes to the church bulletin she was reading. Anita Bendcroft, she learned, was a member of the *Million Dollar Club* at *Century 21 Real Estate*, and we could have any two rooms of carpet cleaned, any size, for $39. Although I'm confident it was entirely inappropriate, and probably a grievous mortal sin, (inasmuch as we were within spitting distance of the church's sanctuary) I was thinking, nonetheless, how very much I would like to take Maria back into one of the confessionals at the rear of the church and have unbridled sex with her. The Italian woman, who must have been reading my "body language," looked up from her Rosary, and gave me an icy scowl. I removed a hymnal from the holder on the seatback in front of me, and discreetly placed it on my lap.

As he occasionally does on special Sundays, Father Maher invited the children in the congregation forward at the beginning of his homily. By asking probing questions of the angelic little tykes, he could usually inspirit charmingly cute and adorable responses that prompted the assembly to swoon. Father fancied himself to be an ecclesiastic Art Linkletter.

"What is *your* name, little girl," he asked a six-year old with her two front baby teeth conspicuously missing.

"Rose," she responded.

"Rose. What a pretty name."

"Yes. My mother named me Rose because she really, really likes roses."

"How wonderful. Your mother named you Rose because she really, really loves roses," Father repeated into his wireless mic for the benefit of the congregation. "And who is this little boy?" Father Maher asked, referring to a toddler who was clinging to the girl like a baby Orangutan to his mother.

"This is my brother Dick."

Horrified, Father Maher abruptly excused the children, took his place at the lectern and delivered an excellent sermon about walking with the risen Jesus.

Maria is a faithful Catholic; me, not so much. I was, however, raised Roman Catholic by my father, who was devout. He displayed a plastic St. Christopher statue on the dashboard of his *Crown Vic*, and never wore a seat belt. Having attended parochial school, and as an altar boy for six of those years, I consider myself to be an unofficial ambassador of the Church, however. I would recommend it to anyone who is searching for a stable, time-tested foundation for their lives, spiritual meaningfulness, and, for you young men out there, a good place to meet girls who like to put out.

This is in contrast to those prudish fundamentalist Christians who believe in a literal interpretation of the Bible whereby, outside of some very narrow parameters, sex is viewed as an evil and destructive force. Catholicism, mercifully, gives one a little more wiggle room in these matters, plus, as a bonus, you get the Pope. I especially liked that Pope John Paul II. He seemed to be a decent enough fellow who said his prayers regularly and went to Mass each Sunday. Although I'll be the first to admit that he was sometimes guilty of wearing his religion on his sleeve, I think he was a good Pontiff, overall, and should certainly be on the inside track to heaven.

Next to going to heaven when you die, the second biggest advantage of being a Roman Catholic is five-o'clock mass. The idea for being able to go to church on Saturday evening, and have it count as a Sunday, is based on scripture. The Sabbath, technically, begins at sundown on the day prior. This is a distinct advantage Catholics have over Protestants, who have to go to church on Sunday mornings, regardless of how hung-over they may be from the previous evening's revelry.

Another little nicety you get with the Catholic faith is confession. It's human nature that confession (for non-psychopaths, that is) lightens the load on one's conscience. It's good to confess stuff. The *problem* with this is that there are certain contributors to guilty consciences, that if you were to confess to your wife, for one, would result in unfortunate and undesirable domestic consequences. Then there may be others, that if confessed to the States Attorney's office, would precipitate a considerable jail term. So, as a practicing Catholic, all you need to do, to avoid all of this grief, is go down to the church on Saturday afternoon and tell the priest, who is hearing confessions that day, how you, for example, twice used the Lords name in vain, knocked over the Oak Park branch of the *First National Bank*, and had unclean thoughts about your cousin.

"Me too!" Father Barsetti once exclaimed when hearing my confession when I was 16.

"So, you also had unclean thoughts about your cousin when you were my age?" I asked, thinking that perhaps this was not as abnormal and perverted as I feared.

"No. *Your* cousin, and just last week."

So, after spilling your guts, you will, in turn, be given a penance, such as doing the Stations of the Cross or some "Our Fathers," and then, you're good to go until your next confession. It's as simple as that.

This is not to say that being a Catholic is without its disadvantages. To my knowledge, it's the only faith that sends you to purgatory right after you die. I don't want to sound like a heretic here (although if I were, I could go to confession and be absolved) but if you ask my opinion, purgatory is just a scheme for the Church to extract a few more bucks, even after you're dead. Here's how it works:

When you croak, instead of floating straight up to heaven on a cloud, as one might expect, you go, instead, to this intermediate place called purgatory. I imagine it to be much like the waiting room at the *Sears Automotive Department* where you sit, drink stale coffee, and read *People Magazine* while they put new tires on your car. Once in purgatory, you're held ransom, listening to the, *voop, voop* of the pneumatic wrenches from the service bay until your relatives and loved ones purchase enough indulgences to buy your way out. It's the same principle employed by many South American prisons. The catch is that nobody's told how much it's going to cost to ransom you, or even if you're still there. So, just to be on the safe side, your loved ones are compelled to keep purchasing indulgences indefinitely.

This is not as much of a rip-off as it may sound like on the surface. Indulgences, you see, are transferable. If the person for whom you have been shelling out, has, unbeknownst to you, already transitioned out of purgatory, then those indulgences may be assigned to a secondary recipient who, in turn, may apply them against his or her ransom expenses. This may involve a small processing fee.[3]

If you're thinking to yourself right now, *I'm sold! I want to convert to Catholicism, but exactly how much is all of this going to cost me?* then you should know that, under certain circumstances, indulgences are sometimes available at substantially discounted prices. In fact, I know of at least two individuals who have never paid full price for an indulgence in their lives. One of them is my Aunt Clara. The other one isn't.

At the church Aunt Clara attends (*Holy Mother of God*), they have a special promotion that they call *First Fridays*. If you come to their special first-Friday-of-the-month masses, for three months in a row, you're given the opportunity to purchase two indulgences for the price of one, with no limits. This is an excellent value and a good opportunity to stock up. It's also a clever way to maximize your bingo winnings.

---

3. A complete delineation of fees, and explanation of terms and conditions are available upon request. Indulgences may be tax deductible. Check with your tax advisor. Offer not valid in Florida or Ohio. Sorry, this offer extends to baptized and confirmed members of the Catholic faith only.

Speaking candidly about matters of the Church, I am guilty of blasphemy. Nonetheless, this is a pardonable sin, provided I didn't drag the Holy Spirit into the mix. Defiant irreverence of the *Holy Spirit*, on the other hand, is an *unforgivable* sin, and something you really want to avoid. Sinning can be a veritable minefield, if you don't know what you're doing. That's why the Church offers helpful Catechism classes. I highly recommend them.

We arrived at the point in the Mass where the priest prayed for the Holly Father in Rome, our leaders in Washington, some victims of a flood along the Mississippi River, and the unborn in the womb, to name a few. He then turned the supplication over to us, in a moment of silence, to pray our own petitions and delineate some of the blessings for which we were truly thankful. I used the opportunity to thank God for Maria and Yazmin, our beautiful home, my fulfilling career and, of course, I was thankful for my Silver Star, without which, none of the other blessings would have been. Once again I glanced over to my beautiful wife, who was kneeling in prayer, her head bowed reverently. Perhaps it was shallow-minded and superficial, but nonetheless, I was appreciative, if not thankful, that Maria had on that wispy spring dress she was wearing, white hose, and my favorite sexy shoes. The old Italian woman, next to whom I was sitting, shot me another disgusted glance, this time making a guttural sound from deep in her throat.

"She's my wife, you old crone!" I responded in a loud voice that broke the sacred silence, and echoed blaringly throughout the hallowed sanctuary.

This is an example, Maria tells all our friends, of why she doesn't like taking me to church with her.

CHAPTER FIFTY

Meeting Malcolm for a Drink

"Ms. Dorsey, would you please connect Malcolm Jackson, of restaurant number 425 to my line," I spoke into the *Teletalk* Model 924 intercom on my desk.

Although her desk sat just outside my open office door, and I could easily converse with her in a normal speaking voice, I just loved playing with that nifty electronic contraption, and did so whenever I had an excuse. Sometimes, when it was slow, (and even when it wasn't) I used it to pretend that I was an air traffic controller. For example:

"Chicago O'Hare Airport Information, 17:54 Zulu weather. Sky clear, visibility 7 miles, wind 080 at 10, altimeter 29.98. ILS or visual approach, Runway 14 left in use and departing 14 left and 14 right. Bird activity in the vicinity of the airport. All departing aircraft contact Chicago Clearance Delivery on 118.5 prior to taxi. Advise on initial contact you have received Information Zulu."

"United five-niner heavy inbound for landing." Ms. Dorsey replied over the intercom, humoring me. "Have traffic in sight. Will squawk Malcom/Juliet Alpha Charlie Kilo Sierra Oscar November at 425. Please advise further instructions if negative contact."

"UNICOM is active," I replied. "Request Malcom/Juliet Alpha Charlie Kilo Sierra Oscar November 425 return call at earliest convenience. Thank you."

"Roger wilco."

While waiting for Ms. Dorsey to place the call, I studied my three-inch thick, 10-pound computer printout of July sales. Overall, business was brisk, and Malcolm's restaurant was no exception.

"I have Mr. Jackson on line one," the intercom crackled.

"Thank you." I punched the flashing button on my phone. "Malcolm! I was just looking at last month's numbers and I see you've been kicking butt."

"It's a lot of work."

"That never changes, my friend."

"Please! Stop referring to me as *friend*. We're business associates. If we were friends, you would have invited me to your wedding, and I would have had an inclination to purchase a gift and attend."

"You would have been the only black family there. I'm sure you wouldn't have felt comfortable."

"Is there a reason for this call? Because, I'm about to hang up."

"I just wanted to know if you have been using our 'mentoring system' protocols to groom a manager? You're going to need an outstanding manager if you intend to open that second location we've been talking about."

"I have, and she's coming along nicely."

"Good. Good. Look Malcolm. Truth is, I wasn't actually calling you today about business. That was just a subterfuge. Although you deny it, you're one of my dearest and most perceptive friends, and I want to talk to you about something personal. I could use some of your sagacious perspective for a troubling predicament I'm facing."

"You and Maria aren't having marital problems, are you? You haven't messed that up now, have you? I love Maria dearly."

"No. Far from it, but I really don't care to discuss this over the phone. Do you want to get together for a beer? It's Friday night, after all."

"Sure. I usually get out of here at 10. How about we meet at *Dirty Dick's* for a *Guinness Stout*?"

"Say 10:30?"

"Plus or minus."

"See you then."

"And remember. We're not friends!"

I disconnected the call by pushing the button for line two on my phone.

"Operator," came the sumptuously sensual sound of Sally's voice. She was our receptionist.

"Outside line, please."

"One moment, please."

Receiving a dial tone, I called Maria at home to explain that I would be getting in late that night. I told her that I was meeting Malcolm for a beer.

"You know," Maria responded, "You really shouldn't keep hounding Malcolm. You're becoming a stalker. It's not endearing."

"Perhaps not, but I could use the benefit of Malcolm's incisiveness on this Silver Star thing."

"Just keep in mind, Bruce: When he says he doesn't like you . . ."

"Yes?"

"Well, I don't think he's kidding. I'm pretty sure he really doesn't like you. Heck! I don't like you all that much, and I'm your wife."

"And you're a jewel of a wife."

"Try not to be too late, and don't drink and drive."

"I'll probably just have coffee. I love you."

After replacing the handset in the cradle, I carefully pried open the back of the shadowbox on my credenza, removed the Silver Star, and placed it in my jacket's side pocket.

Irish folk music greeted me as I stepped inside the pub.

In heaven there is no beer
That's why we drink it here...

I spied Malcolm at the bar.

"Hey, friend. Good to see you," I greeted him with a big bear hug.

"I'm his AA sponsor," Malcolm lied to the barmaid. "It's not uncommon for them to become affectionately demonstrative."

"What did you do to get here so fast? Did you run?"

"Hell, no! A black man in this neighborhood would be shot dead by the police, if seen running. I took a bus."

"You could be shot dead for taking a bus."

"I meant to say I rode the bus."

"Oh. In that case your odds of being shot dead go way down, not more than 10 percent I'd say, so long as you're not wearing dreadlocks. Are you enjoying the music?"

"Just heard a little ditty about some guy who found a great big box floating in the bay."

"Oh, yeah? What did he do with it?"

"He opened it up and got all excited about what he found inside, so he took it to some guy he knew who owned a pawn shop."

"So, did he sell it or use it for collateral on a loan?"

"Neither. When the pawn broker saw what he had in the box, he tossed the fellow out on his ear."

"What did he do then?"

"He took it home and tried to give it to his wife, like it was some sort of thoughtful and spontaneous gift. Big mistake."

"Don't tell me. And she kicked him out too?"

"Just as soon as she saw what was in the box. In retrospect, he should have gone with flowers. A dozen red roses."

"Of course. Always flowers. What a dumb ass. He should have known better than that. And then?"

"He died and tried to take it into heaven with him."

"Don't tell me. Saint Peter wouldn't let him in with it, right?"

"Not even."

"I knew it! I knew it. So what was in the box?"

"That's the odd thing. The song lyrics don't disclose that."

"They never say?"

"Nope. It's like a mystery for the listener to figure out. What do you think could have been in that box?"

"Maybe it was a turd."

"A turd?"

"Yeah. Maybe there was a turd in the box."

"I suppose that could explain a lot."

"Sure. Perhaps we should write another verse to help this guy out:

> *He took the box,*
> *and looked inside,*
> *and uttered oh my word!*
> *It's no wonder why*
> *I'm stuck with this,*
> *nobody wants a turd.*

"How's that sound?"

"Cool. At least we explain what's in the box now. You should have been a lyricist. So, what did you want to talk to me about?"

"I want to talk to you about the Silver Star I received in Vietnam."

"The one on your credenza at the office?"

"Yes."

"Did you want to write a song about it? How about this?
Put a Silver Star on my son's chest. Make him one of America's best . . ."

"No. I want to present it to Bill Hastings' parents . . . although if we *did* write a ballad about it, I could accompany myself on the guitar, and sing it for them."

"That would be pretty tacky. Now, Bill Hastings. Was he the buddy of yours who was killed in the war?"

"Yeah. I'm sure it rightfully belonged to him, after all, only Captain Riley didn't like awarding medals of valor posthumously, so somehow I received it by default."

"So why do you need to discuss it with me? Just do it."

"I was wondering if you believe in providence, and if so, do you think it can be associated with an inanimate object?"

"Like your Silver Star?"

"Like that, yes. And, if I gave that object away, would the recipients benefit with good luck in the same way I did? And equally important, would *my* good fortunes be reversed if I no longer possessed that Silver Star?"

"Look, man. I never knew of any good fortune that came from some 'magic' object, unless you count Aladdin's Lamp. That's just crazy talk. Now if you want to give that medal to the Hastings, I say you just go down there to Kentucky and do it."

"Just do it?"

"Yes. Just go down there and give it to them. The sooner the better, I say. This thing has been eating you up as long as I've known you. You need to put some closure on it."

"Thanks, Malcolm. You're a good fr . . . I mean if you *were* my friend, you'd be a good one to have. That's exactly what I'm going to do. Give this Silver Star to the Hastings."

I reached in my pocket and produced the decoration.

"Wait a minute! You've got the medal with you?"

"Yep. My good luck charm. Now, how about that beer?"

"Sure. I'll have a *Guinness.*"

I waved to the bartender.

"Miss. A *Guinness Stout* for my 'acquaintance' here, and I'll have a black coffee."

The attractive, freckle-faced redhead brought our drinks over.

"That will be a dollar twenty."

"A dollar twenty?" I protested.

"A buck for the *Guinness* and 20 cents for the coffee."

"I'm afraid there must be some mistake, young lady. I think that cup of coffee should be 10 cents."

"I don't know who told you that."

"Captain Riley."

"Never heard of him."

"He was my commander in the army. He told me that 10 cents, and this Silver Star here, would get me a cup of coffee just about anywhere."

I produced the medal.

"Well sir, this isn't just anywhere. This is *Dirty Dick's*, and coffee here is 20 cents."

"How about free refills?"

"Nope. Twenty cents a cup."

"Hey, Malcolm. Did you hear that? Twenty cents for a cup of coffee!"

"That's crazy."

"Forget the taco business. What you and I should do is open up a chain of coffee shops. We could charge 20 cents a cup and get filthy rich."

"Wait! I've got a better idea. Let's charge *30* cents a cup."

"Why stop at 30 cents. Let's make it an even buck."

"A dollar a cup for coffee? Who would pay that much for plain old java?"

"Who said it has to be plain. We could flavor the coffee and foam some steamed milk up in it."

"Well, if you're going to do that, we should charge them two bucks a cup!"

"No. No. How about this idea? We'll top it off with whipped cream, drizzle some caramel over that, and charge $3.50 a cup!"

By this time, Malcolm and I were laughing hysterically, and the bartender signaled the bouncer with a nod. A huge brute wearing a kilt walked over to us. He looked as if he may have been a caber tosser.

"I'm afraid I'm going to have to ask you boys to leave."

Resisting substantial temptation, we desisted from making any wisecracks about Porridge Wag Glaswegian, and went without protest. Out on the street, I put my arm around Malcolm's shoulder, and pulled him close.

"You *do* know, that's the first time I've been bounced from a bar by a fellow wearing a kilt."

"It's my second time," Malcolm replied. "But then again, I'm a person of color."

"A person of color? What happened to being black? I was just getting comfortable with that. So then, you're a colored person now?"

"Hell, no! I *was* a colored person a long time ago, before I was a Negro, but after that, I was black for a while with a lowercase b, then for a while with an uppercase B, and then, I was an African American briefly, but now I'm a person of color."

"I'm sorry, Malcolm, but I'm still having a little trouble distinguishing the nuances between *colored person*, and *person of color*."

"That's because, as a white guy . . ."

"I prefer *a person without color*, if it's all the same to you."

"Very well, then. That's because you people without color (and that sounds ridiculous, by the way) have racism so deeply ingrained in the very most inward reaches of your psyche, that even when you're being uncharacteristically broad-minded, you are, at best, condescending."

"Malcolm, you're a reverse racist, you know. Did anyone ever tell you that? I don't even know why I ever considered you as a friend."

"It's because you're so messed up from the war that you're grasping at straws trying to find someone to be your friend. Now give me a hug and get home to that beautiful wife of yours."

"Get away from me, you jerk. I'm not hugging you. Not after being talked to like that."

"Now, *you're* the one being a jerk."

"No. I'm just trying very hard not to come across as condescending, if it's all just the same to you. After all, I wouldn't want to offend a *person of color*. It might be interpreted as being racist."

"I'm through listening to your *white privilege* bullshit. I'll tell you what. In the future, call someone else when you need advice about what to do with your bogus Silver Star, because, as far as I'm concerned, you can shove it up your ass."

"Well, if that's the way you really feel, I have just one question for you."

"What's that?"

"Does this mean that you won't be writing that ballad about my Silver Star? Because, I've got this catchy little melody in my head that is at once ironic and expositional, with an interesting counterpoint that I think we could build on."

Malcolm rolled his eyes, and without a word, turned his back on me and walked briskly towards the bus stop. I yelled after him, "Don't run!"

CHAPTER FIFTY-ONE

My Mom's Arrest

The Safety Yellow and Green bi-level commuter train's bell clanged an automated syncopation as we crept into the *Chicago and North Western* station, coming to a creaking, straining, scraping halt in parallel with earlier arrivals from the three lines that terminated at Madison, between Clinton and Canal streets. The familiar acrid smell of hot train brakes mingling with the oleaginous odor of diesel filled my nostrils. Stepping over a passed-out drunk and a puddle of urine, I stole my way down the back stairs to the concourse below the elevated tracks, my regular shortcut, and avoided the throngs of fellow commuters in the smoky interior of the station.

As I stepped outside, the cold December air assailed me. The smell of roasting coco beans from the nearby *Blommer Chocolate Company* carried on the breeze.[4] It bore an aroma similar to my Grandpa Schultz's favorite blend of pipe tobacco. A panhandler pushed his plastic cup towards me and jingled the coins he had primed it with. For some reason, on top his hatted head perched a proud red and black rooster. The vagrant caught me gawking.

"It's a gimmick. Every panhandler needs a gimmick these days."

"Where's Dominic?" I asked. "Doesn't he usually work this corner?"

(Dominic's gimmick was playing a couple of inverted empty 5-gallon plastic paint buckets as if they were snare drums.)

"He's taking a little vacation time. I'm just filling in for him until he gets back."

"Is that so? Well, good for him."

"Yeah. Whatever vacation time he accumulates, but doesn't use by the end of the year, he loses."

"Well, that's terrible."

---

4. My mother used to purchase big bags of coco bean husks from the *Blommer Chocolate Company* to mulch her perennial garden. She quit the practice when she discovered it attracted throngs of Norway rats.

"No kidding! I mean he earned it, after all; standing out here in all sorts of weather, having people look down their noses at him. It's a tough vocation, being a panhandler."

"So, is Dominic going anywhere special for his vacation, or just staying in town?"

"As a matter of fact, he's planning on taking his family to the islands."

"Hawaii?"

"No. He's staying local. You know . . . Goose Island, Stony Island, Blue Island. He told me that one of the apartment buildings he owns needs new railings to bring the back porches up to code, so he'll be working on that too."

"He always *has* been a conscientious landlord," I commented. "Maria and I looked at one of his loft conversions before we bought our place in Glen Ellyn."

My bus pulled to the curb, the doors scissored opened with a hiss, and I stepped on board.

"Good morning Mr. Johnson," the driver greeted me as I fed my fare into the box. "Back to public transportation again, I see."

"Let me tell you, Red. With gas prices pushing a buck a gallon, who can afford to drive anymore? Even my mom, the germaphobe, is taking public transportation now. She wipes her seat with disinfectant before sitting down, but she's actually riding the bus and the elevated trains now."

"Talking about your mom, how is she?"

"Great! She's taken up *Tai Chi* now."

"For meditation or for her physical health?"

"Neither. She's more into the combat aspects of *Tai Chi.* Her fantasy is to kick the snot out of an unsuspecting mugger someday."

"Well, if it keeps her active. We all need to stay active."

I worked my way to the back of the swaying bus, grabbing the seatbacks for balance. I found a seat next to Nancy, who was a lunch waitress at my club.

"Hey, Nance," I greeted her.

"Oh! Hi, Mr. Johnson. I missed you yesterday."

"I had a lot of work to do. I ate lunch at my desk. Did I mention to you that the crab cakes I had on Monday were a little on the greasy side? You might want to talk candidly to the chef about it. I don't want to get her in trouble, after all. If I were to complain to the club's manager, that's just what might happen."

"You're so sweet, Mr. Johnson. Some members would have no compunction about causing one of the staff to be disciplined, or even fired, but you're so nice."

"Nice? So that's what you think of me, is it? Well, I'm not going to sit here and be insulted by the likes of you. I'm going to get off this bus at the very next stop!"

"It's your stop, Mr. Johnson."

"And just for the record, I'm actually a real jerk, the truth be known. It's just that it's hard to stay in character when you're married to a woman like my Maria."

Stepping off the bus into the cold, I fastened the top button of my overcoat and walked east towards the lake. Officer Kazmierczak was making his way down East Washington Street writing parking tickets.

"Hey, Rick!" I greeted him. "How have you been?"

"Good. Good. I'm just fine, Mr. Johnson, but did anyone get a hold of you about your mother?"

"My mother?"

"I guess not, then. It came in over the police radio. She's been charged with battery. Seems she kicked the crap out of some poor fellow she thought was a purse-snatcher, but it turned out he just wanted to help her across State Street to get to *Marshal Fields*."

"She beat up a Boy Scout? I didn't even know she was downtown. Is she locked up?"

"No. There was a bond hearing, and she was released on her own recognizance."

"My God!"

I ran to the front door of our office building.

"Jacob!" I interrogated the security guard as I hurried inside. "Is my mother here?"

"Yes, sir. A police car that reeked of *Lysol* dropped her off just 10 minutes ago."

I took the elevator (which also smelled of disinfectant) to the fifth floor. It opened into the reception space.

"Mother!" I called.

"I'm in here," came her amiable voice from my office. "Do you want some coffee? I was just going to make a pot. I have no idea what you pay that secretary of yours for, but she should have the coffee brewing before you walk in the office door each morning."

"Mom. I heard you were arrested! Are you all right?"

"I am, but I'm afraid the other guy wasn't as fortunate. How was I supposed to know? He was in plain clothes . . . and black as the ace of spades."

"Who was in plain clothes?"

"The goddamn Eagle Scout. He should had been wearing his uniform. I didn't even know they allowed coloreds to be scouts."

"You're thinking of homosexuals, Mom."

"Whatever. Now you go wash your hands before you do anything else. I can only imagine how may germs you come in contact with, riding public transportation."

I used my private restroom to wash up but left the door open to continue my conversation with Mom.

"Does Dad know about your run-in with the law this morning?"

"I'm sorry, son, but I don't know a compassionate way to tell you this, so I'll just come out and say it. I think your father may be dead."

"Dead!?"

"Yes. I'm so worried. He was complaining of chest pains this morning when I left the house, and now, he doesn't answer the phone."

"Chest pains? Did you call 911?"

"I would have, but I had a train to catch. I wanted to do some Christmas shopping at *Marshall Field's* and *Carson's*. I'm going to feel so awful now if he died. I just bought him the loveliest money-green silk smoking jacket with free gift-wrapping. I *so* despise making returns. It seems so tacky."

"Mom! Do any of your neighbors have a key to the house?"

"Yes. The Hitchners."

"Do you have their phone number?"

"Don't be silly. They've been our best friends for twenty years. Of course I know their phone number."

She recalled the number as I dialed.

"Okay. Let me think now. It's pound two."

"Pound two! You have the Hitchners on speed-dial?"

"Of course, I do. They're our best friends, you know . . . have been for 20 years."

"But, Mom!"

I dialed the operator.

"Operator. How may I help you?"

"56th District Police station, please."

"Emergency or nonemergency?"

"Emergency, I guess."

The phone played a quick little musical tune, and then I heard a man's voice.

"Nine one one. What's your emergency?"

"My mom thinks my father may be dead."

"What are his symptoms?"

"I don't know for sure. We're downtown in the Loop, and he's at 5126 South Laramie."

"Well, has the trash been getting taken out to the alley, or has it been piling up in the kitchen?"

"I don't know. Like I said, I'm downtown."

"Does he stare at you blankly when you address him?"

"I'm not with him right now, I'm telling you."

"How about the newspapers? Are they accumulating on the front porch? That's often a sign of a victim inside . . . or a foul smell near the house. Is there a foul smell?"

"Look! Can't you send a squad car by to check on him?"

"A car, you say? I'll see."

I could hear the clicking of his computer keyboard.

"Did you want a full-size sedan like a *Crown Victoria* or an SUV such as a *Chevy Suburban*? Oh, look here. I see we also have a *Dodge Diplomat* available, if you prefer."

"I don't care. Whatever's closest."

"I'll send a *Crown Vic*, then. Actually, I see we're having a week-day special on full-sized sedans. They're responding with two officers as opposed to the normal single officer, although, you should be aware that one of them may be a rookie."

"Yeah, fine. A *Crown Vic* would be super, and I have no problem with a rookie. Just send a car, please."

"Okay, then. I'll need your father's address again. If you were calling from that address, it would pop up on my screen just like magic, but since you're calling from the other side of town, you'll need to tell me your parents' address."

I gave him the information he needed.

"Okay. I'm going to disconnect now. Will the responding officers be able to reach you at this phone number?"

"Yes. Thank you."

Dad was fine, as it turned out. He had been running his table saw when the phone rang and never heard it. It was around ground hog day that we received a message on the answering machine from Sergeant Engels, one of the responding officers to our 911 call.

I just wanted to phone you personally to let you know that we have completed our investigation of your father's suspected death. It is our conclusion that, insomuch as he personally answered the door when we called, was able to provide sufficiently persuasive identification, seemed comparatively animated during our interrogation, and consumed a beverage in our presence, no death had occurred and the investigation has therefore been closed.

CHAPTER FIFTY-TWO

Grade School Scandals

It was Yazmin's first day of school at Saint Petronille's. To Maria, it was important that our daughter receive a Catholic education. Having attended a parochial school myself, I dissented, and for good reason. I had had some issues in Catholic schools over the years. I was actually suspended from school during my first week of classes, if you can believe that.

I became dubious about Catholic school when I first walked into kindergarten at Our Lady of the Snows in 1954 and saw that guy up there nailed to a cross. I had kindergarten in the afternoon, and I would just be getting a good fort built or a bonfire going when my mother would call me into the house to get cleaned up for school. It's not as if we ever did anything productive or worthwhile in kindergarten. It wasn't a particularly stimulating venue. Mostly, as I recall, we passed the time cutting up construction paper and pasting it back together into seasonal *objects d' arte,* such as facsimiles of maple leaves in the autumn, snowflakes in the winter, and silhouette portraits of ourselves for Mother's Day gifts. We also pasted together miles of paper chains which, as near as I could figure, were good for absolutely nothing functional (like pulling a car out of a ditch) but I think our teacher believed they had a certain aesthetic appeal. She hung them everywhere, decorating the classroom. To me, they looked like a fire hazard.

As for the other time-honored extracurricular kindergarten activities, melting crayons on the radiator was swell entertainment up to a point, but if you budged in line at recess, were churlish during music, opened even one eye at nap time, or got caught eating the paste, you had to go sit in the cloakroom. I never did understand. If they didn't want us eating the stuff, why the hell did they make it wintergreen flavored?

I spent a lot of time in the cloakroom with Penny Peterson, who was a lifer. She had a permanent seat in there for the time she brought her mother's diaphragm to school for show-and-tell. That was the day that Miss Kovatch, our high-strung kindergarten teacher's assistant, finally lost possession of her faculties and had to go away to that nice place in New Jersey where she could rest.

Actually, we kids could see her meltdown coming for weeks. It was as if she were a nuclear reactor, we all agreed, whose control rods were pulled out too far. Miss Kovatch absolutely went hysterical that day, yelling, "Put that thing down!" but we just kept passing that diaphragm around the room, looking at it, stretching it out, and putting it on our heads like it was a little hat.

Some of the more immature kids in the class seemed inappropriately amused by Miss Kovatch's apparent inability to control her neutron flux or maintain an adequate supply of coolant to her core. I personally took the high road, thanking God that, in our great country, we have places like New Jersey to send these people, like spent nuclear fuel rods.

Now, my father was a scrupulous man, respected all around town and by his brothers in the Knights of Columbus as a reliable and truthful person. He held the rank of Fourth Degree Color Corps Knight. Dad used to warn me that the school kept some sort of an inexpiable file on us kids that would follow us around for the rest of our natural lives. It was like some sort of dark shadow called a "permanent record," and potentially even worse than a dishonorable discharge from the military. He claimed that when Penny was 45 years old, she might be applying for an important job (like president of General Dynamics) and the personnel manager would be able to look back in her permanent record. He would be spellbound, reading along about her grade-point average and her extracurricular activities, when, all of the sudden, there would be the whole diaphragm incident, delineated in graphic detail. It would be the proverbial glass ceiling for Penny's career by the time he got to the footnote about poor Miss Kovatch, and how, at one point, she was on 1,800 mg of Lithium a day, and walked around the booby hatch like a zombie.

However, that had nothing to do with my getting suspended. I got suspended for something entirely unrelated. At class reunions, we fondly refer to it as the *Flying Nun Incident*. It was amazing, as if all the laws of Newtonian physics were suspended in an approximation of the singularity of absolute space-time, and sublimated into some sort of surrealistic air show, only minus the Blue Angels.

I got into some deep shit for that one and was, I must say, made an unfair example of. They tell me the kids at Our Lady of the Snows are still learning from my lesson after all these years. I'm told it's part of incoming student orientation.

For me, public school would have been a better fit. First of all, I wouldn't have to wear a uniform, plus I would have been able to walk home for lunch. While the kids at Our Lady of the Snows were in the multi-purpose room eating peanut butter and jelly sandwiches, I could have been getting grilled cheese and watching cartoons on TV. I could very much relate to Bugs Bunny, that smart-ass rabbit with the New York accent. He was my inspiration. By the time I was in the third grade, I was cracking up the entire class with my clever ad-libs and snappy comebacks.

The most common question I received from teachers in those days was: "Would you like to go down and tell the principal what you just said?"

My standard rejoinder to that was, "With *his* patchy sense of humor, what would be the point?"

Our principal's name was Rubber Legs Chase. At least that was how he was known to the students. The entire faculty had nicknames like that. There was Dog Breath Kirby, Baby Face Burns, and Pops Walters. I don't know for sure where these names originated. They were just passed along by kids' older brothers and sisters. To hear the students talking about these people, you'd think that we were being taught by the Mafia.

The only faculty member not saddled with a derogatory nickname was Mr. Hall. He was a popular young teacher just out of college. The girls all thought he was "dreamy" and the guys liked him because he drove a *Corvette*.

Mr. Hall was dating another young teacher, Twin Peaks Perkins. Although I think it was supposed to be some sort of a secret, it was common knowledge all around the school. Once again, there were two divergent points of view of the relationship, cleaving strictly along the lines of gender. The girls all wondered if the two of them were going to get married, while the boys mostly speculated as to whether or not Mr. Hall had felt her up yet.

A nun, dressed in traditional habit, leaned down, extending her hand, to greet Yazmin. Yazmin screeched, then bolted for the door. I ran after her, finally catching up with our traumatized daughter half a block from the school entrance. Meanwhile, Maria was apologizing profusely to Sister Clara.

"I'm so embarrassed, sister. My husband, who can be so inappropriate at times, has instilled in our daughter an irrational fear of nuns. I don't know what to do with him sometimes."

"I'd suggest grabbing him by the ear, twisting it really hard, then dragging him across the room. Or, slap him silly with an open hand until he's sobbing, or here's an old favorite of mine, crack him across his knuckles with a ruler. And, don't forget, there's no substitute, of course, for good old fashioned public humiliation . . ."

CHAPTER FIFTY-THREE

Selling Poppies

On the television, news reports from the U.S. invasion of Grenada streamed into our family room. I threw my right shoe at the screen, missed, and knocked an expensive Qing Dynasty Chinese Porcelain vase to the floor, shattering the rare artifact. It had been a Christmas gift from my father-in-law.

"Mom's not going to be happy when she sees that," Yazmin commented looking up from her social studies homework.

"It'll be all right. We just need to get our stories straight."

"Our stories straight?"

"Yeah. How about this? We'll tell her that the cat knocked it over."

"I know Mom better than that. She'll never believe that story."

"Why do you say that?"

"Well, to begin with, because we don't *have* a cat, Dad."

"Well, in that case, I don't know how many times I've told you, Yazmin, that you shouldn't play kick ball in the house."

"Dad, if you hate war so much, why did you go in the Army?"

"That's a fair question, dear. The answer, however, is not all that straight forward, but I'll try to answer it for you the best I can."

I turned off the television.

"My generation grew up in the wake of World War II," I explained to Yazmin. "Things were different then. Veterans of the war were ubiquitous in those days. They piloted the planes we flew on vacation, cut our hair at the barbershop, were our scout leaders, teachers, and coached our Little League teams. They were our insurance agents, family physicians, and auto mechanics. I have a good friend whose father was on the *Yorktown* when it was sunk at the battle of Midway. He had lied about his age to enlist, and at sixteen, became a hero, pulling his wounded comrades out of the oil-slicked sea."

Yazmin yawned.

"My own father (your Grandpa Johnson) was a Marine during the war, but never spoke a word of it. What little I know about his military service, your Great Grandfather told me."

"So did you go in the service because your father did?" Yazmin tried for a more succinct answer to her question.

"No, that's not the reason. Actually, I was about to be drafted anyhow, so I just went in and did what they called *volunteering for the draft*; just to get it done and over with."

"May I go outside now?"

"Sure."

I could see she was bored.

"And, if you happen to find a stray cat, feel free to bring it home with you. As a matter of fact, here's a twenty-dollar bill. Perhaps you can motivate one of your little friends to part with their pet for the right money."

"Thanks, Dad!"

The door slammed as Yazmin exited. I retrieved my shoe, descended the basement stairs, and as I rummaged around my workshop for some *Super-Glue*, I thought some more about our conversation, and about some of the World War II vets who had shaped me. The faculty at Brother Rice High School included a former Marine who, like my father, fought in the Pacific, on islands with names like Iwo Jima, Guadalcanal, and Okinawa. Our football coach had been a seasick Army Ranger when he landed on Omaha Beach, June 6, 1944. His assignment: Scale a 100-foot cliff, carrying a 55 pound pack, while taking fire. Whenever we complained that football practice was too tough, he reminded us of this.

Ms. Curtis, the Home Economics teacher, at our sister school, Saint Francis de Sales, had been a Women's Airforce Service Pilot. Although teaching the girls domestic arts, she herself, as a young woman, chose to fly four-engine heavy bombers. Each semester she related her wartime W.A.S.P. experiences to her new students. At Ford's Willow Run aircraft factory, they learned, the 22-year-old Miss Curtis slept on a cot near the hanger-door exit of the 3.5 million square-foot assembly plant. When the B-24H Liberator, to which she had been assigned, rolled off the assembly line, she strapped on her parachute, climbed into the left seat, and flew the virgin craft to a point of overseas embarkation. Thirty-eight Women's Airforce Service Pilots gave their lives in this service.

Another of these World War II Veterans, it turned out, happened to be Maria's and my next-door neighbor in Glen Ellyn. He engaged me in conversation one sunny September Saturday afternoon. I was filling sandbags and building a defensive perimeter.

"Yep," he commented, stroking his chin while observing my neurotic activity. "For years after *I* was discharged, I went to bed each night, cuddling up to a loaded *Luger* 9mm."

"I understand completely."

"On our wedding night, my aroused young bride cooed in my ear, 'Well. It seems like you're sure happy to see me.' I had to explain to her that I had a gun in my bathrobe pocket."

"That's a wacky story. Do you mind if I put it in the book I'm writing?"

"Sure. Go ahead, but change my name if you do," Mr. Dumfarght pleaded. "Tell me, Bruce. Have you ever given any consideration to becoming a member of the Veterans of Foreign Wars?"

The VFW, he explained to me, is an organization open to veterans who had received a combat action ribbon, or a combat infantry badge, or hostile fire/imminent danger pay. At his invitation, I was initiated into the organization later that very same month. At our meetings, I was awed to be in the company of such extraordinary and humble individuals.

The main thing we do at the VFW is raise money for disabled veterans. You may have seen us during the week of Veteran's Day, in our silly hats, "selling" fabric poppies to this end. It works something like this:

We form a gauntlet outside a heavily trafficked store entrance and the only way you can get into the store without being inordinately harassed, is to wear a poppy in the buttonhole of your shirt or blouse. Admittedly this is a variation on extortion but because we are a respected not-for-profit, it's tolerated by the local police, as are the slot machines back at our post.

One year my V.F.W. post sold poppies outside the *Walmart* store on Route 53, south of town. Having never been in a *Walmart* before, the experience was enlightening. *Walmart's* big thing, it seemed, was low prices. Although there wasn't a single piece of merchandise in the entire store that I would care to own, their prices were impressively cheap. Louie, the greeter, explained to me that it was because, with the exception of the five-gallon bags of fluorescent orange cheese puffs, one would be hard-pressed to find a single item in the entire store that was made in the USA.

"Believe it or not," Louie told me, "they pay those Chinese peasants who assemble this crap even less than they pay me."

"For a greeter, aren't you supposed to be the 'face' of *Walmart*?" I asked.

It seemed he had a crummy attitude, and I told him so.

"That's okay," Louie replied, "I'm working off the clock right now."

"What! They make you work off the clock?" I asked, with surprise. "Don't you have a union representative whom you can report this to?"

Louie laughed. "We don't have a union at *Walmart*."

I didn't understand. Where I came from, even union employees had a union.

"Well, you should secure union representation," I insisted. "That way you would have an advocate looking out for your welfare and best interests."

"Some of the night cleaning crew tried that," Louie informed me. "They've all been replaced by undocumented workers from an outside contractor."

Just then, a store patron tried to sneak past without a poppy in evidence.

"Hey lady! Get back here," I ordered. "What do you think you're trying to pull?"

She fled inside, in search of the store manager.

"You're going to have to lighten up," Louie suggested. "This store's sales are down 1% year-to-date from last year. The store manager is on probation. He's barricaded himself in his office, overlooking the floor, armed with an AR-15. If he starts picking off customers, I'm afraid it will only further depress sales."

As we chatted, a police car rolled up and Louie greeted the emerging officer. Evidently, a big problem at *Walmart* is shoplifting. In my 4-hour shift, I saw three people dragged away in handcuffs. It was a curious thing. I was having a hard time trying to figure *that* one out. To me, it didn't make a lick of sense. If these people didn't intend to pay for the stuff, why the hell would they go to *Walmart*? With price, obviously, being no object, so to speak, it would seem to me that shoplifting *Neiman Marcus* or *Von Maur's* would make better sense. There, at least, they would have found fresh, high-quality designer brands plus a knowledgeable and helpful staff.

"How's the standoff going?" The copper casually asked Louie.

"So far so good. Net planned sales are still pretty much on target in spite of the unfortunate situation."

"Well, just let us know if you want a SWAT team. Those Sheriff's Deputy boys are just itching to take someone out ever since they got that new armored personnel vehicle with the 50 cal. mounted on top."

Further conversation with Louie revealed that he was a Pearl Harbor survivor. He had been stationed at Hickam Field on that fateful day. Louie told me how he could have reached up and touched the Japanese dive-bombers; they were that low during the attack. He also told me he was left with a piece of shrapnel in his left buttocks as a souvenir of his being stationed in Hawaii.

"Personally," I jested, "I would have gone with the hula-girl lamp."

"That would have hurt even worse than the hot shrapnel," Louie pointed out.

"I guess you're right."

It made a lot of sense when I really thought about it.

"It must have been horrific."

"That's why you'll never see me driving a *Toyota*," he explained. "I won't even *ride* in a Japanese automobile."

He told me that he drove a *Buick Electra, Park Avenue.*

As I was talking to Louie, an armored truck pulled up to the door we were working. It was subsequently loaded with sacks and sacks of money.

"You better be careful," I quipped, "or you're going to overload that thing and break an axle."

The guard said nothing but gave me a very serious look. I tried to sell him a poppy. In response, he moved his right hand down so that it was touching the leather of his holster, which he unsnapped.

"Don't even think about it," Louie warned me. "They have strict orders to take all the money they can back to Bentonville, Arkansas, and not to leave a nickel more than necessary in the local community."

"You know, Louie, you really *do* have a bad attitude for a greeter. Exactly how much does *Walmart* pay you to insult their business?"

He pulled me close and whispered the answer in my ear. I was shocked!

"Are you kidding me? Do they know that you're a war hero? How do they justify paying you that amount?"

"They justify it because I'm a man," Louie replied. "If I were a woman, I'd be making 70 percent that amount."

"No, that can't be true." I blinked incredulously. "Not in this day and age!"

"Unfortunately, it's all *too* true. You see, my daughter also works here. She's a single mom who lost her job at the local pharmacy when *Walmart* drove them and half the other stores in town out of business.

When I learned she was selling her blood to make ends meet, I decided to get a job to help her out a little financially."

There was a minute or so of silence as I contemplated this conversation we were having. I wondered:

How many other good people (people like Louie) I had met and failed to appreciate their struggles. It couldn't have been easy for a man his age, with a hunk of shrapnel in his butt, to stand all day, as his job required. Moreover, I wondered: how he managed, as he indeed did, to maintain his dignity, having traded the proud uniform of his country's service for a blue Walmart vest.

"Louie. May I ask you a personal question?"

"Sure kid. What is it?"

"How was it for you *after* the war? I mean, after you returned home. Did you have any difficulty adjusting back to civilian life? Did you feel like, like you were angry all of the time or had a chip on your shoulder?"

"And, are you wondering if I was feeling jumpy and easily startled?"

"Yeah! That too."

"Tell me, Boy. You haven't been sleeping well, have you? And, you feel numb and have difficulty focusing. Right?"

"Yes! Yes. How did you know?"

"The same way I know that you've probably been using alcohol in unhealthy excess, and that it will destroy your marriage and render you unemployable if you don't seek help soon."

"Damn Louie! Are you omniscient or something?"

"No. I know this because I've been there too. In WWI they labeled it *Shell Shock.* In my day, it was *Battle Fatigue.* Now, it's called *Posttraumatic Stress Disorder,* but no matter the nomenclature, it's all the same malady."

"What did *you* do to beat it?"

"You'll never beat it son. That's impossible. The war is part of you now. You can't pretend it never happened. The best you can hope for is that it won't beat you."

"How do I do that; keep it from beating me?"

"Get professional help. Don't be ashamed. And, if you're thinking of harming yourself, or someone else, do it today."

The conversation broke off for a long uneasy minute or two.

"You know, Louie," I finally broke the silence, "you're my hero."

I said this as I threaded a poppy through his buttonhole. He adjusted the little fake fabric flower as if it were a boutonnière, then pulled a crinkled dollar bill from his trousers' pocket and stuffed it in my donation can.

"I don't need that," I protested.

"I didn't think you did," he replied. "It's for the *disabled* veterans. That's the other thing you need to know. After you've been helped yourself, it's imperative that you help someone else in turn. That's the deal. It's just how it works."

"How about if I were to write a book about the war, and about adjusting back to civilian life afterwards, you know, to call attention to the problem; perhaps by using sardonic humor as the vehicle . . . and irony?"

"You? You want to write a book? Off the top of my head, son, just the little I've gotten to know you, I'd have to say *that* would be a stupid idea."

"But, perhaps it would be like therapy for me."

"You'd be better off drinking."

CHAPTER FIFTY-FOUR

The Grand Canyon in November

In November of 1983, my friend Bill, whom I've known since kindergarten, called to excitedly tell me he had received some unexpected time off from work. Bill was a Chicago police officer, and along with a uniform allowance, health insurance, and dental, he receives a paid leave of absence whenever he's involved in a shooting, even if he just wings the guy.

Bill called me first knowing that I would likely be available to take a trip with him, as we have been known to do when he's on administrative leave. We make good traveling companions. Bill and I have a lot in common. We grew up in the Garfield Ridge neighborhood together, we both "liked" Sue Fifer in the eighth grade, and we share a deep and enduring love of all things having to do with science. Our underground high school science club, I'm positive, had a lot to do with that. Bill and I never missed a meeting. Without the meddling of a faculty advisor, our young minds were free to soar. We routinely conducted imaginative experiments to unlock the secrets of the cosmos and unleash the power of the universe; all without the burden of having to wear cumbersome eye protection.

Bill and I also had Freshman English together. We had a swell time there in seventh-period English class, checking out the girls, popping our gum (in iambic pentameter, of course), and reading *Hot Rod* magazine while Mrs. Carlson was having an equally genial time up front diagramming compound/complex sentences with prepositional phrases, adjectival phrases, adverbial phrases, and gerundive phrases, not to mention clauses of every kind and variety. If you looked at her blackboard, (which, in fact, I did once early in the semester) you'd think that you had walked into physics class by mistake and someone had put the formula for quantum gravity on the blackboard.

Although English was never my forte, Mrs. Carlson had a flair for making it, if nothing else, entertaining. On one particular afternoon, we had an infectious case of the giggles going around the classroom from something embarrassing Mrs. Carlson said. Having taught freshmen for over 30 years, one would certainly think she'd have known better. It wasn't as if our behavior was unpredictable.

Seemingly oblivious to this reality, she walked right into room 204-B that day, got up in front of the class, stood there with both hands grasping the lectern, and waited until everyone had quieted down and she had the whole room's attention. Glancing around the classroom, she confirmed that all eyes were focused on her before blurting out, "Well, class, I pulled a boner this morning."

There are certain words that you just don't use in the presence of 14-year-olds. *Boner* is near the top of that list. Trying to suppress outright, sidesplitting, rolling in the isles laughter, kids' bodies quivered spasmodically, their eyes were watering, and their faces turned bright red.

Unfortunately, with all this extracurricular amusement, not much was learned that day about the prescribed lesson on singular subjects joined by *or* or *nor*. It is a burden that causes considerable grammatical distress and still haunts me, Bill, and our fellow students, after all these years. It is one of the great consternations of our lives. To this day, you can still identify an alumnus of Mrs. Carlson's seventh-period English class by their proclivity to confuse their correlative conjunctions.

It was just minutes before the final bell of the day when the class had, at last, settled down. Kids were making plans for their afternoon activities. Outside Mrs. Carlson's classroom window, the sky darkened. A strong wind blew up out of the northwest, kicking up litter and bending trees. Cumulonimbus clouds boiled, and the air turned sharply cooler. A deluge followed. Waiting school buses idled outside the main entrance with their headlights on and windshield wipers slapping back and forth. The regular group of cigarette smokers, who congregated just off the school grounds, dashed for cover. When the final bell rang, Mrs. Carlson raised her voice to be heard over the din as students charged for the exit.

"Read chapter 14 for tomorrow and do the exercises on page 167. Expect a quiz on relative clauses."

A clap of thunder rattled the windows. Mrs. Carlson took a moment to ponder the tempest outside.

"I hope everyone remembered to bring their rubbers this morning," she added.

As for our trip west, we decided to take Bill's *Crown Victoria*, since it had cruise control and a bigger trunk, and headed west to check out the Grand Canyon, which we'd heard on the street was becoming a popular destination in Arizona. It was our intention to visit this landmark before its existence became known to the general population, causing it, as often these things do, to become choked with curious tourists and sightseeing Japanese businessmen.

Along the way, we stopped to investigate the Painted Desert. Deciding there was little that a couple of white boys from the south side could do to improve upon it, we traveled on to the Petrified Forest, which was, quite frankly, a disappointment. It appeared to us to be unlike any forest (boreal, coniferous, deciduous, or even petrified, for that matter) that we had ever seen. There wasn't a single living tree to be found in the preserve and surmising that this must have had something to do with the Reagan Administration, we vowed to vote Democrat in the next election.

Arriving at the Bright Angel Lodge on the south rim of the Grand Canyon in a blizzard, we were incredulous. Neither one of us had a clue that it snowed in Arizona. In fact, we had been speculating in the car, while driving though Amarillo, as to whether the lodge would have an outdoor pool or not. What it did have was a concierge with good connections. She could, for a nominal gratuity, procure some coveted tickets for those guests who desired to descend into the canyon on a pack mule. *Why* someone would want to do this we never questioned, as we had heard that this recreation was all the rage and didn't want to miss out on the fun.

Early the next morning, after a hearty breakfast of fried eggs and buffalo sausage, Bill and I found ourselves to be the only customers at the livery. There was a short delay while our mules were fitted with special booties to give them a fighting chance at some traction on the icy trail. Watching the farrier shod our beasts with these devices should have sent up a red flag, but for some inexplicable reason, at the time, it seemed somehow quaint. An hour later, from a greatly different perspective on the snowy trail, this all changed. It seemed then to be more like madness.

Long after the novelty of our adventure had faded, we continued along a circuitous trail, which in places was less than six inches wide. We wound and wound down into the canyon, teetering above 800-foot cliffs while swaying dizzyingly in saddles strapped to animals that were acknowledged to be a chromosome short and seemed to possess no ability to grasp the concept of due prudence.

Too late, I decided I wanted to go home to Chicago. Our guide, meanwhile, explained to us how the strata of rock we passed during our decent were becoming progressively older. One tourist, he quipped, slipped from the trail at around the point of the wooly mammoth, and came to his untimely end in the Triassic Period.

I could tell Bill was feeling just as uncomfortable with our tenuous situation as was I.

"I'm starting to wish that I had fired a warning shot over that guy's head," he confessed to me.

Nevertheless, The Grand Canyon is a natural wonder not to be equaled. The accommodations are comfortable, and the food is good. In the visitor center, you will learn that The Grand Canyon is one of the finest examples of arid-land erosion in the world. Bill and I racked our brains and neither one of us could think of one better. At places over 6,000 feet deep and fifteen miles wide, the Colorado River incises the canyon for 277 miles. The park also contains five major ecosystems: both Upper and Lower Sonoran, Transition, Canadian and Hudsonian. My favorite was the Upper Sonoran while Bill was somewhat partial to the Lower but couldn't choose between it and the Hudsonian.

In the end, we both agreed the Grand Canyon can be adequately viewed and enjoyed from the rim. As a matter of fact, Bill and I agree on most matters of importance, with the possible exception of police profiling. I say that if you encounter a white male officer with a mustache and masking tape over his name tag and badge number, then there is reasonable suspicion, based on experience, that that copper is up to no good. Bill argues that judging a peace officer by the visibility of his or her identification hardware, race, and facial hair is not only politically incorrect, but insensitive, ill-conceived, ineffective, and possibly, a violation of the Fourteenth Amendment to the United States Constitution. To support his case Bill cites Terry v. Ohio, 392 U.S. 1 (1968).

CHAPTER FIFTY-FIVE

My Promotion

"I will continue with my duties as Chairman," Mr. Maciel explained to me over lunch at the club, "But I want you to take over as President and Chief Executive Officer."

Dumbfounded, by this announcement, I couldn't imagine what he might be thinking. I hadn't a clue how to be President. Even my Silver Star, I thought, couldn't help me here.

"I have absolute confidence in you and your ability to carry our company's mission forward."

"Thank you, sir. I'll try not to disappoint you."

"I'm sure you won't."

"But, what's this about a company mission? We have a mission, you say?"

"Yes, of course. I guess I've never been terribly clear on that. I'll need to go over it with you sometime."

"Please do. If we have a mission, I'd be eager to know what it is; I mean if I'm going to be President and all."

"I'll have my secretary pull it from her files and make a copy for you, but in a nutshell, it has to do with providing our franchisees the resources and wherewithal to be successful in their respective markets while realizing a generous rate of return for our stockholders."

"We have stockholders?"

"Of course, we do. Didn't you ever notice the 'Inc.' suffix in our company's name? We're a corporation . . . with stockholders."

I extracted one of my business cards from my pocket and examined it.

"You're right. I never noticed that before. So, we have stockholders then?"

"Yes. In fact, you're *married* to one of the largest shareholders; second only to me. Now, as I was saying, you never have, not in your business dealings, nor in the way you have cared for my Maria, disappointed me. Character counts, you know. I knew you were a man of character the day Maria told me that you had been awarded a Silver Star. They wouldn't hand one of those things over to some meatball, after all."

I thought about some of the meatballs I served with in Vietnam, and some of the items that had been, inadvisably, handed over to them; *like M-79 grenade launchers, fifty caliber machine guns, and Claymore anti-personnel mines.*

"With all due respect, sir. That medal was a fluke. There were numerous guys in my unit who deserved it more than did I; and one in particular."

"Nonsense! There will be no more such talk. Now, Ms. Dorsey, of course, will be receiving a substantial pay increase for her new duties as Administrative Assistant to the President. Your compensation package will need to be voted on by the board of directors. You can trust me when I say it will be generous. They will also need to approve you as CEO. It's purely a formality, however. Now, why are you staring at me with that dumbfounded look on your face?"

"I'm sorry sir, but you say we have a board of directors?"

"I'll delineate all of that before I turn the reins over to you, but rest assured, it's not as bewildering as one might think. Irrespective of the corporate structure, this business is, and always will be, predominately about the food we put on our customers' plates. You did know we have customers, didn't you?"

"Yes. Yes. Of course. I knew about that part. I didn't, however, know we had *plates.*"

"It was a figure of speech."

"Good. You were starting to worry me there for a moment."

Although I sort of looked forward to the challenges my new position would offer, I was, nonetheless, anxious over the prospect. Ms. Dorsey looked up from her typewriter with a look of anticipation on her face as I returned to my office suite.

"How was your meeting?" she asked.

"Let me put it this way. You and I will be getting an extra holiday off from now on, Ms. Dorsey."

"Pardon me?"

"Presidents' Day."

Her expression morphed into a big smile.

"You got the promotion!"

"And you'll be receiving a nice pay increase. Thanks for all you do."

"I'm so happy for you."

"Ms. Dorsey."

"Yes."

"Did you know that we have a board of directors?"

"Absolutely."

"And a mission statement?"

"Well, no. I didn't know that, but I *was* aware of the board of directors."

"I should share the good news with Maria. Please. Get my wife on the phone."

"I'll be happy to do that, but I suspect she already knows."

"Pardon me."

"Maria sits on the corporate board, after all. She's Vice-Chairperson, and one of the nine directors. You didn't know that?"

"No. This has been quite a day of revelation."

I stepped into my office, walked to the desk, and sank into my chair.

"I have Maria on line one," came Ms. Dorsey's voice over the intercom.

"Thank you."

I punched the flashing button.

"Good morning, Maria."

"Dad gave you the promotion, I presume."

"Yes. But, it still needs to be approved by the board."

"Well, I can't speak for any other board members who may be on the fence, but a romantic evening of dinner and dancing, culminated by some passionate love-making, would go a long way towards procuring my vote."

"That's something I want to talk to you about. How come I never knew you were on the board of directors?"

"How come *you* never asked where I was going when I attended those quarterly board meetings?"

"I just assumed you were going to the Hispanic Center to help out like you do. I had no idea you attended corporate board meetings, for goodness sake."

"Then, perhaps, you need to be more interested in your spouse, and less consumed by rehashing your wartime experiences. It's time you let go, and if I may be so presumptuous as to suggest, it's time to resolve, once and for all, this Silver Star conundrum. That medal has no mystical power, Bruce. If you are as ashamed of possessing it under false pretense, as you claim you are, get rid of it. Toss it in the Chicago River or pass it on the Hastings family as you discussed. I don't care, but frankly, I'm fed up with the entire subject."

"Look, the reason I phoned was to ask if you would like to celebrate my promotion with dinner in the Cape Cod Room tonight."

"Instead, how about I *make* dinner. That way we can include Yazmin and celebrate as a family."

"Great! Do I get to choose?"

"Of course."

"Okay then. I'd like Swedish meatballs, pickled Herring, and fruit soup for dessert."

"Sure. And how about, if we don't happen to have the ingredients for that in the house, I make Chili Rellenos, refried beans, and flan for dessert?"

"Yeah. That would be good too."

"Great, because it's your big day, so I want you to pick what we have for dinner, sweetie."

"Oh, Maria."

"Yes?"

"There's just one more thing."

"What is it?"

"Now that I've been promoted, I would appreciate it if you addressed me accordingly."

"Yes, Mr. President."

"That's much better. And, just one more thing . . ."

"Yes?"

"As a board member, did you know we had a mission statement?"

"Of course, I did. This is the 1980s after all. No respectable corporate entity would be without one. But, if you're going to lead this company into the future, Bruce, it won't be with mission statements. You will need to embrace what lies ahead."

"Such as?"

"The worldwide web."

"The worldwide what?"

"Web. The worldwide web."

"Never heard of it."

"Well, you better start educating yourself on it now. In a very short time we will need a company website. It's a new technology they call the *internet*. Our business will need to be at the cutting edge of technology to compete in the 1990s."

"I thought we *were*. I have a *Motorola Bravo* pager and a *Palm Pilot*, after all, and next week my new 1985 *Lincoln Continental Mark VII* is being delivered with the optional $2,995 car phone."

"I know, Bruce, I know. You're quite the Geek."

CHAPTER FIFTY-SIX

The Deal

The New York law/alternative investment management firm, *Duncan, White, Gardner, Williams & Gazarek,* was headquartered in a 1930s vintage art deco suite of offices occupying the entire 22nd floor in the *Bank of Manhattan Trust Building* at 40 Wall Street, in Lower Manhattan. For two and one half years, they had been exploring the potential for acquiring an appreciable block of our restaurants, with the intention of saturating select urban markets. Their anticipated first venture with us would entail the purchase of 27 franchises, with the potential for as many as five hundred in total. This was an exciting prospect. Now, it appeared that *Duncan, White, Gardner, Williams & Gazarek,* (hereinafter referred to as *The Partners*) were ready to pull the proverbial trigger on phase one. So, for me, it was off to New York, New York, where I would be *king of the hill, top of the heap. If I could make it there, I'd make it anywhere.*

I carefully packed my *Hart Schaffner Marx* suit and *vagabond shoes.* Inasmuch as the trip would span our wedding anniversary, Maria traveled with me. We booked a suite at the *Four Seasons.* After concluding my business with *The Partners*, it was our intention to take a carriage ride through Central Park, see the Statue of Liberty, visit Times Square, attend the Met's production of *Otello*, then return to the hotel where we would propose toasts with *Champagne* and generally carry on buoyantly, as if our characters had been written into a Neil Simon comedy. We also wanted to *wake up in a city that never sleeps.*

"Now don't you look handsome," Maria complimented me as she straightened my tie. "I just know you're going to do so well with your meeting."

She moistened her fingers with saliva and used it to plaster down some wayward strands near the part in my hair. I was anxiously apprehensive.

"What if they ask me the ranges in financial performance of the existing franchisees, or, how much litigation we've experienced, or what's our exit strategy?"

"Don't worry. As vice-chairperson of the board of directors, I took the liberty to jot down a few notes for you."

She handed me a small stack of three by five cards.

"You just concentrate on making a good impression and don't concern yourself with such things right now. You can go over my notes in the cab. You should leave now in case there's traffic. If there isn't much, and you arrive early, you can always have a cup of coffee at *P. J. Clarke's*."

She walked me to the elevator and kissed me goodbye.

"Do you want me to call you a cab?" the doorman asked.

"Please."

"Okay. You're a cab."

He raised his gloved hand with two fingers extended and blew into a chrome whistle. A yellow cab shot across three lanes of traffic to get the fare, setting off a cacophony of vehicle horns. I gave the cabbie the address Maria had thoughtfully printed on the top three by five card for me, along with some additional notes: *Don't fidget. Sit up straight in your chair. Be sure to thank The Partners. Don't hit on the receptionist . . .*

Indeed, traffic was light, so I was about fifteen minutes early for my meeting. Rummaging around in my attaché case, I was delighted to find a big fat doobe, which I promptly lit and smoked in the alley, behind a dumpster, before going inside.

"You must have a meeting with *Duncan, White, Gardner, Williams & Gazarek,*" a bag lady commented when she spied me toking up. "I was this close to being made Partner when they fired me for not meeting my billable hour budget. They're a bunch of assholes."

Having achieved a considerable buzz (more so than I was expecting), I boarded elevator B that serviced floors 20 and above. One of Maria's notes explained this would be necessary to reach the 22nd floor. The elevator opened directly into the firm's office lobby. I consulted another three by five card: *Tell the receptionist who you are and that you have an appointment.*

My meeting, I was told, would be with Mr. Gardner. It was explained to me that neither Mr. Duncan nor Mr. White would be able to participate as they were both deceased. I told the receptionist I understood perfectly. She ushered me into a walnut paneled conference room and left me there alone and stoned. From behind one of the numerous paneled doors, I heard a toilet flush. The door opened, and there emerged a tall man who appeared to be in his late 70s.

"Pugh. You're not going to want to go in there for a while," he said, waving his arms. "You'd think I had road-kill for breakfast."

As prescribed by my note cards, I shook the man's hand firmly and looked him in the eye. I was impressed by his countenance. His flowing hair matched the silver gray of his arching mustache. He took a seat in a leather chair by the window, crossing his legs at the knee, and motioned for me to sit in the matching one adjacent, and at an obtuse angle to his. There was a small mahogany table between us. I watched as he produced a huge cigar from his breast pocket, snipped the end, and lit it with a wooden match. He was dressed in a white linen suit adorned with a turquoise and silver string tie. On outward examination, he could have been mistaken for a Mark Twain impersonator. For that reason, I suppose, Pudd'nhead Wilson popped into my brain, and danced around on my THC lubricated psyche for the entirety of our meeting. Even if I *hadn't* just smoked a jay, it would have proved to be quite distracting.

By now, we were sitting in a great cloud of cigar smoke.

"Mr. Gardner," I began, taking the initiative.

"Please. Call me Tom," he insisted.

"Forgive me, but I thought your name was Bill."

"It's William," he replied.

I was confused.

"If your name is William, why then do you wish that I address you as Tom?"

He became terse now.

"I've wished for many things in my day, young man, but never have I wished for you to address me."

"But you requested I call you Tom."

"That's ridiculous. My name is William, but my twin brother was named Thomas. Perhaps you mean to do a meeting with him."

He exhaled an immense plume of smoke.

"Why? Is he in the family business with you?"

"I don't know. I've never met him," he answered.

"You've never met him?"

"Not that I recall," he replied.

As he talked, he was examining the underside of the small table between us.

"Did you know that they attach these things to their bases with lag bolts?"

"I would have guessed them to be doweled and glued," I countered.

"Or a dado mortise," he suggested.

I persisted. "But if he's your twin brother, how can it be that you've never met him?"

He turned the question on me. "Why? Have *you* met him?"

"Me? No."

"See? You don't recall him either, and you're the one who invoked his name. How then do you expect that I would?"

"But he's not my twin," I explained.

"Then who *is* your twin?"

"I don't have a twin."

"Why then do you insist that I do?"

"You told me so."

It seemed that something on the floor was distracting him now.

"I told you to call me Tom."

He disappeared under the table.

"I'll bet you these floor tiles are manufactured with asbestos," he reported. "What do you say we sue the manufacturer? That's what we lawyers do, you know. We sue people."

I acted excited about the idea.

He gave me a curious look.

"Do you think it's fun suing people? Does that amuse you? Have you ever thought what's it's like to be in *their* shoes? Can you imagine the insufferable anxiety that comes with being the defendant in a lawsuit?"

"No," I answered honestly and meekly.

"Fine then. You're our kind of man!"

For over a minute, he sat in silence, puffing his cigar contemplatingly. It made me uneasy, so I decided to take the initiative.

"Very well then, Bill, tell me how you became interested in our restaurants."

"I have no interest in your restaurants whatsoever. Perhaps you're thinking of my twin brother, Tom. We look quite alike, you know."

"Why? Does *he* have an interest in our franchise opportunities?"

"I don't know. As I told you, I've never met him."

I was starting to get the munchies, and there was a tempting variety box from *Dunkin' Donuts* sitting on the sidebar. Marijuana is the gateway drug to apple fritters.

"Let me ask a different question."

"So long as you don't ask to call me Bill. I prefer Tom, you know."

"I understand that you earned your degree in New England. Where did you study?"

"In my dorm room mostly; sometimes the library."

"What I meant to ask is what university did you attend?"

"Yes, indeed, that one."

"Which one?"

"The one from which I received my law degree, of course."

He flicked an ash onto the floor.

"I've been noticing that in consideration of how bright the lights are in here your eyes are abnormally dilated. You might want to see an ophthalmologist about that. I can give you the name of one who we recently, and successfully, defended in a malpractice case. It seems he blinded his victim . . . excuse me . . . patient in one eye with a laser."

I tried to change the subject.

"I'll be fine. I understand that you won a landmark decision for the Sierra Club on behalf of the California condors."

"Actually, I'm a Red Sox fan."

"I was talking about your advocacy."

"I notice that you seem to be doing a lot of talking. I was under the impression that the point here was for *me* to query *you*."

"But how can I have the opportunity to impress upon you the advantages of our organization? You're being very perplexing."

"I presumed that, after I had gleaned some preliminary financial essentials from you, I would start by asking a few probing questions that would reveal to me the extrusive and piquant side of your character. You are a man of character, aren't you."

I fell back on the old reliable, "I have a Silver Star."

"Not impressed," he answered sternly. "I hate war."

I lowered my eyes.

"Please, excuse me, sir."

"Why? Did you fart?"

"No, I believe I offended you."

"Don't worry. I can't smell it."

He was fidgeting with the intercom now.

"They manufacture these things with transistors these days you know. No more waiting for them to warm up."

"Let's try to start over."

"I would suspect you would want to. You haven't made a very favorable impression on me so far, Son."

He stood and had his back to me as he spoke. He was fiddling with the window latch.

"Now, this time you're not going to fart, are you? Because if you do, you should know that this window appears to be painted shut . . . and, I'll bet the paint has lead in it."

"So?"

"I have to say, you don't seem to be a very bright young man. So, we instigate a Class Action lawsuit."

If indeed the paint contained lead, the floor tiles asbestos, I started to worry that the ceiling tiles, with which he was so concerned, might as well. The joint I had smoked was making me feel a little paranoid. I imagined microscopic particles of the stuff snowing down on us as we conversed.

"You did say earlier that you would be entering into a memorandum of understanding with us, didn't you?"

"That was just a joke. You'll need to get used to my sense of humor."

The room by now was a haze of smoke.

"I have to use the can again," he stated. "Here. Hold this for me."

He handed over his cigar and exited through one of conference room's three doors, just seconds before another gentleman entered through one on the opposite side of the room. This man too appeared to be in his late 70s. He looked very like the man in white linen, only with short hair, clean-shaven and he wore a dark blue flannel suit. He also carried a manila file which, I could see, contained one of our glossy franchise brochures. He greeted me with an icy glare.

"We don't permit smoking in here, young man."

CHAPTER FIFTY-SEVEN

How I Lost Maria's Corvette

I have long been enamored by the romance of flight. In my opinion, aviation is one of mankind's great accomplishments. I often wonder what the Wright brothers would think, if they were alive today, to witness the great strides in frequent flyer air miles reward programs that have come about since Kitty Hawk.

Reading the *Glen Ellyn News* one Thursday evening, after tucking Yazmin into bed, I spotted a quarter page add promoting flying lessons:

> *Are you an aspiring aviator? Have you ever wondered what it would be like to fly an airplane? Well, a Discovery Flight might be just the thing for you! Before taking on the full commitment of becoming a licensed pilot, it is a good idea to test the waters. A discovery flight gives you a no-obligation introduction into flight training. For only $29.95 per hour, you can take your first flight lesson today!*

That very next Saturday, I drove Maria's *LT1 Corvette* to Mitchell Field, a quaint, rural general aviation airport about 10 miles from our home. As I piloted the nimble LT-1 Corvette through the pastoral countryside and tidy fields of sweet corn, I fantasized myself to be a crop-duster, spraying great clouds of imidacloprid insecticide in my aerial battle with northern corn rootworm larva. I imagined the little buggers with sinister grins, buck teeth, and thick round glasses.

"This is for Pearl Harbor, you slant-eyed rats!" I cried out.

The sight of a windsock just ahead snapped me back to reality. Pulling up to the front entrance of the flying office, I slipped Maria's *Corvette* into neutral and pulled on the parking brake, leaving the engine running. With its special 2 ½" off-road exhaust system, the ZR-1 optioned LT-1 produced a rich sonorous rumble at idle, and a thunderous roar on hard acceleration.

"Hey, Buddy," I addressed the young fellow dressed in white coveralls who stood by the curb. "After you finish that cigarette, see if you can find a spot to park this baby in a shady spot, but where a tree won't drip sap on her."

I slipped him a five-dollar bill, which he looked at curiously, while I went to find the airport proprietor who I found drinking coffee in the diner next door to the flying office. His name was Bob. The coffee shop was decorated with paintings of World War II training aircraft. Ruth, the 75-year-old cook, I learned, owned and flew a PT-17 *Stearman*. She had spent eight years restoring it.

I was impressed. These were people I wanted to hang out with, people with 100-octane aviation gasoline in their veins. Within a half hour, I had been given a tour of flight services and was assigned my flight instructor, a pimply-faced kid who looked to be no more than 19 years old. He also pumped fuel, mowed the grass and performed other odd jobs around the little airport. He was plunging a plugged toilet when I arrived. I declined shaking his hand. We took our first flight that very afternoon.

For those who have never flown a light trainer, let me explain how it works. For safety, it's essential to walk around the aircraft and carefully inspect it before a flight. It's like buying an "executive-driven" *Chevette* from *Long Chevrolet*.

The first thing to look for, when performing a pre-flight check, is the airplane. Don, my young flight instructor, grabbed a set of keys from the flight office, and off we marched looking for the corresponding aircraft. It seems that he forgot where he parked it. We looked in a couple of obvious places, old metal hangars, one with a tattered windsock on its roof and sparrows nesting in the trusses. We also walked down a long flight line of parked aircraft tethered to the ground, their wheels chocked, some with fitted vinyl tarps covering their engines and canopies.

"What color is it?" I asked, thinking it might help to narrow the search down a bit.

"Red and white," Don answered, "with the identification number *November seven one niner Foxtrot Lima* on the fuselage."

That's the way aviation folks talk, in a special code. It was so cool. I couldn't wait for the day when I too would be talking in code with these flyboys. I would say things like, "Echo, Tango, Alfa fifteen hundred hours squawking Victor five two zero point one four Whiskey Papa," and my watch would always be set on Zulu time.

Meanwhile, Don was still having a hard time finding our airplane.

"Perhaps you had the valet park it but forgot," I suggested.

"We don't have a valet parking here," Don replied, giving me a curious look.

"You don't?"

"No. Never have."

"Who then is that guy in the white coveralls?"

"Him? He's just some vagabond who uses our men's room. The rumor is that he was recently released from prison after serving two years for auto theft."

"Oh shit," I mumbled under my breath.

As it turned out, the craft we were looking for was the last one on the flight line. We began the safety walk-around by checking the engine. Don opened the little metal door in the cowl, exposing the four-cylinder, one-hundred horsepower, Continental model 0-200. He checked the oil, plus we made a visual inspection of the power plant. It looked like a fine engine to me. Don seemed to have some difficulty, however, getting the cowl to latch properly after our check.

"These things can be a little tricky," he informed me. "There, I think I got it."

Next Don opened a small valve under the wing and drained some gasoline to inspect it for color and to remove any water that may have condensed in the fuel tank. The water, being heavier than gasoline, he explained, settles to the bottom. I would have felt a little more comfortable, though, if he had extinguished his cigarette before performing this procedure but Don assured me that what I saw splashing on the ground, was, indeed, mostly water.

"We got a shipment of bad gas awhile back," he explained.

Walking clockwise around the plane (that's clockwise Zulu time you understand), we looked for nicks in the propeller, cracks in the fuselage and loose parts, all of which we found in abundance and all of which Don explained to me were normal for an airplane of this vintage. Next, we slipped inside the craft and belted ourselves in. Don checked to ensure that the parking brake was set, and operated the flight controls to confirm that the flight surfaces were free and clear. He set the fuel mixture to rich, turned the carburetor heat off and primed the engine. Next he turned on the master switch, opened the throttle one-eighth of an inch, popped open the side window and yelled "CLEAR!" to absolutely nobody at all. As far as I could see, the only other people on the airport property that afternoon were Ruth, Bob, and the itinerant carjacker, and they were still back in the diner drinking coffee. The engine cranked and cranked, and then cranked some more. It didn't seem to me like it was going to pop over.

"Maybe you flooded it," I suggested.

Don gave me an annoyed look. Stubbornly, he kept cranking that old Continental engine until, as I knew would happen, the battery died.

"Wait here and don't touch anything," he instructed, getting out of the aircraft and headed towards the coffee shop.

I figured he was going to get some jumper cables but instead he came back with Ruth. She positioned herself at the nose of the aircraft, putting both hands on the prop blade.

"Hey," I reminded Don as he climbed back in the plane, "I'm paying by the hour here you know."

"So was Buddy Holley," he snapped.

"Gas on," Ruth called to Don.

"Gas on," he repeated.

"Switch off."

"Switch off."

"Throttle closed."

"Throttle closed."

"Brakes set."

"Brakes set."

Ruth pulled the prop through a couple of compression cycles, then yelled "Contact!"

"Contact," Don repeated as he hit the ignition switch.

Ruth swung the prop with a heave and the little engine sprang to life. Giving us a wave, she spun around and headed back to the coffee shop. Don was now busy scanning the instrument panel. Admirably, the oil pressure came right up to normal.

"That's amazing," Don commented, pursing his lips and shaking his head. "It almost never does that."

We taxied to a position near the end of the active runway and turned into the wind. Don set the brakes then throttled the engine up to 1,800 rpm. He checked the magnetos, ammeter, and lights. He turned the avionics power switch on, and the radios, and set the transponder to "standby." He also set our compasses, checked our airspeed indicator, vertical speed indicator, and oil temperature. When he got to the suction gauge, he lingered for a few seconds.

"This plane really sucks!" Don shouted close to my ear over the engine noise.

I didn't quite know how to take that.

He then set the altimeter to 768 feet above sea level, closed the window, latched it, and lowered the flaps. I was just beginning to feel comfortable in the hands of what seemed to be a very thorough flight instructor until, as we taxied into position for take-off, Don casually stated, "I only wish we had a little more fuel."

Pushing the throttle forward, Don started the Cessna rolling down the grass runway. We bumped along steadily, gaining more and more speed until, at sixty knots, he pulled back on the yoke and into the air we rose, clearing, by several feet, the Holstein cow grazing on the runway.

"It looks like she's about ready to calve any day now," Don observed, still shouting over the cabin noise as we climbed. "The last two lactations she had bull calves. We're really hoping for a heifer this time."

I nodded, smiled obtusely, then turned to look out the window as we continued our climb into the endless sky. Down below me, in the golden valley, I could see Maria's Corvette racing north along a ribbon of highway. It was like I had stepped into a freakin' Woody Guthrie song. Maria was not going to be happy with me.

"Could you follow that green Corvette down there?" I asked, pointing at the speeding LT-1.

"He's going way faster than this plane will ever do," Don replied.

He said something else after that, but I couldn't quite make it out over the drone of the engine. I'm sure, however, that I probably must have misunderstood him. It was pretty noisy in the cockpit but it sounded like he said, "I had sex with a goat once."

Post Script

Over the next eighteen months, *November seven one niner Foxtrot Lima* and I became good friends. It was as if man and machine were melding into one mechanical/bionic unit. While training on this aircraft, I became, over time, a more and more proficient pilot, and quite the expert, it turned out, at forced landings. We made a lot of forced landings together, that aircraft and me. In fact, we touched down at the Addison golf course so often that I was nominated for membership in the country club. There was some discussion as to whether I would require a golf membership, or if a simple social membership would be sufficient. After considerable debate, the trustees finally decided on the golf membership, with an amendment to the bylaws that all taxiing aircraft would be restricted to the cart path.

CHAPTER FIFTY-EIGHT

My Tri-Pacer

After completing ground school, and 66 hours of student flight time, I passed my PPL written exam easily, and the practical exam by the narrowest of margins. I knew this because during the check flight, my FAA certified examiner, who was evidently a Muslim, repeatedly cried out, in a tortured yowl, "*Allah Akbar. Allah Akbar.*"

This was not helpful.

Although I had meticulously plotted a VFR cross country flight plan that would allow me to indubitably demonstrate my skills as a pilot, not more than 20 minutes into the flight, Muhammad ordered me back to the airport. He asserted that it had something to do with my situational awareness and terrestrial radio broadcast transmitters.

"What are you talking about?" I insisted. "I didn't see any radio towers."

I suspect his eagerness to return to DuPage County Airport had more to do with the 20 ounce latte he consumed during the oral portion of the exam prior to take off.

Extemporaneously plotting a course back to DuPage, I lost 500 feet of altitude before realizing it, and was at 2,500 as we crossed the Fox River at Potawatomie Park. I methodically completed my landing checklist, and made the appropriate radio calls.

November seven one niner Foxtrot Lima, DuPage Control responded. You have traffic at your 1 o'clock, range one mile, same altitude.

"Are you sure you mean my 1 o'clock?" I asked, not seeing any other aircraft.

Try looking just to the right of your 12 o'clock.

"Traffic spotted."

Good. Now try not to hit him.

On a straight-in approach to the airport, I ensured that the aircraft was aligned with the assigned runway, and established my glide slope. A challenging crosswind prevailed. After a slight issue I encountered with some pilot induced oscillations during a nose-wheel first landing, I taxied to our tie-down. Muhammad exited the aircraft and dramatically kissed the ground before dashing to the men's room. Later, in the flight office, while subscribing the requisite papers, he told me that in his 29 years with the FAA, I was the *second* worst pilot he had ever endorsed. (He was the examiner who certified the pilot of Otis Redding's *Model 18 Twin Beech*.)

I'm sittin' on the dock of the bay.

Upon receiving my Private Pilot's License, I used the insurance money from Maria's stolen *Corvette* as a down payment on a 1962 *Piper P-22-150 Tri-Pacer*. By the time Maria found out about this, I was already plying the skies above northeastern Illinois, negotiating the tangled web of Chicago's restricted airspace. This could be a challenge. Once, the *Illinois Air National Guard* even launched a pair of *Cessna 0-2A Skymasters* to escort me away from O'Hare Airport.

United 235 heavy. Abort your landing and execute a 180-degree go-around. It seems we have a cute little single-engine Piper with no transponder out for a Sunday drive over Bensenville.

Executing now. Be advised that, on average, it costs my company $975 to do a go-around. They aren't going to be happy.

Roger, United 235 heavy. Do a $975 go-around.

I'm wheels up and climbing out . . . and you can tell that "flying milk stool," that there's absolutely nothing of sightseeing interest in Bensenville.

Wholly embarrassed by the entire affair, I snuck back to my home airport in Addison, flying low under the radar and navigating by following Illinois Route 53 most of the journey. I encountered the WGN traffic helicopter at North Avenue, and tipped my wings as a greeting. In acknowledgement, she spun hers around in a circle. It was adorable. I spied my airport just ahead. Good. Now, mixture: Rich. Carburetor heat. Speed 70 mph on short final. Just a touch of power. Full flaps. Low 50s over the fence, tail low. Chop the throttle. Bingo! After landing, I taxied to my tie-down and secured the aircraft. Snapping off some limbs from the Cotoneaster hedge by the flight office, I did my best to camouflage the parked airplane from the *Skymasters* circling menacingly overhead. In respect for the horticultural integrity of the landscape, I selected only dead, diseased or crossing branches. This consideration was very much appreciated by Ruth who asked if I could also spray her tea roses with fungicide when I had the chance.

"Next time," I told her. "In fact, I may go ahead and get my aerial applicator's license and hose down the entire airport with *Mefenoxan* for you."

"Would that be safe?"

"Hell yeah. This stuff is virtually inert as compared to *Agent Orange,* and in Vietnam, practically everything outside the major cities smelled and tasted like *Dioxin,* one of the active ingredients in the ubiquitous defoliant. To all intents and purposes, we poured that stuff on our *Rice Krispies* for breakfast! Like they say: What doesn't kill you, makes you stronger."

"But I understand that *Dioxin* exposure *will* kill a person, over time."

"Well, in those unfortunate cases then, it tends *not* to make you stronger," I conceded as I climbed into my car. "See you later aviator!"

Ruth waved goodbye.

I arrived back home to find Maria rummaging through the substantial stack of mail on the console table in the front hall.

"Whatcha doing?" I asked.

"I was just looking for the check from the insurance company for my Corvette. It should have been here weeks ago."

"Don't worry. Give it a little more time. I'm confident *you're in good hands.* A sterling company like that would never put corporate profits above their policyholders' interests."

"Do you ever look at your mail, Bruce? Some of these bills are postmarked months ago."

"I'm going to get to them when I have a chance. I've been pretty busy taking flying lessons, you know."

"Yes, I *do* know. It's all you talk about. You're obsessed."

"Flying is exhilarating."

"Perhaps, but do you really think the ticket seller at the *Glen Theater* or the toll collector on I-90 at Route 31 wants to hear all about your aerial adventures?"

"Well, the waitress at *Big Boy* told me that *she* was impressed and wants to go up with me sometime."

"No, Bruce. Don't get any ideas."

"Talking about restaurants, are you cooking tonight or are we going out to eat?"

"I just assumed we would go out, in-as-much-as it's our anniversary."

"I knew that. As a matter of fact, I was just scouting *Plentywood Farms* in Bensenville when I went up in the *Tri-Pacer* this morning. It looks to be a pretty nice restaurant, at least from 3,000 feet."

"Doris told me they ate there once and the food was good. However, she did add that it was pretty noisy with all of the big jets landing at nearby O'Hare Airport."

> *Coming in from London from over the pond*
> *Flyin' in a big airliner.*

The restaurant, designed by a student of Frank Lloyd Wright, served a palatable Provencal fare and offered competent service. I had the lamb shank, Maria ate Grouper.

"You're not drinking tonight," Maria astutely observed. "Aren't you feeling well?"

"I'm not drinking because I thought it might be romantic to take the *Tri-Pacer* up, fly along the lakeshore, and view the lights of the Chicago skyline at night."

"By romantic you mean . . ."

"No. Like *your* definition of romantic, not mine. Piloting an aircraft is serious business, Maria. One needs minimal distractions and proper task management when flying at night in congested airspace. Besides, it's pretty cramped quarters in the *Tri-Pacer* for what you're implying."

"It was pretty cramped quarters in your *Mustang* at the car wash that one time you browbeat me into it, if you recall. It's a slippery white-trash slope after that, Mister. Literally."

Maria put her hand on my knee. I touched her leg under the table. This talk was getting me worked up.

"That carwash quickie was so hot," she whispered.

"It was for me too, and I suspect it was for the carwash crew to boot."

"I can't say for sure, but I *do* know, it was the only carwash I ever received where *they* tipped *me*!"

"That's it! Let's get out of here before the management is compelled to toss us out."

We skipped dessert, requested our check, and headed straight to our car in a fever. (*Hotter than a pepper sprout.*) The parking attendant spied my *Mustang's* handicap veteran plates and thanked me for my service. I didn't know quite how to respond to something like that. Was I supposed to tell him *you're welcome?* I tried to come up with an appropriate reply but appropriateness is not one of my hallmarks.

"Fuck you," I rejoined as I handed him a $5.00 tip.

He looked dejected.

On the drive to the airport, Marie told me that she really wished I would stop doing things like that. I told her that I was sorry, but that I was afraid that I might be coming down with *Tourette syndrome.* She doubted it. The sun was just setting as we pulled up to the *Tri-Pacer,* her long shadow reaching out to embrace us.

"Why is your airplane covered in Cotoneaster branches?" Maria inquired.

"Camouflage."

"Camouflage! Have you been having flashbacks again, Bruce?"

"No. This was for real. The *Skymasters* were after me. They were circling overhead."

"Oh, Bruce. There are no such things as Sky Masters, or Flying Monkeys, or Darth Vader, or the vanishing hitchhiker in a white dress."

"But she dropped a rose petal in my car. I swear!"

Maria lowered her head. I detected disappointment and sadness in her expression.

"Now. How do you get into this thing?"

She tried tentatively to raise her pretty high-heeled foot enough to get it in the airplane's door but her tight skirt scuttled the plan (much to my delight) while exposing her smooth, shapely leg.

"Like I said. It's pretty confined. You should probably strip down to at least your underwear before you get in."

Maria obligingly removed her blouse and skirt, then squeezed in. I too stripped down to my *Jockeys.*

"I see what you mean," Maria observed. "It *is* tight in here. Perhaps it would be safer if we don't go up tonight."

She moved sensuously closer.

"I agree. I have no idea how I'll be able to keep my turn coordinator centered with you doing *that.*"

To an outside observer, it must have looked strange, that trusty *Tri-Pacer* bouncing up and down on its tricycle landing gear, the rudder flapping wildly back and forth, the elevator going up and down, and the ailerons moving crazily. At one point, Maria bumped the switch that activated the fuselage mounted anti-collision strobe lights.

"This is better than a *Pink Floyd* concert," she moaned.

"It's a good thing neither of us suffer photosensitive epilepsy."

After consummation, and a body-shaking orgasm, Maria opened her door for some fresh air and tumbled to the grassy ground in a sweaty heap.

"Well. That was very romantic, in a white-trash sort of a way," she stated, pushing her damp, sticky hair out of her face. "How was it for you?"

"For me, it was the most fun I ever had in an airplane that never got off the ground. Next, I think we should try the Ferris wheel at Navy Pier."

"And if *that* goes as well as I envision, I say *on to Fantasyland and It's a Small World!*"

"Maria! Should I be concerned about you? Little kids ride that attraction. It's supposed to be wholesome."

"Well, after we're through with it, it'll be an *E-Ticket* ride."

"Really, Maria?"

"No. You're right. You're absolutely right. That would be inappropriate."

"Thanks for seeing it my way. I was really starting to wonder."

"No. You're right. We'll just have to settle for the *Jungle Cruise.*"

A-weema-weh, a-weema-weh, a-weema-weh, a-weema-weh.

CHAPTER FIFTY-NINE

Gallbladder Surgery

The folks at the Federal Aviation Administration are federal employees and can thus be a persnickety lot. Not only do they have volumes of published regulations governing the use of airspace above the United States, they also expect pilots meet certain medical standards. Shortly before my first solo flight, I drank three pots of tea to flush out my system and went in for my third-class aviation medical certificate.

"Hey Doc," I protested while he checked my prostate, taking way longer than I thought to be appropriate. "What the hell are you doing back there?"

"I'm checking your eyesight," he replied. "Now read the third line on the chart over there, hanging on the back of the door."

"You're checking my vision with your finger up my butt?"

"It's called multitasking. Now read."

"B, I, T, E, M . . . Hey Doc. Your eye chart spells *BITE ME*."

"That's curious. I never noticed that before. Oh well. Now, try reading line four for a double letter score."

"OXYPHENBUTAZONE? Is that even a word?"

"Sure! It's an anti-inflammatory medication used to treat arthritis and bursitis. Srimad Pharmaceuticals supplies us these promotional eye charts free of charge."

He pulled off his latex exam glove, turning it inside out in the process, stepped on the peddle that popped open the waste can lid, and tossed it in. He next listened to me on his stethoscope. A serious look formed on his face; something like this: (O_O) Then, he began singing really off-key, and too loud, *"I saw her walking on down the line, you know I saw her for the very first time . . ."*

"What is it, Doc?"

"It sounds like something in between a massive intestinal obstruction and *Hanky Panky* by Tommy James and the Shondells. Does this hurt?"

He pushed on a spot low on my abdomen.

"Only like you stabbed me with a hot fireplace poker," I gasped.

He suggested I see my family physician as soon as possible, which I did the very next day. By then, constant acute pain gripped me. Dr. Howard, who collected vinyl and owned a vintage copy of *Tommy James' Greatest Hits* album, agreed there was something seriously amiss. He sternly cautioned me about the music industry's strict enforcement of piracy laws, suggested I eat more fiber, and promptly sent me by ambulance to *Central DuPage Hospital*. There, a myriad of nurses, doctors, and technicians of every imaginable discipline tried to murder me, but I am happy to report, without success.

Their first attempt on my life came in the emergency-room staging area. It was passive in nature. There, the ominously titled triage nurse decided to just wait me out. I was grouped with the patients who had arrived disemboweled, with severe head trauma, and sucking chest wounds. They calculated that the existing state of medical science was not up to the challenges we presented. We were expected to politely die, quietly, with a minimum of fuss and disturbance to the other patients. I disappointed them. I made a tremendous furor in my effort to convince the nurse I was in the wrong group. This forced the staff (and don't think it doesn't bother me that word is also the name of a virulent and infectious microbe) to fall back on plan B: admitting me.

Once the hospital had the requisite name, address, and telephone number of the nearest relative not living with me, I was officially transferred from outpatient emergency room status to in-patient status. The difference between these two denominations is simple. As an in-patient, no matter how capable one may be of walking about on his or her own accord, a volunteer nevertheless pushes you around the endless maze of hospital corridors in a wheelchair. Usually this volunteer turns out to be a more appropriate candidate for the chair than the passenger. Charlie, the guy who escorted me down to Diagnostic Imaging, was a veteran of the 1918 offensive of the Argonne Forest. He had been with the 91st Infantry Division as a litter bearer. By contrast, as an outpatient, you might have had both legs crushed in a horrific industrial accident, but you would nevertheless be required to *stand* in line to talk to the processing clerk.

After my snails-pace wheelchair ride to Imaging (Charlie celebrated his 108th birthday while we were in transit) I was subjected to a series of tests, none of which I had time to study for. The first of these involved fishing a wire down my esophagus, through my stomach, via my bile tube, into my small intestine and on to parts of my anatomy which, I'm embarrassed to confess, have been part of this old organism for all these years without my knowledge or acquaintance. This procedure afforded me an enlightened empathy for those catfish I used to hook as a kid while fishing with my grandfather. As I reeled in my fish, he would grab the line while I pulled my prize from the water and report, "Whelp, looks like he swallowed the hook."

Now, these hospital folks were continuously checking to see if I was dead yet, as it would be inefficient to allocate valuable resources trying to kill someone who had already expired. I was, in fact, wired up to a sophisticated monitor that employed the latest telemetric technologies. It would promptly announce my demise to the nurse on duty. She would then be able to immediately call down to the kitchen and cancel the lunch I had ordered.

Having determined I still possessed a pulse after the above procedure, they decided the next logical step would be to try killing me from the other end. This involved approximately the same *modus operandi* as before, only with a television camera attached to one end of the wire. Foolishly, I half-expected it to be some sort of miniaturized camera, but for anyone old enough to have enjoyed the *Ed Sullivan Show* on television during the '50s and '60s, it was a vintage *RCA* model TK-40.

Not being able to find anything good on TV, it was time for them to roll out the heavy artillery; nuclear medicine! This is where they injected a giant syringe-full of weapons-grade plutonium into my vein, and excitedly watched a monitor from a lead-lined room in the next county, as the radiation poisoning spread throughout my circulatory system. Subsequently, I now have a half-life of over 1,000 years and a tendency to set off smoke detectors wherever I go. The post-procedural instruction sheet I received, included a curious warning. I am advised against intimacy with any other individual who is "hot." By their definition, that would be someone who had undergone this same procedure within the last 500 years. Evidently there is some risk that the two of us could go critical, like some sort of a human dirty bomb.

What they learned from the nuclear medicine department was that I needed surgery. A generation ago, one's doctor would have extrapolated the same information and come to the identical conclusion by pressing on my abdomen with two fingers. The scheduled surgery was all carefully explained to me in advance, which I appreciated, including the risks. I remember, there was a risk of infection, a risk of brain damage, and a risk of death. It was pretty much the same risks usually associated with riding a Chicago subway.

While recovering from surgery, I shared a room with a guy named Peter. From frank conversations he had with his nurse, that I couldn't help overhearing, I learned way more about his bowl movements than I ever needed to know. He also had a problem controlling his bladder. (If anyone ever happens to be visiting room 5218-B at Central DuPage Hospital, they probably shouldn't sit in the big green chair.)

Peter weighed over 400 pounds. He had just gone through a gastric bypass. Any food that I didn't want, he ate. This was something he wasn't supposed to be doing. Sometimes, after only my first bite, he would ask, "Are you going to finish that?"

There was a curtain between us that I usually kept closed. I didn't want to risk seeing something through the opening of his hospital gown that could potentially have some long-term mental-health consequences for me. Other than that, my room was quite comfortable. I had a TV to watch, and a controller to flip the channels, regulate the volume, adjust my bed, or call a nurse if needed.

One afternoon, Peter was finishing some chicken I couldn't eat when I heard him choking and gasping. From my side of the curtain, it sounded like he was in considerable distress. I frantically pushed the call button, and within the minute, into the room walked a most attractive young nurse. In sharp contrast to Peter, she was the picture of youth and vitality.

"Did you want me?" she asked.

"I do," I confessed, "but I'm afraid that you're too young for me. I haven't seen you around before. Are you new?"

"I just transferred from pediatrics," she explained.

Some disturbing sounds were coming from Peter's side of the room.

"Well, welcome to post-op." I continued our little chat.

I learned that her name was Heather and that she had recently graduated from *Binghamton University*. From behind the curtain that separated us, I could hear Peter thrashing about.

"Is your roommate all right?" Heather inquired.

"Oh, sometimes he just eats too fast," I explained. "Are you originally from the Chicago area?"

"No," she replied. "I'm from New Jersey."

"I went to an air show at the Lakehurst naval station once," I told her. "We have a restaurant near there."

"Did you see the Hindenburg crash?" she asked.

I made a mental note to put some *Grecian Formula* hair color on my shopping list.

Peter, by this time, had finally quieted down. Evidently, I had been wrong when I thought that he was choking. He had some other type of ailment though, but I'm not exactly sure what it was because the hospital uses codes to distinguish maladies. The hospital personnel called Peter's a "code blue."

Minus one or two organs which I was told I didn't need anyway, and which I never knew I had in the first place, the hospital was forced to release me alive. Then again, that's what my grandfather and I used to do with those catfish we caught. After jamming needle-nose pliers down their throats and ripping out the hook, I always suspected it wouldn't be long before that fish would be back at the surface, swimming upside down.

CHAPTER SIXTY

Etiquette at Wakes and Funerals

After my gallbladder surgery, Maria got on a crazy kick to set our personal affairs in order. Her grave concern was the possibility that the next time I died, it might be more successful, so she had our attorney draft a last will and testament for me.

"If you die intestate, or without a will, your estate could become bogged down in probate," she explained to me.

This was the first I had heard about having an estate. I was confused.

"Are you talking about our place on Washington Island? Are you saying that's an estate?"

"Yes. That and all the rest of our assets."

"Wow! I have assets to be concerned with. I feel so grown up now."

"I wouldn't go so far as to say that."

As the day wore on, we became housebound by a nor'easter. Outside, there were a couple of feet of wet heavy snow on the ground, while inside we sipped brandy and had a blazing fire roaring in the hearth. It was very romantic. To the backdrop of Vivaldi, Maria dug out my living will and life insurance papers. She then proceeded to unabashedly re-file them under "pending." When I asked her how she came up with that categorization, she told me to shut up and go shovel the driveway.

Maria also made an appointment for me with the local funeral director. I was to meet with him the following Monday at ten o'clock. My first reaction to this news was a combination of consternation and paranoia until she explained to me that the purpose of my meeting would be to do some "pre-planning." Then it all made perfect sense.

The funeral director, when I showed up for my appointment, escorted me into his richly appointed office and offered up some coffee, which I gladly accepted.

"Decaffeinated, please. Doctor's orders," I told him.

He introduced himself as Mr. Dwyer. As I sipped my steaming *Sanka*, he delineated the rationale for pre-planning.

"When a death occurs in the family," Dwyer explained, "it can be an emotionally stressful and difficult time. This is especially true for the deceased."

I had never looked at it that way before.

"It may be comfortingly consolatory to remember that, when your time comes, you are not the first nor will you be the last to meet this fate."

I remembered what my grandfather used to say along this line: *"Every day, people die who never died before."*

Dwyer continued. "Wakes and funerals, or some variant of them, have long been employed as a vehicle to ease the transition from this life into the uncharted territory beyond. Virtually all cultures and societies, dating back to the roots of civilization, have been known to practice some form of these rituals."

I was all ears. I never expected that pre-planning could be so informative.

"Although this great country is a veritable melting pot of different religions and cultures, in our modern society, there are still some basic protocols that define the rules of socially acceptable intercourse at these ceremonies."

As "intercourse" is one of those words I have difficulty with, I choked on my coffee, and a little of it came out my nose. After I finished my paroxysm, Mr. Dwyer continued.

"Learning these conventions can help an individual to meet the often awkward social situations with confidence and ease, projecting an impression of good manners, and thus good breeding, to those around us."

"How do I get started?" I asked excitedly.

Dwyer handed me a booklet titled *Etiquette at Wakes and Funerals; For the Deceased.*

"Follow along," he suggested, and then continued, "None of us would want the last impression we make, on our friends and family, to be one of crudeness or a lack of decorum. Therefore, some simple, time-honored rules of etiquette should be scrupulously observed at your wake and funeral."

Here the booklet was illustrated with a pleasant line drawing of people attending a wake, dressed in 1950s fashions. I flipped to the back page, curious if this thing had a copyright date or something on it.

"Typically, an individual is waked 3 to 4 days after death occurs. It is, therefore, important, out of consideration for those responsible for your arrangements, that one expires on a timely basis. No one appreciates the individual who drags his or her death out in a protracted and laborious process, nor, conversely, the person who dies quite unexpectedly, with absolutely no warning to one's friends and family."

I started thinking about some of the inconsiderate dead people I had known who could have benefited from pre-planning.

"Punctuality in death, as in life, is a sign of good manners. We have all heard the old cliché, 'He'll be late for his own funeral.' Although some may find that small joke to be mildly jocular, in practice that is most certainly *not* the case!"

Perhaps I'm far too easily amused, but it gave me a chuckle.

"It is of utmost importance that the person being waked arrives well *before* the first guests. Nothing can be more unsettling to a mourner than to find the deceased still being manipulated into the casket upon their arrival."

"This is some good information," I interjected.

Dwyer made brief eye contact with me, then continued reading aloud like a mother to her 4-year-old.

"The time of the wake is often published in the newspaper with the announcement of one's death. A demure individual will be in his or her appointed position at least 45 minutes prior to that time to accommodate the possibility of an early guest or two, especially those who have traveled a long distance and may have allowed extra time for contingencies."

I wondered if Maria had any idea of how much I was learning.

"Wakes may last for many hours, so it is equally important to make oneself perfectly comfortable in anticipation of the ceremony. Nowadays, all but the cheapest caskets are equipped with ample cushioning and often a sophisticated suspension system, similar in many ways to a modern mattress. Take advantage of this. Nobody appreciates a corpse that squirms and fidgets."

I wasn't going to get one of those "cheesy" caskets, I decided right then and there.

"In that same vain, it is highly recommended that you not consume, immediately prior to your death, any foods that have been known to give you gas."

I never thought about that before.

"Could I have a little more coffee?" I asked.

Dwyer called out the door to a young man in his middle 20s appeared, identically dressed. He seemed to be assessing my health. I had the uneasy impression he was hoping to get some overtime that week.

"Mr. Johnson would like some more decaffeinated," instructed the funeral director.

The young man disappeared down the hall and the narrative continued.

"Probably, if you live to a formidable age, you will have attended many wakes and funerals of others. Do not be disappointed if they fail to reciprocate. Their absence is to be expected and should not be considered insolent or disobliging."

The coffee arrived. As it was handed to me, I wondered if it was *really* decaffeinated. For all I knew, it could have been laced with amphetamines.

The funeral director thanked the young man for me and continued.

"Probably the most asked question on the subject of wakes and funerals concerns the proper attire for these occasions. As in life, certain dress codes should be strictly observed in death. Although some religious persuasions may dictate clothing for burial (for example, a shroud for Orthodox Jews) there are some simple guidelines that should be followed for the well-dressed deceased."

I wondered if I could wear my colorful Hawaiian shirt that Maria hated so much.

"For a man, one can never go wrong with a conservative business suit, gray, black or dark blue in color."

Just like these guys were dressed!

"Avoid broad stripes, bold plaids, and bright colors."

There went the Hawaiian shirt.

"A good rule of thumb, for the man of faith, is to wear something that you might wear to church. Never wear a morning coat, cutaway or a dinner jacket to your funeral. A tuxedo would only be appropriate for those rare individuals for whom such would be associated with in life (for example a ringmaster in the circus), and then, under no circumstances, should one be buried in a *rented* tuxedo."

I wasn't quite sure what a morning coat looked like, but I was positive that I didn't own one.

"Your tie should be of a conservative nature and must bear no design, leave perhaps a quiet stripe. If it applies, a man's club tie would be a very suitable accoutrement. Avoid paisleys, bold polka dots, and most assuredly, graphics or verbiage of any type; for example: 'Shit Happens.' In his casket, a man should look dignified."

That made me wonder if the mortician had any little tricks for getting rid of the permanent smirk on my face that Maria accused me of sporting. He read on.

"Most funerals include a procession to the cemetery. Unless the graveyard is immediately adjacent to the place where you are being waked, as is still the case in some rural areas of our country, an automobile procession is typically the practice. In such a procession, there are frequently specific vehicles assigned to the immediate family, and dignitaries, should there be any in attendance."

I was pretty sure that there weren't going to be any dignitaries at my funeral.

"In *all* cases, though, the deceased rides in the hearse, and then, always in the back, never up front with the driver."

At this point in the booklet, a drawing depicted what appeared to be a 1955 or 1956 *Cadillac* populated with a bevy of somber-looking occupants, the women wearing mid-calf dresses and the men, fedoras.

"Although it is quite understandable that one would desire to look around and drink in one last view of this world before being condemned to eternal darkness." (as a Catholic, at least I didn't have to worry about *that*) "It is at best, unseemly."

I was happy to see we were close to the end of the booklet. Learning about wakes and funerals was now starting to become tedious and I wanted to get on to the part where I got to pick out my casket.

"No matter how new one may be to the experience of dying, a few simple rules of etiquette, in combination with a dose of good common sense, will help to make, what otherwise might be a disagreeable situation, if nothing else, decorous."

The booklet concluded with a beautifully lithographed, fold-out depiction of a sunset. It was so serene that I brought it home with me and had it double-matted and nicely framed. It now hangs in my library, over the fireplace. Maria thinks it's morbid and tawdry. I, on the other hand, like the way it complements my cherished collection of *Thomas Kinkade* paintings.

CHAPTER SIXTY-ONE

The Decision

"I'm going to do it!" I announced to Ms. Dorsey as I entered my outer office, my *Wall Street Journal* under my arm. "I've talked it over with Maria, and Malcolm, and they agree. The next time I have business in Cincinnati, I'm going to phone the Hastings, procure an invitation, and present them with that confounded Silver Star on my credenza. I don't want or need it anymore. It never really belonged to me in the first place."

"From what you've told me, it would be the right and noble thing to do; offering it to the Hastings."

"Absolutely. Now, come on in. I want you to take some dictation. I don't think it would be inappropriate to give them a note along with the medal, do you?"

"No. I think a note would be fine. It would add a compassionate, personal touch, in my opinion."

"Good. I'm glad you agree. I have a lot of respect for your perspective."

We walked together into my office. I smacked my newspaper down on my desk with a loud crack. Ms. Dorsey took her usual seat in the more comfortable Ruby Red oversized leather club chair by the window. She crossed her legs and placed the steno pad on her lap. For a 56-year-old woman, she had great legs. With a nod, she indicated that she was ready.

"Dear Pastor and Mrs. Hastings," I began. "Here is the Silver Star that should have been your son Bill's. Not only did our nefarious government leaders cheat him of his precious life, but they defrauded Bill of his medal for valor as well. Those criminal monsters in Washington, who concocted and carried on that iniquitous campaign to inflict pain and suffering on a population of good and simple people, taking your son's life and countless others in the process, should be hunted down as war criminals for the atrocities they prescribed, and hanged. No. Make that brought before a firing squad and shot."

I paused to collect my thoughts.

"Could you read back what we've got so far please, Ms. Dorsey?"

"Of course."

She flipped back a page and read.

"Dear Pastor and Mrs. Hastings; Your son Bill was the bravest man I ever knew. He fought proudly and died honorably in the service of his country."

"Good. Good. I think that's fine just as it is. It's succinct, and to the point. There's absolutely no reason to say anything more. Now choose an appropriate complimentary closing, whatever you think is best, and type that up, please, on some of that special, sort of translucent linen stationery we have. I won't need to see a draft first. You may make any editorial changes you deem necessary. That's all for now. Thank you, Ms. Dorsey."

"I have just a couple of items for *you*, however. Last month's financial reports are there on your desk, you have a lunch meeting with the sales rep from WGN radio at 10, and Malcolm Jackson phoned yesterday, after you had left the office."

"Thank you. Would you please see if you could get him on the line for me?"

I picked up the framed Silver Star that had been sitting on my credenza for the past 15 years, leaned back in my chair with my feet on the desk, and contemplated it. I tried to think of even *one* good fortune I enjoyed that couldn't be tied back to this object in some way. I could come up with none. I had met Maria, thanks to my Silver Star. As a consequence of that, I procured my job with her father's business. And what about our daughter Yazmin, the fruit of Maria's and my union? What a blessing she has been. I enjoyed a comfortable, secure home, and the financial resources to support a few worthwhile charities and do a little traveling with my family. If I were to relinquish my Silver Star, I still worried, my good fortune might change for the worse. Maria could bump into an old high school sweetheart, rekindle their romance, and take off to the Bahamas with him. Yazmin might join a cult, become brainwashed, and shave her head. What if I got fired, and lost all of our savings to some smooth-talking money manager who actually ran an elaborate Ponzi scheme? I could become one of those bitter, homeless, drug-addicted Vietnam veterans who make a pilgrimage to the wall of shame in Washington for the purpose of leaving some enigmatic object at its base. And, what if I developed some sort of huge, disfiguring, and non-operable tumor on my neck from my exposure to Agent Orange?

"I have Mr. Jackson on line one," came Ms. Dorsey's voice over the intercom.

"Thank you." I pushed the flashing button on my phone.

"Malcolm! What's happening?"

"You, my man, *you*. Look, I'll get straight to the point, Bruce. As you know, I've been supporting the Boy's and Girl's Clubs of Chicago since even when I was still a washroom attendant. Now that my restaurants are providing me with a good cash flow, I've been trying to do more, but it's still not enough. I was thinking that, perhaps, on the corporate level we could do something further to make a real difference for these kids."

"Malcolm. Say no more. I'll put it on the agenda for our next board meeting. Did you know that we had a board of directors?"

"Yeah. I knew that, and Maria sits on it, doesn't she?"

"Yes. Yes. Well, we always like for some of our charitable giving to go to the local community. It's common knowledge the good these clubs do for the young people in our city. If you could, however, prepare a short presentation for our board, I would appreciate it."

"Absolutely. I'd be happy to do it."

"Good. Good. I'll have Ms. Dorsey phone you with the time and date of our next meeting."

"Thanks, Bruce. I really appreciate it."

"Hey, Malcolm; one more thing before you hang up."

"Sure. What is it?"

"I've definitely decided to give my Silver Star to the Hastings. I'm going to do it the next time I have business in Kentucky."

"I'm pleased to hear that. Let me know how it goes."

"I wrote a letter, too."

"A letter?"

"To go with the Silver Star."

"I thought there was already a letter that went with it; from Richard M. Nixon."

"Yeah, but he's a dick. I thought that a personal note from me would be more meaningful."

"I'm not so sure of that, Bruce. This concerns me. What, just exactly, did you *say* in your letter?"

"Don't worry. I allowed Ms. Dorsey her customary editorial discretion."

"Thank God for that! You had me worried there for a moment."

"Let me know if you want to get together for a beer sometime."

"Sure! Sounds good to me. There are still plenty of drinking establishments in this town that haven't banished us, you know."

"Of course, there are. They're mostly 'biker' bars, but that's all right. I used to ride a little *Honda* one-sixty when I was in high school."

"Really? What did you have? A *Scrambler*?"

"No. I had a 1965 *Honda Dream*."

"You must have been a bad ass."

"You bet I was. My mother insisted, however, that I always wear this goofy helmet that made me look like a space alien."

"Bummer. How'd that go over with the chicks?"

"The ones from this planet? Not so well."

"You take care now. We'll talk."

"Okay. Later Bro."

"And, by the way, I'm not your bro."

"Sure, you are. We're friends. We're like soul brothers."

"What are you talking about? You're nothing close to being a soul brother. You're a dorky white guy. We have a business relationship. That's all. Business!"

"But you invited me to your daughter's recital."

"And I never would have done it had I known that you'd consequently think we were friends and start stalking me. I knew you liked opera. She was playing a piece by *Bizet*. Look, Bruce. Just accept it. We're not soulmates or whatever it is you think we are."

I replaced the phone's handset in its cradle, thinking about my conversation with Malcolm.

"Ms. Dorsey," I buzzed my secretary. "Do we have a *Yellow Pages* here in the office?"

"The receptionist has one up front. What did you want to look up?"

"I'm thinking about buying a motorcycle. See if you can find out where the nearest *Harley Davidson* dealership is located."

"If you do that, I'm telling your wife, you know."

"Very well. In that case then, instead of the yellow pages, please bring me the agenda for the next board meeting. I'd like to add a topic for discussion."

"Now that's much better, Mr. Johnson. I'll bring it in at once."

CHAPTER SIXTY-TWO

Ice Skating on Lake Ellyn

Our Glen Ellyn home sat perched on a glacial moraine overlooking picturesque Lake Ellyn, a favorite winter venue for speed-skaters. Maria and I, therefore, purchased Yazmin a pair of *Planert's Northlight* racing skates for Christmas. As excited about the present as I was, Yazmin was unimpressed. Speed-skating did not hold the same mystique for her as it did for me. Maria warned me that this could be the case when I excitedly wrapped the gift.

"I just hope, Bruce, that you won't be too disappointed if she would prefer a pair of pretty white figure skates with colorful little pom-poms."

I didn't get it. Back in 1963, speed-skating on McKinley Park Lagoon was a favorite and wholesome winter recreation for us junior-high kids. Every day after school and on weekends, so long as there was good ice, we skated until dark and our fingers and toes were nearly frostbitten. I'm not talking about playing hockey. We didn't play hockey. There was a good reason why hockey never interested us. For a bunch of white boys from the southwest side, this may seem an anomaly, but hockey was too exclusive a sport. It did not include both sexes. Back in those days, for some inexplicable reason, only boys played hockey, so instead, to rise above the sexist attitudes of the day, and be more inclusive of the girls, we stole their hats.

It seems a curious contest, looking back on it now, but that's what we did. The young men would loop and turn, weaving in and out between the girls we encountered, like the courting dance of male Antarctic Penguin. In a display of our finest athletic ice-skating skills, we tried to impress the young ladies with our virility and our ability, our grace and our stamina. The truth be known, these midwinter games were actually more about sex than anything else. We may not have realized it at the time, but this preening was, in fact, a rudimentary mating ritual; an early stage of the selection process. We were beginning our search for a partner to ultimately carry our genes on to the next generation.

Here's how it worked: A boy, as he skated in between the group of girls, would single out one that had a special appeal. Perhaps it would be the healthy glow of her cheeks in the frosty cold. Maybe her jeans fit just right, or if her jacket was open, it might have been the way her breasts improved the lines of her sweater. Yes, it was most definitely all about sex. But, our hormonal impulses back then were not only immature, they were a mystery to us. So, when we singled out a distinct young lady who had just that special appeal, we would do what came naturally. We would swoop in and steal her hat.

The hope was, of course, that the chemistry between the boy and his selected target would be just right, betting his young ego on the mutuality of this attraction. Ideally, the girl would be thinking to herself, as the young man zeroed in for the strike, "I sure wouldn't mind getting my hat stolen by *him*." The huge risk inherent in this activity was, you should understand, the looming possibility that she *could* be thinking, "I hope to God that dork doesn't try to steal my hat."

I trust you can appreciate the degree of anxiety that accompanies the recreation of hat stealing. It requires grit, determination, and nerves of steel. This is why, I suppose, some boys, instead, play hockey.

Either way, the hat thief would quickly receive his answer. The desired response was that, having had her hat swiped, the girl would shriek, and commence to chase the boy across the ice. This indicated she was mutually attracted to the young man. The boy would then gleefully skate backwards, dangling the stolen hat out as bait for the pursuing girl. At some strategic point, he would allow himself to be overtaken and tackled. The couple would then tumble to the ice. There would be a lot of subsequent physical contact involved. This, after all, was the motivation for the entire ceremony. Perhaps, in the fall, her legs would entwine around his torso. They might land with her mouth close to his. Maybe his hand would brush against a breast. Conceivably, one of the parties might be seriously impaled on a skate blade and although I'm confident that somewhere within the realm of this latter possibility there is a pertinent lesson to be learned that would be not only sparklingly clever but also brimming with wit and irony, I am disappointed to acknowledge that eludes me at the moment.

On the other hand, if the unfortunate boy had seriously misjudged the situation, if the object of his tender passion had no interest in him, she would just stand there hatless while the humiliated young man skated off unpursued. To my knowledge, there was no good way to salvage any dignity from this disgraceful situation. In the worst cases, a girl might roll her eyes and look completely disgusted until the boy skated back and ignominiously returned her garment. This could be emotionally devastating, and pervert the normal, healthy, sexual development of an adolescent male. There could be serious mental health consequences. The disesteemed boy might be inclined to sulk home, skipping dinner, retreat to his bedroom, lock the door, and commence to compulsively stealing his own hat. (Back in 1963, these unfortunate casualties of the sexes were commonly, and insensitively, referred to as "losers." Today, you may better know them as video gamers.)

In fact, it turned out that this primitive sexual behavior was a good predictor of the future, and the social niches my classmates and I would ultimately occupy when we were promoted to high school and beyond. There were girls, who regularly skated at McKinley Park, with reputations for letting just about any boy steal their hats. Some guys were known to go for a tumble with a girl, and then never steal her hat again. Bill Ferrell spent most of his time in the warming house sipping hot *Ovaltine* and eating popcorn while half the guys in town were stealing *his* girlfriend's hat and, convicted of animal hoarding during her declining years, Sue Aster was a lifelong spinster who never wore a hat while ice-skating.

Then, of course, I don't want to forget Sue Becker and Beth Smith, who, I would be remiss if I failed to mention, very much enjoyed stealing each other's hats.

Excitedly, I watched Yazmin as she opened her "special" gift on Christmas morning. The fire I built crackled on the hearthstone. Recorded Yule carols played softly in the background. Outside, a fresh blanket of snow covered the earth.

"Oh, ice skates," she pronounced appeasingly, "and a triple cable fur pom-pom beanie! Thanks, Mom. Thanks, Dad."

"You're very welcome, dear," Maria responded, with a soft satisfied smile. *"De nada, mi hija."*

"Well," I warned Yazmin, "I know you're eager to try out your new skates, but I want you be careful out there on the ice, young lady."

"I know Dad, I promise that I will only skate on ice thick enough to safely support me, as determined by the Glen Ellyn Park District officials."

"Yeah. Well that too, but what I had more in mind was that I don't want you be flaunting that new beanie hat around those lascivious young men, like a trollop."

"A trollop?"

Her expression evinced confusion.

"It's like a slut," Marie explained, factually.

"Dad! You think I'm a slut?"

"No. I *didn't* say that."

Yazmin turned and ran to her room crying. I heard her bedroom door slam shut.

"It's getting to be a Christmas tradition," Maria addressed me matter-of-factly, "making Yazmin cry. Remember last year when you suggested that she abstain from the holiday cookies (*galletas de Navidad*), inasmuch as she was getting a little chunky? And the year before that when, after consuming an excessive number of *Smirnoff Bloody Marys*, you roasted *Mr. Potato Head* to a cinder in her new *Easy-Bake Oven*?"

"Well, I'll admit that last Christmas I was a bit out of line, and the year before that too, but this year, all I did was . . ."

"Call your 13-year-old daughter a slut. I have absolutely *no* idea *why* that would upset her."

CHAPTER SIXTY-THREE

Temptation

I never, in all my years, received even a snippet of serviceable or constructive advice from my father, and only once from my mother. Even then, *that* was incomplete. (She admonished me to look one way before crossing the street.) So, I was astonished when my dad, delirious, while in his hospital bed recovering from a parlous bout with salmonella-derived food poisoning, drew me close and, in a trembling voice, urged, "Son, don't eat your mother's Caesar Salad with raw egg."

"Okay, Dad."

"And also, don't look directly into the sun when viewing an eclipse."

"I'll remember that."

"And if your English muffin gets stuck in the toaster, don't try to dig it out with a butter knife; not without unplugging the appliance first."

"Fine."

"And Bruce . . ."

"Yes, Dad?"

"Don't ever do anything that would jeopardize your marriage to Maria."

"Like what are you saying?"

"I know you do a lot of traveling on business. There may be times when you're feeling lonely being away from home. When that happens, don't be taking up with any unsavory women. I know they're out there, and it can be a temptation. Don't even think about it. Look at me. I've been married to your mother for close to 40 years now, and until that nurse's aide with the red hair gave me a sponge bath this morning, I never gave another woman a second thought."

"I would never consider it, Dad."

"Good. Because she's quite a gal, you know."

"The redhead?"

"No. Your Maria."

"Why are you telling me this?"

"You need to be careful. There are unscrupulous women out there."

"I never got the impression that you approved of Maria, she being Mexican and all."

"I *don't* approve of her being Mexican, but your mother and I, nonetheless, agree she's been a good wife and wonderful mother, and as a stay-at-home mom, she hasn't stolen any jobs from God-fearing American men."

"She's a native-born U.S. citizen, Dad."

"Don't start in on me with that 14th Amendment crap now. I just paid you a compliment about your wife. Can't you just accept that for what it is without trying to start an argument?"

"I'm sorry."

"Apology accepted."

"Well, I need to get going, Dad. You take care of yourself, and I'll call you later."

"Just one more thing, son."

"What is it? I really need to get to the airport."

"Always put on clean underwear; in case you're in an accident and have to go to the hospital."

I was heading back to Kentucky for a goodwill tour of our mid-south locations. Ms. Dorsey had chosen the resort and spa where I was to be staying because it was within an easy drive of six of our restaurants.

As I packed my attaché case with sales reports, a *Texas Instruments Model BA-35 Business Analyst* calculator, and my Silver Star, Ms. Dorsey briefed me on my accommodations.

"The hotel dress code calls for a jacket and tie after 6 p.m. in all public areas. There is both an indoor and outdoor pool, tennis, golf, saddle horse stables, cycling, hiking, trap shooting, and wild boar hunting with a guide only. Did you want me to phone ahead to reserve any of those activities?"

"No thank you. As intriguing as the wild boar hunting sounds, I think I'll just stay within my comfort zone and stick to my usual routine."

"Drinking martinis?"

"Exactly. What model rental car were you able to procure?"

"That was a bit of a problem, but I *was* able to find a car rental company that does not include you on their "blacklist." They're not number one, you should know, and they don't try harder, and they don't have a kiosk at the airport. You will need to take a taxi to the *Ugly Duckling* car lot to pick up your 1972 *Cadillac Eldorado*. I typed the address on a 3 X 5 card and put it with your papers. As I understand it, they are in a pretty tough neighborhood, so you may have to try a few cabs before you find one that will venture into that part of town."

"Are you serious? *Ugly Duckling?*"

"Yes. Now, you better get going, or you will miss your plane."

After a comfortable flight to Cincinnati in the first class cabin of a Boeing 727-200, and subsequently disturbing cab ride from the airport through a war-torn section of the city, we pulled up to the *Ugly Duckling* car lot. Ms. Dorsey was not kidding. The neighborhood *was* rough. Gang signs were spray-painted on every conceivable surface. The car lot was enclosed with a 12 foot high cyclone fence topped with razor wire. Spent 9 mm shell casings littered the apparently blood-stained sidewalk.

"My secretary reserved a car for me," I informed the heavily tattooed, 300 lb. plus attendant.

A 357 magnum *Colt Python* with a six-inch barrel lay on the counter within easy reach of the brute. I noticed that it was fully cocked.

"Did you know that there's a chalk outline of a body on the sidewalk in front of your establishment?" I advised the attendant.

"Oh. That's not for real. Some anti-violence, anti-gun protesting nun was painting those all around town to draw attention to gun deaths in the city."

"How did that work out? Did she get good press?"

"You bet she did. Someone shot her. It made all the papers. Here we go. I see that you requested a luxury vehicle. It took a while to locate one for you, but our auto recovery team was able find a nice specimen, illegally parked, in the 300 block of Martin Luther King Drive. The ignition switch, unfortunately, has been punched out, but our service department has provided a No. 2 slotted-head screwdriver. There's a little trick to starting the car, but you'll get the knack of it in no time."

He slid some papers in front of me.

"You will be fully responsible for gasoline, and charged six dollars per day, plus eight cents per mile. Initial here that you are accepting the car with 365,273 miles on the odometer. Also confirm, by your initials here, that you understand the vehicle's registration may not exactly match its VIN number, which may or may not be obscured from being exposed to the ultra-violet rays of the sun, as sometimes occurs with a model of this vintage. For your convenience, you need not return the car here. Just phone us with the ending mileage, wipe off your fingerprints, and leave the vehicle in any of the three airport parking lots. We will charge your credit card accordingly. Be sure to take your paperwork with you. Do not leave it in the car."

After executing the contract with my signature, I was escorted to the waiting *Caddy*. It was equipped with a massive after-market chrome grill, and a continental spare tire kit. The car squatted down to within one inch of the pavement and sported old-school custom wire wheels. Holding the fuzzy steering wheel with my left hand, I inserted the screwdriver into the void where the ignition switch once resided. A substantial spark arced from within, succeeded by a little puff of blue smoke. The engine exploded to life with the sound of a broadside salvo of cannons from the *USS Constitution*. The rental agent opened the gate and gave me a big grin and a thumbs up. The *Caddy* scraped bottom as I pulled into the street. Had it been equipped with mufflers, I'm confident they would have been ripped from the car. I honked the horn and waved to "Bruno" as I pulled into traffic. It played a tune like the one announcing the appearance of the contenders of the *Kentucky Derby*. After discovering that nifty feature, I proceeded to honk at every opportunity at attractive women I encountered. I couldn't wipe the smile off my face.

During my relaxing stay at the venerable *Mount Airy Resort*, I ate most of my dinners in the grill room, eschewing the finer dining venue, which I deemed more elegant than I desired for eating alone. One evening, after finishing my meal of lobster bisque, crab cakes, seared ahi tuna and avocado tartare, I ordered a brandy.

"Your *Grand Marnier*, sir," the waiter announced.

"Thank you. Would it be alright if I took this to the terrace and enjoyed it there?"

"Of course, sir. You go ahead and find a comfortable seat that suits you, and I'll bring your brandy. Be aware, however, that there is an existential threat of rain later this evening."

"What do you mean by an *existential* threat?"

"It means that there exists a threat of rain."

"So what you're saying then is that there's a threat of rain."

"Exactly. *Existential* adds absolutely no meaning to the sentence. It is only there for effect; to sound more sophisticated."

"So, what you're saying is, if I want to sound sophisticated, all I need to do is insert the word *existential* into my sentences here and there?"

"Yes, but there's an existential drawback to that."

"Like?"

"You may be perceived as being existentially pretentious."

"Well. I certainly want to avoid any existential perceptions like that."

I walked as we conversed through the pillared archway out onto the terrace with the waiter in tow. He carried my drink on a small *Bakelite* tray decorated with Roman goddesses. After settling into a comfortable wicker chair with a panoramic view of the grounds, I was handed my brandy.

"Thank you."

"You're very welcome, sir. Will there be anything else?"

"No. This is very nice; at an existential level. Thank you."

"Very well."

Sitting across from me, I noticed an attractive woman in her early 30s. Her blonde hair, which she wore up, contrasted her rich tan. She was wearing a short black dress, dangling earrings, pearls and nylons. With her legs crossed at the knee, she made little circles with the toe of her black pumps, popping her heal in and out of the shoe. I wasn't certain if she was trying to provoke me, but, intended or not, she was, effectively, accomplishing exactly that.

A friendly smile formed on her lips as I, inadvertently, made eye contact. I'm positive that she had caught me admiring her legs. I smiled back, rose from my chair, turned, and nearly sprinted to my room, leaving my drink behind. After fumbling nervously with the key, I pushed open the door, clicked the deadbolt, hooked the security chain, and picked up the phone. I dialed for an outside line, then our home number.

"Johnson/Maciel residence," Maria answered the phone.

"Oh, Maria!"

"What's up with you calling twice in one day?"

"Maria. I love you so much."

"And, I love you."

"I miss you terribly."

"What happened? Did some attractive woman make eyes at you and give you a scare?"

"How did you know?"

"The important thing to remember is that I *did* know. You can't hide anything from me, Bruce. I know you all *too* well, and it's a good thing you didn't accede to that woman, because, with all due respect, your life wouldn't be worth living if you had, lucky Silver Star or not."

"Do you have someone tailing me?"

"Just remember. It's three strikes and you're out, mister, and your second strike was when your ex-girlfriend showed up at our wedding reception."

"What was my first strike?"

"Being born."

"That's pretty harsh."

"That's the way it is, mister. I overlooked your handing the keys for my Corvette over to a car thief, and publishing in the *Glen Ellyn News* that I'm married to a lesbian woman trapped in a man's body, but I have zero tolerance for infidelity."

"I understand. I think I'll watch the news, then go to bed. I'll call you in the morning. I have a free day tomorrow so I phoned the Hastings and arranged a visit to present my Silver Star to them. It was either that or wild boar hunting. I'm going to tell them that I'm now convinced it was intended for their son, Bill, and not me."

"Follow your conscience, but remember dear, you have, to be frank, an engrossment on the subject of that Silver Star. Not everyone might share the importance you place on it."

"I understand, and thanks. I *do* love you."

"Good night, Bruce. Let me know how it goes tomorrow."

"Are you sure you don't have one of those private eyes with the camera and telephoto lens shadowing me?"

"Why would I do that, honey? I trust you. Sweet dreams. And, you might want to draw your blinds if you're going to lie there on your bed like that in your underwear."

CHAPTER SIXTY-FOUR

The Presentation

Pulling in the now familiar tree-lined drive to the Hastings' farmette, a soothing sense of tranquility engulfed me, acutely contrastive to my previous boneheaded social call. Astutely counseled by my sagacious wife, I phoned first this visit, and prudently procured an invitation. After years of soul-searching, a long overdue, and very personal, transaction would execute in the coming hour or so. I was resolute. Unequivocally, I had decided to pass my Silver Star on to whom I believed to be the rightful possessors and, I was at last, decisively at absolute peace with the decision.

Hearing my car crunching along the Indiana limestone aggregate driveway, the pastor and Mrs. Hastings emerged through the front door like cuckoos onto the expansive veranda, sporting a porch swing, two rocking chairs, and a wringer-style *Maytag Model J2L Commander* washing machine. I parked in the shade of a sprawling Kentucky Coffee Tree and waved like a ninny as I exited my *Ugly Duckling* rental car.

"Hello. I hope I didn't run over one of your chickens," I called to the *American Gothic* partners posing phlegmatically on the porch. Mrs. Hastings stood stoically, one shoulder slightly behind her reverential spouse.

"Don't worry. They heard you coming a mile away, as did we. Mother here thought you were a moonshine runner. Come on up. We want you to meet Linda Sue."

Shyly, a woman, about my age, perhaps a few years younger, emerged from the house, joining the Hastings on the porch. She was a pretty, freckle-faced woman with strawberry-blonde hair worn in braids. One of the straps of her cotton sundress fell provocatively from her shoulder as she offered her right hand. She self-consciously covered her mouth with her other as she smiled bashfully. Her two top front teeth, I could see, were grossly misaligned.

"Linda Sue was engaged to Bill when he was killed," Mrs. Hastings explained to me.

"Oh. Were you his cousin then?" I quipped, only to think better of it, regrettably too late.

Pastor Hastings scowled, observing my conspicuous discomposure and sensing the chagrin I felt for the indelicate joke.

"Please disregard that," I appealed. "I can be abashedly inappropriate at times."

"In these parts, we call that closing the barn door after the cattle are out."

"Back in Chicago, where barn doors are *recherché*, that crack would have been considered hilarious, however."

"But, to answer your question, they *were* second cousins. Linda Sue is married to Cooter Cody now. He runs the garage over in Beaver Lick. They have two fine sons and a lovely daughter."

"I'm pleased to meet you."

I took her extended hand in mine and squeezed it gently. She smiled meekly with eyes cast downward. Her hand was softer than I expected. She smelled of *Bounce* dryer sheets . . . original scent.

"Likewise. Bill wrote of you often."

She spoke with an accent like Loretta Lynn.

"Is that your car," she inquired.

"Well, it's a rental."

"My husband has a low regard for those. He says that *Jesus* wouldn't be able to coax more than 235 horsepower out of that engine's 8.5:1 compression ratio.

"Is that so? I intend to write a letter to the company, and I'll be sure to include that. But, getting back to Bill . . ."

"I especially remember him mentioning you and your leave to Nashville during basic training. I wish I could have met him there."

"We saw an episode of the Grand Ole Opry being taped for TV," I remarked.

She stared at me blankly.

"TV . . . television. It's like radio but with moving images projected on a cathode ray screen."

"I know what a television is, silly. We have one in our house, and a big, tall antenna that pulls in Channel 12 all the way from Cincinnati, Ohio."

"Is that a CBS affiliate?"

"I think so."

"Then, I bet, you've watched the *Beverly Hillbillies*? Isn't that Jed Clampett a riot? And Granny! I just love her. The show is still in reruns, you know. It's a classic."

"I won't watch it. I think the show demeans people who dwell in the rural, mountainous areas of Appalachia by fostering negative stereotypical connotations."

"Hum. Now you see, I came away with an all-together different interpretation. I thought the show was downright hysterical."

"Well, I didn't."

This conversation wasn't going well at all, but that, unfortunately, never stopped me.

"Perhaps you missed the episode where Jed buys the Los Angeles freeway. It was hilarious. You see, this con man . . ."

"We'll never see eye to eye on this."

"I'm sorry. I shouldn't have brought it up."

"Bill thought of you as one of his dearest friends."

"Then I have to say, he had poor judgment in that regard," I quipped.

"I was just thinking the same thing," Linda Sue replied.

I could tell, she was dead serious.

Mr. and Mrs. Hastings ushered us inside as we conversed. We found our seats in the parlor.

"I remember the cookies you baked. They were good."

"What were your favorites?"

"Hands down, the peanut butter cookies with the fork marks on top. Although, I have to tell you, I did find a strawberry blond hair baked into one. I think you owe me a replacement dozen."

"Next time I bake a batch. I'm happy you enjoyed them. That was so like Bill to share with his buddies."

"I don't know how to say this, or even if I should. You're right. He *was* a good guy, but, to be perfectly candid with you, Bill wasn't one to share."

"No?"

"No. He was pretty much a selfish jerk when it came to 'care packages' from home."

"I can't believe that."

"I'm sorry. So, it was out of pure necessity, mind you, that we intercepted your cookies from the mail before he could get his acquisitive hands on them. I'm ashamed to confess this, but I need to get it off my chest. Only now, on meeting you, do I see what an unscrupulous thing it was to do."

"Did he ever receive *any* of my cookie shipments?"

"Well, the first one; the one he wouldn't share with us."

"So, after that, he never got to eat any of my cookies?"

"Oh, no! We weren't like Bill. We *shared* our cookies. He enjoyed them very much. He just had no idea you baked them. He thought they were from Loren's mom."

"You guys were unconscionable."

"It was war. War can raise havoc with a person's moral code. It changes him."

"Not Bill. He was a Christian. His faith was his basis; his unchanging faith. It was his guiding light."

"I don't mean to be argumentative, but it would seem pretty difficult to me to reconcile one's Christian faith with some of the iniquitous things we did in that war."

"What about you, Bruce? Are you a Christian?"

"I'm Catholic."

"I'm so very sorry about that. I'll pray for you. I'll pray that you'll find Jesus. Would you like that?"

"Well, you see, I *like* Jesus, but he *loves* me, so that makes it a little awkward."

The atmosphere in the room was getting too intense.

"I've got an idea," I joked, to lighten things up. "How about we talk about politics."

"I have a photo, Bill sent me, of the two of you together. Do you want to see it?"

"Sure," I lied.

She produced the tattered snapshot from a pocket on the front of her sundress and handed it to me. The image was of the two of us, shirtless, our arms around each other's shoulders, smiling like nitwits at the camera. Bill was wearing his "dog tags," I wasn't. The photo must have been snapped after I had lost mine while scrambling aboard an evac chopper extracting us from an untenable situation near Dak To. The sounds of projectiles piercing the aluminum skin of the Huey, that day, convinced me that I didn't want to stop and look for them in the elephant grass.

Embarrassingly, tears welled up in my eyes as I viewed the photo. It felt as if one was about to roll down my cheek. I didn't know which would be ignominious; to let that happen, or risk calling even more attention to myself by wiping my eye with a handkerchief.

"You *are* staying for dinner, aren't you?" Mrs. Hastings inquired. I could smell it cooking.

"What are you having?" I asked. "I'm on a very strict diet; doctor's orders, you know."

I wanted to give myself an "out" in case they were serving something of a marsupial genus, as I had heard could be the case in this neck of the woods.

"Stewed chicken with dumplings. Is that permitted on your diet?"

"Oh, yes. That sounds great."

"Do you have health problems?"

"Post combat traumatic stress syndrome."

"There's a special diet for that?"

"Well, I can't eat C-rations. They conger up all sorts of sour memories; especially the chopped ham and scrambled eggs."

"Did you think we would serve C-rations?"

"No. Not at all."

"I know. I bet you were afraid we'd cook a raccoon."

"Well, not quite. I was thinking more along the line of possum."

"Well, fear not. When the pastor went out to tend the chickens this morning, it seemed that one of the roosters had gotten his neck stuck in the wire and was strangled while trying to extricate himself."

"If he was already dead when you found him, isn't that sort of like eating road kill?"

"I suppose you could look at it that way, but then again, road kill has an undeserved negative connotation. There's nothing wrong with eating a deer, for example, that was struck by a car, so long as you know it's been freshly killed."

"So, we're having chicken then. Right?"

"Yes. Father plucked and gutted him, and I stewed the bird for dinner. He was too old to roast. Excuse me while I put the food on the table. We'll eat in five minutes or so. Did you want to wash up?"

I looked around awkwardly.

"It's okay. Don't panic. We have running water. You don't need to go outside to the pump. The bathroom is behind that door over there."

In the bathroom, I splashed some cold water on my face, hoping it would mitigate some of the redness around my eyes. Putting my hand on the doorknob, I paused, taking a deep breath, before returning to the gathering.

"Well. Dinner sure smells good. I'm looking forward to some home-cooking after being on the road for the past week."

"Is your wife a good cook?"

"She tries. But, in all honesty, she's a *terrible* cook; probably the worst I've ever encountered."

"I hope you never tell her that."

"I may be crazy, but I'm not stupid."

We took our places at the dining room table. Just in case I wasn't feeling uncomfortable enough, we all held hands in a circle and prayed before we ate. Now, I'm not talking about "thank you for this food and for God's bounty, Amen." No, we prayed for the whole of the Hastings clan, most of the population of Beaver Lick, our representatives in Washington DC, and for the Kentucky Supreme Court to overturn a "feminist agenda" inspired law that encouraged women to leave their husbands, kill their children, practice witchcraft, destroy capitalism, and become lesbians. When Pastor Hastings mentioned his son, Bill, in the petition, Linda Sue squeezed my hand. I squeezed back and was mortified when the tender touching stirred a strong sexual impulse in me.

"And may our wicked thoughts be redirected to the goodness and grace of Jesus Christ, our Lord," Pastor Hastings concluded. "Amen."

Although the dinner was delicious, my appetite was pathetic.

"You sure don't eat much, Boy," Pastor Hastings observed. "What's in the box you've been clutching to your breast since you arrived? Is that a hostess gift that you neglected to present to Mother? Is it candy? She has quite a sweet tooth, you know."

Looking at her teeth, this disclosure did not surprise me.

"No. Actually, this is a Silver Star. It's the medal of valor Bill earned, but was never awarded, due to his unseasonable death. I've been holding it for all these years now. Forgive me. I was thinking you might want to display it up there next to his photo on the fireplace mantel."

"Well, that's a very nice gesture," Mrs. Hastings commented as she took the medal from me, glanced at it, then passed it to her husband. "It's so sweet of you."

Somehow, I had envisioned that there would be a little more emotion attached to the act of transferring the award to its new owners.

"Yes. Thank you very much, Son. We'll put this with his baseball glove and some of the other items we've saved of Bill's."

For some reason, it just wasn't registering with these country-fried hay seeds, the significance of the object they were holding.

"That's the third-highest military decoration that can be awarded for valor in the face of the enemy," I desperately tried to explain to them.

"Tell me this, Son," Pastor Hastings asked in a tranquilizing voice. "You were there with Bill. Were those people *really* our enemy?"

A deep sense of remorse came over me. I didn't want to answer his question. In fact, I now desperately wanted to leave. The vast majority of Vietnamese with whom I had come in contact, the ones who hadn't been corrupted by American affluence, were just a simple people who had been dominated by the French, then the Japanese during World War II, then the French again, and finally, the USA before winning their sovereignty in 1975. A staggering two million Vietnamese died for their country's independence.

"No. They actually weren't," I answered succinctly.

An awkward silence engulfed the room. My eyes darted from Pastor Hasting's tumble polished agate-decorated string tie, to (inappropriately) Linda Sue's smooth skin and alluring cleavage, to the framed Silver Star, which had formerly, and proudly, decorated my office, but now lay ignominiously upon a stack of mail house catalogs, next to a sewing basket and some old socks that awaited darning.

There was some polite conversation about my job, how I enjoyed it, and what it was like to live in the Chicago metropolitan area.

"I can't even imagine what it would be like living in such a big city," Mrs. Hastings commented. "I get nervous driving into Beaver Lick to go to the *Piggly Wiggly*."

"Well, thank you for visiting us . . ."

Pastor Hastings rose abruptly and extended his right hand to me. I had been hoping for some homemade pie for desert but it looked like that wasn't going to be.

"It was so very nice to meet you, but I hope you can understand that this should be closure now. You go forward and live your life as best you can, with the burdens you carry, and we'll live ours amidst the vacuum Bill's death created in our family. It's all we can do. There needn't be, and indeed, it would be best if there were to be no further communications between us. I trust you understand?"

"Yes. Yes, of course," I replied, dumbfounded.

What a bunch of fucking country bumpkins! I couldn't get to my rental car fast enough. I waved one last goodbye as I pulled out onto the gravel road and accelerated away, spitting up some stones in the process. I couldn't believe what a stupid thing I had just done. To a wholly ungrateful family, I had just boneheadedly handed over the very object that had precipitated everything good in my life. It was gone forever, now. What the hell was I thinking? And if that wasn't bad enough, they were a bunch of bible-thumping, homophobic, Baptist yokels who ate road kill, voted Republican, and married their second cousins. I made a fist and hit the dashboard as hard as I could. The glove box popped open. As I reached over to close it, I heard a sharp crack, like the report of a rifle. The car pulled hard to the right. Coasting to the side of the road, I got out to find what I suspected, a blowout of my right front tire. Taking deep breaths, and exhaling loudly through my pursed lips, I counted to 10 before kicking a big dent in the driver's door.

So, Bill Hastings had finally received his Silver Star. It made me think about Captain Riley and how much he detested awarding those things posthumously.

THE END

www.ingramcontent.com/pod-product-compliance
Lightning Source LLC
Chambersburg PA
CBHW050857130726
47900CB00013B/129